P9-DWH-391

PIONEER HOMESTEAD APTS.
835 E. HANSEN
P.O. BOX 552
JACKSON, WYOMING 83001

Breathing
Room

ALSO BY SUSAN ELIZABETH PHILLIPS

This Heart of Mine

Just Imagine

First Lady

Lady Be Good

Dream a Little Dream

Nobody's Baby but Mine

Kiss an Angel

Heaven, Texas

It Had to Be You

WILLIAM MORROW
An Imprint of HarperCollins*Publishers*

Breathing Room

Susan Elizabeth Phillips

BREATHING ROOM. Copyright © 2002 by Susan Elizabeth Phillips. All rights reserved. Printed in the United States of America. No part of this book may be used or reproduced in any manner whatsoever without written permission except in the case of brief quotations embodied in critical articles and reviews. For information address HarperCollins Publishers Inc., 10 East 53rd Street, New York, NY 10022.

Designed by Shubhani Sarkar

ISBN 0-06-621122-0

To Michael Spradlin and Brian Grogan

Every author should be lucky enough to have the two of you
in her corner. This is just in case you don't know
how much I appreciate you.

Acknowledgments

I am so grateful to Alessandro Pini and Elena Sardelli for showing me the beauties of Tuscany. Bill, I couldn't have had a better companion on those unforgettable walks than you, even if you had to squeeze those (fabulous) shoulders into the tiny Italian showers. I am especially grateful that Maria Brummel came into my life at just the right time to help with the Italian translations. (Thanks, Andy, for having the good sense to marry such a wonderful young woman.) Thank you, too, Michèle Johnson and Cristina Negri for your invaluable help when I needed it most.

Once again, my fellow writers came to my aid with their knowledge and insight, especially Jennifer Crusie, Jennifer Greene, Cathie Linz, Lindsay Longford, and Suzette Vann. Jill Barnett, Kristin Hannah, Jayne Ann Krentz, and Meryl Sawyer, I can't imagine doing this job without the friendship and phone calls. Barbara Jepson, you were the best present I've ever given myself. Without the many things you do for me so efficiently and cheerfully, I'd have no time to write.

Thanks, Zach Phillips, for sharing your wisdom about metaphysics and human behavior patterns. Lydia, you're not only the best sister in the world but the best listener, too. We'll always have Paris! Steven Axelrod, I'm eternally grateful for the way your steady hand keeps us on course. Ty and Dana, sharing your happiness has brought me such joy this past year. To the "Seppies" on my website bulletin board—you're the world's best cheerleaders. Cissy Hartley and Sara Reyes have done an incredible job creating and maintaining my website. And to all the readers who write me such wonderful letters and send that encouraging e-mail, thank you so much. It's a great way to start the day.

It is long past time for me to recognize the talented and enthusiastic people at William Morrow and Avon Books who so frequently go above and beyond the call of duty for me. Carrie Feron, my gifted editor and guardian, has also been a wonderful friend. I am deeply indebted to all of the people who market and sell my books, design my beautiful covers, and cheer me on. These include Richard Aquan, Nancy Anderson, Leesa Belt, George Bick, Shannon Ceci, Geoff Colquitt, Ralph D'Arienzo, Karen Davy, Darlene Delillo, Gail Dubov, Tom Egner, Seth Fleischman, Josh Frank, Jane Friedman, Lisa Gallagher, Cathy Hemming, Angela Leigh, Kim Lewis, Brian McSharry, Judy Madonia, Michael Morrison, Gena Pearson, Jan Parrish, Chadd Reese, Rhonda Rose, Pete Soper, Debbie Stier, Andrea Sventora, Bruce Unck, and Donna Waitkus. You're the best!

Breathing Room

1

Dr. Isabel Favor prized neatness. During the week she wore exquisitely tailored black suits with tasteful leather pumps and a strand of pearls at her throat. On weekends she favored tidy sweater sets or silk shells, always in a neutral palette. A well-cut bob and an assortment of expensive beauty products generally tamed her blond hair's inclination to rearrange itself into disobedient curls. If that failed, she resorted to narrow velvet headbands.

She wasn't beautiful, but her evenly spaced light brown eyes sat exactly where they should, and her forehead rose in proportion to the rest of her face. Her lips were a shade too lavish, so she camouflaged them with nude-toned lipstick and dotted foundation on her nose to mute an unruly splash of freckles. Good eating habits kept her complexion creamy and her figure slender and healthy, although she would have preferred slimmer hips. In nearly every respect she was an orderly woman, the exception being a slightly uneven right thumbnail. While she no longer bit it to the quick, it was markedly shorter than her other nails, and nibbling at its edges remained the only habit from her very untidy childhood that she'd never entirely been able to conquer.

As the lights in the Empire State Building went on outside her office windows, Isabel tucked her thumb inside her fist to resist temptation. Lying on her art deco desk was that morning's issue of Manhattan's favorite tabloid. The feature article had festered inside her all day, but she'd been too busy to brood. Now it was brooding time.

AMERICA'S DIVA OF SELF-HELP IS DRIVEN, DEMANDING, AND DIFFICULT

> The former administrative assistant to well-known self-help author and lecturer Dr. Isabel Favor says her employer is the boss from hell. "She's a total control freak," declares Teri Mitchell, who resigned from her position last week. . . .

"She didn't resign," Isabel pointed out. "I fired her after I found two months' worth of fan mail she didn't bother to open." Her thumbnail crept to her teeth. "And I'm not a control freak."

"Coulda fooled me." Carlota Mendoza emptied a brass wastebasket into the receptacle on her cleaning cart. "You're also—what was those other things she said—driven and demanding? *Sí*, those, too."

"I am not. Get the top of those light fixtures, will you?"

"Do I look like I got a ladder with me? And stop biting your nails."

Isabel tucked away her thumb. "I have standards, that's all. Unkindness is a flaw. Stinginess, envy, greed—all flaws. But am I any of those things?"

"There's a bag of candy bars hidden in the backa your bottom drawer, but my English isn't too good, so maybe I don' understand this greed stuff."

"Very funny." Isabel didn't believe in eating her feelings, but it had been a horrible day, so she slid open her emergency drawer, pulled out two Snickers bars, and tossed one to Carlota. She'd simply put in extra time with her yoga tapes tomorrow morning.

Carlota caught the candy bar and leaned against her cart to tear it open. "Just outta curiosity . . . you ever wear jeans?"

"Jeans?" Isabel smooshed the chocolate against the roof of her mouth, taking a moment to savor it before she replied. "Well, I used to." She set down the candy bar and rose from the desk. "Here, give me that." She grabbed Carlota's dust cloth, kicked off her pumps, and tugged up the skirt of her Armani suit so she could climb onto the couch to reach a wall sconce.

Carlota sighed. "You're gonna tell me again, aren't you, about how you put yourself through college cleaning houses?"

"And offices and restaurants and factories." Isabel used her index finger to get between the scrollwork. "I waited tables all through graduate school, washed dishes—oh, I hated that job. While I wrote my dissertation, I ran errands for lazy rich people."

"What you are now, except without the lazy part."

Isabel smiled and moved on to the top of a picture frame. "I'm trying to make a point. With hard work, discipline, and prayer, people can make their dreams come true."

"If I wanted to hear all this, I'da bought a ticket to one of your lectures."

"Yet here I am giving you my wisdom for free."

"Lucky me. You done yet? 'Cause I got other offices to clean tonight."

Isabel stepped down from the couch, handed over the dust cloth, then rearranged the cleaning bottles on the top of the cart so Carlota wouldn't have to reach so far for the ones she needed. "Why did you ask about jeans?"

"Just trying to picture it in my mind." Carlota popped the rest of the Snickers into her mouth. "All the time you look ritzy, like you don't know what a toilet is, let alone how to clean one."

"I have to maintain an image. I wrote *Four Cornerstones of a Favorable Life* when I was only twenty-eight. If I hadn't dressed conservatively, no one would have taken me seriously."

"You're what, sixty-two now? You need jeans."

"I just turned thirty-four, and you know it."

"Jeans and a pretty red blouse, one of them tight ones to show off your boobs. And some really high heels."

"Speaking of hookers, did I tell you those two ladies who hang out by the alley showed up at the new job program yesterday?"

"Those whores'll be back on the street by next week. I don' know why you waste your time with them."

"Because I like them. They're hard workers." Isabel kicked back in her chair, forcing herself to concentrate on the positive instead of that humiliating newspaper article. "The Four Cornerstones work for everybody, from streetwalkers to saints, and I have thousands of testimonials to prove it."

Carlota snorted and turned on the vacuum, effectively ending their conversation. Isabel shoved the newspaper in the trash, then gazed toward the lighted niche in the wall to her right. It held a magnificent Lalique crystal vase etched with four interlocking squares, the distinctive logo of Isabel Favor Enterprises. Each square represented one of the Four Cornerstones of a Favorable Life:

Healthy Relationships

Professional Pride   Financial Responsibility

Spiritual Dedication

Her critics attacked the Four Cornerstones as too simplistic, and she'd been accused more than once of being both smug and sanctimonious, but she didn't take anything she'd earned for granted, so she'd never felt smug. As for being sanctimonious, she was no charlatan. She'd built her company and her life by applying those principles, and it gratified her to know that her work was making a difference in people's lives. She had four books to her credit, with a fifth coming out in a few weeks; a dozen audiotapes; lecture tours scheduled through next year; and a hefty bank account. Not bad for a mousy little girl who'd grown up in emotional chaos.

She gazed at the tidy piles on her desk. She also had a fiancé, a wedding that she'd been promising to plan for a year, and paperwork she needed to attack before she could go home for the night.

She waved good-bye as Carlota wheeled away her cart, then picked up a thick envelope from the Internal Revenue Service. It should have gone to Tom Reynolds, her accountant and business manager, but he'd called in sick yesterday, and she didn't like letting things pile up.

Which didn't mean that she was driven, demanding, *or* difficult.

She slit the envelope with a monogrammed letter opener. The press had been calling all day for her comments on the newspaper article, but she'd taken the high road and refused to respond. Still, the negative publicity made her uneasy. Her business was built on both the respect and affection of her fans, which was why she tried her hardest to live an exemplary life. An image was a fragile thing, and this article would damage hers. The question was, how badly?

She pulled out the letter and began to read. Halfway through, her eyebrows shot up, and she reached for her telephone. Just when she'd thought her day couldn't get worse, now she had a screw-up with the IRS. And it looked like a doozy—a bill for $1.2 million in back taxes.

She was scrupulously honest with her taxes, so she knew that it was one of their maddening computer errors, which didn't mean it would be simple to straighten out. She hated to pester Tom when he was sick, but he'd need to attend to this first thing in the morning.

"Marilyn, it's Isabel. I need to speak with Tom."

"Tom?" Her business manager's wife's speech was slurred, as if she'd been drinking. Isabel's parents used to sound like that. "Tom's not here."

"I'm glad he's feeling better. When do you expect him back? I'm afraid we have an emergency."

Marilyn sniffed. "I—I should have called you earlier, but . . ." She burst into tears. "But I—I couldn't . . ."

"What's wrong? Tell me."

"It's T-Tom. He's—he's—" Her sobs caught in her throat like a jackhammer stuck in blacktop. "He's r-r-run off to South America with m-m-my s-sister!"

And, as Isabel discovered less than twenty-four hours later, all of Isabel's money.

Michael Sheridan stayed with Isabel while she dealt with the police and endured a long series of painful meetings with the IRS. He wasn't just Isabel's attorney but the man she loved, and she'd never been more grateful to have him in her life. Yet even his presence wasn't enough to avert disaster, and by the end of May, two months after she'd received that damning letter, her worst fears had been confirmed.

"I'm going to lose everything." She rubbed her eyes, then dropped her purse onto the Queen Anne chair in the living room of her Upper East Side brownstone. The room's warm cherry paneling and oriental rugs glowed in the soft light of her Frederick Cooper lamps. She knew that earthly possessions were fleeting, but she hadn't expected them to be *this* fleeting.

"I'll have to sell this place—my furniture, my jewelry, all my antiques." Then there was the disbanding of her charitable foundation, which had been doing so much good at a grassroots level. Everything gone.

She wasn't telling Michael anything he didn't know, just trying to make it real so she could cope, and when he didn't respond, she regarded him apologetically. "You've been quiet all night. I've exhausted you with my complaining, haven't I?"

He turned away from the window where he'd been gazing down on the park. "You're not a complainer, Isabel. You're just trying to reorient yourself."

"Tactful, as always." She gave him a rueful smile and straightened a tapestry pillow on the sofa.

She and Michael weren't living together—Isabel didn't believe in that—but sometimes she wished they were. Living apart meant they saw too little of each other. Lately they'd been lucky to manage their weekly Saturday-night dinner date. As for sex . . . She couldn't remember how long it had been since either of them had felt the urge.

The moment Isabel had met Michael Sheridan, she'd known he was her soul mate. They'd both grown up in dysfunctional families and worked hard to put themselves through school. He was intelligent and ambitious, as orderly as she was, and just as dedicated to his career. He'd been her sounding board as she'd refined her lectures on the Four Cornerstones, and two years ago, when she'd written a book about the Healthy Relationship Cornerstone, he'd contributed a chapter offering the male point of view. Her fans knew all about their relationship and were always asking when they were getting married.

She also found comfort in his pleasant, unassuming looks. He had a thin, narrow face and neatly trimmed brown hair. He was only a little over five feet nine, so he didn't tower above her, something that made her uneasy. He was even-tempered and logical.

Most of all, he was contained. With Michael there were no dark mood swings or unexpected outbursts. He was familiar and dear, a little stuffy in the best possible way, and perfect for her. They should have been married a year ago, but they'd both been too busy, and they got along so well that she'd seen no need to rush. Marriage couldn't help but be chaotic, even those that had been well thought out.

"I got the sales report on my new book today." She tried hard not to give in to the bitterness that kept trying to worm its way to the surface.

"It was just bad timing."

"I'm a joke on *Letterman*. While I was writing about the Financial Responsibility Cornerstone, my business manager was embezzling my money." She kicked off her shoes, then pushed them under the chair to keep from tripping over them. If only her publisher had been able to stop shipment, she could at least have been spared this final public humiliation. Her last book had spent sixteen weeks on the *New York Times* bestseller list, but this one was sitting unread on bookstore shelves. "I've sold, what, a hundred copies?"

"It's not that bad."

Except it was. Her publisher had stopped returning her calls, and ticket sales for her summer lecture tour had tanked so badly she'd been forced to cancel. Not only was she losing her material possessions to the IRS, but she had lost the reputation it had taken her years to build.

She took a deep breath against the panic that kept threatening to overwhelm her, and tried to look toward the positive. Soon she'd have all the time in the world to plan her wedding. But how could she marry Michael knowing that he'd be supporting them until she got back on her feet? *If* she got back on her feet . . .

She was too committed to the principles of the Four Corner-stones to let negative thoughts paralyze her. This was something they needed to discuss. "Michael, I know it's getting late, and you said you were tired, but we have to talk about the wedding."

He fiddled with the volume on her sound system. He'd been under a lot of stress at work, and her own troubles weren't helping. She reached out to touch him, but he stepped away. "Not now, Isabel."

She reminded herself that they'd never been a touchy-feely couple, and tried not to take his rejection to heart, especially since she'd put him through so much lately. "I want to make your life easier, not harder," she said. "You haven't mentioned anything lately about the wedding, but I know you're upset with me for not having set a date. Now I'm bankrupt, and the fact is, I'm having a hard time dealing with the idea of someone else supporting me. Even you."

"Isabel, please . . ."

"I know you're going to say it doesn't make any difference—that your money is my money—but it makes a difference to me. I've been supporting myself since I was eighteen, and—"

"Isabel, stop."

He hardly ever raised his voice, but she was coming on like a bulldozer, so she didn't blame him. Her assertiveness was both her strength and her weakness.

He turned toward the windows. "I've met someone."

"Really? Who?" Most of Michael's friends were lawyers, wonderful people but a little boring. It would be nice to add someone new to their circle.

"Her name is Erin."

"Do I know her?"

"No. She's older than I am, nearly forty." He turned back to her.

"And, God, she's a mess—a little overweight, and she lives in this crazy place. She doesn't care about makeup or clothes, and nothing ever matches. She doesn't even have a college degree."

"So what? We're not snobs." Isabel picked up the wineglass Michael had left on the coffee table earlier and carried it into the kitchen. "And let's face it, you and I can be a little uptight."

He followed her, speaking rapidly and with a kind of energy she hadn't heard in months. "She's the most impulsive person I've ever met. She cusses like a sailor and likes the worst movies. She tells terrible jokes, and she drinks beer, and . . . But she's comfortable with herself. She"—he took a deep breath—"she makes me comfortable, too, and . . . I love her."

"Then I'm sure I will, too." Isabel smiled. Smiled hard. Smiled forever. Smiled until her jaw froze, because as long as she smiled, everything would be all right.

"She's pregnant, Isabel. Erin and I are going to have a baby. We're getting married at City Hall next week."

The wineglass dropped into the sink and shattered.

"I know this isn't a good time, but . . ."

Her stomach cramped. She wanted to stop him. Stop time itself. Turn back the clock so none of this was happening.

He looked pale and miserable. "We both know this hasn't been working out."

The air wheezed in her lungs. "That's not true. It's been— It's—" She couldn't breathe.

"Except for business meetings, we barely see each other."

She sucked in air. Clamped her fingers around the gold bangle she wore at her wrist. "We've been . . . been busy, that's all."

"We haven't had sex in months!"

"It's just— That's only temporary." She heard the same edge of hysteria in her voice that she'd heard so frequently in her mother's, and she struggled to hold herself back, to stay in control. "Our relationship has . . . It's never been based just on sex. We've talked about that. This is— It's temporary," she repeated.

He took a short, swift step forward. "Come off it, Isabel! Don't lie to yourself. Our sex life isn't programmed into your fucking PalmPilot, so it doesn't exist."

"Don't talk to me about PalmPilots! You take yours to bed at night!"

"At least it gets warm in my hand!"

She felt as if he'd slapped her.

He wilted. "I'm sorry. That was unnecessary. And untrue. Most of the time it was all right. It's just . . ." He made a small, helpless gesture. "I want *passion.*"

She grasped the side of the counter. "Passion? We're grown-ups." She tried to steady herself, tried to breathe. "If you're not happy with our sex life, we can . . . we can get counseling." But there'd be no counseling. This woman was carrying Michael's baby. The baby Isabel had someday planned on bearing.

"I don't want counseling." His voice dropped. "It's not my problem, Isabel. It's yours."

"That's not true."

"It's . . . You're schizo when it comes to sex. Sometimes you get into it. Other times it feels like you're doing me a favor and you can't get it over with fast enough. Even worse, sometimes it feels like you're not there at all."

"Most men would appreciate a little variety."

"You need to control everything. Maybe that's why you don't like sex that much."

She couldn't bear the look of pity he gave her. She should pity him. He was running off with a badly dressed older woman who liked awful movies and drank beer. And wasn't schizo about sex. . . .

She heard herself falling apart. "You're so wrong. I crave sex! I live for it! Sex is all I think about."

"I love her, Isabel."

"It's not really love. It's—"

"Don't tell me what I'm feeling, damn it! You always do that. You think you know everything, but you don't."

She didn't think that. She only wanted to help people.

"You can't control this, Isabel. I need a normal life. I need Erin. And I need the baby."

She wanted to curl up and howl from the pain of it. "Then take her. I don't ever want to see you again."

"Try to understand. She makes me feel—I don't know . . . safe. Sane. You're *too much*! You're too much of everything! And you make me crazy!"

"Good. Get out."

"I'd hoped we could do this civilly. Stay friends."

"We can't. Get out of here."

And he did. Without another word. He just turned his back and walked out of her life.

She began to choke. She stumbled to the sink and turned on the water, but she couldn't breathe. She staggered to the kitchen window and struggled with the latch, then pushed her head out into the air shaft. It was raining. She didn't care. She gulped in air and tried to find the words to pray, but they weren't there. And that's when it hit her.

Healthy Relationships
Professional Pride
Financial Responsibility
Spiritual Dedication

All Four Cornerstones of a Favorable Life had crashed in on top of her.

2

L orenzo Gage was viciously handsome. Hair as dark and thick
as devil's velvet set off silver-blue eyes so cold and piercing
they looked feral. His thin black brows shot into dangerous
angles, and his forehead spoke of an ancient aristocracy tinged with
corruption. His lips were cruelly sensuous, while his cheekbones
could have been carved by the knife he held in his hand.

Gage made his living killing people. His specialty was women.
Beautiful women. He beat them, tortured them, raped them, and
murdered them. Sometimes a bullet to the heart. Sometimes slice-
and-dice. This was one of those.

The redhead who lay in his bed wore only a bra and panties. Her
skin gleamed like ivory against his black satin sheets as he gazed
down at her. "You betrayed me," he said. "I don't like it when
women betray me."

Terror filled her green eyes. All the better.

He leaned down and flicked the sheet from her thighs with the
tip of his dagger. The gesture galvanized her. She screamed, rolled
away, and shot across the room.

He liked it when they fought back, and he let her reach the door before he caught her. She struggled in his arms. When he grew bored with her resistance, he backhanded her. The vicious snap knocked her across the room. She fell onto the bed, breasts heaving, those lovely thighs separating. He showed no emotion beyond a subtle flicker of anticipation. Then his brutally sculpted lips curled in a cruel smile, and one hand flicked open his silver belt buckle.

Gage shuddered. His stomach was unpredictable when it came to atrocities, and unlike the audience in the movie theater, he knew what was coming. He'd hoped the Italian dubbing would distract him enough from the carnage on the screen so he could actually watch his last film, but the remnants of a nasty hangover combined with a serious case of jet lag conspired against him. It was a bitch being Hollywood's favorite psychopath.

In the old days John Malkovich had done the job, but from the moment the public had set eyes on Ren Gage, they'd wanted to see more of this villain with a face to die for. Until tonight he'd avoided *Slaughter Alliance*, but since the critics had only mildly detested it, he'd decided to give it a shot. Big mistake.

Rapist, serial killer, assassin for hire. Hell of a way to make a living. In addition to the women he'd mortally abused, he'd tortured Mel Gibson, slammed a tire iron into Ben Affleck's kneecap, given Pierce Brosnan a nearly fatal chest wound, and gone after Denzel Washington in a nuclear-powered helicopter. He'd even killed Sean Connery. He'd burn in hell for that one. Nobody messed with Sean Connery.

Still, the stars got even with him before the picture was over. Ren had been garroted, set on fire, beheaded, and castrated—that one had hurt. Now he was being publicly drawn and quartered for driving America's movie sweetheart to suicide. Except—wait a minute—that was his real life, wasn't it? His very own, very real, very fucked-up life.

All the screaming was making his head pound. He glanced back up at the screen in time to watch blood spray as the redhead bit the dust. *Tough luck, sweetheart. That's what you get for being taken in by a pretty face.*

Neither his head nor his stomach could tolerate more, and he slipped out of the darkened movie theater. His pictures did big business internationally, and as he eased into the milling crowd that was enjoying the warm Florentine night, he glanced around to make certain no one recognized him, but the tourists and locals were too busy enjoying the busy street life to take notice.

The last thing he wanted to do was deal with fans, so he'd taken time to alter his appearance before he'd left his hotel room, even though he'd been functioning on less than two hours of sleep. He'd slipped in some brown contact lenses to hide his trademark silver-blue eyes and let his dark hair—still long and sleek from the picture he'd finished shooting in Australia two days earlier—hang free. He'd also neglected to shave, hoping the stubble would camouflage a chiseled jaw that might have been passed down from his Medici ancestors. Although he'd rather have worn jeans, he'd costumed himself in the elegant garb of a wealthy Italian: black silk shirt, dark trousers, exquisite loafers with a scratch across one toe because he was as careless with clothes as he was with people. Keeping a low profile was a relatively new experience. Generally, if there was a spotlight around, he liked to make certain it was shining on him. But not right now.

He should go back to the hotel and sleep till noon, but he was too restless. If his cronies had been around, he might have headed for a club, but then again maybe not. Club life had lost its appeal. Unfortunately, he was a night owl, and he hadn't yet figured out what to do instead.

He passed the window of a butcher shop. A stuffed boar's head stared at him through the glass, and he looked away. The last couple of days had been a bitch. Karli Swenson, his former girlfriend and one of Hollywood's favorite actresses, had killed herself the week before at her Malibu beach house. Karli had a long history with cocaine, so he suspected that her suicide was drug related, which pissed him off so much he still couldn't mourn her. One thing he did know for sure—she hadn't killed herself because of him.

Even when they were dating, Karli had cared a lot more about what was going up her nose than she'd ever cared for him, but audiences adored her, and the tabloids wanted a sexier story than drugs. No surprise, they'd decided he was it. Hollywood's career bad boy whose heartless ways with women had driven sweet Karli to her grave.

Since those bad-boy stories had helped build his career, he couldn't blame the media, but he still didn't like how exposed this was making him feel. That was why he'd decided to go to ground for the next six weeks or so, until shooting for his next picture started.

He'd originally planned to call up an old girlfriend, head for the Caribbean, and get down to the serious business of resuming the sex life he'd put on hiatus a few months before filming on his last picture had started. But the uproar over Karli's death made him want to put more distance between himself and the States, so he'd decided to go to Italy instead. It was not only the country of his ancestors but also the place where the initial filming on his next picture would begin. He'd get a chance to soak in some atmosphere, slip into the skin of a new character. And he wasn't bringing along any publicity-hungry old girlfriends to get in his way.

What the hell. He could tolerate his own company for a few weeks until the heat from Karli's suicide died down and he felt more like getting back into the swing of things. For now, the idea of moving around incognito was novel enough to keep him entertained.

He looked up and realized he'd wandered into the center of Florence, the crowded Piazza della Signoria. He couldn't remember

the last time he'd been alone. He made his way across the cobblestones to Rivoire and found a table under the awning. The waiter
appeared to take his order. Considering his hangover, he should
stick with club soda, but he seldom did what he was supposed to,
and he ordered a bottle of their best Brunello instead. The waiter
took too long delivering it, and Ren snarled at him when he reap-
peared. His ugly mood came from lack of sleep, booze, and the fact
that he was tired all the way to his bones. It came from sweet, sad
Karli's death, and a general feeling that all the money and all the
fame still weren't enough—that no spotlight could ever shine bright
enough. He was jaded, restless, and he wanted more. More fame.
More money. More . . . something.

He reminded himself his next film would give it to him. Every
actor in town wanted to play the villainous Kaspar Street, but only
Ren had been offered the job. It was the role of a lifetime, the
chance for top billing.

Slowly his muscles unwound. Making *Night Kill* would involve
months of hard work. Until filming began, he intended to enjoy
Italy. He'd relax, eat well, and do what he did best. Leaning back in
his chair, he took a sip of wine and waited for life to entertain him.

As Isabel gazed up at the pink and green dome of the Duomo outlined against the night sky, she decided that Florence's most
famous landmark looked garish instead of grand. She didn't like
this city. Even at night it was crowded and noisy. Italy might have a
tradition as the place where soul-bruised women came to heal, but
for her, leaving New York had been a terrible mistake.

She told herself to be patient. She'd arrived only yesterday, and
Florence wasn't her ultimate destination. That had been determined by fate and her friend Denise's change of mind. For years

Denise had dreamed about coming to Italy. Finally she'd applied for a leave of absence from her Wall Street job and rented a house in the Tuscan countryside for the months of September and October. She'd planned to use the time to begin work on a book about investment strategies for single women. *"Italy is the perfect place for inspiration,"* Denise had told Isabel over the glazed pear and endive salad at Jo Jo's, their favorite lunch spot. *"I'll write all day, then eat fabulous food and drink great wine at night."*

But shortly after Denise had signed the lease on the Tuscan farmhouse of her dreams, she'd met the man of her dreams and declared that she couldn't possibly leave New York now. Which was how Isabel had ended up with a reasonably priced two-month rental on a farmhouse in Tuscany.

It couldn't have come along at a better time. Life in New York had grown unbearable. Isabel Favor Enterprises no longer existed. Her office was closed; her staff had moved on. She had no book contract, no lecture tour, and very little money. Her brownstone, along with nearly everything else she owned, had fallen to the auctioneer's gavel so she could pay off her tax debt. Even the Lalique crystal vase engraved with her logo was gone. All she had left were her clothes, a broken life, and two months in Italy to figure out how to start over.

Someone bumped against her, and she jumped. The crowds had thinned out, and the New Yorker inside her no longer felt safe, so she headed down the Via dei Calzaiuoli to the Piazza della Signoria. As she walked, she told herself she'd made the right decision. Only a clean break from the familiar could clear her mind enough so that she could stop feeling as though all she wanted to do was cry. Finally she'd be able to move ahead.

She had a definite plan for how she would begin the process of reinventing her life. *Solitude. Rest. Contemplation. Action.* Four parts, just like the Four Cornerstones.

"Can't you ever be impulsive?" Michael had once said. *"Do you have to plan everything?"*

A little over three months had passed since Michael had left her for another woman, but his voice poked into her consciousness so frequently she could hardly think anymore. Last month she'd caught a glimpse of him in Central Park with his arm around a badly dressed pregnant woman, and even from fifty feet away Isabel could hear the sound of their laughter, a little giddy, silly almost. In all their time together, he and Isabel had never once been silly. Isabel was afraid she'd forgotten how.

The Piazza della Signoria was as crowded as the rest of Florence. Tourists milled around the statues, while a pair of musicians strummed their guitars near Neptune's Fountain. The forbidding Palazzo Vecchio, with its crenellated clock tower and medieval banners, loomed over the nighttime bustle just as it had been doing since the fourteenth century.

The leather pumps she'd paid three hundred dollars for last year were killing her, but going back to the hotel was too depressing. She spotted the beige and brown awnings of Rivoire, a café that had been mentioned in her guidebook, and made her way through a group of German tourists to find an outside table.

"Buona sera, signora. . . ." The waiter was at least sixty, but that didn't stop him from flirting with her as he took her wine order. She would have loved a risotto, but the prices were even higher than the calorie count. How many years had it been since she'd had to worry over menu prices?

When the waiter left, she centered the salt and pepper shakers on the tablecloth, then moved the ashtray to the edge. Michael had looked so happy with his new wife.

"You're too much," he'd said. *"Too much of everything."* So why did she feel as if she were too little?

She drank the first glass of wine more quickly than she should have and ordered another. Her parents' long-term love affair with personal excess had made her wary of alcohol, but she was in a strange country, and the emptiness that had been growing inside her for months had become unbearable.

"It's not my problem, Isabel. It's yours . . ."

She'd promised herself she wouldn't brood about this again tonight, but she couldn't seem to get past it.

"You need to control everything. Maybe that's why you don't like sex that much."

That was so unfair. She liked sex. She'd even started toying with the idea of taking a lover to prove it, but she recoiled from the idea of sex outside a committed relationship. It was another legacy from watching her parents' mistakes.

She wiped away the smear her lipstick left on her wineglass. Sex was a partnership, but Michael seemed to have forgotten that. If he hadn't been satisfied, he should have discussed it with her.

Her thoughts were making her even more unhappy than she'd been when she entered the piazza, so she finished her second glass of wine and ordered another. One night of excess would hardly turn her into an alcoholic.

At the next table two women smoked, gestured, and rolled their eyes over the absurdity of life. A group of American students just behind them gorged on pizza and gelato, while an older couple gazed at each other over thimble-size aperitifs.

"I want passion," Michael had said.

The implication was too painful to contemplate, so she studied the statues on the other side of the piazza, copies of *The Rape of the Sabines,* Cellini's *Perseus,* Michelangelo's *David.* Then her eyes settled on the most amazing man she'd ever seen. . . .

He sat three tables away, a portrait of Italian decadence in a rumpled black silk shirt with dark stubble on his jaw, long hair, and

La Dolce Vita eyes. Two elegantly tapered fingers curled around the stem of the wineglass that dangled indolently from his hand. He looked rich, spoiled, bored—Marcello Mastroianni stripped of his clown face and chiseled into perfect male beauty for an avaricious new millennium.

There was something vaguely familiar about him, although she knew they'd never met. His face could have been painted by one of the masters—Michelangelo, Botticelli, Raphael. That must be why she felt as if she'd seen him before.

She studied him more closely, only to realize he was studying her in return. . . .

3

Ren had been watching her ever since she arrived. She'd rejected two tables before she found one that pleased her, then rearranged the condiments as soon as she was seated. A discriminating woman. She wore the stamp of intelligence as visibly as her Italian shoes, and even from here she radiated a seriousness of purpose that he found as sexy as those overly lavish lips.

She looked to be in her early thirties, with understated makeup and the simple but expensive clothes favored by sophisticated European women. Her face was more intriguing than beautiful. She wasn't Hollywood emaciated, but he liked her body—breasts in proportion to her hips, tapered waist, the promise of great legs underneath her black slacks. Her blond hair had highlights she hadn't been born with, but he'd bet that was the only thing fake about her. No artificial fingernails or false eyelashes. And if those breasts were stuffed with silicone, she'd be showing them off instead of keeping them tucked away underneath that tidy black sweater.

He watched her finish one glass of wine and start on another.

She took a nibble on her thumbnail. The gesture seemed out of character for such an earnest woman, which made it weirdly erotic.

He studied the other women in the café, but his eyes kept returning to her. He sipped his wine and thought it over. Women found him—he never went after them. But it had been a long time, and there was something about this one.

What the hell . . .

He leaned back in his chair and gave her his patented smoldering gaze.

Isabel felt his eyes on her. The man oozed sex. Her third glass of wine had lifted the leading edge of her dismal mood, and his attention lifted it a bit higher. Here was a person who knew something about passion.

He shifted his weight slightly and raised one dark, angular eyebrow. She wasn't used to such a blatant come-on. Gorgeous men wanted counseling from Dr. Isabel Favor, not sex. She was too intimidating.

She moved the silverware half an inch to the right. He didn't look American, and she had no international following, so he wouldn't have recognized her. No, this man wasn't interested in Dr. Favor's wisdom. He just wanted sex.

"It's not my problem, Isabel. It's yours."

She looked up, and his lips curved. Her bruised heart, numbed by the wine, feasted on that slight smile.

This man doesn't think I'm schizo, Michael. This man recognizes a powerfully sexual woman when he sees one.

He locked his eyes with hers and deliberately touched the corner of his mouth with his knuckle. Something warm unfolded inside her, like a layer of puff pastry plumping in an oven. She watched, fascinated, as his knuckle drifted toward the slight indentation in his bottom lip. The gesture was so blatantly sexual she should have been offended. Instead, she took another sip and waited to see what he'd do next.

He rose, picked up his glass, and walked slowly toward her. The two Italian women at the next table stopped their conversation to watch. One uncrossed her legs. The other shifted in her chair. They were young and beautiful, but this fallen Renaissance angel zeroed in on her.

"Signora?" He gestured toward the chair across from her. *"Posso farti compagnia?"*

She felt herself nod, even as her brain ordered her to turn him away. He slid into the chair, as seductive as a black satin sheet.

Up close he was no less devastating, but his eyes were a little bloodshot, and the stubble on his jaw seemed more a product of fatigue than a fashion statement. Perversely, his ragged edges intensified his sexuality.

She was only mildly startled to hear herself address him in French. *"Je ne parle pas l'italien, monsieur."*

Whoa . . . One part of her brain ordered her to get up and walk away right now. The other part told her not to be in such a hurry. She did a quick survey to see if anything obvious would give her away as an American, but Europe was filled with blondes, including ones like her who'd had light streaks added to perk up their spirits. She was dressed in black, as he was—slim trousers and a cropped, sleeveless cotton sweater with a funnel neck. Her uncomfortable shoes were Italian. The only jewelry she wore was a thin gold bangle with the single word BREATHE inscribed inside, to remind her to stay centered. She hadn't eaten, so he couldn't have witnessed that telling transfer of fork from left hand to right that Americans made when they cut their meat.

What does it matter? Why are you doing this?

Because the world as she knew it had collapsed around her.

Because Michael didn't love her, and she'd had too much wine, and she was tired of being frightened, and she wanted to feel like a woman instead of a failed institution.

"*È un peccato.*" He shrugged in that wonderful Italian way. "*Non parlo francesca.*"

"*Parlez-vous anglais?*"

He shook his head and brushed his chest. "*Mi chiamo Dante.*"

His name was Dante. How appropriate in this city that had once been the home of the poet Dante Alighieri.

She tapped her own chest. "*Je suis . . . Annette.*"

"*Annette. Molta bella.*" He lifted his glass in a sexy, silent toast.

Dante . . . The name warmed her belly like hot syrup, and the night air turned to musk.

His hand touched hers. She gazed down at it but didn't draw away. Instead, she took another sip of wine.

He began toying with the tips of her fingers, letting her know this was more than a casual flirtation. This was a seduction, and the fact that it was calculated bothered her for only a moment. She was too demoralized for subtlety.

"*Hold your body precious,*" the Spiritual Dedication Cornerstone advised. "*You're a treasure, God's greatest creation. . . .*" She absolutely believed that, but Michael had bruised her soul, and this fallen angel named Dante promised a dark kind of redemption, so she smiled at him and didn't move her hand away.

He leaned farther back in his chair, at ease with his body in a way few men were. She envied his physical arrogance.

Together they watched the American students grow more boisterous. He ordered a fourth glass of wine for her. She shocked herself by flirting a little with her eyes. *See, Michael, I know how to do this. And do you know why? Because I'm a lot more sexual than you think I am.*

She was glad the language barrier made conversation impossible. Her life had been filled with words: lectures, books, interviews. PBS played her videos whenever they had a fund drive. She'd talked, talked, talked. And look what it had gotten her.

His finger slipped beneath her hand and stroked the cradle of her palm in a gesture that was purely carnal. Savonarola, that fifteenth-century enemy of everything sensual, had been burned at the stake in this very piazza. Would she burn?

She was burning now, and her head was spinning. Still, she wasn't so drunk that she didn't notice that his smile never made it to his eyes. He'd done this a hundred times before. This was about sex, not sincerity.

That's when it struck her. He was a gigolo.

She started to snatch away her hand. But why? This simply spelled everything out in black and white, something she usually appreciated. She lifted her wineglass to her lips with her free hand. She'd come to Italy to reinvent her life, but how could she do that without erasing the ugly tape of Michael's accusation that kept playing in her head? The tape that made her feel shriveled and lacking. She fought back her despair.

Maybe Michael was responsible for their sexual problems. Hadn't Dante the gigolo shown her more about lust in a few minutes than Michael had shown her in four years? Maybe a pro could accomplish what an amateur hadn't been able to. At least a pro could be trusted to push the proper buttons.

The fact that she was even thinking about this should shock her, but the past six months had numbed her to shock. As a psychologist, she knew for certain that no one created a new life by ignoring old problems. They simply came back to bite again.

She knew she shouldn't make a decision about something this important when she wasn't sober. On the other hand, if she were sober, she'd never consider it, and that suddenly seemed like the worst mistake she could make. What better use could she find for the little money she had left than to put the past to rest so she could move ahead? This was the missing piece of her plan to reinvent herself.

Solitude, Rest, Contemplation, and *Sexual Healing*—four steps all leading to a fifth, *Action*. And all, more or less, in keeping with the Four Cornerstones.

He took his time finishing his wine, stroking her palm, sliding his finger beneath her gold bangle and over the pulse at her wrist. Abruptly he grew bored with the game and flung a handful of bills on the table. He rose and slowly extended his hand.

Now was the time to decide. All she had to do was keep her hand on the table and shake her head. A dozen other women sat within breathing distance, and he wouldn't make a fuss.

"Sex will not fix what's broken inside you," Dr. Isabel said when she lectured. *"Sex without a deep and abiding love will only leave you feeling sad and small. So fix yourself first. Fix yourself! Then you can think about sex. Because if you don't—if you try to use sex to hide your addictions, to hurt the people who've abused you, to heal your insecurities so you can feel whole—you'll only make what's broken inside you hurt that much worse. . . ."*

But Dr. Favor was a bankrupt failure, and the blonde in the Florentine café didn't have to listen to her. Isabel rose and took his hand.

Her knees felt wobbly from the wine as he led her out of the piazza into the narrow streets. She wondered how much a gigolo charged, and hoped she had enough. If not, she'd use her overextended credit card. They walked in the direction of the river. Once again she experienced that nagging sense of familiarity. Which of the Old Masters had captured his face? But her brain was too fuzzy to remember.

He pointed to a Medici shield on the side of a building, then gestured toward a tiny courtyard where white flowers grew around a
fountain. Tour guide and gigolo in one erotic package. The universe
provided. And tonight it had provided the missing link in her plan
to create a new life.

She didn't like men towering over her, and he was a head taller
than she, but he'd be horizontal soon, so that wouldn't be a problem. She suppressed a flicker of panic. He could be married, but he
barely seemed civilized, let alone domesticated. He could be a mass
murderer, but despite the Mafia, Italian criminals tended to prefer
theft to slaughter.

He smelled expensive—clean, exotic, and enticing—but the
scent seemed to come from his pores instead of a bottle. She had a
vision of him pressing her against one of the ancient stone buildings, lifting her skirt, and pushing into her, except that would get it
over with too quickly, and getting it over with wasn't the point. The
point was being able to silence Michael's voice so she could move
forward with her life.

The wine had made her clumsy, and she tripped on nothing. Oh,
she was a smoothie, all right. He steadied her, then gestured toward
the door of a small, expensive hotel.

"Vuoi venire con me al'albergo."

She didn't understand the words, but the invitation was clear.

"I want passion!" Michael had said.

Well, guess what, Michael Sheridan? So do I.

She pushed past Dante and marched into the tiny lobby. Its
exquisite appointments were reassuring—velvet drapes, gilded
chairs, terrazzo floor. At least she'd be having her sordid sex on
clean sheets. And this wasn't the kind of place a lunatic would
choose to murder a naïve, undersexed female tourist.

The desk clerk handed him a key, so he was already registered. A high-class gigolo. Their shoulders brushed in the tiny elevator, and she knew that the heat in the pit of her stomach came from more than wine and unhappiness.

They stepped out into a dimly lit hallway. As she gazed at him, a bizarre image flashed through her mind of a black-garbed man firing an assault weapon.

Where had that come from? Although she didn't feel entirely safe with him, neither did she feel as though she were in physical danger. If he'd planned to murder her, he'd have done it in one of the alleys they'd passed, not with an assault weapon in a five-star hotel.

He led her to the end of the corridor. His hand on her arm was firm, a silent signal, perhaps, that he was now in charge.

Oh, God . . . What was she doing?

"Good sex, great sex, needs to be just as much about our brains as it is about bodies."

Dr. Isabel was right. But this wasn't about great sex. This was about raunchy, forbidden, dangerous sex in a strange city with a man she'd never see again. Sex to clear her mind and wash away her fear. Sex to reassure her that she was still a woman. Sex to mend the broken places so she could move ahead.

He opened the door and flipped on a light switch. His women paid him well. This was no simple hotel room but an elegant suite, although a bit untidy, with his clothes tumbling from an open suitcase and his shoes lying in the middle of the floor.

"Vuoi un poco di vino?"

She recognized the word *"vino"* and meant to say yes, but she got confused and shook her head instead. The motion was too fast, and she nearly lost her balance.

"Va bene." A small, courteous nod, and then he walked past her into the bedroom. He moved like a creature of the dark, sleek and

damned. Or maybe she was the one damned because she didn't leave. Instead, she followed as far as the doorway and watched him go to the windows.

He leaned out to push the shutters back, and the breeze ruffled the long, silky strands of his hair while the moonlight glazed it with silver. He gestured outside. *"Vieni vedere. Il giardino è bellissimo di notte."*

Her feet felt like alcohol-soaked rags as she set her purse on the dresser and went over to stand at his side. She gazed down and saw half a dozen tables in the flower-filled courtyard, their umbrellas collapsed for the night. Beyond the walls she heard traffic, and she thought she detected the musty scent of the Arno.

His hand slipped under her hair. He'd made the first move.

She could still leave. She could let him know this was a big mistake, a colossal mistake, the mother of all mistakes. How much money did you leave a gigolo who hadn't completed the job? And what about a tip? Should she leave—

But he was just holding her. And holding wasn't bad. It had been a long time. He felt a lot different from Michael. That unpleasant height, of course, but also a very pleasant muscularity.

He lowered his head, and she began to back away, because she wasn't ready for the kissing to start. Then she reminded herself this was to be a purging.

His lips touched hers at just the right angle. The slide of his tongue was perfect, neither too timid nor too suffocating. It was a great kiss, elegantly executed, no slurping sounds. Pretty much flawless. Too flawless. Even in her haze she knew that there was nothing of himself in it, just an effortless display of professional expertise. Which was good. Exactly what she would have expected if she'd had enough time to expect anything.

What was she *doing* here?

Shut up and let the man do his job. Think of him as a sex surrogate. Reputable therapists use them, don't they?

He certainly believed in taking his time, and her blood began to move a little faster. She gave him points for gentleness.

His hand slid under her sweater before she was ready, but she didn't try to redirect him. Michael was wrong. She didn't have to take control. Besides, Dante's touch felt good, so she couldn't be all that dysfunctional, could she? He flicked the catch of her bra, and she began to tense. *Relax and let the man work. This is perfectly natural, even if he is a complete stranger.*

He pushed aside the cups and stroked her spine. She was going to let him do this. She was going to let him brush his finger over her nipple. Yes, just like that. He was very skillful. . . . Taking plenty of time. Maybe she and Michael had been too quick to race to the end, but what could you expect from goal-oriented workaholics?

Dante seemed to appreciate fondling her breasts, which was nice. Michael had enjoyed them, but Dante seemed more of a connoisseur.

He drew her away from the window toward the bed and pushed up her sweater. Before, he'd been able only to touch her breasts. Now he could see them as well, and that felt intrusive, but if she pulled her sweater back down, she might be proving Michael's point, so she kept her hands at her sides.

He cradled her breast. Lifted it, molded it, then bent his head and drew the nipple deep into his mouth. Her body began to break away from its moorings.

She felt her slacks drifting over her hips. It was her nature to be cooperative, and she slipped off her shoes. He stepped back just enough to take off her sweater, then her bra. He was a wizard with women's clothes. No fumbling or wasted motions, everything perfect right down to the meaningless Italian endearments he was whispering in her ear.

She stood before him in beige lace panties and a gold bangle with the word BREATHE inscribed inside. He removed his shoes and socks—no awkwardness there—and unbuttoned his black silk shirt with the slow expertise of a male stripper, exposing one perfectly defined muscle after another. She could see that he worked out to keep the tools of his trade in good order.

His thumbs settled over her nipples, which were still moist from his mouth. He plucked them between his fingers, and she floated away from herself, which was a good place to be—the farther the better. *"Bella,"* he whispered, the sound a deep male purr.

His hand trailed over the beige lace between her legs and began to rub, but she wasn't ready for that. Dante needed to go back to gigolo school.

She'd no sooner thought it than the tip of his finger began a slow tracing around the lace. She clutched his arm for support against the sudden weakness in her legs. Why did she always think she knew how to do other people's jobs better than they did? This was one more reminder that she wasn't an expert at everything, or even anything—not that she needed many more reminders about that.

He flicked back the covers with an elegant twist of his wrist, drew her down, then reclined beside her, the motion so exquisitely executed it might have been choreographed. He should write a book: *Sex Secrets of Italy's Top Gigolo.* They should both write books. Hers would be called *How I Proved I Was All Woman and Reclaimed My Life.* Her publisher could sell them as a boxed set.

She was paying for this, and he'd touched her, so it was time to touch back, even though they hardly knew each other and it seemed presumptuous.

Stop it!

She began her tentative exploration with his chest, then his back. Michael worked out, but not like this man.

Her hands crept to his abdomen, which was tightly ridged like an athlete's. His trousers were gone—when had he gotten rid of them?—and his boxers were black silk.

Just do it!

She touched him through the thin fabric and heard the quick catch of breath. Real or feigned, she didn't know. One thing, however, wasn't an illusion. He'd been born with a natural gift for the gigolo trade.

She felt her panties being slipped off. *Did you expect to keep them on?* He shifted his weight and began kissing the inner slope of her thigh. A warning bell clanged. Her tension grew as his mouth moved higher. She grabbed his shoulders and pushed him away. There were some things she couldn't submit to, not even to clear out the past.

He gazed up at her. In the dim light she saw the question in his expression. She shook her head. He shrugged and reached toward the bedside table.

She hadn't once thought about condoms. Apparently she'd developed a death wish along with her other hang-ups. He slipped it on as smoothly as he did everything else, then began to draw her close, but she seized what little sanity she had left and held up two fingers.

"Due?"

"*Deux, s'il vous plaît.*"

With a look that had "crazy foreigner" written all over it, he reached for another condom. This time his motions weren't effortless. He had to struggle to fit latex over latex, and she looked away because his clumsiness made him seem human, and she didn't want that.

His hand brushed her hip, then her thighs. He pressed them open again, ready to practice more refinements on her, but this intimacy was too much for her. A tear leaked from the corner of her eye. She turned her head and blotted it on the pillow before he noticed. She wanted an orgasm, damn it, not drunken, self-pitying tears. An exquisite orgasm that would clear her mind so she could give her full attention to reinventing her life.

She tugged to pull him on top of her. When he hesitated, she tugged harder, and finally he did as she wanted. His hair brushed her cheek, and she heard the rough rasp of his breathing as he slipped a finger inside her. It felt good, but he was too close, and the wine sloshed uneasily in her stomach, and she should have made him lie on his back so she could get on top.

His touch grew slower, more tantalizing, but she wanted to get where they were going, and she pulled on his hips to urge him inside her. At last he moved his legs and resettled.

She realized right away that it wouldn't be an easy fit, not like with Michael. She gritted her teeth and wiggled against him until his self-control gave way and he embedded himself inside her.

Even then he wouldn't move along, so she tilted her hips, urging him to hurry, to get her where she needed to be, to finish up so she could be done with this before the sober whispers invading her wine-soaked brain turned into shouts and she had to deal with the fact that she was violating everything she believed in and *this was wrong!*

He angled, pulled back, and gazed down at her with hot, glazed eyes. She closed her own eyes so she wouldn't have to look at him, as superb as he was. He slipped his hands between their bodies and rubbed her, but his patience only made everything worse. The wine curdled in her stomach. She pushed his arm away and moved her hips. Eventually he took the hint and began a slow, thorough thrusting. She bit her lip and counted backward, counted forward, pushed his hand away again, and fought the bleakness of self-betrayal.

Eons passed before he convulsed. She endured his shudders and waited for the moment when he would roll to his side. When it finally came, she leaped from the bed.

"Annette?"

She ignored him and shoved herself into her clothes.

"Annette? *Che problema c'è?*"

She reached into her purse, threw a handful of bills on the bed, and fled from the room.

4

Eighteen hours later her blinding headache still hadn't eased. She was somewhere southwest of Florence trying to drive a stick shift Fiat Panda through the dark night on a strange road marked with signs in a language she couldn't read. Her knit dress had bunched under the seat belt, and she'd been too groggy to do her hair. She hated herself like this—messy, disorganized, depressed. She wondered how many disastrous missteps an intelligent woman could take and still keep her head up. Considering the current condition of her head, this woman had taken a few too many.

A sign flashed by before she could read it. She slowed, pulled off to the side of the road, and made herself back up. No worry about hitting anyone coming from behind, since she hadn't seen another car for miles.

The Tuscan countryside was reputed to be exquisitely beautiful, but she'd made the trip after dark, so she hadn't seen much. She should have gotten an earlier start, but she hadn't been able to drag herself out of bed until late afternoon. Then she'd simply sat in front of the window and stared, trying to pray but unable to do so.

The Panda's headlights came to rest on the sign. CASALLEONE. She turned on the dome light to look at the directions and saw that she'd somehow managed to stumble back onto the proper road. God protected fools.

So where were you last night, God?

Someplace else, that was for certain. But she couldn't blame God or even all the wine she'd drunk for what had happened. Her own character defects had driven her to monumental stupidity. She'd rejected everything she believed in, only to discover that Dr. Favor had been right as usual. Sex couldn't heal the broken places.

She pulled back out onto the road. Like so many other people's, her broken places originated in childhood, but how long could you keep blaming your parents for your own failures? Her parents had been college professors who'd thrived on chaos and emotional excess. Her mother was boozy, brilliant, and intensely sexual. Her father: boozy, brilliant, and hostile. Despite being authorities in their respective academic fields, neither could achieve tenure. Her mother had a tendency to indulge in affairs with her students, and her father had a penchant for getting into shouting matches with his colleagues. Isabel had spent her childhood being dragged from one college town to the next, an unwilling witness to lives that had spun out of control.

While other children yearned to escape their parents' discipline, Isabel craved a structure that never came. Instead, her parents used her as a pawn in their battles. In a desperate act of self-preservation, she'd turned her back on them at eighteen. She'd been on her own ever since. Six years ago her father had died of liver failure, and her mother had followed not long after. She'd done her duty at the end, but she hadn't mourned them as much as she'd mourned the waste of their lives.

Her headlights picked out a narrow, winding street with pictur-esque stone buildings set close to the road. As she drove farther, she saw a collection of shops shuttered for the night. Everything in the town seemed old and quaint except for the giant Mel Gibson movie poster plastered on the wall of a building. In smaller letters beneath the title, she made out the name Lorenzo Gage.

That's when it hit her. Dante hadn't reminded her of a figure in a Renaissance painting. He'd been a ringer for Lorenzo Gage, the actor who'd recently driven her favorite actress to suicide.

Her stomach felt queasy again. How many of Gage's movies had she seen? Four? Five? Way too many, but Michael loved action films, the more violent the better. Now she'd never have to see another one.

She wondered if Gage felt any remorse for Karli Swenson's death. It would probably add to his box-office appeal. Why were nice women so fascinated with bad boys? The rescue fantasy, she supposed—the need to believe they were the only women powerful enough to transform those losers into husbands and fathers. Too bad it wasn't that easy.

She cleared the edge of the town, then turned on the dome light again to see the rest of the directions: *"Follow the road from Casalleone for about two kilometers, then turn right at the rusty Ape."*

Rusty ape? She envisioned King Kong with a bad dye job. Two kilometers later her headlights picked out a lumpy shape off to the side of the road. She slowed and saw that the rusty Ape wasn't of the gorilla variety, but the remnants of an *Ah-pay*, one of those tiny vehicles beloved by European farmers. This particular junker had once been the famous three-wheeled Ape truck, although its trio of tires had disappeared long ago.

As she turned, stones clicked against the undercarriage. The directions mentioned the entrance of the Villa dei Angeli, "Villa of the Angels," and she took the Panda around another series of uphill curves before she saw the open iron gates marking the villa's main drive. The gravel road she was looking for lay just beyond. It was barely more than a path, and the Panda lurched as it rolled downhill, then took a sharp curve.

A structure rose in front of her. She slammed on the brakes. For a moment she simply stared. Finally she turned off the ignition, killed the lights, and dropped her head against the back of the seat. Despair welled inside her. This crumbling, neglected pile of stones was the farmhouse she'd rented. Not beautifully restored, as the description from the real-estate agent had indicated, but a dilapidated heap that looked as if cows still lived inside.

Solitude. Rest. Contemplation. Action. Sexual healing was no longer part of her plan. She wouldn't even think about it.

The house offered solitude, but how could she rest, let alone find an atmosphere conducive to contemplation, when she was locked inside a ruin? And she needed contemplation if she intended to come up with an action plan to get her life back in gear. Her mistakes piled higher and higher. She could no longer remember what it had felt like to be competent.

She rubbed her eyes. At least she'd solved the mystery of why the rent was so cheap.

She barely summoned the energy to get out of the car and drag her suitcases toward the door. Everything was so quiet she could hear herself breathe. She would have given anything for the friendly blare of a police siren or the gentle roar of a plane flying out of La Guardia, but she heard only the chirping of crickets.

The rough wooden door was unlocked, just as the rental agent had indicated it would be, and it creaked like a bad movie sound effect. She braced herself for a flock of bats to come flying out at her, but she was greeted with nothing more ominous than the musty scent of old stones.

"Self-pity will paralyze you, my friend. So will a victim mentality. You're not a victim. You're filled with a magnificent power. You're—"

Oh, shut up! she told herself.

She fumbled along the wall until she found a switch that turned on a floor lamp with the wattage of a Christmas-tree bulb. She glanced around just long enough to note a cold, bare tile floor, a few ancient furnishings, and an unwelcoming stone staircase. At least there were no cows.

She couldn't cope with any more tonight, so she grabbed her smallest suitcase and made her way upstairs, where she found a functioning bathroom—thank you, Mother God—and a small, stark bedroom that looked like a nun's cell. After what she'd done last night, nothing could have been more ironic.

Ren stood on the Ponte alla Carraia and gazed down the Arno at the bridges that had been built to replace the ones the Luftwaffe had blown up during the Second World War. Hitler had spared only the Ponte Vecchio, built in the fourteenth century. Once Ren had tried to blow up London's Tower Bridge, but George Clooney had taken him out first.

The wind whipped a short lock of hair over his forehead. He'd had it cut that afternoon. He'd also shaved and—since he intended to avoid lighted public spaces tonight—removed his brown contact lenses. Now, however, he felt exposed. Sometimes he wanted to step out of his own skin.

The Frenchwoman last night had spooked him. He didn't like misjudging people. Although he'd gotten the anonymous sex he'd wanted, something had been drastically wrong. He managed to find trouble even when he wasn't looking for it.

A pair of street toughs ambled toward him from the other side of the bridge, looking him over as they came closer to decide how big a fight he'd put up if they tried to take his wallet. Their swagger

reminded him of his own youth, although his crimes had been limited more to self-destruction. He'd been a punk with a silver spoon
up his ass, a kid who'd figured out early on that misbehavior was a
good way to get attention. The more things changed, the more they
stayed the same. Nobody got more attention than the bad guy.

He reached for his cigarettes, even though he'd quit six months
ago. The crumpled pack he pulled from his pocket held exactly one,
all he let himself carry these days. It was his emergency stash.

He lit it, flicked the match over the side of the bridge, and
watched the boys come closer. They disappointed him by exchang-
ing uneasy glances and passing on.

He drew the smoke deep into his lungs and told himself to forget
about last night. But he couldn't quite manage it. The woman's light
brown eyes had shone with intelligence, and all that buttoned-up
sophistication had excited him, which was probably why he'd neglected to pick up on the fact that she was a wacko. At the end he'd
gotten this gut-churning feeling that he was somehow attacking
her. He might rape women on the silver screen, but in real life that
was one outrage even he couldn't imagine.

He left the bridge behind and wandered along an empty street,
taking his foul mood with him, even though he should be on top of
the world. Everything he'd worked toward was about to happen. The
Howard Jenks film would give him the credibility that had eluded
him. Although he had more than enough money to live the rest of
his life without working, he loved the whole business of making
films, and this was the role he'd been waiting for, a villain who
would be every bit as memorable to audiences as Hannibal Lecter.
Still, he had those six weeks to get through before *Night Kill* started
filming, and the city felt claustrophobic around him.

Karli . . . The woman last night . . . The sense that nothing he'd
achieved meant anything . . . God, he was sick of being depressed.

He tucked the cigarette in the corner of his mouth, shoved his hands into his pockets, hunched his shoulders, and kept walking. James-fucking-Dean on the Boulevard of Broken Dreams.

The hell with it. Tomorrow he was leaving Florence and heading for the place that had drawn him here.

5

Isabel turned over in bed. Her travel clock said nine-thirty, so it should be morning, but the room was dark and gloomy. Disoriented, she gazed toward the windows and saw that the shutters were closed.

She rolled to her back and studied the combination of flat red roof tiles and rough wooden beams above her head. Outside she heard something that might have been the distant rumble of a tractor. That was all. No reassuring clank of garbage trucks or musical shouts of taxi drivers cursing each other in Third World languages. She was in Italy, sleeping in a room that looked as if its last occupant had been a martyred saint.

She tilted her head far enough back to see the crucifix hanging on the stucco wall behind her. The tears she hated started leaking out. Tears of loss for the life she'd lived, the man she'd thought she loved. Why hadn't she been smart enough, worked hard enough, been lucky enough to hold on to what she'd had? Even worse, why had she defiled herself with an Italian gigolo who looked like a psychopathic movie star? She tried to fight the tears with a morning prayer, but Mother God had turned a deaf ear to her delinquent daughter.

The temptation to pull the covers over her head and never get up was so strong that it frightened her into dropping her legs over the side of the bed. Cold tile met the soles of her feet. She made her way across the dreary room into a narrow hallway with a utilitarian bathroom at one end. Although small, it had been modernized, so maybe this place wasn't quite the ruin she'd imagined it to be.

She bathed, wrapped herself in a towel, and returned to her martyred saint's cell, where she slipped into a pair of gray slacks and matching sleeveless top. Then she walked over to the window, unlocked the shutters, and pushed them back.

A shower of lemony light drenched her. It streamed through the window as if it had been poured from a bucket, the rays so intense she had to close her eyes for a moment. When she opened them, she saw the rolling hills of Tuscany lying before her.

"Oh, my . . ." She rested her arms on the stone ledge and took in the mosaic of buff, honey, and pewter-colored fields, broken here and there by rows of cypress, like pointed fingers against the sky. There were no fences. The boundaries between the harvested wheat fields, the groves of trees, and the vineyards were formed by a road here, a valley there, a simple curve of land somewhere else.

She was gazing out over Bethlehem. This was the Holy Land of the Renaissance artists. They'd painted the landscape they knew as the background for their Madonnas, angels, mangers, and shepherds. The Holy Land . . . right outside her window.

She took in the distant view, then studied the land closer to the house. A terraced vineyard extended off to the left, while a grove of gnarled olive trees grew beyond the garden. She wanted to see more, and she turned away from the window, then stopped as she saw how the light had changed the character of the room. Now the whitewashed walls and dark wooden beams were beautiful in their sparseness, and the simple furniture spoke more eloquently of the past than a volume of history books. This wasn't a ruin at all.

She moved into the hallway and down the stone steps to the ground floor. The living room, which she'd barely glanced at the night before, had the rough walls and vaulted brick ceiling of an old European stable, something it had probably once been, since she seemed to recall reading that the tenants of Tuscan farmhouses had lived above their animals. The space had been beautifully converted into a small, comfortable living area without losing its rustic authenticity.

Stone arches wide enough for farm animals to pass through now served as windows and doors. The rustic sepia wash on the walls was the real version of the faux treatment New York's finest interior painters charged thousands to reproduce in uptown co-ops. The old terra-cotta floor had been waxed, polished, and smoothed by a century or more of wear. Simple dark-wooden tables and a chest sat along the wall. A chair with a muted floral print rested across from a couch covered in earth-toned fabric.

The shutters that had been closed last night when she'd arrived were now thrown open. Curious to see who had done it, she passed through a stone arch into a large, sunny kitchen.

The room held a long, rectangular farm table nicked and scarred by a few centuries of use. Red, blue, and yellow ceramic tiles formed a narrow backsplash over a rustic stone sink. Below, a blue-and-white-checked skirt hid the plumbing. Open shelves displayed an assortment of colorful pottery, baskets, and copper utensils. There was an old-fashioned propane stove and a set of wooden cupboards. The rough French doors that opened to the garden had been painted bottle green. This was everything she'd imagined an Italian country kitchen to be.

The door opened, and a woman in her sixties walked in. She had a dumpling figure, doughy cheeks, dyed black hair, and small dark eyes. Isabel quickly demonstrated her crackerjack mastery of the Italian language.

"Buon giorno."

Although the Tuscan people were known for their friendliness, the woman didn't look friendly. A gardening glove hung from the pocket of the faded black dress she wore with heavy nylon stockings and black plastic mules. Without a word, she removed a ball of string from the cupboard and went back outside.

Isabel followed her into the garden, then stopped to absorb the view of the farmhouse from the back. It was perfect. Absolutely perfect. *Rest. Solitude. Contemplation. Action.* There could be no better place for it.

The old stones of the house glowed a creamy beige in the sharp morning light. Vines clung to the mortar and curled near the tall green shutters at the windows. Ivy climbed a drain spout. A small dovecote perched on the roof, and silver lichen softened the rounded terra-cotta tiles.

The main part of the structure was built in a simple, unadorned rectangle, the typical style of the *fattoria,* or Italian farmhouse, that she'd read about. A one-story room bumped haphazardly off the end, probably a later addition.

Even the dour presence of the woman digging with her trowel didn't detract from the shady enchantment of the garden, and the knots inside Isabel began to loosen. A low wall built of the same golden stones as the house marked the far perimeter, with the olive grove sloping away beyond it, and the vista Isabel had seen from her bedroom window behind that. A wooden table with an old marble top sat in the shade of a magnolia tree, a perfect place for a lazy meal or for simply contemplating the view. But that wasn't the only refuge the garden offered. Nearer the house, a wisteria-covered pergola sheltered a pair of benches where Isabel could envision herself curled up with pen and paper.

Gravel paths meandered through the garden's flowers, vegetables, and herbs. Glossy basil plants, snowy white impatiens, tomato vines, and cheery roses grew near clay pots overflowing with red and pink geraniums. Bright orange nasturtiums formed a perfect partnership with the delicate blue flowers of a rosemary shrub, and silvery sage leaves made a cool backdrop to a cluster of red pepper plants. In Tuscan fashion, lemon trees grew in two large terra-cotta urns sitting on each side of the kitchen door, while another set of urns held hydrangea bushes heavy with fat pink blooms.

Isabel gazed from the flowers to the bench beneath the pergola, to the table under the magnolia where a pair of cats lounged. As she breathed in the warm scent of earth and plants, the sound of Michael's voice in her head grew silent, and a simple prayer began to take shape in her heart.

The woman's dark mutter broke the peaceful mood, and the prayer drifted away. Still, Isabel felt a glimmer of hope. God had offered her the Holy Land. Only a fool would turn her back on a gift like that.

She drove into town with a much lighter heart. Finally something had happened to ease her despair. She stocked up on food at a small *negozio di alimentari*. When she returned, she found the woman in the black dress working in the kitchen, washing up some dishes Isabel hadn't left there. The woman shot her an unfriendly look and went out the back door—a serpent in the Garden of Eden. Isabel sighed and unpacked her groceries, arranging everything neatly in the cupboard and tiny refrigerator.

"*Signora? Permesso?*"

She turned to see a pretty young woman in her late twenties with sunglasses perched on top of her head standing in the arch between the kitchen and the dining area. She was petite, and her clear olive skin made an unusual contrast with her fair hair. She wore a peach blouse, a slim, biscuit-colored skirt, and the killer shoes favored by Italian women. The beautifully curved heels tapped on the old tiles as she approached. "*Buon giorno*, Signora Favor, I am Giulia Chiara."

As Isabel nodded in response, she wondered if everyone in Tuscany walked into strangers' homes unannounced.

"I am the *agente immobiliare*." She hesitated, searching for the English words. "The real-estate agent for this house."

"I'm glad to meet you. I like the house very much."

"Oh, but no . . . is not a good house." Her hands flew. "I tried to telephone you many times last week, but I could not find you."

That was because Isabel had disconnected her phone. "Is there a problem?"

"*Si*. A problem." The young woman licked her lips and tucked a lock of hair behind her ear, revealing a small pearl stud in her lobe. "I'm very sorry to tell you, but you cannot stay here." Her hands moved in the graceful gestures Italians employed for even the simplest of conversations. "Is not possible. This is why I try to call you. To explain this problem and tell you I have another place for you to stay. If you'll come with me, I will show you."

Yesterday Isabel wouldn't have cared about leaving, but now she cared very much. This simple stone house with its peaceful garden held the possibility of meditation and restoration. She wasn't giving that up. "Tell me what the problem is."

"There is . . ." A small arc with her hand. "Work needs to be done. Is not possible for anyone to be here."

"What kind of work?"

"Much work. We must dig. There is problems with the sewer."

"I'm sure we can work around it."

"No, no. *Impossibile.*"

"Signora Chiara, I've paid two months' rent, and I intend to stay."

"But you would not like it. And Signora Vesto would be most upset to have you unhappy."

"Signora Vesto?"

"Anna Vesto. She would be very displeased if you were uncomfortable. I have found you a nice house in town, yes? You will enjoy it very much."

"I don't want a house in town. I want this one."

"I'm so sorry. Is not possible."

"Is that Signora Vesto?" Isabel pointed toward the garden.

"No, that is Marta. Signora Vesto is at the villa." She made a small gesture toward the top of the hill.

"Is Marta the housekeeper here?"

"No, no. Is no housekeeper here, but in town there is very good housekeepers."

Isabel ignored that. "Is she the gardener?"

"No, Marta keeps the garden, but is not the gardener. There is no gardener. In town is possible for you to have a gardener."

"Then what does she do here?"

"Marta lives here."

"I understood I'd have the house to myself."

"No, you would not be alone here." She walked to the kitchen door and pointed at the one-story addition at the back of the house. "Marta lives there. Very close."

"But I'd be alone in the middle of all those people in town?" Isabel said, taking a wild guess.

"*Si!*" Giulia beamed, her smile so charming Isabel hated to put a damper on it.

"I think it would be best if I spoke with Signora Vesto. Is she at the villa now?"

Giulia looked relieved to pass the ball. "*Si, si,* that would be best. She will explain to you why you cannot stay, and I will come back to take you to the house I have found for you in town."

Isabel took pity on her and didn't argue. She'd save that for Signora Anna Vesto.

She followed the path up from the farmhouse to a long, cypress-lined drive. The Villa dei Angeli sat at the end, and as Isabel caught sight of it, she felt as if she'd been transported into the film version of *A Room with a View.*

Its salmon-pink stucco exterior, as well as the wings that sprouted here and there, were characteristic of grand Tuscan homes. Lacy black grillwork covered the ground-floor windows, while the long shutters on the upper floor had already been closed against the heat of the day. Nearer the house, the cypress gave way to the rigid formality of clipped box hedges, classical statues, and an octagonal fountain. A double set of stone staircases with massive balustrades led to a pair of polished wooden doors.

Isabel climbed the stairs, then lifted a lion's-head brass knocker. While she waited, she gazed down at a dusty black Maserati convertible parked near the fountain. Signora Vesto had expensive tastes.

No one answered, and she knocked again.

A voluptuous middle-aged woman with discreetly colored red hair and tilted Sophia Loren eyes gave Isabel a friendly smile. "*Si?*"

"*Buon giorno, signora.* I'm Isabel Favor. I'm looking for Signora Vesto."

The woman's smile faded. "I'm Signora Vesto." Her plain navy dress and sensible shoes made her more likely to be the house-keeper than the person who owned the Maserati.

"I rented the farmhouse," Isabel said, "but there seems to be a problem."

"No problem," Signora Vesto replied briskly. "Giulia has found you a house in town. She will see to everything."

She kept her hand on the door, clearly wanting to hurry Isabel away. Behind her a set of large, obviously expensive suitcases sat in the entrance hall. Isabel was willing to bet that the villa's owners had either just arrived or were about to leave.

"I signed a rental agreement," she said, speaking pleasantly but firmly. "I'm staying."

"No, *signora*, you will have to move. Someone will come this afternoon to help you."

"I'm not leaving."

"I'm very sorry, *signora*, but there is nothing I can do."

Isabel realized that it was time to get to the top of the chain of command. "I'd like to speak with the owner."

"The owner is not here."

"What about those suitcases?"

She looked uneasy. "You must leave now, *signora*."

The Four Cornerstones were made for moments like this. *"Behave politely, but decisively."* "I'm afraid I can't leave until I speak with the owner." Isabel pushed her way into the entrance hall and received a brief impression of high ceilings, a gilt and bronze chandelier, and a grand staircase before the woman jumped in front of her.

"Ferma! You can't come in here!"

"People who try to hide behind their authority do so out of fear, and they need our compassion. At the same time, we can't let their fears become our own."

"I'm sorry to upset you, *signora*," she said as compassionately as she could, "but I must speak with the owner."

"Who told you he was here? No one is to know this."

The owner was a man then. "I won't say anything."

"You must go at once."

Isabel heard Italian rock and roll coming from the back of the house. She headed toward an ornately carved archway with green and red marble inlays.

"Signora!"

Isabel was tired of people messing with her—a crooked accountant, a faithless fiancé, a disloyal publisher, and her fair-weather fans. She'd lived in airports for those fans, taken the podium through a bout of pneumonia for them. She'd held their hands when their kids did drugs, curled her arms around them while they struggled with depression, and prayed for them through desperate illnesses. But the minute a few dark clouds had shown up in her own life, they'd run like rabbits.

She charged through the house, down a narrow gallery where ancestral portraits in heavy frames juggled for space with baroque landscapes, across an elegant reception room wallpapered in brown and gold stripes. She whipped by grim frescoes of hunting scenes and grimmer portraits of martyred saints. Her sandals left scorch marks on the marble floors and singes in the fringes of the kilim rugs. A Roman bust trembled on its pedestal as she rushed by. *Enough is enough!*

She came to a halt inside a less formal salon at the back of the house. The polished chestnut floors were laid in a herringbone pattern, and the frescoes showed harvest scenes instead of boar hunts. Italian rock music accompanied the shafts of sunlight spilling in through long open windows.

At the end of the room an arched doorway much grander than the one in the farmhouse opened to a loggia, the source of the blaring music. A man stood inside the arch, his shoulder resting against the frame as he gazed out toward the sunlight. She squinted against the glare and saw that he wore jeans and a rumpled black T-shirt with a hole in the sleeve. His profile was so classically chiseled it might have belonged on one of the room's statues. But something about his rebel's slouch, the liquor bottle tilted to his mouth, and the pistol dangling from his free hand told her this might be a Roman god gone bad.

With a wary eye on the gun, she cleared her throat. "Uh . . . *scusi?* Excuse me."

He turned.

She blinked against the sun. Blinked again. Told herself it was only a trick of the light. Just a trick. It couldn't be. It couldn't. . . .

6

But it was. The man who'd called himself Dante stood slouched in the doorway. Dante of the hot, glazed eyes and decadent touches. Except this man's hair was shorter, and his eyes were a silvered blue instead of brown.

"Son of a bitch."

She heard American English—movie-star English—spoken in the deep, familiar voice of the Italian gigolo she'd met the night before last in the Piazza della Signoria. Even then it took a moment before she understood the truth. Lorenzo Gage and Dante the gigolo were the same man.

"You . . ." She swallowed. "You're not . . ."

He gazed at her with assassin's eyes. "Shit. Leave it to me to pick up a stalker."

"Who are you?" But she'd seen his movies, and she already knew the answer.

"Signore Gage!" Anna Vesto burst into the room. "This woman! She would not leave when I told her to. She is—she is—" The English language couldn't contain her indignation, and she released a torrent of Italian.

Lorenzo Gage, the philandering movie star who'd driven Karli Swenson to suicide, was also Dante, the Florentine gigolo, the man she'd allowed to taint a corner of her soul. She slumped into one of the chairs along the wall and tried to breathe.

He growled at the housekeeper in Italian.

She replied with wild gestures.

Another growl from him.

The woman huffed and swept from the room.

He stomped out onto the loggia and snapped off the music. When he returned, a lock of inky hair had fallen over his forehead. He'd left the bottle behind, but the pistol still hung from his hand.

"You're trespassing, sweetheart." His lips barely moved, and his deadly drawl sounded even more menacing in real life than it did in digital SurroundSound. "You really should have called first."

She'd had sex with Lorenzo Gage, a man who'd bragged in a magazine article that he'd "screwed five hundred women." And she'd let herself become five hundred and one.

Her stomach heaved. She buried her face in her hands and whispered words she'd never before spoken to another human being, never even thought to speak. "I hate you."

"That's how I make my living."

She sensed him coming closer and dropped her hands, only to find herself staring at the pistol.

It wasn't exactly pointed at her, but it wasn't exactly *not* pointed at her either. He held it loosely near his hip. She saw that it was an antique, probably several hundred years old, but that didn't necessarily make it any less deadly. Look what he'd nearly done to Julia Roberts with a samurai sword.

"Just when I think the press can't sink any lower. What happened to your *non parler anglais*, Frenchy?"

"The same thing that happened to your Italian." She sat straighter, finally focusing on what he was saying. "The press? You think I'm a reporter?"

"If you wanted an interview, all you had to do was ask."

She jumped up from the chair. "You think I went through all *that* just to get a *story*?"

"Maybe." Faint alcohol fumes wafted her way. He planted his foot on the chair she'd vacated. She gazed at the pistol resting on his thigh and tried to decide whether he was threatening her or he'd forgotten it was there.

"How did you find me, and what do you want?"

"I want my house." She took a step back, then was angry with herself for doing it. "Is this how you get your kicks? Disguising yourself so you can pick up women?"

"Believe it or not, Fifi, I can do that without a disguise. And I was worth a hell of a lot more than those fifty euros you left."

"A matter of opinion. Is that gun loaded?"

"Beats me."

"Well, put it down." She gripped her hands.

"I don't think so."

"Am I supposed to believe you'll shoot me?"

"Believe whatever you want." He yawned.

She wondered how much he'd had to drink and wished her legs didn't feel so boneless. "I won't tolerate being around guns."

"Then leave." He sprawled into the chair, legs extended, shoulders slouched, pistol on his knee. A perfect portrait of decadence in the Villa of the Angels.

No power on earth would make her leave until she understood what had happened. She clenched her hands tighter to keep them from trembling and managed to drop into the chair across from him without knocking it over. She finally knew what hatred felt like.

He studied her for a moment, then pointed the pistol toward a wall-size tapestry of a man on horseback. "My ancestor, Lorenzo de' Medici."

"Big deal."

"He was a patron of Michelangelo. Botticelli, too, if the historians are right. When it comes to Renaissance men, Lorenzo was one of the best. Except . . ." He stroked the stock with his thumb and regarded her with narrow-eyed menace. "He let his generals sack the city of Volterra in 1472. Medicis aren't good people to piss off."

He was nothing more than an egocentric movie star going through his paces, and she wouldn't be intimidated. Not much, anyway. "Save your threats for the ticket buyers."

The menace vanished, replaced by boredom. "Okay, Fifi, if you're not the press, what are you up to?"

Now that she'd dug in, she realized she couldn't talk about the night before last—not yet, not ever. The house. That's why she'd come here in the first place.

"I'm here to settle a disagreement about the house I rented." She tried to put more authority behind her words, something that came normally to her but wasn't so easy now. "I paid for two months, and I'm not leaving."

"Why, exactly, am I supposed to care about this?"

"It's your house."

"You rented this house? I don't think so."

"Not this house. Your farmhouse. But your employees are trying to kick me out."

"What farmhouse?"

"The one down the hill."

His lip curled. "I'm supposed to believe the woman I *accidentally* met in Florence two nights ago just happened to rent a house I own. Maybe you'd better come up with a better story."

Even she found it hard to swallow, except that the tourist heart of Florence was small, and she'd run into the young couple she'd met in the Uffizi at two other sites that same day. "Sooner or later every tourist in Florence ends up in the Piazza della Signoria. We just happened to get there at the same time."

"Lucky us. You look familiar. I thought so last night."

"Do I?" This was a topic she didn't care to pursue. "I rented your farmhouse in good faith, but as soon as I arrived, I was told to leave."

"Are you talking about that place where old Paolo used to live, down by the olive grove?"

"I don't know who old Paolo is. A woman named Marta seems to be living there now, which I don't like but am prepared to tolerate."

"Marta . . . Paolo's sister." He spoke as if he'd dredged up a distant memory. "Yeah, I guess that is part of this property."

"I don't care who she is. I paid my money, and I'm not leaving."

"Why are you being kicked out?"

"Something about trouble with a sewer."

"I'm surprised you want to stay, considering what happened between us. Or maybe you're just pretending to be pissed off."

His words jolted her back to reality. Of course she couldn't stay. She'd violated the essence of who she was with this man, and it would be unbearable to run into him again.

A crushing sense of disappointment joined her other painful emotions. In the farmhouse garden she'd experienced her first peace in months, and now it was being ripped away from her. She still had a little pride. If she had to leave, she'd at least do it in a way that wouldn't let him think he'd won. "You're the actor, Mr. Gage. Not me."

"I guess that remains to be seen." A crow cawed a warning note from the gardens. "If you're staying, you'd better keep away from the villa." He rubbed his thigh with the barrel of the pistol. "And don't let me find out you're lying. You won't like the consequences."

"That sounds like a line from one of your horrible movies."

"Glad to know I have a fan."

"I've only seen them because of my ex-fiancé. Unfortunately, I didn't make the connection between his bad taste in films and his sexual wanderlust until it was too late." Now, why had she said that?

He propped an elbow on the arm of the chair. "So our sexcapade was your way of getting back at him."

She began to deny it, but he'd hit too close to the truth.

"Let me see . . ." He laid the pistol on the table. "Exactly who was the wronged party two nights ago? Was it you, the vengeful female, or me, the innocent pawn in your lust for revenge?"

He was actually enjoying himself. She rose so she could look down at him, then wished she hadn't, because her legs still weren't steady. "Are you drunk, Mr. Gage?"

"I'm way past drunk."

"It's barely one o'clock."

"Ordinarily you'd have a point, but I haven't been to bed yet, so this is technically still nighttime drinking."

"Whatever works for you." She had to either sit down again or get out of here, so she headed for the door.

"Hey, Fifi."

She turned, then wished she hadn't.

"The thing is . . ." He picked up the polished marble ball that had been resting on a stone plinth next to him and ran his thumb over it. "Unless you want my fans crawling all around that little farmhouse, I suggest you keep your mouth shut about my being here."

"Believe it or not, I have better things to do than gossip."

"Let's make sure it stays that way." He squeezed the marble ball in his fist in case she hadn't gotten the message.

"Overacting a bit, aren't you, Mr. Gage?"

The menace evaporated, and he laughed. "Nice meeting you, Fifi."

She made it to the salon door without bumping into anything, but she couldn't resist one glance back.

He was tossing the marble ball from one hand to the other, a gorgeous Nero fiddling while Rome burned.

The stitch in her side forced her to slow down before she reached the farmhouse. Gravel had sifted through the toes of her Kate Spade sandals, probably the last pair she'd ever be able to afford. She was glad she hadn't crumbled in front of him, but the fact was, she had to leave. If she packed up now, she could be back in Florence by four o'clock.

And then what?

The house came into view. Bathed in golden light, it looked solid and comforting, but also somehow magical. It looked like a place where the vision of a new life could be born.

She turned away and followed a branch of the path into the vineyard. The deep purple grapes, fat with juice, hung heavy on the vines. She picked one and put it in her mouth. It burst against her tongue, startling in its sweetness. The seeds were so small she didn't bother spitting them out.

She pulled off a small cluster and walked deeper into the vineyard. She needed her sneakers. The heavy clay soil felt like rocks beneath her thin sandals. But she wouldn't think of what she needed, only of what she had—the Tuscan sun over her head, warm grapes ripe in her hand, Lorenzo Gage in the villa at the top of the hill. . . .

She'd given herself away so cheaply. How would she ever get past that?

Not by running away.

Her stubborn streak set in. She was tired of her sadness. She'd never been a coward. Was she going to let herself be chased away from something precious by a degenerate movie star? The encounter had been meaningless to him. He obviously disliked her, so he'd hardly come searching her out. And she needed to be here. Every instinct told her this was the place she had to stay, the only place where she could find both the solitude and the inspiration that would let her figure out how to set her life on a new course.

Right then she made up her mind. She wasn't afraid of Lorenzo Gage, and she wouldn't let anyone force her to leave here until she was ready.

Ren put away the seventeenth-century flintlock he'd taken out to examine just before Fifi had barged in. He could still hear the echo of those efficient little heel taps as she'd swept from the room. He was supposed to be the devil, but unless he was mistaken, Ms. Fifi had left the scent of brimstone behind her.

He chuckled, then closed the cabinet door. The pistol was a beautiful piece of workmanship, one of many priceless objects in the villa. He'd inherited the place two years ago, but this was his first chance to visit since his Aunt Philomena had died. He'd originally planned to sell the property, but he had good memories from his three visits here as a kid. It didn't seem right to sell the place without seeing it again. He'd been impressed with both the housekeeper and her husband when he'd spoken with them on the phone, and he'd decided to wait.

He retrieved his bottle of scotch from the table on the loggia so he could resume the drinking Ms. Fifi had interrupted. He'd enjoyed giving her a hard time. She was so uptight she vibrated, yet her visit had left him feeling almost relaxed. Weird.

He stepped through one of the loggia's three arches out into the garden and made his way along the clipped hedges toward the swimming pool, where he sank into a chaise. As he absorbed the quiet, he thought about all the people who usually surrounded him: his faithful posse of assistants, business managers, and the bodyguards the studios occasionally wanted him to keep around. A lot of celebrities encircled themselves with aides because they needed reassurance that they were stars. Others, like himself, did it to make life easier. Aides kept overzealous fans at bay, which was useful but came at a price. Few people spoke the truth to the person responsible for their paycheck, and all the brown-nosing had gotten old.

Ms. Fifi, on the other hand, didn't seem to know anything about brown-nosing, and that had been oddly restful.

He'd pushed aside the bottle of scotch without uncapping it and sank deeper into the chaise. Slowly his eyes drifted shut. Very restful . . .

Isabel cut a wedge from the aged pecorino she'd purchased in town. This was the sheep's cheese so beloved by the Tuscan people. While she'd counted out her money to pay for it, the female store clerk had pressed a tiny pot of honey on her. "It is the Tuscan way," she'd said. "Honey with the cheese."

Isabel couldn't imagine it, but wasn't she trying to be less rigid? She arranged the cheese and honey pot on a ceramic plate, along with an apple. All she'd eaten today were those few grapes she'd picked on the way back from the villa three hours ago. Her encounter with Gage had stolen her appetite. Maybe a little food would make her feel better.

She discovered half a dozen crisp linen napkins in a drawer, removed one, then arranged the others in a tidier pile. She'd already unpacked her suitcases and organized the bathroom. Although it was barely four o'clock, she opened the Chianti Classico she'd picked up in town. Chianti could only be termed *classico*, she'd learned, if it had been pressed from grapes grown in the Chianti region that lay a few miles to the east.

She found stemless wineglasses in the cupboard. She wiped off a water spot, filled one, and carried everything out to the garden.

The delicate scents of rosemary and sweet basil drifted up from the gravel path as she made her way toward the old table that sat in the shade of the magnolia. Two of the garden's three cats came up to greet her. She settled down and gazed out over the ancient hills. The plowed fields that had been grayish brown in the morning had turned to lavender in the late-afternoon sun. So beautiful.

Tomorrow she would begin to follow the schedule she'd set up for the next two months. She didn't need to check the notes she'd made to remember how she planned to organize her days.

- Awaken at 6:00
- Prayer, Meditation, Gratitude, and Daily Affirmations
- Yoga or brisk walk
- Light breakfast
- Morning chores
- Work on a new book
- Lunch
- Sight-seeing, window-shopping, or other pleasurable activity (Be impulsive)
- Revise morning writing
- Dinner
- Inspirational reading and evening chores

- Bed at 10:00
- REMEMBER TO BREATHE!

She wouldn't worry about the fact that she had no idea what kind of book she would write. That's why she needed to stay here, so she could unblock her mental and emotional channels.

The wine was full and fruity, and it melted on her tongue, but as she leaned back to savor it, she noticed a dusty film on the marble tabletop. She jumped up and went back inside for a rag. When she'd wiped it off, she sat back down again.

She inhaled the wine and the rosemary. In the distance a road curled against the hills in a pale, smoky trail. This beautiful place . . . To think that only yesterday she hadn't wanted to be here.

On top of a hill off to her right she noticed what might have been part of a village but now looked like ruins with a crumbling wall and the remains of a watchtower. She started to get up so she could find her opera glasses, then reminded herself she was supposed to be relaxing.

She took a cleansing breath, settled back in her chair, and reached inside herself for contentment.

It wasn't there.

"Signora!"

The cheery voice belonged to a young man coming her way through the garden. He was in his late twenties or early thirties, and slender. Another handsome Italian. As he came closer, she saw liquid brown eyes, silky black hair caught back in a low ponytail, and a long, beautifully shaped nose.

"Signora Favor, I am Vittorio." He introduced himself expansively, as if his name alone should bring her pleasure.

She smiled and returned his greeting.

"May I join you?" His accent indicated he'd learned his elegant, lightly accented English from British teachers instead of American ones.

"Of course. Would you like some wine?"

"Ah, I would love some."

He stopped her as she began to rise. "I've been here many times," he said. "I'll get it. Sit and enjoy the view."

He returned in less than a minute with the bottle and a glass. "A beautiful day." A cat rubbed against him as he settled at the end of the table. "But then, all our Tuscan days are beautiful, are they not?"

"It seems that way."

"And you are enjoying your visit?"

"Very much. But it's more than a visit. I'll be staying here for several months."

Unlike Giulia Chiara, Anna Vesto, and the dour Marta, he looked delighted with the news. "So many Americans, they come on their tour buses for a day, then leave. How can one experience Tuscany like that?"

It was hard to ignore so much enthusiasm, and she smiled. "One cannot."

"You have not yet tried our pecorino." He dipped the spoon on her plate into the honey pot and drizzled a dab on her wedge of cheese. "Now you will be a proper Tuscan."

He looked so eager that she didn't have the heart to disappoint him, even though she suspected he'd been sent here to dislodge her. She took a bite and discovered the snap of the cheese and the honey's sweetness made them perfect companions. "Delicious."

"The Tuscan cuisine is the best in the world. Ribollita, panzanella, wild boar sausage, fagioli with sage, Florentine tripe—"

"I think I'll take a pass on the tripe."

"Take a pass?"

"Avoid."

"Ah, yes. We eat perhaps more of the animal here than you do in the States."

She smiled. They began chatting about the cuisine as well as local attractions. Had she been to Pisa yet? What about Volterra? She must tour some of the wineries in the Chianti region. As for Siena . . . its Piazza del Campo was the most beautiful in Italy. Did she know about the Palio, the horse races that took place each summer in the Campo itself? And the towered city of San Gimignano was not to be missed. Had she seen it yet?

She had not.

"I will show you everything."

"Oh, no."

"But I am a professional guide. I do tours all over Tuscany and Umbria. Group and private. Walking tours, cooking tours, wine tours. Did no one offer you my services?"

"They've been too busy trying to evict me."

"Ah, yes. The sewer. It's true you didn't come at the best time, but there is much to see nearby, and I will take you sight-seeing during the day so you can escape the dirt and the noise."

"I appreciate the offer, but I'm afraid I can't afford a private guide."

"No, no." An elegant gesture of dismissal. "We will go only when I have no other clients, a gesture of friendship. I will show you all the places you cannot find on your own. You will not have to worry about driving on strange roads, and I will translate for you. A very good bargain, you will see."

An extraordinary bargain. One, coincidentally, that would get her out of the farmhouse. "I couldn't possibly impose on you like that."

"But it is not an imposition. You can pay for the petrol, yes?"

Just then Marta emerged from the room at the back. She snapped off a few sprigs from a basil plant and carried them into the kitchen.

He took a sip of his Chianti. "I have tomorrow free. Would you like to go to Siena first? Or perhaps Monteriggioni. An exquisite little town. Dante writes of it in the *Inferno*."

Her skin prickled at the name. But Dante the gigolo didn't exist, only Lorenzo Gage, a playboy movie star who'd been her partner in shame. Now that she'd met him, she didn't find it hard to believe that he'd driven Karli Swenson to suicide. Isabel was going to do her best to make sure she never saw him again.

"Actually, I've come here to work, and I need to get started tomorrow."

"Work? This is too bad. Still, we must all do what we have to." He smiled good-naturedly, finished his wine, then jotted a phone number on a piece of paper he pulled from his pocket. "If you need anything at all, you will call me."

"Thank you."

He gave her a dazzling smile, then a wave as he walked away. As least he was prepared to dislodge her with charm, or maybe she was being too suspicious. She fetched her copy of Yogananda's *Autobiography of a Yogi* but ended up reading her travel guide instead. Tomorrow would be soon enough to reinvent her career.

It had begun to grow dark by the time she went inside, and fragrant smells filled the kitchen. She entered just as Marta placed a bowl filled with a hearty-looking soup on a tray covered in snowy linen. The tray also held a glass of Isabel's Chianti, judging by the bottle next to it, as well as a serving of sliced red tomatoes garnished with dark, wrinkled olives and a crusty slab of bread. Any hopes Isabel had that the food might be intended for her faded, however, as Marta walked out the door with it. One of these days, Isabel really should learn how to cook.

She slept well that night, and the next morning she awakened at eight instead of six as she'd intended. She jumped out of bed and hurried to the bathroom. Now she'd have to cut her prayer and meditation session short or she'd never be able to catch up with her schedule. She turned on the faucet to splash her face, but the water refused to warm up. She hurried downstairs and tested the sink. It was the same. She searched for Marta so she could tell her they had no hot water, but the garden was empty. She finally located the card Giulia Chiara had left.

"Yes, yes," Giulia said when Isabel reached her. "Is very difficult for you to stay there while so much work must be done. At the house in town you will not have to worry about such things."

"I'm not moving to town," Isabel said firmly. "I spoke with . . . the owner yesterday. Would you please do your best to have the water fixed as soon as possible?"

"I will see what I can do," Giulia said, with obvious reluctance.

Casalleone had an old Roman wall, a church bell that rang on the half hour, and children everywhere. They called out to one another in the playgrounds and romped next to their mothers along the narrow cobbled streets that wound in a maze. Isabel drew out Giulia's card and checked the address against the sign. Although the street name was similar, it wasn't the same.

A day had passed since she'd talked to the real-estate agent, and she still had no hot water. She'd called Anna Vesto, but the house-keeper had pretended not to understand English and hung up. Marta seemed oblivious to the problem. According to Isabel's schedule, she should be writing now, but the issue with the water had distracted her. Besides, she had nothing to write. Although she usually thrived on self-discipline, she'd gotten up late again this morning, she hadn't meditated, and the only words she'd written in two days had been notes to friends.

She approached a young woman who was walking across the village's small piazza with a toddler in hand. *"Scusi, signora."* She held out Giulia's card. "Can you tell me where the Via San Lino is?"

The woman picked up her child and hurried away.

"Well, excuu-se me." She frowned and headed toward a middle-aged man in a ratty sport coat with elbow patches. "*Scusi, signore.* I'm looking for the Via San Lino."

He took Giulia's card, studied it for a moment, then studied Isabel. With something that sounded like a curse, he pocketed the card and stomped away.

"Hey!"

The next person gave her a "*non parlo inglese*" when she asked the location of the Via San Lino, but then a beefy young man in a yellow T-shirt offered directions. Unfortunately, they were so complicated that she ended up at an abandoned warehouse on a dead-end street.

She decided to find the grocery store with the friendly clerk that she'd visited yesterday. On the way toward the piazza, she passed a shoe store and a *profumeria* that sold cosmetics. Lace curtains draped the windows of the houses that lined the street, and laundry hung on lines overhead. "Italian dryers," the travel guide had called the clotheslines. Because power was so expensive, families didn't have electric dryers.

Her nose led her into a tiny bakery, where she bought a fig tart from a rude girl with purple hair. When she came out, she gazed up at the sky. The high, fluffy clouds looked as though they should be printed on blue flannel pajamas. It was a beautiful day, and she wouldn't let even a hundred surly Italians spoil it for her.

She was on her way up the cobbled hill toward the grocery when she spotted a newsstand with racks of postcards displaying vineyards, splashy fields of sunflowers, and charming Tuscan towns. As she stopped to choose a few, she noticed that several of the postcards depicted Michelangelo's *David*, or at least a significant part of him. The statue's marble penis stared back at her, both front and side views. She pulled one from the rack to examine it more closely. He seemed a little shortchanged in the genitalia department.

"Have you already forgotten what one looks like, my child?"

She spun around and found herself staring into a pair of ancient steel-framed eyeglasses. They belonged to a tall, black-robed priest with a bushy, dark mustache. He was an exceptionally ugly man, not because of the mustache, although that was unsightly enough, but because of a jagged red scar that drew the skin so tightly along his cheekbone it pulled down the corner of one silver-blue eye.

One very familiar silver-blue eye.

7

Isabel resisted the urge to shove the postcard back into the rack. "I was just comparing this with something similar I saw recently. The one on the statue is so much more impressive." Oh, now, that was a lie.

The sun glimmered off the lenses of his glasses as he smiled. "There are some pornographic calendars on that back rack, in case you're interested."

"I'm not." She replaced the postcard and set off up the hill.

He fell into step beside her, moving as gracefully in the long robes as if he wore them every day, but then Lorenzo Gage was accustomed to being in costume. "If you want to confess your sins, I'm all ears," he said.

"Go find some schoolboys to molest."

"Sharp tongue this morning, Fifi. That'll be a hundred Hail Marys for insulting a man of God."

"I'm reporting you, Mr. Gage. It's against the law in Italy to impersonate a priest." She spotted a harried young mother emerging from a shop with a set of twins in hand and called out to her. "*Signora!* This man isn't a priest! He's Lorenzo Gage, the American movie star."

The woman looked at Isabel as if *she* were the lunatic, snatched up her children, and hurried away.

"Nice going. You probably traumatized those kids for life."

"If it's not against the law, it should be. That mustache looks like a tarantula died on your lip. And don't you think the scar's a little over the top?"

"As long as it lets me move around freely, I don't really care."

"If you want anonymity, why don't you just stay at home?"

"Because I was born a wanderin' man."

She inspected him more closely. "You were armed the last time I saw you. Any weapons underneath that robe?"

"Not if you don't count the explosives taped to my chest."

"I saw that movie. It was awful. That whole scene was just an excuse to glorify violence and show off your muscles."

"Yet it grossed a hundred and fifty million."

"Proving my theory about the taste of the American public."

"People who live in glass houses, Dr. Favor . . ."

So he'd figured out who she was.

He pushed the steel-framed glasses up on his perfect nose. "I don't pay much attention to the self-help movement, but even I've heard of you. Is the doctorate real or phony?"

"I have a very real Ph.D. in psychology, which qualifies me to make a fairly accurate diagnosis: You're a jerk. Now, leave me alone."

"Okay, now I'm getting pissed." He lengthened his stride. "I didn't attack you that night, and I'm not apologizing."

"You pretended to be a gigolo!"

"Only in your vivid imagination."

"You spoke *Italian*."

"*You* spoke *French*."

"Go away. No, wait." She rounded on him. "You're my landlord, and I want my hot water back."

He bowed to a pair of old women strolling arm in arm, then blessed them with the sign of the cross, something she was fairly certain would keep him locked in purgatory for an extra millennium or so. She realized she was standing there watching, which made her an accessory, and she started walking again. Unfortunately, so did he.

"Why don't you have any hot water?" he asked.

"I have no idea. And your employees aren't doing anything about it."

"This is Italy. Things take time."

"Just fix it."

"I'll see what I can do." He rubbed the phony scar on his cheek. "Dr. Isabel Favor . . . Hard to believe I've been to bed with America's New Age guardian of virtue."

"I'm not New Age. I'm an old-fashioned moralist, which is why I find what I did with you so repugnant. But instead of dwelling on it, I'm going to chalk it up to trauma and try to forgive myself."

"Your fiancé dumped you, and your career hit the skids. That qualifies you for forgiveness. But you really shouldn't have cheated on your taxes."

"My accountant's the cheat."

"You'd think somebody with a Ph.D. in psychology would be smarter about the people she hires."

"You'd think. But as you might have noticed, I've developed a black hole when it comes to people smarts."

His chuckle had a diabolic edge. "Do you let a lot of men pick you up?"

"Go away."

"I'm not being judgmental, you understand. Just curious." He blinked his good eye as they came out of the shady street into the piazza.

"I've never let a man pick me up. Never! I was just—I was crazy that night. If I picked up some awful disease from you . . ."

"I had a cold a couple of weeks ago, but other than that . . ."

"Don't be cute. I saw that charming quote of yours. By your own admission, you've— Let's see, how did you put it? 'Screwed over five hundred women'? Even assuming some degree of exaggeration, you're a high-risk sex partner."

"That quote's not even close to accurate."

"You didn't say it?"

"Now, see, there you've got me."

She shot him what she hoped was a withering glare, but since she didn't have much practice with that sort of thing, it probably fell short.

He blessed a cat that strolled by. "I was a young actor trying to stir up a little publicity when I gave a reporter that quote. Hey, a guy's got to make a living."

She itched to ask how many women there'd really been, and the only way she managed to restrain herself was to speed up her pace.

"A hundred max."

"I didn't ask," she retorted. "And that's disgusting."

"I was kidding. Even I'm not that promiscuous. You guru people have no sense of humor."

"I'm not a guru people, and I happen to have a very well developed sense of humor. Why else would I still be talking to you?"

"If you don't want to be judged by what happened that night, you shouldn't judge me that way either." He grabbed her sack and poked inside it. "What's this?"

"A tart. And it's mine. Hey!" She watched him take a big bite.

"Good." He spoke with his mouth full. "Like a juicy Fig Newton. Want some?"

"No thank you. Feel free to help yourself."

"Your loss." He demolished the tart. "Food never tastes as good in the States as it does here. Have you noticed that yet?" She had, but she'd reached the grocery, and she ignored him.

He didn't follow her inside. Instead, she watched through the window as he knelt to stroke the ancient dog who ambled down the step to greet him. The friendly clerk of the honey pot was nowhere in sight. In her place stood an older man wearing a butcher's apron. He glared at her as she handed over the list she'd made with the aid of an Italian dictionary. She realized that the only friendly person she'd encountered all day was Lorenzo Gage. A terrifying thought.

He was leaning against the side of the building reading an Italian newspaper when she came out. He tucked it under his arm and reached for her grocery sacks.

"No way. You'll just eat everything." She headed for the side street where she'd left her car.

"I should evict you."

"On what grounds?"

"For being—what's the word?—oh, yeah . . . bitchy."

"Only to you." She raised her voice toward a man taking the sun on a bench. "*Signore!* This man isn't a priest. He's—"

Gage grabbed her groceries and said something in Italian to the man, who clucked his tongue at her.

"What did you tell him?"

"That you're either a pyromaniac or a pickpocket. I always get those words mixed up."

"You're not funny." Actually, he was, and if he'd been anyone else, she would have laughed. "Why are you stalking me? I'm sure there are dozens of needy women in town who'd love your company." A dapper man in the doorway of a Foto shop stared at her.

"I'm not stalking. I'm bored. And you're the best entertainment in town. In case you haven't noticed, people here don't seem to like you."

"I've noticed."

"It's because you look snotty."

"I don't look one bit snotty. They're just closing ranks to protect their own."

"You look a little snotty."

"If I were you, I'd ask to see the rental records on your farm-house."

"Just what I want to do on my vacation."

"Something underhanded is going on, and I think I know exactly what it is."

"I feel better already."

"Do you want to hear this or not?"

"Not."

"Your farmhouse is supposed to be available for rent, right?"

"I suppose."

"Well, if you investigate, I think you'll discover that's not been happening."

"And you're just aching to tell me why."

"Because Marta regards the house as her own, and she doesn't want to share it with anyone."

"Dead Paolo's sister?"

Isabel nodded. "People in small towns stick together against outsiders. They know how she feels, and they've been protecting her. I'd be surprised if she's ever paid you a cent of rent for the place, not that you need it."

"There's a big hole in your conspiracy theory. If she's kept the house from being rented, how come you—"

"Some kind of snafu."

"Okay, I'll go down there and throw her out. Do I have to kill her first?"

"Don't you dare throw her out, even though she's not my favorite person. And you'd better not start charging her rent either. *You* should pay *her*. That garden's incredible." She frowned as he grabbed one of her grocery sacks and began rummaging through it. "The point I'm trying to make—"

"Is there any more dessert in here?"

She snatched it back. "The point is, I'm the innocent party. I rented the farmhouse in good faith, and I expect hot water in return."

"I told you I'd take care of it."

"And I'm *not* snotty. They would have been hostile to anyone who'd rented the house."

"Can I get back to you on that?"

She didn't like his smugness. She had a reputation for being unflappable, but in comparison to him, she felt very . . . flappable. She swiped at him to retaliate. "That's an interesting scar on your cheek."

"You're using your shrink voice, aren't you?"

"I'm wondering if the scar might be symbolic."

"Meaning?"

"An outward representation of the internal scars you're carrying around. Scars caused by—oh, I don't know—lechery, depravity, debauchery? Or maybe just a guilty conscience?"

She'd been thinking of the way he'd treated her, but as his amusement faded, she realized she'd hit a nerve, and she suspected that nerve had Karli Swenson's name written all over it. She'd actually managed to forget about the actress's suicide. Gage obviously hadn't, and the corner of his mouth tightened.

"Just part of my actor's bag of tricks."

She felt him distance himself, which was exactly what she wanted, but the flash of unguarded pain she'd seen on his face before he'd wiped it away bothered her. She had many faults, but deliberate cruelty wasn't one of them. "I didn't mean—"

He checked his watch. "Time for me to hear confessions. *Ciao,* Fifi."

As he turned to walk away, she reminded herself that he'd taken a dozen pokes at her, so she had no reason to make amends. Except that the poke she'd taken had drawn blood, and she was a healer by nature, not an executioner. Still, she was dismayed to hear herself call out to him. "I'm going to Volterra tomorrow to do some sightseeing."

He looked back and cocked a brow. "Is this an invitation?"

No! But her conscience prevailed over her personal needs. "It's a bribe to get my hot water back."

"All right, I accept."

"Fine." She cursed herself. There must have been a better way to make amends than this. "I'm driving," she said begrudgingly. "I'll pick you up at ten."

"In the morning?"

"Is that a problem?" A problem for her. According to the schedule, she should be writing at ten o'clock.

"You're kidding, right? That's before dawn."

"Sorry you can't make it. Maybe some other time."

"Okay, I'll be ready." He started off, then looked back. "You're not going to pay me to have sex with you again, are you?"

"I'll do my best to resist the temptation."

"Attagirl, Fifi. See you at dawn."

She climbed into her car and shut the door. As she stared glumly through the windshield, she reminded herself that she had a Ph.D. in psychology, which qualified her to make a fairly accurate diagnosis: She was an idiot.

Ren ordered an espresso at the counter of the bar on the piazza. He carried the tiny cup to a round marble table and settled in to enjoy the luxury of sitting undisturbed in a public place. After giving the drink a few moments to cool, he downed it in one gulp just as his *nonna* used to. It was strong and bitter, exactly the way he liked it.

He wished he hadn't let the feisty Dr. Favor get to him there at the end. He'd coasted along with ass-kissers for so long that he'd forgotten what it was like to have to pay attention, but if he intended to hang around with her, he'd better get back into the habit. She sure wasn't impressed by his fame. Hell, she didn't even like his movies. And that moral compass strapped to her back was so heavy she could barely stand up straight. So did he really intend to spend the day with her tomorrow?

Yeah, he really did. How else was he going to get her naked again?

He smiled and toyed with his cup. The idea had taken hold the moment he'd seen her with that postcard. Her forehead had been furrowed in concentration, and she'd been nibbling those full lips she tried to downplay with boring lipstick. Her streaky blond hair had been neat as a pin except for a wayward lock curling across her cheek. Neither the pricey little cardigan she'd knotted around her shoulders nor her buttoned-up, toast-colored dress did all that great a job of concealing a body that was way too curvy to be wasted on a do-gooder.

He kicked back in his chair and let the idea settle in. Something had gone wrong the first time he and the good doctor had made love, but he'd make sure it didn't go wrong again, which meant he might have to take it a little slower than he'd like.

Contrary to popular opinion, he had a conscience, and he gave it a quick check. Nope. Not even a twinge. Dr. Fifi was an adult, and if she hadn't been attracted to him, she wouldn't have gone off with him that night. Still, she was resisting him right now, and did he really want to work hard enough to get past that?

Yeah, why not? She intrigued him. Despite her sharp tongue, she had a decency about her that was oddly alluring, and he'd bet the farm that she believed what she preached. Which meant that—unlike last time—she'd expect some sort of relationship first.

God, he hated that word. He didn't do relationships, at least not with any degree of sincerity. But if he were just straightforward enough, without letting down his guard for a second, and—it went without saying—being completely devious the whole time, he might be able to slide through the relationship thing.

It had been a long time since he'd been around a woman who interested him, not to mention one who offered genuine entertainment. Last night he'd had his first decent sleep in months, and so far today he hadn't felt the need to pull out his emergency cigarette. Besides, anybody could see that Dr. Fifi would benefit from a little corruption. And he was just the man for the job.

A rush of hot water greeted Isabel the next morning. She reveled in a warm bath, taking her time as she shampooed her hair and shaved her legs. But her gratitude toward her landlord faded when her hair dryer wouldn't go on, and she discovered the house had no electricity.

She stared in the mirror at her towel-dried hair. Blond ringlets had already started to form at her ears. Without her hair dryer and brush, she'd end up with a headful of curls that all the gels and conditioners in the world couldn't tame. In twenty minutes she'd look just as messy as her mother used to look after she'd come home from one of her extracurricular tutoring sessions with a studly undergrad.

The psychological roots behind Isabel's need for order weren't buried very deeply. Being a neat freak was a fairly predictable outcome for someone who'd grown up in chaos. She considered phoning the villa and canceling the trip, but Gage would think she was afraid of him. Besides, she wasn't that neurotic about her hair. She simply didn't like the way untidiness made her feel.

To compensate, she dressed in a simple black mock-neck sundress cut high on her shoulders. With the addition of slimly sculpted mules, her gold BREATHE bangle, and a natural straw sun hat pulled low over her curls, she was ready to go. She wished she'd been able to meditate that morning to calm herself first, but her mind had refused to quiet.

Although she'd planned to arrive at the villa fifteen minutes late, just for the pleasure of making Mr. Movie Star wait, she was habitually punctual, and at 10:05, she started to hyperventilate and had to head for her car. She glanced into the rearview mirror as she pulled up to the front entrance of the villa. The curls peeking out from beneath her hat made her want to rush back to the farmhouse and organize something.

She noticed a man skulking in the shrubbery—a very badly dressed tourist, by the look of him. She felt an unwilling flash of sympathy for Gage. Despite his disguise yesterday, he hadn't been able to keep his hiding place a secret from his fans.

The fan wore an ugly checked sport shirt, baggy Bermuda shorts that nearly brushed his knees, and thick, crepe-soled sandals with white socks. A Lakers cap shadowed his face, and a camera hung from a strap around his neck. His purple fanny pack sagged like a bruised kidney at his waist. He spotted her car and began walking toward it, shifting his weight from side to side in the awkward gait of the overweight and out of shape.

She braced herself for a confrontation, then looked more closely. With a groan, she banged her forehead against the top of the steering wheel.

He stuck his head in the door and grinned. "Morning, Fifi."

8

I refuse to be seen in public with you!"

His knees bumped the dash as he folded himself into her Panda. "Believe me, you'll enjoy the day more this way. I know this is going to be hard for you to believe, but the Italians love my films."

She gazed at his geeky outfit. "You have to lose the fanny pack."

"I can't believe I'm out of bed this early when I don't have to work." He slouched down in the seat and closed his eyes.

"I mean it. The fanny pack goes. I can deal with the white socks and those sandals, but not that fanny pack." She looked again. "No, I can't deal with the white socks either. They both have to go."

He yawned. "Okay, let's see . . . how will the story play out on *Entertainment Tonight*?" He dropped his voice into television-announcer mode. "The recently disgraced Dr. Isabel Favor, who's apparently not as wise as she wants her legions of worshippers to believe, was seen in Volterra, Italy, with Lorenzo Gage, Hollywood's dark prince of dissolute living. The two were spotted together—"

"I love the fanny pack." She threw the Panda into gear.

"What about the sandals and white socks?"

"A retro fashion statement."

"Excellent." He squinted, then fumbled with the zipper on the pack. She wondered how someone so tall fitted into a Maserati.

"What were you doing in the shrubbery?"

He stuck on a pair of clunky black sunglasses. "There's a bench back there. I was taking a nap." Despite his complaining, he looked healthy and rested. "Nice hair this morning. Where did the curls come from?"

"A sudden and mysterious electrical failure that rendered my hair dryer ineffective. Thanks for the hot water. Now may I have my electricity back?"

"You don't have electricity?"

"Strangest thing."

"It could be accidental. Anna said they've had water problems at the farmhouse all summer, which is why they need to dig."

"And why she told you I have to move to town."

"I believe she mentioned it. Dump the hat, will you?"

"Not a chance."

"It'll draw too much attention to us. Besides, I like those curls."

"Be still, my heart."

"You don't like curls?"

"I don't like messiness." She gave his clothes a telling glance.

"Ah."

"What?"

"Nothing. Just 'ah.' "

"Keep your 'ahs' to yourself so I can enjoy the scenery."

"Be glad to."

It was a beautiful day. Hills stretched to the horizon on either side of the road. Oblong bales of wheat sat in one field. A tractor moved through another. They passed acres of sunflowers drying in the sun but not yet plowed under. She would've loved to see them in bloom, but then she would've missed the sight of the grapes ready for harvest.

"My friends call me Ren," he said, "but today I'd appreciate it if you'd call me Buddy."

"That's gonna happen."

"Or Ralph. Ralph Smitts from Ashtabula, Ohio. It has a certain ring to it. If you have to wear a hat, I'll buy you something a little less eye-catching when we get there."

"No thanks."

"You're one uptight chick, Dr. Favor. Is that a building block of your philosophy? 'Thou shalt be the most uptight chick on the planet'?"

"I'm principled, not uptight." Just saying it made her feel stuffy, and she wasn't stuffy, not really, not in her heart anyway. "What do you know about my philosophy?"

"Nothing until I got on the Web last night. Interesting. From what I read in your bio, you built your empire the hard way. I've got to hand it to you. Nobody seems to have given you anything for free."

"Oh, I got a lot for free." She thought of all the people who'd inspired her over the years. Whenever she'd reached a low point in her life, the universe had always sent her an angel in one form or another.

Her foot slipped off the accelerator.

"Hey."

"Sorry."

"Either pay attention to the road or let me drive," he grumbled. "Which you should have done in the first place, because I'm the man."

"I noticed." She gripped the wheel more tightly. "I'm sure my

life story is boring compared to yours. Didn't I read that your
mother's royalty?"

"A countess. One of those meaningless Italian titles. Mainly she
was an irresponsible international playgirl with too much money.
She's dead now."

"I've always been fascinated with the influences of childhood.
Do you mind an intrusive question?"

"You want to know what it was like growing up with a mother who
had the maturity level of a twelve-year-old pothead? I'm touched
by your interest."

She'd imagined herself staying aloof today instead of chatting
away. Still, what else could he do to her? "Professional curiosity
only, so don't get sentimental on me."

"Let's see, maternal influence . . . I can't remember the first
time I got drunk, but it was around the time I grew tall enough to
pick up the liquor glasses her party guests left around." She didn't
hear any bitterness, but it had to be lurking around in there somewhere. "I smoked my first joint when I was ten, and a lot more after
that. I'd seen a few dozen porn films before I was twelve, and don't
think that doesn't screw up your adolescent sexual expectations. In
and out of boarding schools all along the East Coast. Totaled more
cars than I can count. Arrested for shoplifting twice, which was
ironic because I had a fat trust fund and way too much disposable
income for a snot-nosed punk. But, hey, anything to get attention.
Oh . . . snorted my first line of coke when I was fifteen. Ah, the
good old days."

A lot of pain hid behind his chuckle, but he wasn't going to let
her see a bit of it. "What about your father?" she asked.

"Wall Street. Very respectable. He still goes to work every day.
The second time around he made sure he married more responsi-
bly—a blueblood who wisely kept me as far away as possible from

their three kids. One of them's a decent guy. We see each other occasionally."

"Did any angels show up in your childhood?"

"Angels?"

"A benevolent presence."

"My *nonna*, my mother's mother. She lived with us off and on. If it weren't for her, I'd probably be in prison now."

As it was, he seemed to have made his own kind of creative prison, playing only villainous parts, maybe to reflect his self-image. Or maybe not. Psychologists had a bad habit of oversimplifying people's motivations.

"What about you?" he asked. "Your biography said you've been on your own since you were eighteen. Sounds tough."

"It built character."

"You've come a long way."

"Not far enough. I'm currently broke." She reached for her sunglasses, hoping to deflect the conversation.

"Worse things can happen than being broke," he said.

"I'm guessing you're not speaking from personal experience."

"Hey, when I was eighteen, the interest check from my trust fund was lost in the mail. It got pretty ugly."

She'd always been a sucker for self-deprecating humor, and she smiled, even though she didn't want to.

Half an hour later they reached the outskirts of Volterra, where a castle of forbidding gray stone appeared on the hill above them. Finally a safe topic of conversation. "That must be the *fortezza*," she said. "The Florentines built it in the late 1400s over the original Etruscan settlement, which dated to around the eighth century B.C."

"Been reading our guidebook, have we?"

"Several of them." They passed an Esso station and a tidy little house with a satellite dish perched above its red roof tiles. "Somehow I'd pictured the Etruscans as cavemen with clubs, but this was a fairly advanced civilization. They had a lot in common with the Greeks. They were merchants, seafarers, farmers, craftsmen. They mined copper and smelted iron ore. And their women were surprisingly liberated for the time."

"Thank God for that."

There was nothing like a history lesson to keep things impersonal. She should have thought of this earlier. "As the Romans moved in, the Etruscan culture was gradually assimilated, although some people think the modern Tuscan lifestyle is more a reflection of its Etruscan roots than its Roman ones."

"Any excuse for a party."

"Something like that." She followed the parking signs past a pretty walkway lined with benches and found a spot at the end of the lot. "They don't let cars in the city, so we have to park out here."

He spoke around a yawn. "There's a great museum in town filled with some world-class Etruscan artifacts that should strike your fancy."

"You've been here?"

"Years ago, but I still remember it. The Etruscans were one of the reasons I majored in history before I flunked out of college."

She eyed him suspiciously. "You already knew those things I was talking about, didn't you?"

"Pretty much, but it gave me a chance for a quick nap. By the way, the original Etruscan city was built around the ninth century B.C., not the eighth. But, hey, what's a hundred years here and there?"

So much for showing off her knowledge. They got out of the Panda, and she saw that one corner of his sunglasses was wrapped with tape. "Didn't you wear a disguise like this in that movie where you tried to rape Cameron Diaz?"

"I believe I was trying to murder her, not rape her."

"I don't mean to sound critical, but doesn't all that sadism get to you after a while?"

"Thank you for not being critical. And sadism has made me famous."

She followed him through the parking lot toward the sidewalk. He moved with the rolling gait of a much heavier man, another illusion from his actor's tool box. It seemed to be working, because no one was paying any attention to him. She told herself to be quiet and leave it alone, but old habits were hard to break. "That's still important to you, isn't it?" she said. "Despite all the inconvenience. Being famous."

"If there's a spotlight around, I generally enjoy having it pointed in my direction. And don't pretend not to know what I'm talking about."

"You think attention is what motivates me?"

"Isn't it?"

"Only as a means of getting my message across."

"I believe you."

He clearly didn't. She looked up at him, knowing she should let it go. "Is that all you want your life to be about? Staying in the spotlight?"

"Spare me your self-improvement lectures. I'm not interested."

"I wasn't going to lecture."

"Fifi, you live to lecture. Lecturing is your oxygen."

"And that threatens you?" She followed him down the cobblestones.

"Everything about you threatens me."

"Thank you."

"It wasn't a compliment."

"You think I'm smug, don't you?"

"I've observed a tendency."

"Only around you, and that's deliberate." She tried not to enjoy herself.

They turned into a narrower street that looked even older and more quaint than the ones they'd been on. "So did you get your Four Cornerstones in a thunderbolt from God," he asked, "or did you read them on a greeting card somewhere?"

"From God, thanks for asking." She gave up on her attempt to stay aloof. "Not in a thunderbolt, though. We moved around a lot when I was a child. It kept me fairly isolated, but it gave me time to observe people. As I got older, I started working different jobs to put myself through school. I read and kept my eyes open. I saw people succeed and fail—in jobs, in personal relationships. The Four Cornerstones grew out of all that observation."

"I don't imagine fame came instantly."

"I started writing about what I was observing around the time I entered graduate school."

"Academic papers?"

"At first. But that began to feel too limiting, so I condensed my ideas for some of the women's magazines, and that's how the Four Cornerstones were born." She was rattling on, but it felt good to talk about her work. "I'd begun putting the lessons to use in my own life, and I liked what was happening, the way I felt more centered. I organized some discussion groups on campus. They seemed to help people, and they kept getting bigger. A book editor started attending one of them, and everything took off from there."

"You enjoy what you do, don't you?"

"I love it."

"Then we have something in common after all."

"You truly enjoy those parts you play?"

"See, there you go with that snotty thing again."

"It's just hard to imagine loving a job that glorifies violence."

"You forget that I usually die in the end, which makes my films morality tales. That should be right up your alley."

The crowd jostled them apart as they entered the piazza. She gazed around at the open stalls displaying everything from baskets overflowing with fruits and vegetables to brightly colored toys. Pots of herbs scented the air, along with braids of garlic and strands of peppers. Clothing vendors sold silk scarves and leather purses. Colorful bags of pasta rested next to jewel-like bottles of olive oil. She passed a pushcart holding an array of earth-toned soaps that were studded with lavender, poppy seeds, and lemon peel. As she stopped to smell the lavender ones, she spotted Ren near a wire birdcage. She thought of other actors she'd known. She'd heard them talk about how they had to look internally to find the seeds for the character they were playing, and she wondered what Ren saw inside himself that let him portray evil so convincingly. Leftover feelings from his deviant childhood?

As she approached, he gestured toward the canaries. "I'm not planning their demise, in case you were worried."

"I suppose two small birds aren't enough of a challenge for you." She touched the latch on the cage door. "Don't get a big head about this, but objectively speaking, you seem to be a terrific actor. I'll bet you could play a great hero if you set your mind to it."

"Are we back to that again?"

"Wouldn't it be nice to save the girl for a change instead of brutalizing her?"

"Hey, it's not just women. I'm an equal-opportunity brutalizer. And I tried saving the girl once, but it didn't work. Did you ever see a movie called *November Time*?"

"No."

"Neither did anyone else. I played a noble but naïve doctor who stumbles on some medical chicanery while he's fighting to save the heroine's life. It tanked."

"Maybe it was a bad script."

"Or maybe not." He glanced down at her. "Here's the life lesson I've learned, Fifi: Some people are born to play the hero, and some are born to play the bad guy. Fighting your destiny only makes life harder than it needs to be. Besides, people remember the villain long after they've forgotten the hero."

If she hadn't caught that flicker of pain on his face the day before, she might have let it go, but delving into people's psyches was second nature to her. "There's a big difference between playing the bad guy on-screen and playing him in real life, or at least feeling as if you are."

"Not very subtle. If you want to know about Karli, just ask."

She hadn't been thinking just of Karli, but she didn't back off. "Maybe you need to talk about what happened. Darkness loses some of its power when you shine light on it."

"Wait here for me, will you? I have to throw up."

She didn't take offense. She simply lowered her voice and spoke more softly. "Did you have anything to do with her death, Ren?"

"You're not going to shut up, are you?"

"You just told me all I had to do is ask. I'm asking."

The look he shot her was withering, but he didn't walk away. "We hadn't even spoken in over a year. And when we were dating, it wasn't a grand passion for either of us. She didn't kill herself because of me. She died because she was a junkie. Unfortunately, the less savory members of the media wanted a sexier story, so they invented one, and since I've been known to play fast and loose with the truth myself when it comes to the press, I can hardly cry foul, can I?"

"Of course you can." She said a quick prayer for the soul of Karli

Swenson, only a few words, but in light of her current spiritual black hole, she was thankful she could pray at all. "I'm sorry for what this has put you through."

The chink in his self-protective armor had been a small one, and his villain's sneer returned. "Spare me the sympathy. Bad press only adds to my box-office appeal."

"Gotcha. All sympathy retracted."

"Don't do it again." He took her arm to guide her through the crowd.

"If there's one thing I've learned, it's not to antagonize anyone with a fanny pack."

"Funny."

She smiled to herself. "See those people staring at us. They can't figure out why a babe like me is walking around with such a geek."

"They think I'm rich and you're a little treat I bought for myself."

"A little treat? Really?" She liked that.

"Stop looking so happy about it. I'm hungry." He took her arm and steered her into a tiny *gelateria*, where a glass case held round tubs filled with the rich Italian ice cream. Ren addressed the teenager behind the counter in pidgin Italian laced with a hokey Deep South accent that made Isabel snicker.

He shot her a quelling look, and a few moments later they emerged from the shop with double cones. She dabbed at the mango, then the raspberry, with the tip of her tongue. "You could have consulted me about what flavor I wanted."

"Why? You'd just have ordered vanilla."

She'd have ordered chocolate. "You don't know that."

"You're a woman who likes to play it safe."

"How can you say that after what happened?"

"Are we back to our night of sin?"

"I don't want to talk about it."

"Proving my point. If you didn't like to play it safe, you wouldn't still be obsessing over what turned out to be a less than memorable experience."

She wished he hadn't put it that way.

"If the sex had been great—now, that would have been worth obsessing about." His steps slowed, and he slipped off his sunglasses to gaze down at her. "You know what I mean by great, don't you, Fifi? The kind of sex that makes you so wild all you want to do is stay in bed for the rest of your life. The kind of sex where you can't get enough of the other person's body, where every touch feels like you're being rubbed with silk, where you get so hot and—"

"You've made your point!" She told herself this was simply Ren Gage showing off his tricks and, in general, trying to aggravate her with those smoldering eyes and that husky, seductive voice. She took a slow breath to cool off.

A teenager shot by on a scooter, and the sun melting from the golden stones fell warm on her bare shoulders. She smelled herbs and fresh bread in the air. His arm brushed hers. She licked her cone, swirling the mango and raspberry against her taste buds. Every one of her senses felt alive.

"Trying to seduce me?" He pushed his glasses up on his nose.

"What are you talking about?"

"That thing you're doing with your tongue."

"I'm eating my gelato."

"You're diddling with it."

"I'm not diddl—" She stopped and gazed up at him. "Is this turning you on?"

"Maybe."

"It is!" Sparks of happiness rushed through her. "Watching me eat this is turning you on."

He looked irritated. "I've been a little sex-deprived lately, so it doesn't take much."

"Sure. It's been, what? Five days?"

"Don't even think about counting that pitiful encounter."

"I don't see why not. You were satisfied."

"Was I?"

She no longer felt quite so happy. "Weren't you?"

"Have I hurt your feelings?"

She noticed he didn't sound too worried about it. She tried to decide whether she should be honest or not. *Not.* "You've destroyed me," she said. "Now, let's go to the museum before I completely fall apart."

"Snotty *and* sarcastic."

Compared to New York's glittering monuments to the past, the Guarnacci Etruscan Museum was unimpressive. The small lobby was shabby and a little gloomy, but as they began inspecting the contents of the glass cases on the ground floor, she saw a vast display of fascinating artifacts: weapons, jewelry, pots, amulets, and devotional objects. More impressive, however, was the museum's extraordinary collection of alabaster funeral urns.

She remembered seeing a few urns prominently displayed at other museums, but here hundreds jostled for space in the old-fashioned glass cases. Designed to hold the ashes of the deceased, the rectangular urns varied from about the size of a rural mailbox to something closer to a toolbox. Many were topped by reclining figures—some female, some male. Mythological scenes, as well as depictions of everything from battles to banquets, were carved in relief on the sides.

"The Etruscans didn't leave any literature," Ren said when they finally climbed the stairs to the second floor, where they found even more urns crowded into the old-fashioned cases. "A lot of what we know about their daily lives comes from these reliefs."

"They're certainly more interesting than our modern cemetery markers." Isabel stopped in front of a large urn with the figures of an elderly couple reclining on the top.

"The *Urna degli Sposi*," Ren said. "One of the most famous urns in the world."

Isabel gazed at the couple's lined and wrinkled faces. "They look so real. If their clothes were different, they could have been a couple we passed on the street today." The date indicated was 90 B.C. "She looks like she adored him. It must have been a happy marriage."

"I've heard such things exist."

"But not for you?" She tried to remember if she'd read whether he'd been married.

"Definitely not for me."

"Ever tried it?"

"When I was twenty. A girl I grew up with. It lasted a year, and it was a disaster from the start. How about you?"

She shook her head. "I believe in marriage, but not for me." Her breakup with Michael had forced her to face the truth. It hadn't been time constraints that had kept her from planning their wedding; it had been her subconscious warning her that marriage wouldn't be good for her, even with a better man than Michael had proved to be. She didn't believe that all marriages were as chaotic as her parents' had been, but marriage was disruptive by nature, and her life would be better without it.

They wandered into the next room, and she stopped so suddenly he bumped into her. "What's that?"

He followed the direction of her eyes. "The museum's prize."

In the center of the room a single glass case held an extraordinary bronze statue of a young boy. The nude was about two feet tall but only a few inches wide.

"This is one of the most famous Etruscan artifacts in the world," he said as they approached. "I was eighteen the last time I saw it, but I still remember it."

"It's beautiful."

"It's called *Shadow of the Evening. Ombra della Sera.* You can see why."

"Oh, yes." The boy's elongated form was reminiscent of a human shadow at the end of the day. "It looks so contemporary, like a piece of modern art."

"It's from the third century."

There was little detail to the piece, adding to its modern aura. The bronze head with its short hair and sweet features might have appeared female if not for the small penis. The boy's long, thin arms were clasped to his sides, and his legs had tiny bumps for knees. The feet, she noticed, were a bit large in comparison to the head.

"The fact that it's a nude makes the statue unusual," he said. "There's not even a piece of jewelry to indicate status, which was important to the Etruscans. It's probably a votive figure."

"It's extraordinary."

"A farmer plowed it up in the nineteenth century and used it as a fireplace poker before someone finally recognized it for what it was."

"Imagine a country where things like this can be plowed up."

"Houses all over Tuscany have secret stashes of Etruscan and Roman artifacts hidden away in their cupboards. After a few glasses of grappa, the owners will usually pull them out if you ask."

"Do you have a stash at the villa?"

"As far as I know, the artifacts my aunt collected are all out on display. Come up for dinner tomorrow night and I'll show them to you."

"Dinner? How about lunch?"

"Afraid I'll turn into a vampire after dark?"

"You've been known to."

He laughed. "I've had enough funeral urns for today. Let's eat."

She took one last look at *Shadow of the Evening*. Ren's knowledge of history bothered her. She preferred her original impression of him as oversexed, self-absorbed, and only moderately intelligent. Still, two out of three wasn't bad.

Half an hour later they were sipping Chianti at a sidewalk café. Drinking at lunch felt hedonistic, but then so did being with Lorenzo Gage. Not even the geek clothes and taped sunglasses could completely camouflage that decadent elegance.

She dredged one of her gnocchi through a sauce of olive oil, garlic, and fresh sage. "I'm going to gain ten pounds while I'm here."

"You've got a great body. Don't worry about it." He devoured another of the razor clams he'd ordered.

"A great body? Hardly."

"I've seen it, Fifi. I'm entitled to an opinion."

"Would you stop bringing that up?"

"Relax, will you? It's not like you killed someone."

"Maybe I killed a little corner of my soul."

"Spare me."

His faint air of boredom grated on her. She set down her fork and leaned closer. "What I did violated everything I believe in. Sex is sacred, and I don't like being a hypocrite."

"God, it must be hard being you."

"You're going to say something smarmy, aren't you?"

"Just making an observation about how tough it has to be to stay on that narrow path to perfection."

"I've been taunted by bigger bullies than you, and I'm impervious. Life is precious. I don't believe in drifting through it."

"Well, charging through it doesn't seem to be working right now, does it? From what I can see, you're disgraced, broke, and unemployed."

"And where has your live-life-for-the-moment philosophy

gotten you? What have you contributed to the world that you're proud of?"

"I've given people a few hours of entertainment. That's enough."

"But what do you *care* about?"

"Right now? Food, wine, and sex. The same things you do. And don't even try to deny the sex. If it hadn't been important, you wouldn't have let me pick you up."

"I was drunk, and that night didn't have anything to do with sex. It was about confusion."

"Bull. You weren't that drunk. It was about sex." He paused, cocked an eyebrow at her. *"We're* about sex."

She swallowed. "We're not about sex."

"Then what are we doing here right now?"

"We've just formed an odd sort of friendship, that's all. Two Americans in a foreign country."

"This isn't a friendship. We don't even like each other that much. What's between us is sizzle."

"Sizzle?"

"Yeah, sizzle." He drew out the word until it sounded like a caress.

A little shiver passed through her, which made it a challenge to sound offended. "I don't sizzle."

"I noticed."

Well, she'd left herself wide open for that one.

"But you want to." He suddenly seemed very Italian. "And I'm prepared to help."

"My eyes are misting from emotion."

"I'm just saying that I'd like a second shot."

"I'll bet."

"I don't want blemishes on my employment record, and I didn't do the job you hired me for."

"I'll settle for a refund."

"Against company policy. We only give even exchanges." He smiled. "So you're not interested?"

"Not at all."

"I thought honesty was basic to the Four Cornerstones."

"You want honesty? All right. Admittedly you're a great-looking man. Dazzling, actually. But only in that impossible, movie-star, fantasy way. And I outgrew movie-star fantasies when I was thirteen."

"Is that how long you've had your sexual hang-ups?"

"I hope you're done with lunch, because I am." She tossed her napkin onto the table.

"And here I thought you were too evolved to get huffy."

"You thought wrong."

"All I'm proposing is that you stretch your boundaries a little. Your bio says you're thirty-four. Don't you think that's a little old to carry around so much baggage?"

"I don't have sexual hang-ups."

The knowing arch of his brow made her uncomfortable. He stroked the corner of his mouth. "In the interest of serving another human being—a philosophy you should appreciate—I'm prepared to help you work through every one of those hang-ups."

"Hold on. I'm trying to remember if I've ever had a more insulting offer. No. This is it."

He smiled. "It's not an insult, Fifi. You turn me on. There's something about the combination of a great body, a first-class brain, and a snotty personality that does it for me."

"I'm getting all misty again."

"When we met in town yesterday, I had this fantasy of seeing you naked again, and—I hope I'm not being too explicit here—spread-eagled." The slow smile that curled the edges of his mouth looked more boyish than evil. He was having a great time.

"Ahh . . ." She tried for sophistication—young Faye Dunaway—but he was definitely getting to her. This man was bottled sex, even when he was being outrageous. She'd always applauded people who were clear about their goals, so it seemed wiser to let the more rational Dr. Favor take over. "You're proposing that we establish a sexual liaison."

He stroked the corner of his mouth with his thumb. "What I'm proposing is that we spend every minute of every night for the next few weeks engaged in either foreplay, afterplay, or . . . play." He lingered over the word, teasing it with his lips. "What I'm proposing is that all we talk about is sex. All we think about is sex. All we do is—"

"Are you making this up on the spot, or is it from a script?"

"Sex until you can't walk and I can't stand up straight." His voice delivered a thousand volts of smolder. "Sex until we're both screaming. Sex until every hang-up you have is gone and your only goal in life is to come."

"My lucky day. Free smut." She tilted her sunglasses higher on her nose. "Thanks for the invitation, but I think I'll pass."

His index finger made a leisurely journey around the rim of his wineglass, and his smile spoke of conquest. "I guess we'll see about that, won't we?"

9

Even Ren's tough morning workout didn't burn off his restless energy. He took a slug from the water bottle and gazed at the pile of brush Anna wanted moved away from the villa's garden. She'd planned to ask her husband, Massimo, who supervised the vineyard, to do it, or her son, Giancarlo, but Ren needed activity, and he'd volunteered.

The day was hot, the Madonna-blue sky cloudless, but even as he fell into the rhythm of the task, he couldn't shake off thoughts of Karli. If he'd tried harder to reach her, she might still be alive; but he'd always taken the easy way out. He'd been careless with women, careless with friendships, careless about everything except his work.

"I don't want you around my children," his father had said when Ren was twelve. Ren had retaliated by stealing the old man's wallet.

Granted, he'd cleaned up his act in the past ten years, but old habits were hard to break, and he'd always have a sinner's heart. Maybe that was why he felt so relaxed around Isabel. She wore her goodness like armor. She might feel vulnerable now, but she was tough as iron, so tough that even he couldn't corrupt her.

He loaded up the wheelbarrow again and pushed it to the edge of the vineyard, where he emptied it into one of the empty metal drums used to burn brush. As he set it on fire, he gazed in the direction of the farmhouse. Where was she? A day had passed since they'd gone to Volterra, and she still didn't have electricity, mainly because he hadn't bothered to tell Anna to get it fixed. Hey, good deeds hadn't gotten him where he was today, and this seemed the easiest way to get Ms. Perfect on his turf.

He wondered if she'd wear her hat when she finally came charging up the hill to confront him about her power problems, or if she'd let those curls she hated fly free. Stupid question. Nothing about Isabel Favor would ever fly free. She'd be buttoned up neat as a pin, looking capable and sophisticated, and she'd probably be waving a sheaf of legal papers that threatened to lock him up for life for being a slumlord. So where was she?

He briefly considered going down to the farmhouse to check on her, but that defeated the purpose. No, he wanted Ms. Perfect coming to him. A villain always preferred luring the heroine to his lair.

Isabel found a small chandelier decorated with metal flowers tucked away in a cupboard. Its white paint had flaked with age, and the original bright colors had faded to dusty pastels. She removed the old lightbulbs and fitted the sockets with candles, then found some strong cord and hung it from the magnolia tree.

When she was done, she looked around for something else to keep herself busy. She'd finished her hand wash, organized the books on the shelves in the living room, and tried to bathe the cats. So far her schedule was a joke. She couldn't summon the concentration to write, and meditating was an exercise in futility. All she

heard was that seductive, low-pitched voice luring her to decadence.

*"Sex until we're both screaming. . . . Sex until every hang-up you
have is gone . . ."*

She reached for the dish towel to polish the glassware and considered phoning Anna Vesto again, but she suspected that Ren was
calling the shots now. Walking up to the villa to confront him in
person was exactly what he wanted her to do—making her dance to
his tune. But even electricity wasn't worth that. He might have cunning on his side, but she had the Four Cs on hers.

Suppose she lost her mind and gave in to the urge to dance with
him on the dark side? It didn't bear thinking about. She'd sold her
soul once. She wouldn't do it again.

A movement outside caught her attention. She made her way to
the open kitchen door and watched two workmen come into the
olive grove. She'd never welcomed a distraction more, and she
went down to investigate.

"Are you here to see about the electricity?"

The older man had a road-map face and wiry, graying hair. The
younger was stocky, dark-eyed, and olive-skinned. He set down his
pick and shovel as she approached. "Electricity?" He looked her
over in the way of Italian males. "No, *signora*. We come to see about
problem with the well."

"I thought the problem was with the sewer."

"*Si,*" the older man said. "This is my son's bad English. I am
Massimo Vesto. I take care of the land here. And this is Giancarlo.
We do the survey now to see if we can dig."

She glanced at the pick and shovel. Odd surveying equipment.
Or maybe Massimo had his English mixed up as well.

"Will be much noise," Giancarlo said, flashing his teeth at her.
"Much dirt."

"I'll live with it."

She returned to the villa. A few minutes later Vittorio appeared, his long black hair swinging free in the breeze.

"Signora Favor! Today is your lucky day."

By the time the afternoon heat drove Ren inside, he was in a black mood. According to Anna, Isabel had driven off in a red Fiat with a man named Vittorio. Who the hell was Vittorio, and why was Isabel going anyplace when Ren had his own plans for her?

He took a swim, then returned his agent's phone call. Jaguar wanted him for commercial voice-over work, and *Beau Monde* was considering a cover story. More important, the script for the Howard Jenks film was finally on its way.

Ren had talked at length with Jenks about the role of Kaspar Street. Street was a serial killer, a darkly complex man who preyed on the very women he fell in love with. Ren had signed on to the project without seeing the final script because Jenks, who was notoriously secretive about his work, hadn't finished tinkering with it. Ren couldn't remember ever having been more excited about a film than he was about *Night Kill*. Not so excited, however, that he could forget about Isabel and the man in the red Fiat.

Where was she?

"Thanks, Vittorio, I had a wonderful afternoon."

"It was my pleasure." He beamed his charmer's smile. "Soon I will show you Siena, and then you will know you have seen heaven."

She smiled as she watched him drive away. She still couldn't decide how deeply involved he was in the effort to remove her. His behavior had been above reproach, charming and just flirtatious enough to be flattering but not encroaching. He'd told her his clients had canceled for the day, and insisted on taking her to see the tiny town of Monteriggioni. As they'd wandered through the charming little piazza, he'd made no effort to talk her into moving into Casalleone. Still, he'd managed to get her out of the house for the afternoon. The question was, what had happened while she'd been gone?

Instead of going inside, she walked down to inspect the olive grove. She couldn't see any signs of digging, but the ground had been trampled near a stone-front storehouse built into the side of the hill. Scuff marks in the dirt outside the wooden door indicated they'd been here, but she couldn't tell whether or not they'd gone inside, and when she tried the latch, she discovered it was locked.

She heard the crunch of gravel and glanced up to see Marta standing at the edge of the garden watching her. She felt guilty, as if she'd been caught snooping. Marta stared at her until Isabel finally moved away.

That night she waited until the old woman had disappeared into her room before she began her search for the key to the storehouse. But without electricity she couldn't see into the drawers or the backs of cupboards, so she decided to try again in the morning.

As she headed upstairs to bed, she wondered what Ren was doing. Probably making love with a beautiful *signora* from the village. The idea depressed her more than she wanted it to.

She leaned outside to open the shutters that Marta insisted on closing every night and saw the steady glow of incandescent light seeping through the slats covering the older woman's window. Apparently not everyone in the farmhouse had lost electrical power.

She tossed and turned all night, obsessing about electricity and Ren and pretty Italian women. As a result, she didn't awaken until nearly nine, once again throwing off her schedule. She took a quick shower and then, her frustration at the boiling point, called the villa and asked for him.

"Signore Gage is not available," Anna said.

"Could you tell me what's being done about my electricity?"

"It will be taken care of." She broke the connection.

Isabel itched to charge up to the villa and confront him, but he was wily, and she couldn't shake the feeling that he was trying to manipulate her. Look at the way he'd lured Jennifer Lopez into his evil clutches.

She hurried to the garden, filled a tub with soapy water, and marched off to catch a cat. If she didn't keep busy, she would jump right out of her skin.

Ren reached into his pocket for his emergency cigarette, then realized he'd already smoked it, not a good sign, since it was barely eleven in the morning. He had to admit that she'd proved harder to manage than he'd figured. Maybe he should have taken into account the fact that she was a psychologist. But, damn it, he wanted her coming to him, not the other way around.

He could either wait her out, which he no longer had the patience for, or concede this round. The idea galled him, but in the long run what difference did it make? One way or another they were going to fulfill their sexual destiny.

He decided to take a walk in his olive grove. Just a casual walk. No big deal. If she happened to be in the garden, he'd say something like, *Hey, Fifi, is that electricity problem all taken care of? It isn't? Well, damn . . . Tell you what, why don't you come up to the house with me, and we'll talk to Anna together?*

But luck wasn't with him. All he saw in the garden was a trio of angry cats.

Maybe a shot of espresso and a newspaper would settle him down, although what he really wanted was another cigarette. As he climbed into his Maserati, visions of a red Fiat danced through his head. With a scowl, he shoved the key into the ignition and started down the drive.

He'd just reached the end when he saw her. He slammed on his brakes and jumped out. "What in the *hell* are you *doing*?"

She gazed up at him from underneath the brim of her straw hat. Despite her work gloves, she looked more dignified than a queen. "I'm picking up roadside litter." She plopped an empty *limonata* bottle into the plastic sack she was carrying.

"Why in God's name are you doing that?"

"Please don't invoke God's name in anger. She doesn't like it. And litter is a blight on the environment, no matter what country it's in."

The gold bangle on her wrist glimmered in the sunlight as she reached into a clump of wild fennel for a crumpled cigarette wrapper. Her spotless white-on-white print top was tucked into a pair of trim, buff-colored shorts that showed off her shapely legs. All in all, she looked a little dressy for the litter squad.

He crossed his arms and gazed down at her, finally beginning to enjoy himself. "You don't have a clue how to relax, do you?"

"Of course I know how to relax. This is very relaxing. It's contemplative."

"Contemplative, my ass. You're strung so tight you twang."

"Yes, well, not having even the most *basic* of modern conveniences could make anyone tense."

He went into full Actors Studio—a blank stare followed by a nearly imperceptible widening of the eyes capped with a subtle frown. "Are you trying to tell me your electricity isn't fixed? I don't believe this. Damn it, I told Anna to take care of it. Why didn't you let me know there was still a problem?"

They didn't pay him the big bucks for nothing. She studied him for a moment and then bit. "I assumed you knew."

"Thanks a lot. I guess that shows what you think of me."

He should have quit while he was ahead, because her eyes narrowed with suspicion. He made a quick grab for his cell and placed a call to his housekeeper, deliberately speaking English.

"Anna, I'm talking to Isabel Favor, and there's no electricity at the farmhouse. Get it fixed by the end of the day, will you? I don't care what it costs."

He disconnected and leaned against the side of the car. "That should take care of it. Let's go for a drive while you're waiting. I'll check everything out when we get back to make sure it's done."

She hesitated, then turned her attention to his Maserati. "Okay, but I get to drive."

"Forget it. You drove last time."

"I like to drive."

"So do I, and it's my car."

"You'll speed."

"Arrest me. Will you get in, for chrissake?"

"Blasphemy isn't just a sacrilege," she pointed out with what he regarded as an unnecessary degree of relish. "It's the sign of someone's having a limited command of the English language."

"Whatever. And the reason you want to drive is that you like to control everything."

"The world works better that way."

Her deliberately smug smile made him chuckle. And she was probably right. If Dr. Favor were in charge of the world, at least it would be tidier.

"First you have to help me finish picking up this litter," she said.

He started to tell her to forget it, because no woman on earth was worth this much aggravation, but then she bent over, and her trim little shorts molded to her hips, and the next thing he knew, he had a piece of tire tread in one hand and a broken beer bottle in the other.

He chose back roads that wound east past quaint farmhouses, then dipped into the valleys that held the vineyards of the Chianti region. Near Radda he donned a ball cap and his geek sunglasses as a quick disguise and made Isabel do the talking when they stopped at a small winery. The owner served them glasses of his '99 reserve at a table that sat in the shade of a pomegranate tree.

At first no one in the small group of tourists at the other occupied table paid any attention to them, but then a young woman wearing silver earrings and a University of Massachusetts T-shirt began watching them. He braced himself when she rose from her chair, but as it turned out, his cap and glasses had done the job—he wasn't the one she wanted.

"Excuse me. Aren't you Dr. Isabel Favor?"

He felt an unfamiliar surge of protectiveness, but Isabel merely smiled and nodded.

"I can't believe it's you," the woman said. "I'm sorry to interrupt, but I heard you speak when you came to UMass, and I have all your books. I just wanted you to know that you really helped me when I was having chemo."

For the first time Ren noticed how thin the woman was, and pale. Something inside him tightened as he saw Isabel's expression soften. He thought of the comments he received from his own fans. *"Dude, me and my friends loved it when you pulled out that guy's guts."*

"I'm so glad," Isabel said.

"I'm really sorry about all your problems." The visitor bit her bottom lip. "Would you mind— My name is Jessica. Would you pray for me?"

Isabel rose and hugged her. "Of course I will."

His throat constricted. Isabel Favor was the genuine article. And he'd set out to corrupt her.

The woman returned to her table, and Isabel settled into her chair. She dipped her head and gazed into her wineglass. With a sense of shock, he realized she was praying. Right there in front of everybody, for chrissake.

He reached for a cigarette, then remembered he'd already smoked his daily ration. He drained his wineglass instead.

She looked up and gave him a soft, confident smile. "She's going to be fine."

She might as well have slammed a tire iron into his head, because right then he knew he couldn't do it. He couldn't seduce a woman who prayed for strangers, and picked up highway litter, and only wanted good things for everybody. What was he thinking? It would be like seducing a nun.

A really hot nun.

He'd had enough. He'd drive her back, drop her off at the farmhouse, and forget her. For the rest of his vacation he'd act as though she didn't exist.

The idea depressed the hell out of him. He liked being with her, and not just because she turned him on and made him laugh, but also because her decency was oddly seductive, like a freshly painted wall just waiting for a little graffiti.

She gave him a smile that didn't quite work. "It's women like her who've helped me get through these past six months, knowing that my books and lectures have meant something to them. Unfortunately, there aren't enough left to fill an auditorium."

He pulled himself out of his mental confusion. "You've probably become a guilty pleasure. They still like what you have to say, but you're not the flavor of the month, and they don't want to be unfashionable."

"I appreciate the vote of confidence, but I think most people prefer taking advice from someone whose life isn't a shambles."

"Okay, that, too."

She was quiet on the way back, which made him suspect she was praying again, and wasn't that just a fucking inspiration? Maybe he should pack up and fly back to L.A. But he didn't want to leave Italy.

When they reached the farmhouse, he roused himself from his gloomy thoughts and went through the motions of checking the power. The lights came on as they were supposed to. He went outside, ostensibly to make sure the exterior lights were working. "This is nice," he said, gazing out at the garden.

"You've never been here?"

"A long time ago. I stayed at the villa a couple of times when I was a kid. My aunt brought me down here once to meet old Paolo. Grouchy son of a bitch, as I remember."

A series of high-pitched squeals split the air. He looked up and saw three children running down the hill from the villa. Two noisy little girls and a boy—all of them barreling straight toward him and screaming at the top of their lungs.

"Daddy!"

10

Ren took a step backward as the girls hurled themselves at his legs, their giggles shrill enough to cut glass. Only the boy held back.

Isabel felt light-headed. *Daddy?* Ren had never said a thing about having children. He'd admitted to a short-term marriage when he was young, but three children didn't look short-term to her.

She glanced up and saw a woman appear at the top of the hill. She stood silhouetted against the sky, a toddler in her arms, the breeze plastering the skirt of her cotton dress to her very pregnant belly.

"Daddy! Daddy! Did you miss us?" the older girl shrieked in American English, while the younger collapsed in giggles.

Ren jerked away as if the children were radioactive and gazed at Isabel with something that looked like panic. "I swear to God, I've never seen them before in my life."

Isabel tilted her head toward the top of the hill. "Maybe you'd better tell her that."

Ren looked up.

The woman waved, her long dark hair fluttering in the breeze. "Hey, lover!"

He shielded his eyes. "Tracy? Damn it, Tracy, is that you?"

"You said 'damn.'" The youngest girl, who looked to be around four or five, butted his legs.

"He's allowed to, you dope," the boy said.

"You can back off now, kids," the woman called down. "We've terrified him enough."

"He looks mad, Mom," the younger girl said. "Are you mad, mister?"

"You'd better watch out," the boy declared. "He kills people. Even girls. He cuts out people's eyeballs, don't you?"

"Jeremy Briggs!" the woman exclaimed without moving from her perch at the top of the hill. "You know you're not allowed to see R movies."

"It was PG-thirteen."

"You're eleven!"

Isabel turned on Ren. "You cut out someone's eyeballs in a PG-thirteen movie? Nice going."

He gave her a glare that suggested the next eyeballs he cut out might belong to her.

"Whadja do with them?" the littlest girl asked. "Didja eat 'em? I hurted my pee-pee on the airplane."

The two older children snickered, while Ren turned pale.

"I hurted it on the seat arm," she continued, unfazed. "Wanna see my dolphin panties?"

"*No!*"

But she'd already raised the skirt of her checked sundress. "I got whales, too," she pointed out.

"Very pretty." Isabel was beginning to enjoy herself. Watching Mr. 2-Kool twitch was the most fun she'd had all day. "Surely you've seen whales on a lady's undergarments before, Ren."

His dark eyebrows slammed together in one of his trademark scowls.

The children's mother shifted the toddler to her other hip. "The only way I can make it down that hill is on my backside, so you'd better come up here. Brittany, put those panties back on. Your body's private, remember?"

Sure enough, the dark-haired cherub had stripped down with all the cool of a table dancer. Ren took one look, then shot up the hill as if both Denzel and Mel were after him. The boy began to follow, then changed his mind and headed for the Maserati parked near the farmhouse.

"You got any dolphins?" the cherub asked Isabel.

"Brit'ny, that's not polite," her sister said.

Isabel smiled at both girls and helped the little one back on with her panties. "No dolphins. Just some tan lace."

"Can I see?"

"I'm afraid not. Your mother's right about bodies being private." Which was another good reason not to share hers with Ren Gage, although he hadn't mentioned sex all afternoon. Maybe he'd decided she was too much work. Or maybe, like Michael, he'd simply decided she was too much of everything.

With Brittany's clothes back in place, Isabel took the girls' hands and steered them up the hill before she missed any more of the conversation that had just started to take place there. She noticed that Ren's doomsday scowl hadn't detracted one bit from those hearts-afire good looks.

"I must have missed your phone call telling me you were coming, Tracy."

The woman rose on her toes and planted a kiss on his cheek. "Well, hello to you, too."

Her silky dark hair fell to her shoulders in a tumble. Her skin was

Snow White pale, her bright blue eyes slightly tilted and shadowed, as if she hadn't slept well for a while. She wore a rumpled but fashionable scarlet maternity dress and pricey low-heeled sandals. Her toenails were unpolished and her sandals run over ever so slightly at the heels. Something about the way she held herself combined with the careless manner in which she wore her clothes screamed old money.

"Daddy!" The toddler in her arms squealed and held out his arms to Ren, who backed up so fast he bumped into Isabel.

"Relax," Tracy said. "He calls every man that."

"Well, make him stop. And what kind of mother tells her kids to do something perverted like running up to a stranger and calling him . . . that word they called me?"

"I take my amusements where I can find them. It cost me five bucks a kid."

"It wasn't funny."

"I enjoyed it." She regarded Isabel with interest. Her pregnant belly and exotic eyes made her look like a goddess of sexuality and fertility. Isabel began to feel a little withered. At the same time she sensed an air of sadness lurking behind the woman's lighthearted tone.

"I'm Tracy Briggs." She held out her hand. "You look familiar."

"Isabel Favor."

"Of course you are. Now I recognize you." She gazed at them both with open curiosity. "What are you doing with him?"

"I'm renting the farmhouse. Ren is my landlord."

"No kidding." Her expression indicated she didn't believe a word of it. "I only read one of your books—*Healthy Relationships in Unhealthy Times*—but I liked it a lot. I've . . ." She bit her bottom lip. "I've been trying to get my head together about leaving Harry."

"Tell me you're not running away from another husband," Ren said.

"I've only had two." She turned to Isabel. "Ren's still mad because I left him. Just between us, he was a terrible husband."

So this was Ren's ex-wife. One thing seemed clear. Whatever sparks had once burned between them had gone out. Isabel felt as if she were watching a brother and sister bicker, instead of former lovers.

"We got married when we were twenty and stupid," Ren said. "What does anybody that young know about being married?"

"I knew more than you." Tracy nodded down the hill toward her son, who'd climbed into the front seat of Ren's Maserati. "That's Jeremy, my oldest. Steffie's next. She's eight." Steffie had a pixie cut and a vaguely anxious air. She and her sister had begun drawing circles in the gravel with the heels of their sandals. "Brittany's five. And this is Connor. He just turned three, but he still won't use the potty, will you, big guy?" She smacked the toddler's fat diaper, then patted her own swollen belly. "Connor was supposed to be our caboose. Surprise, surprise."

"Five kids, Trace?" Ren said.

"Stuff happens." Once again she bit her lip.

"Didn't you only have three when we talked a month ago?"

"It was two months ago, and I had four. You never pay attention when I talk about them."

Steffie, the eight-year-old, let out a piercing shriek. "*Spider!* There's a spider!"

" 'Snot a spider." Brittany crouched down in the gravel.

"Jeremy! Get out of that—"

But Tracy's command came too late. The Maserati, with her son inside, had already begun to roll.

Ren started to run. He made it to the bottom of the hill just in time to watch his expensive sports car crunch into the side of the farmhouse, where the front end folded like an origami bird.

Isabel had to give him credit. He dragged Jeremy out of the car and checked to make sure the eleven-year-old wasn't hurt before he inspected the damage. Tracy, in the meantime, was waddling down the hill—pregnant belly, toddler, and all. Isabel hurried to grab her arm before she fell, and they managed to reach Ren and Jeremy without mishap.

"*Jeremy Briggs!* How many times have I told you to leave other people's cars alone! You just wait till your father hears about this." Tracy took a couple of gulps of air, then seemed to run out of steam. Her shoulders slumped, and her eyes filled with tears.

"*Spider!*" Steffie howled from the hill behind them.

The toddler noticed his mother's distress and started to cry.

"*Spider! Spider!*" Steffie yowled.

Ren looked over at Isabel, his expression comically helpless.

"Hey, Mr. Ren!" Brittany called down from the top of the hill. "Look at me!" She waved her panties like a flag. "I got seahorses, too."

Tracy let out a noisy sob, then reached out and whacked Ren in the chest. "*Now* do you see why we're moving in?"

"She can't do this!" Ren stopped pacing long enough to spin on Isabel as if this were all her fault. They were in the rear salon at the villa with the doors open to the garden and children running everywhere. Only Anna seemed happy. She laughed over the girls, rubbed Jeremy's head, picked up the toddler, and set off to the kitchen with him to prepare dinner for everyone.

"Go upstairs and tell Tracy to leave!"

"Somehow I don't think she'll listen." Isabel wondered when he'd figure out that he was fighting a losing battle. The characters he played on-screen might be able to evict a pregnant woman and her four children, but in real life Ren seemed like a softer touch. That didn't mean, however, that he intended to be gracious about it.

"We haven't been married for fourteen years. She can't just move in here with all these kids."

"She seems to have done it."

"You heard me try to book a hotel for her, but she grabbed the receiver out of my hand and hung up."

Isabel patted Steffie's shoulder. "That's enough bug spray, honey. Let me have the can before you give us all cancer."

Steffie reluctantly handed it over, then looked apprehensively around her feet for more spiders.

Ren growled down at the eight-year-old girl. "It's September. Shouldn't all of you be in school?"

"Mom's homeschooling us till we get back home to Connecticut."

"Your mother can barely add."

"She adds okay, but she has trouble with long division, so Jeremy and I have to help her." Steffie walked over to the couch and gingerly lifted the pillow to look beneath it before she sat down. "Could I have my bug spray back, please?"

Isabel's heart turned over for the little girl. She stealthily passed the can to Ren, then sat beside her and drew her into a hug. "You know, Steffie, the things we think we're afraid of aren't always what's really bothering us. Like spiders. Most of them are pretty friendly insects, but a lot has happened in your family lately, and that might be what's really worrying you. We all feel afraid sometimes. It's okay."

Ren muttered something that was definitely not okay. As Isabel continued talking softly with Steffie, she spied Jeremy through the French doors grimly slamming a tennis ball against the side of the villa. It was only a matter of time before he broke a window.

"Everybody, watch me!" Brittany shot into the room and threw herself into a series of cartwheels, heading straight for a cabinet filled with Meissen porcelain.

"Watch out!" Ren rushed forward and caught her just before she crashed.

"Look on the bright side," Isabel said. "She's wearing her panties."

"But she's taken off everything else!"

"I'm the champ!" The five-year-old leaped to her feet and extended her arms in a victory V. Isabel smiled and gave her a thumbs-up. Just then the air was filled with the unmistakable sound of breaking glass, followed by Tracy's shriek from upstairs: *"Jeremy Briggs!"*

Ren turned the can of bug spray to his head and pressed the valve.

It was a long evening. Ren threatened to cut off Isabel's electricity forever if she abandoned him, so she stayed at the villa while Tracy remained locked in her room. Jeremy entertained himself by torturing Steffie with phantom spiders, Brittany hid her clothes, and Ren complained the entire time. Everywhere he went, he left clutter behind him—sunglasses, discarded shoes, a sweatshirt—the debris of a man accustomed to having servants pick up after him.

With the appearance of the children, Anna underwent a personality transformation, laughing and plying everyone with food, even Isabel. She and Massimo lived in a house about a mile away with their two grown sons and a daughter-in-law. Since she'd be going home after dinner, she asked Marta to come up from the farmhouse to spend the night. Marta, too, seemed like a different woman in the presence of the children.

Anna quickly adopted Connor as her special pet, and he stayed at her side except when he disappeared into a corner to load his diaper. The three-year-old, Isabel had learned, already had an excellent vocabulary. His favorite expression was "Potty is very, very bad."

Even though Ren gave the girls no encouragement, they badgered him for attention. He ignored them as much as he could but finally gave in to Jeremy's pleas to teach him some martial-arts moves. It was well after dark before they were all tucked into bed.

Isabel managed to slip away to the farmhouse while Ren was on the phone. She tumbled into bed and fell instantly asleep, only to be awakened at one in the morning by a crash followed by a curse. She bolted upright in bed.

The light snapped on in the hall, and Ren poked his head in. "Sorry. I banged my duffel against the chest and knocked over a lamp."

She blinked and pulled the sheet to her shoulders. "What are you doing here?"

"You don't seriously believe I'm staying up there, do you?" He bristled with indignation.

"Well, you can't move in here."

"Watch me." He disappeared.

She shot out of bed, her silk gown fluttering behind her as she went after him.

He'd thrown his duffel on the bed in the next room, which was smaller than her own room but just as plain. The gregarious Italians didn't believe in wasting their decorating money on solitary spaces like bedrooms when they could spend it on the kitchens and gardens that were their gathering places. As she rushed in, he stopped unpacking long enough to take in the ivory lace bodice that clung to her breasts and the delicate, ankle-length skirt. "You got any dolphins under that?"

"None of your business. Ren, the villa's huge, and this house is small. You can't—"

"Not huge enough. If you think I'm staying under the same roof with a nutty pregnant woman and her four psycho kids, you're crazier than they are."

"Then go somewhere else."

"Exactly what I'm doing." Once again his eyes went on an exploratory mission. She waited for him to say something provocative, but he surprised her. "I appreciate the way you stuck around tonight, although I could have done without those lists you kept shoving at me."

"You threatened to turn off my electricity if I left."

"You can't fool me, Doc. You'd have stayed anyway, because you're a sucker for cleaning up other people's messes." He pulled out a messy stack of T-shirts. "That's probably why you like hanging around with me, except in my case you're fighting a losing battle."

"I *don't* like hanging around with you. I'm *forced* to hang around with you. Okay, maybe I like it a little bit." Her fingers itched to pick up the T-shirt he'd just dropped to the floor, but she resisted. "You can sleep here tonight, but tomorrow you're moving back into the villa. I have work to do, and you'll only get in the way."

He propped a shoulder against the doorjamb and crossed his ankles, his gaze traveling from her ankles to her breasts. "Too big a distraction for you, right?"

Her skin grew warm. He was the devil incarnate. This was the way he lured women to their deaths. "Let's just say I need to concentrate on the spiritual at the moment."

"You do that." He gave her his most sinister smile. "And don't even think about what happened to Jennifer Lopez when she slept in the room next to mine."

She shot him a look that told him exactly how infantile she thought he was, and swept past him. Just as she got to the hallway, she noticed the small lamp sitting on the chest directly in front of her. Even before she heard his evil chuckle, she knew he could see right through her nightgown.

"Definitely no dolphins. You're killing me, Fifi."

"A distinct possibility."

The next morning Isabel made a glass of freshly squeezed orange juice for herself and carried it out to one of the blue metal chairs that sat in a sunny spot near the house. Dew still clung to the leaves of the olive trees, and a few stray ribbons of mist drifted in the valley below. She uttered a little prayer of gratitude—the least she could do—and began to take her first sip of juice just as Ren emerged from the house in all his rumpled glory.

"Had to get up early today so I could run before it gets too hot." He yawned.

"It's nearly nine."

"That's what I mean."

She set down the orange juice and watched the hem of his gray sleeveless T-shirt rise as he began to stretch. His stomach rippled with hard muscle, and a thin line of dark hair disappeared into a pair of black running shorts. She drank in every inch of him—cheekbones, pirate's stubble, athlete's chest, and all.

He caught her watching him. As he crossed his arms over his chest, she could see that he was already enjoying himself. "Do you want me to turn around so you can get the back view?"

She retaliated with her shrink voice. "Do you think I want you to turn around?"

"Oh, yeah."

"Being so dazzling must be difficult. You never know whether people want to be with you because of your character or only because of your appearance."

"Definitely appearance. I have no character."

She couldn't let that pass. "You have a very strong character. Most of it is twisted, true, but not all of it."

"Thanks for nothing."

And wasn't it a miracle how a good night's sleep could increase a woman's capacity to annoy? She imitated his oily smile. "Would you mind turning to the side so I can enjoy your profile?"

"Stop being a wise-ass." He collapsed in the chair next to her, where he drained the glass of juice she'd taken ten minutes to squeeze.

She frowned. "I thought you were going for a run."

"Don't rush me. Tell me none of Tracy's little monsters have shown up here."

"Not yet."

"They're smart little buggers. They'll find us. And you're going up there with me after I get cleaned up, so you can be there while I have it out with her. I've decided to tell her you're recovering from a nervous breakdown, and you need peace and quiet. Then I'm loading everybody up in that Volvo she's driving, and sending them on their way to a great hotel, all expenses paid."

Somehow Isabel didn't think it would be that easy. "How did she find you?"

"She knows my agent."

"She's an interesting woman. How long did you say you were married?"

"One miserable year. Our mothers were friends, so we grew up together, got into trouble together, and also managed to flunk out of college at the same time. Since we didn't want to get kicked off the parental gravy train and actually have to work for a living, we decided to get married to divert their attention." He set down the empty glass. "Do you have any idea what happens when two spoiled brats get married?"

"Nothing pleasant, I'm sure."

"Door slamming, temper tantrums, hair pulling. And she was even worse."

Isabel laughed.

"She got remarried two years after our divorce. I've seen her a couple of times when she's come out to L.A., and we talk every few months."

"An unusual relationship for a divorced couple."

"For a few years afterward we didn't talk at all, but neither of us has any brothers or sisters. Her father died, and her mother's a nutcase. I guess nostalgia for our dysfunctional childhoods keeps us in contact more than anything else."

"You'd never seen her children or her husband?"

"I saw the two older ones when they were little. Never met her husband. One of those corporate types. He sounds like a real stiff." He moved his weight to one hip, withdrew a folded piece of paper from the pocket of his shorts, and flipped it open. "I found this in the kitchen. You want to explain?"

She must possess a subconscious desire to be tortured, or she'd never have left that lying around. "Give it to me."

Naturally he held it just out of her reach. "You need me even worse than I thought." He began to read from the schedule she'd drawn up her first day here. " 'Get up at six o'clock.' Why the hell would you want to do that?"

"I don't, apparently, because I've only been up since eight."

" 'Prayer, meditation, gratitude, and daily affirmations,' " he went on. "What's a daily affirmation? No, don't tell me."

"Affirmations are positive statements. A benevolent kind of

thought control. For example, here's one: 'No matter how much Lorenzo Gage annoys me, I'll remember that he, too, is one of God's creatures.' Not God's best work perhaps, but . . ."

"And what's this 'Remember to breathe' crap?"

"It's not crap. It's a reminder to stay centered."

"Whatever that means."

"It means staying calm. Refusing to be buffeted by every gust of wind that blows your way."

"Sounds boring."

"Sometimes boring is good."

"Uh-huh." He tapped the page. " 'Inspirational reading.' Like People?"

She let him have his fun.

" 'Be impulsive.' " He arched one of those exquisite eyebrows. "That's gonna happen. And according to this schedule you should be writing now."

"I'm planning." She fiddled with the button on her blouse.

He folded the list and zeroed in on her with eyes that were far too perceptive. "You don't have a clue what you're going to write about next, do you?"

"I'm starting to make notes for a new book."

"About what?"

"Overcoming personal crisis." It was the first thing that popped into her head, and it seemed a logical choice.

"You're kidding."

His expression of disbelief made her testy. "I do know something about it. In case you haven't noticed, I'm overcoming my own."

"I must have missed that part."

"That's your problem. You miss a lot."

His irritating sympathy was back. "Stop pushing so hard, Isabel. Take some time off, and don't try to force everything. Relax and have a little fun for a change."

"And how would I do that? Oh, wait, I know. By going to bed with you, right?"

"That'd be my choice, but I guess everyone has a different idea of entertainment, so you can pick your own. No, on second thought, it'll work out better for both of us if you let me do the picking."

"Time's a-wasting if you're going for that run."

He settled deeper into the chair. "You've been through a lot these past six months. Don't you think you deserve a little breathing room?"

"The IRS wiped me out. I can't afford breathing room. I have to get my career back on track so I can earn a living, and the only way I can do that is to work at it." Even as she said it, she could feel little fingernails of panic trying to dig into her.

"There's more than one way to work."

"Your suggestion would be to do it on my back, right?"

"You can get on top if you want."

She sighed.

He rose from the chair and turned toward the olive orchard. "What are Massimo and Giancarlo doing down there?"

"Something about a new sewer or a well, depending on the translation."

He yawned again. "I'm going for my run, and then we're both talking to Tracy. And don't argue unless you want the untimely death of a pregnant woman and her four obnoxious kids on your conscience."

"Oh, I'm not going to argue. I wouldn't miss watching you go up in flames for the world."

He scowled at her and took off.

An hour later she was changing the sheets on her bed when she heard him return and disappear into the bathroom. She smiled and crept to the door. It wasn't long before she heard him yowl.

"I forgot to tell you," she called out sweetly. "We don't have any hot water."

Tracy stood in the middle of the bedroom she'd taken over. Suitcases, clothes, and assorted toys littered the floor around her. While Ren leaned against the wall frowning at both of them, Isabel began separating the dirty clothes from the clean.

"Do you see why I divorced him?" Tracy looked red-eyed and tired, but still luscious in a mulberry bathing suit and matching cover-up. Isabel wondered how it felt to have such effortless beauty. Tracy and Ren were a matched set.

"He's a cold, unfeeling son of a bitch. That's why I divorced him."

"I'm not unfeeling." Ren definitely sounded unfeeling. "But I told you, with Isabel's delicate nervous condition . . ."

"Do you have a delicate nervous condition, Isabel?"

"Not unless you count a major life crisis." She dropped a T-shirt into the dirty pile, then began refolding a stack of clean underwear. The children were in the kitchen with Anna and Marta, but much like Ren, they'd left signs of their presence everywhere.

"Are the kids bothering you?" Tracy asked.

"They're terrific. I'm enjoying them very much." Isabel wondered if Tracy understood that her children's various behavior problems were almost certainly rooted in the tension they'd picked up from their parents.

"That's not the point," Ren said. "The point is that you barged in here without any warning and—"

"Will you think about someone other than yourself for once?" Tracy threw down a GameBoy, disturbing Isabel's carefully folded pile. "I can't lock up four active children in a hotel room."

"Suite! I'll get you a suite."

"And you're my oldest friend. If a person's oldest friend won't help her when she's in trouble, who will?"

"Newer friends. Your parents. What about your cousin Petrina?"

"I've detested Petrina ever since we were debutantes. Don't you remember how she tried to hit on you? Besides, none of those people happen to be in Europe right now."

"Which is another reason you should fly home. I'm no expert on pregnant women, but I understand they need familiar surroundings."

"Maybe in the eighteenth century." Tracy made a helpless gesture toward Isabel. "Could you recommend a good therapist? Twice I've married men with stone where their hearts should be, so I obviously need help. Although at least Ren didn't screw around on me."

Isabel moved the clothes she'd folded out of the line of fire. "Your husband's been unfaithful?"

Tracy's voice grew unsteady. "He won't admit it."

"But you think he's having an affair."

"I caught them together. A hot little Swiss miss from his office. He . . . hated it when I got pregnant again." She blinked hard. "This is his revenge."

Isabel felt herself developing a good solid dislike for Mr. Harry Briggs.

Tracy tilted her head so that her hair fell over one shoulder. "Be reasonable, Ren. I'm not moving in here forever. I just need a few weeks to get my head together before I have to face everybody back home."

"A few *weeks*?"

"The kids and I'll spend all our time at the pool. You won't even know we're here."

"*Mommmmyyy!*" Brittany streaked in, naked except for purple socks. "Connor threw up!" She shot back out again.

"Brittany Briggs, you come back here!" Tracy rushed after her, hips waddling. "Brittany!"

Ren shook his head. "It's hard to believe that's the same girl who used to throw a fit if her maid woke her before noon."

"She's a lot more fragile than she's letting on. That's why she's come to you. You realize, don't you, that you have to let her stay?"

"I've got to get out of here." He grabbed her arm, and she barely had time to snatch her straw hat from the bed before he pushed her out the door. "I'll buy you an espresso in town and one of those pornographic calendars you like so much."

"Tempting, but I need to start making notes for my new book. The one on overcoming personal crisis," she added.

"Trust me. Somebody who entertains herself picking up litter doesn't have the foggiest idea how to overcome crisis." He headed down the stairs. "One day you're going to admit that life's too messy to fit inside those tidy little Cornerstones of yours."

"I've seen exactly how messy life can be." She sounded defensive, but she couldn't seem to help it. "I've also seen how applying the Cornerstones can make things better. It's not just me, Ren. I have testimonials." And how pathetic did that make her sound?

"I'll bet you do. And I'm sure the Cornerstones work in a lot of situations, but they're not going to work for everybody all the time, and I don't think they're working for you right now."

"They're not working because I'm not applying them properly." She caught her bottom lip between her teeth. "I also might need to add a few new steps."

"Will you just relax?"

"Like you?"

"Don't knock it till you've tried it. At least I have a life."

"You make awful movies where you do hateful things. You have to wear disguises to go out in public. You have no wife, no family. Is that what you call having a life?"

"Well, if you're going to get picky about it." He crossed the marble floor to the front door.

"You can deflect other people with wisecracks, but it doesn't work with me."

"That's because you've forgotten how to laugh." He twisted the knob.

"Untrue. You're making me laugh right now. *Ha!*"

The door swung open to reveal a strange man standing on the other side.

"You wife-stealing bastard," the intruder growled. And then he drew back his arm and swung.

11

sabel flew across the marble floor, but the man had only caught
a shoulder, and Ren was already back on his feet, every muscle
in his body focused on annihilation. She shot an incredulous
look at his assailant. "Are you *out of your mind?*"

Ren made a leap for him just as the words the man had spoken
sank into Isabel's brain. "Ren, stop! Don't hit him."

He already had the man by the throat. "Give me one good reason."

"It's Harry Briggs. You can't kill him unless Tracy says so."

His grip eased, but he didn't let go, and fury still glimmered in
his eyes. "Do you want to explain that punch before or after I take
you apart?"

She had to give Briggs credit for standing his ground in the face
of what could be a very painful death. "Where is she, you son of a
bitch?"

"No place where you can touch her."

"You made her miserable once. You're not going to do it again."

"Dad!"

Ren quickly released his hold as Jeremy rushed in. The boy dropped the broken roof tile he'd been carrying and flung himself into his father's arms, the sulky expression he wore most of the time vanishing.

"Jeremy." Briggs drew him close, sinking his hands into his son's hair and closing his eyes for a moment.

Ren rubbed his shoulder and watched.

Despite the foolhardy punch he'd thrown, Harry Briggs didn't look too dangerous. He stood a few inches shorter than Ren, with a slim build and pleasant, regular features. As Isabel studied him, she sensed a neat freak like herself, except this one had fallen into a bad spell. His straight, conservatively cut brown hair hadn't been near a comb recently, and he needed a shave. Behind his wire-rimmed glasses, his eyes were tired, and he'd worn his rumpled khakis and tan polo shirt a day too long. He didn't look like a philanderer, but that wasn't exactly something you could see on a person's face. He also seemed to be one of the least likely men on earth to be married to a dazzler like Tracy.

As he rubbed his son's shoulders, she noticed a serviceable watch and a plain gold wedding band. "Have you been taking care of everybody?" he asked Jeremy.

"I guess."

"We need to talk, buddy, but I have to see your mother first."

"She's down at the pool with the brats."

Harry tilted his head toward the front door. "See if I put any dings in the car while I was driving down here, will you? There were some gravel roads."

Jeremy looked troubled. "You won't leave or anything without me, will you?"

Once again Harry touched his son's hair. "Don't worry, pal. Everything's going to be fine."

As the boy set off, Isabel noticed that Harry hadn't answered his question. When Jeremy was out of earshot, he turned his attention back to Ren, and all the softness he'd displayed to the boy vanished. "Where's the pool?"

The heat of Ren's anger seemed to have burned off, although she suspected it could reignite at any moment. "Maybe you'd better cool down first."

"Never mind. I'll find her myself." Harry stalked past them.

Ren picked up the piece of broken roof tile Jeremy had dropped, stared at it for a moment, then gave a martyr's sigh. "We can't leave him alone with her."

Isabel patted his arm. "Life's never simple."

Tracy saw Harry coming. Her heart did an instinctive skip-hop before it settled into the pit of her stomach. She'd known he'd show up sooner or later. She just hadn't expected him to find her so quickly.

"*Daddy!*" The girls came flying out of the water. Connor squealed when he spotted him, and his fat diaper bobbled from side to side as he rushed to greet his favorite person in the world, not knowing that same person hadn't wanted him to be born.

Harry somehow managed to scoop up all three. He was particular about his clothes, but not when it came to the kids, and he didn't seem to mind getting wet. The girls lavished him with sloppy kisses. Connor knocked his glasses askew. Tracy's heart ached as she watched him return their kisses and offer them the same single-minded attention he'd given her in the days when they'd still been in love.

Ren appeared. It didn't hurt to look at him the way it did to look at Harry. This older Ren was tougher and smarter than the boy who'd taught her how to smoke a joint, but he was also more cynical. She couldn't imagine how this business with Karli Swenson had affected him.

Isabel came to his side looking cool and capable in her sleeveless blouse, biscuit-colored slacks, and straw hat. Her boundless competence would have been intimidating if she weren't so kind. The kids had adored her on sight, generally a good sign of a person's character. Just like every other woman who stepped into Ren's orbit, she was fascinated by him, but unlike the others, she was fighting it. Tracy gave her high marks for trying, even if she didn't stand a chance, not when Ren's desire was so obvious. In the end she wouldn't be able to resist him, which was a shame, because a fling wouldn't be enough for her. She was the kind of woman who wanted all the things Ren didn't have to give, and he'd eat her up before she realized it. Not just in a good way either.

It was less agonizing to feel sorry for Isabel than herself, but Harry was here now, and she could only hold off her pain for so long. *Who are you?* she wanted to ask. *Where is the sweet, tender man I fell in love with?*

She hoisted herself out of her chair, 158 pounds of beached whale. Fifteen more pounds and she'd outweigh her husband. "Girls, take Connor and go find Signora Anna. She said she was making cookies."

The girls clung tighter to their father and glared at her resentfully. From their point of view she was the wicked witch who'd taken them away from him. A hard, tight knot stuck in her throat.

"Go on," he said to the girls, still not looking at her. "I'll come in and see you soon."

They didn't give him trouble like they gave her, and she wasn't surprised when they took Connor and set off toward the house. "You shouldn't have come here," she said when they were gone.

He finally looked at her, but his eyes were as cold as a stranger's. "You didn't leave me any choice."

This was the man she'd shared her life with, the man she'd believed would always love her. They used to stay in bed all weekend, talking and making love. She remembered the joy they'd shared when Jeremy and the girls were born. She remembered the family outings, the holidays, the laughter, the quiet times. Then she'd gotten pregnant with Connor, and things had begun to change. But even though Harry hadn't wanted more children, he'd still fallen in love with their youngest son the moment he'd slipped from her body. At first she'd been certain he'd fall in love with this one, too. Now she knew different.

"We talked about it, and we agreed. No more kids."

"I didn't get pregnant by myself, Harry."

"Don't you dare blame this on me. I wanted a vasectomy, remember? But you threw a fit, so I backed off. My mistake."

She cupped her hand over his mistake and rubbed the taut skin.

"Would you like me to help you pack," he said levelly, "or do you want to do it yourself?"

He was as remote as a distant planet. Even after all these months she couldn't get used to his coldness. She remembered the day he'd told her that his company wanted him to go to Switzerland and oversee an important acquisition. Not only did it mean the promotion he'd been working toward, but it would also give him an opportunity to do the kind of work he was best at.

Unfortunately, her pregnancy stood in his way. He'd be gone from August through November, and the baby was due at the end of October. Since Harry Briggs always did the right thing, he said he was turning down the job. But she'd refused to let him be a martyr, and she told him she was packing up the kids and coming with him. Women had babies in Switzerland, didn't they? She'd have hers there, too.

It had been a mistake from the beginning. She'd hoped their time away from home would bring them close again and mend the hurts, but it had only driven them further apart. The apartment the company had found was too small for a large family. The kids had no one to play with, and as the weeks passed, their misbehavior escalated. She planned weekend excursions—EuroDisney, boat trips down the Rhine River, cable-car rides—but she ended up taking the children by herself, because Harry worked constantly. He was gone nights, Saturdays, even sometimes on Sunday. Still, she hadn't fallen apart until two days ago, when she'd caught him at a restaurant with another woman.

"Do you want me to help you pack?" he repeated, in the overly patient voice he used when he was reprimanding one of the children.

"I'm not leaving, Harry, so I don't need to pack."

"Yes you do. You're not staying here." No emotion registered on his face. She heard no pain in his voice, no caring, nothing but the cold, flat statement of a man compelled to do his duty.

"Watch me."

Ren was standing just behind Harry, and he frowned. She knew he didn't want her here, but if he said a word about it in front of Harry, she'd never forgive him.

Harry's eyes stayed on her even as he addressed Ren. "I'm surprised you want her. Setting aside the fact that she's seven and a half months pregnant, she's just as spoiled and irrational now as she was when you were married to her."

"As opposed to being a controlling, cheating bastard?" she shot back.

A muscle twitched in the side of his jaw. "Very well. I'll pack the children's things myself. Feel free to stay as long as you like. The kids and I will do fine without you."

Her ears rang, and her breath caught on a hiss. "If you think for one minute that you're going to walk off with my children . . ."

"That's exactly what I think."

"Over my dead body."

"I can't imagine why you'd object. You've done nothing but complain about them since we arrived in Zurich."

The injustice nearly choked her. "I never get a break! I'm with them all day and all night. And all weekend while you're cuddled up with your anorexic girlfriend!"

Her anger didn't even make him flinch. "It was your choice to come with me, not mine."

"Go to hell."

"If that's the way you want it, I'm leaving. I'll take the four children we have. You can keep the new one."

Tracy felt as if he'd slapped her. *This is it,* she thought. *This is the darkest moment of my life.*

She heard Isabel make a quiet sound of distress. Ren, her old childhood friend, stepped forward. "You're not taking anybody anywhere, pal."

Harry's jaw set in the stubborn line Tracy had seen so often. He knew that Ren could flatten him without even breathing hard, but he was Harry, and he turned toward the house anyway.

Ren began to move. Tracy started to cry out, but Isabel got to it first. "Both of you, stop right there!"

Isabel sounded like every authority figure Tracy had spent her childhood rebelling against, but she'd never been more grateful for anyone's interference.

"Ren, please step aside. Harry, come back here, would you? Tracy, you need to sit down."

"Who are you?" Harry said, cold and hostile.

"I'm Isabel Favor."

Tracy wasn't clear exactly how Isabel made it happen, but Ren moved aside, Harry walked back toward the pool, and Tracy sank down at one of the tables.

Isabel took another step forward, speaking softly but firmly.

"The two of you need to stop trading insults and start talking about what matters."

"I don't believe that either of us asked for your opinion," Harry said, prickly as hell.

"I am," Tracy heard herself say. "I'm asking."

"I'm not," Harry retorted.

"Then I'll speak on behalf of your children." Isabel projected a confidence that Tracy envied. "Although I'm not an expert on child behavior, I think I can safely say that what the two of you are doing is going to damage five small lives in ways you can't even imagine."

"Parents get divorced all the time," Harry retorted, "and their kids turn out fine."

Pain shot into the very depths of Tracy's heart. *Divorce.* As bad as it had gotten, neither of them had ever spoken that word, not until now. But what had she expected? She'd left, hadn't she? Still, she'd never imagined this. She'd just wanted to get Harry's attention. She'd wanted to cut through that layer of ice that had formed a block around him so thick she didn't know how else to chisel through it.

Harry no longer looked quite as detached, but it was hard to tell what he was feeling. He kept his emotions neatly tucked away until it was convenient for him to deal with them. She, on the other hand, hung hers out for the world to see.

"People do get divorced," Isabel said. "And sometimes it's unavoidable. But when five children are involved, don't you think parents need to suck it up and do their best to figure out how they can stay together? I know it may seem tempting right now, but you both forfeited your chance to run off and follow your bliss a long time ago."

"That's not what this is about," Tracy retorted.

If anything, Isabel's expression grew more sympathetic. "Do you hit each other? Is there physical abuse?"

"Of course not," Harry snapped.

"No. Harry won't even set a mousetrap."

"Is either of you abusive to your children?"

"No!" they said together.

"Then everything else can be solved."

Tracy's bitterness rose to the surface. "The problems we have are too big to be solved. Betrayal. Adultery."

"Immaturity. Paranoia," Harry countered. "And problem-solving requires logic. That leaves Tracy out."

"It also requires some knowledge of human emotions, and Harry hasn't felt an emotion in years."

"Are you listening to yourselves?" Isabel's gentle shake of the head left Tracy feeling faintly ashamed. "You're both adults, and it's obvious you love your children. If your marriage isn't working the way you want it to, then fix it. Don't run away from it."

"It's too late for that," Tracy said.

Isabel's expression remained sympathetic. "Right now you can't afford a disposable relationship. You have sacred responsibilities, and no amount of wounded pride justifies walking away from them. Only the most selfish and immature parents would use beautiful children as weapons in a power struggle."

Harry had never been called immature in his life, and he looked as though he'd swallowed a mouthful of guppies. Tracy had more experience, so it didn't sting quite so badly.

Isabel bore in. "It's time to transfer your energy from arguing to figuring out how you're going to live together."

"Ignoring the fact that you are completely out of line," Harry said, "what kind of life would it be to grow up with parents who can't stand living together?"

His words made Tracy want to cry. He was bailing out on her. Harry Briggs, the most hardworking, stubborn, decent man she'd ever known, was bailing out.

"You *can* live together," Isabel said firmly. "You just have to fig-ure out how you're going to do it." She zeroed in on Harry. "You have some priorities to sort out, I think. Call up the people you work with and tell them you won't be in for a few days."

"You're wasting your breath," Tracy said. "Harry never misses work."

Isabel ignored her. "There are plenty of bedrooms in the villa, Mr. Briggs. Pick one and unpack."

Ren's eyebrows shot up. "Hey!"

Isabel ignored Ren's protest. "Tracy, you need some time to yourself. Why don't you take a drive? Harry, your children have missed you. You can spend the afternoon with them."

Harry was indignant. "Wait a minute. I'm not going to—"

"Oh, yes, you are." Physically, Isabel might be the smallest person beside that pool, but she was angry now, and that made her formidable. "You'll do this because you're decent and because your children need you. And if *that's* not good enough"—she bore down on him—"you'll do it because I'm telling you to." She held his eyes for what must have seemed like forever, then turned and marched away. Ren, who hated emotional upheaval nearly as much as Harry did, couldn't follow her fast enough.

Harry swore under his breath. Being alone with him was more than Tracy could tolerate right now, and she rushed toward the house. Isabel was right. She needed to be by herself for a while.

Church bells rang in the distance, and Tracy's heart felt so bruised it was hard to breathe. *What happened to us, Harry? Our love was supposed to last forever.*

But forever seemed to have passed them by.

Ren followed Isabel as she swept through the villa's garden and down the slope toward the vineyard. The soft bounce of her hair beneath her straw hat was at odds with her purposeful stride. Ren wasn't normally attracted to warrior goddesses, but nothing about his attraction to her had been normal from the beginning.

Why couldn't an ordinary woman have rented that farmhouse? A good-time woman who understood that sex, was just sex, and didn't have squirrelly ideas about how everybody in the world should live their lives. Most of all, a woman who didn't *pray* when she was with him. Today he'd received the distinct impression she was actually praying for *him*, and what kind of crap was that to have to put up with from a woman you wanted for sex?

He pulled up next to her. "I just saw the Four Cornerstones in action, didn't I?"

"They're both wounded right now, but they have to get over it. Personal responsibility is at the heart of any well-lived life."

"Remind me never to piss you off. Oh, wait, I already did that." He resisted the urge to destroy that silly hat. Women like Isabel shouldn't wear hats. They should go about the world bareheaded, with a sword in one hand, a shield in the other, and a chorus of angels singing the "Hallelujah Chorus" behind them. "Was it my imagination or did you really call those little monsters from hell 'beautiful children'?"

Instead of smiling, she looked so troubled he wanted to stick a red rubber ball on his nose and grab a seltzer bottle.

"You think I should have stayed out of it, don't you? That I was pushy and dictatorial. Possibly even driven, demanding, and diffi-cult?"

"You took the words right out of my mouth." He didn't really mean it. She'd been terrific with them. Still, if he gave her an inch, she'd take over the world. "Didn't any of those psych classes teach you to butt out of other people's lives unless they ask you for advice?"

As her steps slowed, she seemed to get angry all over again. "When did we get the idea that disposable marriages were all right?

Shouldn't people have figured out by now that it's not going to be easy? Marriage takes hard work. It takes sacrifice and commitment. Couples need—"

"He's screwing around on her."

"Is he? Am I the only one who's noticed that Tracy doesn't seem to be the most reliable source? And from what I saw today, they haven't talked through a single one of their issues. Did you hear either of them mention a word about counseling? Because I didn't. What I saw was wounded pride wrapped up in all kinds of hostility."

"Which—and correct me if I'm wrong—doesn't seem like the best way to keep a marriage going."

"Not if the hostility's genuine. I grew up that way, and believe me, that kind of warfare poisons everything it touches, especially children. But Tracy and Harry aren't in my parents' league."

He didn't like to think about her growing up with hostility. It was one thing for him to have been raised by jerks—he'd learned to tune it out. But she cared too deeply about the people around her, and it made her more vulnerable.

Her expression grew stormier. "I hate it when people try to bail out without a fight. It's emotional cowardice, and it violates everything our lives should be about. They loved each other enough to conceive five children, but now they want to throw up their hands and take the easy way out. Doesn't anybody have a backbone anymore?"

"Hey, don't get mad at me. I'm just your sex partner, remember?"

"You're not my sex partner."

"Not at this exact moment, but the future's looking good. Except you have to stop that praying crap. It turns me off. You, however, turn me on."

She lifted her face to the heavens. "Please, God, don't strike this man with lightning, even though he deserves it."

He smiled, glad he'd finally managed to cheer her up. "Knock it off. You want me. Admit it. You want me so bad right now that you can't stand it."

"Women who want you end up dead and buried."

"The strong survive. Unbutton your blouse."

Her lips parted, and her eyes got big. Momentarily, at least, he'd made her forget the Briggses' troubles.

"What did you say?"

"It's not smart to argue with me. Just unbutton it."

In less than a heartbeat her expression shifted from confused to calculating. She had his number, and if he weren't careful, she'd carve it in his chest with the tip of one of those polished little fingernails.

He gave her a half-lidded sneer, then thinned his lips with just enough menace to get her blood pumping.

Her jaw set in a stubborn line that boded no good.

He shifted his weight until he loomed over her, something he'd already figured out she didn't like. Then he lifted his hand and, with sinister slowness, traced her jugular with his thumb.

Now her nostrils flared.

Damn, he was having a good time. Except . . . *what the hell was he doing?* He went out of his way to avoid intimidating women in real life, yet here he was deliberately baiting this one in the most aggressive way he could. Even more surprising, the indignant sparks in those honey-brown eyes indicated she just might be appreciating his effort.

He switched to his whispery, beyond-the-crypt voice. "I believe I gave you an order."

"So you did."

She was snotty as all hell. Okay, now she was asking for it. "There's no one around. Do what I said."

"Unbutton my blouse?"

"Don't make me repeat myself."

"Let me think about it." She didn't. "No."

"I hoped I wouldn't have to do this." He trailed his finger past the open button at the collar of her blouse. She wasn't so indignant, he noticed, that she backed away. "It seems I'm going to have to remind you of the obvious." He built the tension with a long pause. God, he hoped he was turning her on, because he sure as hell was turning himself on. "It seems I'm going to have to remind you of how much you want to. Of how it's going to feel."

Her lashes flickered, and that full bottom lip parted from its mate. *Oh, yeah . . .*

She moved a fraction of an inch closer. "I, uh, stand reminded."

He suppressed a smile. *Not so sassy now, are you, sweetheart?* "Let's be sure about that."

He gazed at those puffy lips and thought about how good they were going to feel against his own. "Imagine the sun beating down on your bare breasts. Feel me watching you. Touching you." He was sweating beneath his shirt, and his groin felt thick and heavy. "I'm going to pick the fattest grapes I can find and squeeze the juice on your nipples. Then I'm going to lick off every drop."

The honey in her eyes darkened to syrup. He tipped her chin, bent his head beneath the brim of her hat, and closed his mouth over hers. It was so much better than he remembered. He tasted sun, the grape juice he'd imagined, and a heady dose of righteous, turned-on woman. He felt a primitive urge to take her right in the vineyard. To lay her down in the ancient soil of his ancestors, shaded by these old vines. To plunge into her the way one of his Medici ancestors might have taken a willing peasant woman. Or an unwilling one, for that matter, but he sure didn't have to worry about that right now, because this woman had molded herself right to him.

He pushed off her hat, let it fall to the ground, and tunneled his fingers through her disorderly curls. She was killing him, and he released her just enough to whisper against her lips. "Let's go to the house."

"Let's . . . not." Even to Isabel's own ears her words sounded like a sigh. But she didn't want to go anyplace. She wanted to kiss. And then she wanted to open her blouse just as he'd said, and let him do exactly what he wanted with her breasts.

The scents and sensations overwhelmed her. The heat of the Tuscan sun, the smell of ripe grapes, of soil, and, mostly, of man. She felt drunk with him, his kiss, his erotic verbal foreplay, the hint of menace that shouldn't have excited her but did—and she had no intention of analyzing that. His tongue slipped past her teeth into her mouth. A soul kiss. Exactly the right term for a kiss that was too intimate to be offered to just anyone.

His hands were on her hips now, pulling her against his erection. "Unbutton," he whispered. And she couldn't resist.

She did it slowly, working from bottom to top. He inched back enough to let the fabric part, revealing her lacy, nude-toned bra. There was no triumph in his eyes, merely honest male anticipation. She flicked the center clasp, pushed the lacy cups away, and let the sun fall on her breasts.

He made a quiet sound of suppressed need, lifted his hands, and cradled her breasts so they lay like pale ivory offerings in his palms. His thumbs brushed the nipples, and they pebbled. He reached into the vines and plucked a grape.

She didn't understand what he was doing until he squeezed the grape between his fingers. The juice spurted, then trickled in a gleaming rivulet down the slope of her breast and over the tip. She shuddered. Tried to catch her breath. But he wasn't done.

Slowly, he rubbed the sun-hot pulp over the nipple, making

circles, each one coming closer to the erect tip. She let out a hiss of pleasure when he reached his goal.

He slipped the bruised fruit—pulp and skin—over the end and squeezed. Grape. Pulp. Tiny seeds. He rolled it all between his fingers, abrading her flesh in the sweetest pain she'd ever felt. Her breath came quicker, and edgy waves of pleasure cut through her bloodstream. His tongue licked at the inside of her mouth, then slipped away to her breast. He played there, sucking and teasing, eating what was left of the fruit, tormenting her flesh, until she couldn't bear it any longer.

"God . . ." He breathed the word like a prayer, drawing back to gaze at her. Juice stained his cheek. His eyes were heavy-lidded and slumberous, his lips slightly swollen. "I want to push a grape inside you and eat it from your body."

Her pulses kicked. She was heady with need and a ferocious joy. This was what real passion felt like, this mindless saturnalia of the senses. He cupped her through her slacks and rubbed. She arched against his hand in a slow, holy dance. Her flesh was sticky from the juice, and her body felt as swollen as the grapes.

Abruptly, he jerked away. The sudden motion left her dazed and disoriented. With a rough growl he grabbed her hat from the ground, thrust it at her, and spun her toward the farmhouse. "I'm way too old for this."

He was *rejecting her?*

"Signore Gage!"

She glanced back and saw Massimo approaching. Not a rejection, after all, but a hideously untimely interruption. She clutched her blouse together and hurried to the farmhouse, stumbling on the path. She'd never experienced anything like this, and she wanted more.

She reached the farmhouse, rushed to the bathroom, and turned on the cold water. She splashed her face, then rested the heels of her hands on the sink to catch her breath. The memory of her own voice mocked her.

"If we don't ever push the parameters of our lives, how can we grow as human beings, my friends? God smiles at us when we reach for the stars, even if we don't quite manage to touch them. Our very willingness to make the attempt shows we aren't taking life for granted. That we've kicked up our heels, howled at the moon, and honored the sacredness of this gift we've been given. . . ."

She peeled off her crumpled, juice-stained blouse. Her lust for Lorenzo Gage wasn't sacred. On the other hand, her desire to howl at the moon had become irresistible.

After she'd tidied herself, she jumped into the Panda and drove to town. As she wandered through the market that had been set up in the piazza, she tried to turn her jumbled feelings into a prayer, but the words wouldn't take shape. She could pray for other people again, but she still couldn't manage to pray for herself.

Breathe. . . . She focused on the piles of fresh produce, where eggplants lay sleek and fat in their purple skins, and ruby heads of radicchio nested between lacy bundles of leaf lettuce. Tubs of wrinkled black olives sat next to pyramids of apples and pears. Straw baskets held porcini mushrooms with earth still clinging to the stems. Gradually, she could feel herself calm.

Until she'd come to Tuscany, she hadn't thought much about her inadequacies as a cook, but in a culture where food was everything, she was missing out on something important and life-affirming. Maybe she could redirect some energy by taking a few cooking classes when she wasn't writing. And despite Ren's scoffing, she *would* write.

She approached the market's flower stalls and chose a country bouquet. As she paid for it, she noticed Vittorio emerging from a shop across the piazza with Giulia Chiara, her ineffective real-estate agent. As she watched, he drew Giulia against him and kissed her, a kiss of passion, not friendship.

They were both young and attractive, so there was nothing surprising about their being together, especially since Casalleone was a small town. But when Isabel had mentioned Giulia in connection with the various utility problems, Vittorio hadn't said a word.

"Thanks for ditching me."

A pulse jumped in her throat. She turned and saw a tall, shabbily dressed workman with a frayed eye patch and a flat cap pulled over his dark hair. She wished he'd left her alone until she'd had a chance to reorient herself. "I had things to do. How did you get here? I thought your car was in the garage."

"I borrowed Anna's." He acted as if their erotic encounter hadn't been more than a handshake, another reminder of the emotional chasm that existed between them. And she intended to make love with this man . . .

The knowledge jarred her, and she banged her elbow against a metal post.

"Watch yourself."

"I'm trying to!" She'd spoken too loudly, and several people turned to stare at her. She had a death wish. That was the only explanation. But what was the use in pretending? The incident today proved that it was only a matter of time before she gave in to something that was guaranteed to add even more turbulence to her life. Unless . . .

Unless she was very clear about her goal. This would be a time to celebrate her body. Only her body. She would keep her spirit, her heart, and especially her soul safely tucked away. Not that it would be too difficult, since Ren wasn't interested in any of those parts. What a dangerous man. He reeled women in, then dismembered them. And she was voluntarily giving him space in her life.

Because she still felt vulnerable, she blistered him with a frown. "Do you just happen to keep things like eye patches lying around, or did you steal that from someone who actually needs it?"

"Hey, the minute the guy fell down, I gave him back his white cane."

"You're demented." But her irritation faded.

"Look at all this great food." He surveyed the market stalls. "I'm not eating with anybody named Briggs tonight, so I'll let you cook for me."

"I wish. Unfortunately, I've been too busy building my empire to learn anything about cooking." She looked around and saw that Vittorio and Giulia had disappeared.

"I must be losing my hearing. Is there actually something you don't know how to do?"

"Lots of things. For example, I haven't the slightest idea how to gouge out someone's eyeballs."

"Okay, you win this round." He took the bouquet from her and sniffed. "Sorry about that interruption earlier. *Really* sorry. Massimo wanted to give me a progress report on the grapes and to ask my opinion about when we should pick them, knowing full well that I have no clue. He suggested you might like to help with the *vendemmia*."

"What's that?"

"The harvest. It'll start in about two weeks, depending on weather, the position of the moon, birdcalls, and a few other things I don't understand. Everyone helps out."

"It sounds like fun."

"It sounds like work, something I'd rather avoid. You, on the other hand, will no doubt volunteer to organize the entire event, even though you know absolutely nothing about harvesting grapes."

"I do have a talent."

He snorted and started negotiating with an old woman selling eggplant. Once that purchase was complete, he began gathering up other vegetables, ripe pears, a gnarled wedge of pecorino, and a crusty loaf of pane toscano. His meat purchase was accompanied by a great deal of discussion with the butcher and the butcher's wife about the pros and cons of various preparation methods.

"Do you really know how to cook, or are you faking it?" she finally asked.

"I'm Italian. Of course I know how to cook." He steered her away from the butcher. "And this evening I'm making you a great dinner."

"You're only half Italian. The rest of you is a rich movie star who grew up on the East Coast surrounded by servants."

"And a grandmother from Lucca with no granddaughter she could pass the old ways on to."

"Your grandmother taught you to cook?"

"She wanted to keep me busy so I wouldn't impregnate the maids."

"You're not nearly as rotten as you want me to believe."

He gave her his bone-melting smile. "Baby, all you've seen is my good side."

"Stop it."

"That kiss really threw you into a tailspin, didn't it?"

"Oh, yes." He laughed, which made her more peevish, so she threw Michael's words at him. "I'm schizo when it comes to sex. Sometimes I get into it, and sometimes I can't get it over with fast enough."

"Cool."

"It's not funny."

"Will you just relax? Nothing's going to happen that you don't want to."

Exactly what she was afraid of.

1 2

Ren went upstairs to get rid of his eye patch and change out of his laborer's garb. Isabel finished unpacking the groceries and straightened up the mess he left in his wake. She wandered over to gaze out the garden door. The workers had disappeared from the olive grove, and Marta seemed to have moved into the villa for a while. This was a good time to locate the key to the storehouse.

She searched the kitchen drawers and cupboards, then moved on to the living room, where she finally discovered a wire basket containing half a dozen old-fashioned keys bound together with a piece of twine.

"What's up?"

She jumped as Ren appeared behind her. He'd changed into jeans and a lightweight oatmeal cotton sweater. The hot water, she'd already noted, had magically returned. "I'm hoping one of these is the key to the storehouse."

He followed her back through the kitchen and out into the garden. "Is there a reason this matters?"

A pair of crows squawked in protest as they headed for the olive grove. "I thought everyone was trying to get rid of me so Marta wouldn't have to share the house, but now it appears to be more complicated than that."

"At least in your imagination."

They reached the grove, and she began to look for evidence of digging. It didn't take long to notice that the ground near the storehouse was more trampled today than it had been yesterday.

Ren gazed at the footprints. "I remember poking around down here once when I was a kid. I liked the way the storehouse was built into the side of the hill. I think it was used to keep wine and olive oil."

She tried the keys. Finally she found one that fit, and she turned it in the old iron lock. The wooden door dragged on its hinges as she pushed against it, and Ren moved her aside to give it a little muscle. They stepped into the dim, musty interior and saw old barrels, crates piled with empty wine bottles, and a few odds and ends of furniture stacked around. As her eyes adjusted to the light, she noticed scuff marks in the dirt.

Ren noticed them, too, and stepped around a broken table to take a closer look. "Someone's moved these crates away from the wall. Go up to the house, will you, and see if you can find a flashlight? I want a better look."

"Here." She pulled out the small flashlight she'd stuck in her pocket.

"Do you have any idea how annoying that is?"

"I'll try not to do it again."

He played the flashlight across the walls, pausing to study the places where the rock had been reinforced with stones and mortar. "Look at this."

She moved closer and saw scratch marks around the stones, as if someone had tried to pry them out. "Well, well . . . What do you think of my imagination now?"

He ran his fingers over the marks. "Maybe you'd better tell me what this is about."

She gazed around the dark space. "Didn't you try to kill somebody once in a place like this?"

"Brad Pitt. Worst luck, he got me instead. But in a contest between you and me, Fifi, I'm going to win, so start talking."

She brushed away a spiderweb and walked over to investigate the opposite wall. "Massimo and Giancarlo are supposed to be digging a well in the olive grove, but this doesn't look like the olive grove to me."

"It sure is an odd place for a well."

They poked around a bit more but found nothing else suspicious. She followed him out into the sunshine, where he switched off the flashlight. "I'm going to have a talk with Anna," he said.

"She'll stonewall you."

"This is my property, and if there's something going on, I want to know about it."

"I don't think confronting her is the best way to get information."

"You have a better way? Stupid question. Of course you do."

She'd already thought it over. "It might be more productive to act as though we haven't noticed anything odd, then make ourselves scarce and watch what happens from someplace we can't be seen the next time Massimo and Giancarlo show up."

"Spy, you mean. Now, that has to violate every Cornerstone you ever made up and a few you haven't even thought about."

"Not exactly true. The Personal Relationship Cornerstone calls for aggressively pursuing your goals, and the Professional Responsibility Cornerstone encourages out-of-the-box thinking. Also, something very dishonest seems to be going on here, and the Spiritual Discipline Cornerstone advocates total honesty."

"Spying, of course, being a great way to practice that."

"Which has always been a problem with the Four Cs. They don't give you a lot of wiggle room."

He laughed. "You're making this way too complicated. I'm talking to Anna."

"Go ahead, but I'm telling you right now, you won't get anywhere."

"Is that so? Well, you've forgotten one thing, Ms. Know-It-All."

"And what's that?"

"I have ways of making people talk."

"Then be my guest."

Unfortunately, his ways didn't work with Anna Vesto, and Ren returned to the farmhouse later that evening with no more information than when he'd left.

"I told you so," she said to punish him for the afternoon she'd spent sitting in the arbor thinking about that vineyard kiss instead of working on an outline for her book about overcoming personal crisis.

He refused to take the bait. "She said there'd been some small landslides, and the men can't start digging until they make certain the hill's stable."

"Strange that they had to go inside the storehouse—undoubtedly the most stable part of that slope—to begin making reinforcements."

"My thoughts exactly."

They were standing in the kitchen, where Ren had just begun dinner preparations. He'd moved into her house, mess and all, and she hadn't done anything to stop it.

She took a sip of the wine he'd poured, and leaned against the counter to watch as he pulled the chicken he'd bought from the small refrigerator. He sharpened a wicked-looking carving knife with a steel he found in a drawer. "When I mentioned to Anna that the storehouse didn't seem like the most logical place to start making reinforcements, all I got were shrugs, along with the suggestion that Italian workmen knew a lot more about landslides and well-digging than a worthless American movie star does."

"Except more politely stated."

"Not much. Then that five-year-old exhibitionist came running in and flashed me. I swear, I'm not going up there again without a personal bodyguard—meaning you."

"Brittany's just trying to get attention. If everyone would ignore her negative behavior and reinforce the positive, she'd stop doing it."

"That's easy for you to say. You're not the one being stalked."

"You do have a way with women." She smiled and took another sip of wine. "How are Tracy and Harry doing?"

"She wasn't there, and Harry ignored me." He pushed aside a yellow plate holding the pears he'd bought at the market. "Okay, this is how we're going to solve the mystery of what's going on around here. We're announcing to everyone that we're driving to Siena for the day. Then we'll pack up the car, head off, and when we get far enough away, double back and find a vantage point where we can watch the olive grove."

"Interesting plan. *My* plan, as a matter of fact."

"Actually, that's what *I'm* going to do." He took a whack at the chicken breast. "You're staying in the car and driving to Siena."

"Okay."

He cocked one of those screen-idol eyebrows. "In the movies this is where the liberated woman tells the macho hero that he's crazy if he thinks he's going on that dangerous mission without her."

"Which is why you, the bad guy, are always able to abduct those foolhardy females."

"I don't think you have to worry too much about Massimo or Giancarlo abducting you. Tell Father Lorenzo the truth. You don't want to compromise your principles with spying, so you're making me do the dirty work."

"Good theory, but wrong. When it comes to a choice between boiling in the hot sun all day and strolling through the shady streets of Siena, guess which one I'd rather do?" Besides, strolling the streets of Siena wouldn't present the same temptation as spending hours alone with Ren. Even though she'd almost positively decided to have an affair with him, she wanted to give herself another chance to regain her sanity.

"You're the most unpredictable woman I've ever met."

She took an olive from the bowl on the counter. "Why are you so anxious to send me off to Siena?"

He pushed aside a thigh with the edge of his blade. "Are you nuts? About five minutes into the stakeout you'd be dusting the weeds and rearranging the leaf piles. Then, when you finished all that, you'd start trying to tidy me up, and I'd have to shoot you."

"I know how to relax. I can do it if I concentrate."

He laughed. "So do you plan to just stand around entertaining me, or do you want to learn something about cooking?"

She smiled despite herself. "I've actually been thinking about taking a few cooking classes."

"Why take classes when I'm here?" He washed the chicken from his hands in the sink. "Start cleaning those vegetables, then cut up the pepper."

She gazed at the chicken he'd just finished dismembering. "I'm not sure I want to do any activity with you that involves knives."

He laughed, but as he gazed down at her, his amusement faded.

For a moment he seemed almost troubled, but then he dropped his head and slowly, thoroughly, kissed her. She tasted wine on his lips and something else that was distinctly Lorenzo Gage—strength, cunning, and a thinly veiled vicious streak. Or maybe she'd made up that last one to try to terrify herself out of what she wanted to do with him.

He took his time drawing away. "Are you ready to start talking about cooking, or do you intend to keep distracting me?"

She made a grab for the small spiral-bound notebook she'd left on the table. "Go ahead."

"What's that?"

"A notebook."

"Well, put it away, for chrissa—for Pete's sake."

"These are supposed to be lessons, aren't they? I need to understand the principles first."

"Oh, I'll just bet you do. Okay, here's a principle for you: She who works, eats. She who writes crap in a notebook, starves. Now, get rid of that and start slicing up those vegetables."

"Please don't use the word 'slice' when we're alone." She opened the nearest drawer. "I need an apron."

He sighed, grabbed a dish towel, and wrapped it around her waist. But when he'd finished tying it, his hands stayed on her hips, and his voice developed a husky note. "Get rid of your shoes."

"Why?"

"Do you want to learn to cook or not?"

"Yes, but I don't see— Oh, all right." If she protested, he'd just say she was being rigid, so she kicked off her sandals. He smiled as she tucked them under the table, but she didn't see anything amusing about leaving a pair of shoes out where anyone could trip over them.

"Now, open that top button."

"Oh, no. We're not doing—"

"Quiet." Instead of arguing, he reached out and did the job himself. The material fell away just enough to reveal the swell of her breasts, and he smiled. "Now you look like a woman a man wants to cook for."

She thought about buttoning it back up, but there was something intoxicating about standing here in a fragrant Tuscan *cucina*, wineglass in hand, rumple-haired, unbuttoned, barefoot, surrounded by beautiful vegetables and an even more beautiful man.

She set to work, and as she rinsed and sliced, she was conscious of the worn, cool tiles beneath her feet and the tickle of evening air brushing the tops of her breasts. Maybe there was something to be said for looking like a slattern, because she loved the way he kept gazing at her. It was oddly satisfying to be appreciated for her body instead of her brain.

They got their wineglasses mixed up, and when he wasn't looking, she discreetly turned his so she could drink from the place where his lips had touched. The silliness pleased her.

Outside the garden door the evening turned the hills to lavender. "Have you already signed for your next film?"

He nodded. "I'll be working with Howard Jenks. We start filming in Rome, then move on to New Orleans and L.A."

She wondered when they'd begin, but she didn't like the idea of having an invisible clock ticking over her head, so she refrained from asking. "Even I've heard of Howard Jenks. I assume this won't be your standard slasher film."

"You assume right. It's the part I've been waiting my whole career to tackle."

"Tell me about it."

"You won't like it."

"Probably not, but I want to hear anyway."

"This time I won't be playing your garden-variety psychopath."

He began describing the role of Kaspar Street, and by the time he'd finished, she had chills. Still, she could understand his excitement. This was the kind of complex role actors stood in line for. "But you still haven't seen the final script?"

"It should be here any day. It's an understatement to say that I'm anxious to see what Jenks has done with it."

He slid the chicken into the oven, then began placing the vegetables in a separate roasting pan. "As horrible as Street is, there's almost something poignant about him. He genuinely loves the women he murders."

Not her idea of poignant, but for once she was going to keep her mouth shut. Or almost shut. "I don't think it's good for you to always play such horrible men."

"As I believe you've mentioned before. Now, dice up those tomatoes for the bruschetta." He pronounced the word with the hard *k* of the Italians instead of the soft *sh* most Americans used.

"All right, but if you ever want to talk about—"

"Chop!"

While she was doing that, he cut thin slices from yesterday's bread, then drizzled them with olive oil, rubbed them with a clove of garlic, and showed her how to toast them over the open flame of the stove. As they turned golden brown, he added bits of ripe olive and slivers of fresh basil to the tomatoes she'd diced, then spooned the mixture on the bread slices she arranged on a majolica plate.

While the rest of the dinner cooked in the oven, they carried everything into the garden, along with the earthenware jug holding the flowers she'd bought at the market. Gravel dug into her bare feet, but she didn't bother going back for her shoes. They settled at the stone table, where the cats came up to investigate.

She leaned back and sighed. The last rays of light clung to the hills, and long purple shadows fell over the vineyard and the olive grove. She thought of the Etruscan statue in the museum, *Shadow of the Evening,* and tried to imagine that young boy roaming lean and naked over the fields.

Ren took a sloppy bite of bruschetta, then stretched out his legs and spoke with his mouth full. "God, I love Italy."

She closed her eyes and breathed a soft amen.

A whiff of breeze carried the cooking smells from the oven into the garden. Chicken and fennel, onion and garlic, the sprig of rosemary Ren had tossed on top of the roasting vegetables.

"I don't appreciate food when I'm home," he said. "In Italy there's nothing more important."

Isabel knew what he meant. At home her life had been too highly scheduled for her to enjoy a meal like this. She was out of bed at five for yoga, then in the office before six-thirty so she could write a few manuscript pages before her staff arrived. Meetings, interviews, phone calls, lectures, airports, strange hotel rooms, falling asleep over her laptop at one in the morning trying to write a few more pages before she turned out the light. Even Sundays had become indistinguishable from weekdays. That Divine Slacker might have had time to rest on the seventh day, but He didn't have Isabel Favor's workload.

She let the wine roll over her tongue. She tried so hard to approach life from a position of strength, but all that effort had come at a price. "It's easy to forget simple pleasures."

"But you've done your best." She heard something that sounded like sympathy in his voice.

"Hey, I've got a world to run." She said the words lightly, but they still tried to catch in her throat.

"Permesso?"

She turned to see Vittorio coming through the garden. With his black hair tied in a ponytail and his elegant Etruscan nose, he looked like a gentle Renaissance poet. And walking just behind him was Giulia Chiara.

"Buona sera, Isabel." He opened his arms in greeting.

She smiled automatically, discreetly fastened her top button, and rose to have her cheeks kissed. Even though she didn't trust Vittorio, there was something about him that made her look forward to his company. Still, she doubted it was coincidental that he'd shown up tonight with Giulia. He knew that Isabel had spotted them together, and he was here to do damage control.

Ren looked less than friendly, but Vittorio didn't seem to notice. "Signore Gage, I am Vittorio Chiara. And this is my beautiful wife, Giulia."

He'd never said a word about being married, let alone being married to Giulia. He'd never even told Isabel his last name. Most men who hid the existence of wives did it so they could hit on other women, but Vittorio's flirtatiousness had been harmless, so he'd had another reason.

Giulia was dressed in a plum-colored miniskirt and striped top. She'd tucked her light brown hair behind her ears, and gold hoops swung from her lobes. Ren's scowl gave way to a smile, which made Isabel resent Giulia even more than she'd resented her for the unanswered phone calls.

"My pleasure," Ren said. Then, to Vittorio, "I see word's gotten out that I'm here."

"Not too much. Anna is very discreet, but she needed help with preparations for your arrival. We're family—she is my mother's sister—so she knows I'm very trustworthy. The same is true of Giulia." He lavished his wife with a smile. "She is the best *agente immobiliare* in the area. Homeowners from here to Siena trust her to handle their rental properties."

Giulia gave Isabel a strained smile. "I understand you were trying to find me. I've been out of town and didn't get your messages until this afternoon."

Isabel didn't believe it for a moment.

Giulia tilted her head at a charming angle. "I trust Anna took care of everything while I was away."

Isabel made a noncommital murmer, but Ren was suddenly all hospitality. "Would you like to join us?"

"Are you sure we won't be a bother?" Vittorio was already steering his wife toward a chair.

"Not at all. Let me get some wine." Ren set off for the kitchen and quickly returned with more glasses, the wedge of pecorino, and some fresh slices of bruschetta. Before long they were settled around the table laughing at Vittorio's stories of his experiences as a guide. Giulia added her own tales centering on the wealthy foreigners who rented villas in the area. She was more reserved than her husband but just as entertaining, and Isabel began to set aside her earlier resentment and enjoy the young woman's company.

She liked the fact that neither of them questioned Ren about Hollywood, and when Isabel was guarded about her own work, they didn't press. After several trips to the kitchen to check the oven, Ren invited them to stay for dinner, and they accepted.

While he sautéed the porcini, Giulia put out the bread, and Vittorio opened a bottle of sparkling mineral water to accompany the wine. It was getting dark, so Isabel found some chunky candles to set in the middle of the table, then asked Vittorio to climb on a chair and light the candles in the chandelier she'd hung in the trees. Before long, glimmers from the flames were dancing through the magnolia leaves.

Ren hadn't misrepresented his abilities as a chef. The chicken was perfect, juicy and flavorful, and the roasted vegetables held subtle undertones of rosemary and marjoram. As they ate, the chandelier swayed gently from the tree limb above them, and the flames flickered happily. Crickets sang, the wine flowed, and the stories grew more outrageous. It was all very relaxed, very merry, very Italian. "Pure bliss." Isabel sighed, as she bit into the last of the meaty porcini.

"Our *funghi* are the best in the world," Giulia said. "You must come and hunt the porcini with me, Isabel. I have secret places."

Isabel wondered if Giulia's invitation was genuine or another gambit to get her away from the house, but she was too relaxed to care.

Vittorio chucked Giulia under the chin. "Everyone in Tuscany has secret places to find porcini. But it's true. Giulia's *nonna* was one of the most famous *fungarola* in the area—what you would call a mushroom hunter—and she passed on everything she knew to her granddaughter."

"We will all go, yes?" Giulia said. "Very early in the morning. It is best after we've had a little rain. We will put on our old boots and take our baskets and find the best porcini in all of Tuscany."

Ren brought out a tall, narrow bottle of golden vinsanto, the local dessert wine, along with the plate of pears and a wedge of cheese. One of the candles in the tree chandelier sputtered out, and an owl made a soft *whoo* nearby. The meal had passed the two-hour mark, but it was Tuscany, and no one seemed in a rush to finish. Isabel took a sip of vinsanto and sighed again. "The food has been too delicious for words."

"Ren's cooking is much better than Vittorio's," Giulia teased.

"Better than yours, too," her husband responded, mischief in his smile.

"But not as good as Vittorio's *mamma's*."

"Ah, my *mamma's*." Vittorio kissed his fingers.

"It is a miracle, Isabel, that Vittorio is not one of the *mammoni*." At Isabel's puzzled expression, Giulia explained, "These are the . . . How do we say this in English?"

Ren smiled. "The mama's boys."

Vittorio laughed. "All Italian men are mama's boys."

"So true," Giulia replied. "By tradition, Italian men live with their parents until they marry. Their mamas cook for them, do their laundry, run their errands, treat them like little kings. Then the men don't want to get married because they know younger women like me won't cater to them like their *mammas*."

"Ah, but you do other things." Vittorio traced her bare shoulder with his finger.

Isabel's own shoulder tingled, and Ren gave her a slow smile that made her blood rush. She'd seen that smile on the screen, usually just before he led some unsuspecting woman to her death. Still . . . not the worst way to go.

Giulia leaned against Vittorio. "Fewer Italian men get married all the time. This is why we have such a low birthrate in Italy, one of the lowest in the world."

"Is that true?" Isabel asked.

Ren nodded. "The Italian population could decrease by half every forty years if the trend doesn't change."

"But it's a Catholic country. Doesn't that automatically mean lots of children?"

"Most Italians don't even go to mass," Vittorio replied. "My American guests are always shocked to learn that only a small percentage of our population truly practices Catholicism."

The headlights of a car coming down the lane interrupted their conversation. Isabel glanced at her watch. It was after eleven, a little late for visitors. Ren rose. "I'll see who it is."

A few minutes later he came into the garden with Tracy Briggs, who gave Isabel a tired wave. "Hey, there."

"Sit down before you collapse," Ren growled. "I'll get you something to eat."

While Ren went inside, Isabel performed the introductions.

Tracy wore another expensive but rumpled maternity dress and the same run-down sandals she'd had on yesterday. Despite that, she looked gorgeous.

"How was the sight-seeing?" Isabel asked.

"Lovely. No kids."

Ren emerged holding a plate piled with leftovers. He slapped it in front of her, then filled a glass with water. "Eat and go home."

Vittorio looked shocked.

"We used to be married," Tracy explained as the last of the candles sputtered out overhead. "Ren has leftover hostility."

"Take all the time you want," Isabel said. "Ren is being insensitive as usual." Not so insensitive, however, that he didn't make sure Tracy had plenty to eat.

Tracy looked longingly toward the farmhouse. It's so peaceful down here. So adult."

"Forget it," he said. "I've already moved in, and there's no room for you."

"You haven't *moved in,*" Isabel said, even though she knew he had.

"Relax," Tracy said. "As much as I enjoyed getting away from them, I've been missing them like crazy for hours."

"Don't let us keep you a minute longer."

"They're asleep by now. No reason to hurry back."

Except to begin making peace with your husband, Isabel thought.

"Tell me where you went today," Vittorio said.

The conversation moved on to the local sites, with only Giulia remaining silent. Isabel realized she'd been subdued ever since Tracy had appeared, almost resentful. Since Tracy had been friendly, Isabel didn't understand it.

"I'm tired, Vittorio," she said abruptly. "We need to go home."

Isabel and Ren walked them out to their car, and by the time they got there, Giulia had recovered her good cheer enough to invite them to their house for dinner the following week. "And we will go *funghi* hunting soon, yes?"

Isabel had been enjoying herself so much she'd managed to forget that Giulia and Vittorio were part of the forces trying to get her out of the house. Still, she agreed.

As the couple drove off, Tracy headed for her own car, munching a bread crust on the way. "Time to get back."

"I'll take the children for a while tomorrow if you'd like," Isabel said. "That'll give you and Harry a chance to talk."

"You can't," Ren said. "We have plans. And Isabel doesn't believe in sticking her nose into other people's business, do you, Isabel?"

"On the contrary, I live to interfere."

Tracy gave her a tired smile. "Harry will be halfway to the Swiss border by lunch, Isabel. He won't let a little thing like talking to his wife interfere with his job."

"Maybe you're underestimating him."

"Or maybe not." Tracy hugged her, then Ren, who gave her shoulder a comforting squeeze and helped her into her car. "I'll give Anna and Marta a big tip for watching the kids today," she said. "Thanks for dinner."

"You're welcome. Don't do anything stupider than usual."

"Not me."

As Tracy drove away, Isabel's stomach took a roller-coaster dip. She wasn't ready to be alone with Ren, not until she'd had a little more time to come to terms with the fact that she'd nearly decided to let herself become another notch on his splintery bedpost.

"You're getting jittery again, aren't you?" he said as she headed for the kitchen.

"I'm just going to clean up, that's all."

"I'll pay Marta to do it tomorrow. Stop being so nervous, for God's sake. I'm not going to jump you."

"You think I'm afraid of you?" She grabbed a dish towel. "Well, think again, Mr. Irresistible, because whether or not our relationship goes any further is my decision, not yours."

"I don't even get to vote?"

"I know how you're voting."

His smile sent out a sexy smoke signal. "And I've got a pretty good idea how you're voting, too. Although . . ." The smile faded. "We both need to make sure we're clear about where we're going with this."

He wanted to warn her off, as though she were too naïve to figure out that he wasn't proposing a long-term relationship. "Save your breath. The only thing I could possibly—and I emphasize 'possibly,' because I'm still thinking about it—the only thing I could possibly want from you is that amazing body, so you'd better let me know right now if I'll break your heart when I dump you afterward."

"God, you're a brat."

She gazed up. "You're not, God. Forgive Ren for being disrespectful."

"That wasn't a prayer."

"Tell Her."

He had to know it wouldn't take much effort on his part to make her forget she wasn't quite ready to take that final step. One more of those well-practiced kisses would do the trick. She watched him try to make up his mind whether or not to press her, and she didn't know whether she was glad or sorry when he headed for the stairs.

Tracy used the banister to haul herself upstairs. She felt like a cow, but then she always felt like a cow by her seventh month—a big, healthy Elsie cow with round eyes, a shiny nose, and a daisy chain around her neck. She loved being pregnant, even with her head hanging over the toilet, her ankles swollen, and the sight of her feet nothing but a memory. Until now she'd never worried much about the stretch marks that had spread like lightning bolts across her belly or her big, leaky breasts, because Harry had pronounced them beautiful. He'd said pregnancy made her smell like sex. Obviously he didn't find her sexy now.

She walked down the long corridor toward her room. The heavy moldings, frescoed ceilings, and Murano glass fixtures weren't her style, but they suited the dark elegance of her ex-husband. Considering the way she'd barged in on him, he wasn't being as much of a prick as she'd expected, which proved that you could never predict exactly how people would behave, even the ones you knew the best.

She opened the door to her bedroom, then stopped just inside as light from the hallway fell on her bed. Harry lay on his back in the middle of her mattress, the raspy sounds coming from his mouth not exactly snores, but not exactly not-snores either.

He was still here. She hadn't been completely certain he'd stick around for the rest of the day. She allowed herself a moment of hope, but it didn't last long. Only his sense of obligation had kept him from leaving right away. He'd drive off first thing in the morning.

In looks, Harry was ordinary compared with Ren. His face was too long, his jaw too stubborn, and his light brown hair beginning to thin on top. The creases at the corners of his eyes hadn't been there the night of that dreary cocktail party twelve years ago when she'd accidentally on purpose tipped a glass of wine into his lap.

The moment she'd seen him, she'd made up her mind to get his clothes off, but he hadn't made it easy. As he'd later explained, men like him weren't used to having beautiful women hitting on them. But she'd known what she wanted, and she'd wanted Harry Briggs. His quiet intelligence and steady outlook had been the perfect antidote to her wild, aimless life.

Now Connor lay across his chest, the fingers of one chubby hand caught in the neck of his father's undershirt. Brittany was pressed against his other side, the final remnant of her tattered blankie draped over his arm. Steffie had curled into a tight, insect-fighting ball near his legs. Only Jeremy was missing, and she suspected that it had taken a supreme act of will to keep him in his room instead of cuddled up with his father and the "brats."

For twelve years Harry had been the calm to her fire, putting up with all the drama and emotional excess that made up who she was. Despite their love for each other, it hadn't been an easy match. Her untidiness drove him crazy, and she hated the way he withdrew when she tried to get him to express his feelings. She'd always been secretly afraid he'd eventually leave her for someone more like himself.

Connor stirred and rolled farther up on his father's chest. Harry instinctively drew him closer. How many nights had they spent with kids in their bed? She never turned them away. It hadn't seemed logical that the most secure people in a family, the parents, were permitted to find comfort together at night but the smallest and most vulnerable were expected to sleep alone. After Brittany was born, they'd moved their king-size mattress to the floor so they didn't have to worry about babies falling out at night and hurting themselves.

Her friends had been incredulous. "How can you ever have sex?" But the doors in their house had solid locks, and she and Harry had always managed to find a way. Always, that was, until this last pregnancy, when he'd finally gotten fed up with her.

He stirred and opened his eyes. They were unfocused until they settled on her. For a moment she thought she saw a flicker of that familiar, steadfast love, but then his expression went blank, and she saw nothing at all.

She turned away and went off to find an empty bed.

In a small stone house on the outskirts of Casalleone, Vittorio Chiara pulled his wife closer to his side. Giulia liked to sleep with her fingers in his hair, and that's where they were now, woven through the long strands. But she wasn't asleep. His chest was damp beneath her cheek, so he knew she'd been crying, and her silent tears broke his heart.

"Isabel will be gone by November," he whispered. "We'll do the best we can until then."

"What if she doesn't leave? For all we know, he might sell the house to her."

"Don't borrow trouble, *cara*."

"I know you're right, but . . ."

He stroked her shoulder to quiet her. A few years ago he would have made love to her, but that wasn't so much fun anymore. "We've waited a long time," he whispered. "November isn't far off."

"They're nice people."

She sounded so sad he couldn't bear it, and he said the only thing he could think of that might cheer her up. "I'll be in Cortona on Wednesday night with those Americans I'm taking out. Can you meet me?"

She didn't reply for a moment, but then she nodded against his skin. "I'll be there," she said, sounding just as sad as he felt.

"This time it'll work, you'll see."

Her breath skittered across his skin. "If only she'd go away."

Something woke Isabel up. She stirred in bed, then began to drift back off, only to hear it again, a clicking against the window. She turned on her side and listened.

At first she heard nothing, but then it came again: the sound of pebbles being tossed against the glass. She got up and made her way across the tiles. Outside the window only the faintest sheen of moonlight illuminated the garden. And then she saw it.

A ghost.

It moved through the olive grove, a vaporous apparition. She thought about waking Ren, but going anywhere near his bed didn't seem like the best idea. Better to wait until morning.

The ghost moved behind a tree, then drifted out again. Isabel waved, shut the window, and went back to bed.

13

Tracy reveled in the luxury of waking up without being poked by a five-year-old or lying in a damp spot from Connor's leaky diaper. If he didn't potty train soon, she was putting him in Depends.

She heard a catcall from Jeremy followed by Steffie's shrill scream. He was teasing her again, and Brittany was probably running around naked, and Connor got diarrhea if he ate too much fruit at breakfast, but instead of getting up, she buried her face in the pillow. It was still early. What if Harry hadn't left yet? She couldn't bear the thought of watching him drive away.

She closed her eyes and tried to force herself back to sleep, but the baby was stomping on her bladder, so she dragged herself out of bed and made her way to the bathroom. The moment she sat on the toilet seat, the door flew open and Steffie burst in.

"I hate Jeremy. Make him stop teasing me."

Brittany appeared—dressed for once, but with Tracy's lipstick smeared over her mouth. "Mommy! Look at me!"

"Pick me up!" Connor demanded, padding in, too.

And then Harry was there, standing in the doorway gazing down at her. He hadn't made it to the shower yet, and he wore jeans with one of his sleeping T-shirts. Only Harry Briggs could have T-shirts he'd specifically designated for sleeping, old ones he considered too worn for regular daytime wear but too good to throw out. Even in his sleeping T-shirt he looked better than she did, sitting on the pot with her gown bunched at her waist.

"Could I have a little privacy, please?"

"I hate Jeremy. He called me a—"

"I'll talk to him. Now, leave. All of you."

Harry stepped back from the door. "Go on, kids. Anna said breakfast would be ready in a minute. Girls, take your brother."

The kids reluctantly filed out, and she was left with Harry, the person she least wanted standing around right now. "Everybody means you, too. Why are you still here?"

He regarded her through his glasses. "Because my family's here."

"Like you care about that." She was never at her best in the morning, and today she felt particularly shrewish. "Get out. I have to pee."

"Go right ahead." He sat on the edge of the tub and waited.

Sooner or later pregnant women were robbed of every shred of dignity, and this was one of those times. When she was done, he handed her a precisely folded stack of toilet paper. She rumpled it just to make the point that everything in life couldn't be as neat as he wanted. She wiped, flushed, and stood up to wash her hands, all without looking at him.

"I suggest we talk now while the children are eating breakfast. I'd like to be on the road by noon."

"Why wait until noon when you can go right now?" She squeezed toothpaste onto her brush.

"I told you yesterday. I'm not leaving without the children."

He couldn't work and care for the children at the same time, they both knew that, so why was he doing this? He also knew she wouldn't let an army of stone-hearted husbands take her kids from her. He was trying to manipulate her into going back to Zurich.

"Okay, take them. I need a vacation." She began brushing her teeth as if she didn't have a care in the world.

In the mirror she saw him blink behind the lenses of his glasses. He hadn't expected that. She noticed that he'd found time to shave. She loved the smell of his skin in the morning, and she yearned to bury her face in his neck.

"All right," he said slowly.

In a fit of sadomasochism she laid down her toothbrush and cupped her belly. "Except this one. We agree. As soon as this one's born, it's all mine."

For the first time he couldn't meet her eyes. "I'm—I shouldn't have said that."

"Apology not accepted." She spat in the sink and rinsed. "I think I'll take back my maiden name—for me and for the baby."

"You hate your maiden name."

"You're right. Vastermeen is a terrible name." He followed her from the bathroom to the bedroom, giving her a chance to devastate him as he'd devastated her. "I'll go back to Gage. I always liked the sound of Tracy Gage." She shoved a suitcase out of her way. "I hope the baby's a boy so I can name him Jake. Jake Gage. You can't get much stronger than that."

"Like hell."

She'd finally managed to pierce his wall of indifference, but the fact that she was hurting him didn't give her satisfaction. Instead, she felt like crying. "What difference does it make? This is the baby you don't want, remember?"

"Just because I'm not happy about this pregnancy doesn't mean I won't accept the baby."

"Am I supposed to be grateful?"

"I'm not going to apologize for my feelings. Damn it, Tracy, you're always accusing me of being out of touch with my emotions, but the only emotions you want me in touch with are the ones you like." She thought he was finally going to lose a little of that self-control, but then he reverted to the cool, unemotional tone that drove her wild. "I didn't want Connor either, but now I can't imagine life without him. Logic says I'll feel the same way about the new one."

"And thank God for logic." She snatched her swimsuit from a pile on the floor.

"Stop being so childish. The real reason you're upset is that you haven't been getting enough attention, and God knows you like attention."

"Go to hell."

"You knew before we left Connecticut that I'd be working most of the time."

"But you neglected to mention that you'd also be screwing around on me."

"I wasn't screwing around."

The overly patient note in his voice set her teeth on edge. "Did you explain that to your little hottie at the restaurant?"

"Tracy . . ."

"I saw you with her! The two of you cuddled up in that corner booth. She was kissing you!"

He had the gall to look annoyed. "Why didn't you come rescue me instead of leaving me with her? You know I'm not good in awkward social situations."

"Oh, yeah . . . it looked real awkward." She grabbed her sandals.

"Come off it, Tracy. Your drama-queen routine's getting old. She's the new VP for Worldbridge, and she drinks way too much."

"Lucky you."

"Stop being a spoiled brat. You know I'm the last man on earth who'd have an affair, but you had to invent a Greek tragedy out of a drunken woman's slobbering because you've been feeling neglected."

"Yeah, that's right. I'm just having a little sulk here." Somehow it had been easier to deal with the idea of infidelity than his devastating emotional abandonment, but she'd probably known all along he hadn't been having an affair. "The truth is, Harry, you started freezing me out months before we left home. The truth is, Harry . . . you've bailed out on our marriage, and you've bailed out on me."

She wanted him to deny it, but he didn't. "You're the one who left, and you're not turning this on me. And where did you go running? Right to your party-boy ex-husband."

Tracy's relationship with Ren was Harry's only insecurity. For twelve years he'd dodged meeting him, and he got frosty when she talked to him on the phone. It was so unlike him.

"I ran to Ren because I knew I could count on him."

"Is that so? Well, he didn't look like he was all that happy to see you."

"You couldn't understand what Ren Gage is feeling in a million years."

She finally had him at a disadvantage, so he naturally decided to change the subject. "You're the one who insisted I take the job in Zurich. And you also insisted on coming with me."

"Because I knew how much it meant to you, and I wasn't going to have it thrown back in my face that I'd sabotaged your career because I got pregnant again."

"When have I ever thrown anything back at you?"

Never. He could have blasted her with a long list of grievances from the early days of their marriage, when she was still figuring out how to love someone, but he'd never done it. Until she'd gotten pregnant with Connor, he'd always been so patient with her. She desperately wanted that patience back. Patience, reassurance, and, most of all, the love she'd always thought was unconditional.

"That's right," she said bitterly. "I'm the one who holds grudges. You're perfect, which is why it's a shame you got stuck with such an imperfect wife." She threw her swimsuit over her shoulder, grabbed her cover-up, and fled to the bathroom. When she came out, he'd disappeared, but as she headed for the kitchen to check on the children, she heard him call out to Jeremy in the garden. They were playing catch.

Just for a moment she let herself pretend that everything was all right.

"You saw a what?"

"A ghost." Isabel took in Ren's sweat-soaked T-shirt. It was a deep navy, and it turned his eyes a particularly ominous shade of silver. She gazed at him for a moment too long before she began putting away the plates Marta had left on the drainboard after she'd come down from the villa to clean up. "Definitely a ghost. How can you run in this heat?"

"Because I got up too late to run when it was still cool. What kind of ghost?"

"The kind that throws pebbles at my window and runs around in the olive trees wearing a white sheet. I waved."

He wasn't amused. "This has gone on long enough."

"Agreed."

"Before I went running, I called Anna and told her you and I were going to Siena today. That should give everybody plenty of warning that the house'll be empty." He grabbed the glass of freshly squeezed orange juice she'd foolishly left unguarded, downed it, and headed for the stairs. "I need ten minutes to shower, and then I'll be ready to leave."

Twenty minutes later he returned in jeans, a black T-shirt, and his Lakers cap. He stared suspiciously at her gray drawstring knit pants, sneakers, and the charcoal T-shirt she'd reluctantly filched from him. "You don't look like you're dressed for sight-seeing."

"Camouflage." She grabbed her sunglasses and headed for her car. "I changed my mind and decided to go on the stakeout with you."

"I don't want you with me."

"I'm going anyway. Otherwise you'll fall asleep and miss something important." She opened the driver's door. "Or you'll get bored and start pulling the legs off a grasshopper or setting butterflies on fire or—what was that thing you did in *Carrion Way*?"

"I have no idea." He moved her aside and climbed behind the wheel himself. "This car's a disgrace."

"Not all of us can afford a Maserati." She walked around to the other side and slid in. The incident with the pseudoghost last night indicated an uncomfortable degree of desperation, and she had to see this through, even if it meant being alone with him in a place where those mind-shattering kisses wouldn't be interrupted by grape growers, children, or housekeepers.

Only the two of them. Just thinking about it made her blood pound. She was ready—more than ready—but first they needed to have a serious conversation. Regardless of what her body was saying, her brain knew she had to set limits. "I brought some things for a nice picnic. They're in the trunk"

He shot her a disgusted look. "Nobody but girls brings a picnic to a stakeout."

"What should I have brought?"

"I don't know. Stakeout food. Cheap doughnuts, a thermos of hot coffee, and an empty bottle to pee in."

"Silly me."

"Not a pop bottle either. A *big* bottle."

"I'm going to try to forget that I'm a psychologist."

Ren waved to Massimo as he pulled up the drive, then swung toward the villa. "I need to see if the script's arrived yet from Jenks. I'll also make our pending absence known."

She smiled as she watched him disappear into the house. She'd laughed more in these few days with Ren Gage than in all three years she'd spent with Michael. Her smile faded as she poked at the leftover wounds from her broken engagement. They hadn't healed yet, but they hurt in a different way. It wasn't the hurt of a broken heart, but the hurt of wasting so much time on something that had never been right from the beginning.

Her relationship with Michael had been like a pool of stagnant water. Never any churn or hidden eddies, no rocks jutting up to force either of them to change direction or move in new ways. They'd never quarreled, never challenged each other. There'd been no excitement and—Michael was right—no passion either.

With Ren it would all be passion . . . passion churning through an ocean full of rocks. But just because the rocks were there didn't mean she had to let herself run into any of them.

He returned to the car looking luscious and harried. "The little nudist found my shaving cream and squirted herself a bikini."

"Inventive. Was the script there?"

"No, damn it. And I think I have a broken toe. Jeremy found my hand weights and left one on the stairs. I don't know how Tracy puts up with them."

"I think it's different when they're your own." She tried to imagine Ren with children and saw gorgeous little demons who'd tie up baby-sitters, set off stink bombs, and prank-call the elderly. Not a pretty picture.

She gazed over at him. "Remember that you weren't any prize as a kid."

"True. The shrink my father sent me to when I was eleven explained that the only way I could get either of my parents' attention was by acting up. I perfected misbehavior early on to keep myself in the spotlight."

"And you carried that same philosophy into your career."

"Hey, it worked for me as a kid. Everybody remembers the villain."

This wasn't the time to talk about their relationship, but it might be a good time to put a gentle rock in his path—not to capsize him, merely to make him more aware. "You understand, don't you, that we develop dysfunctions as children because we see them as essential to our survival?"

"Uh-huh."

"Part of our maturity process is getting past that. Of course, the need for attention seems to be a common factor with most great actors, so in this case your dysfunction became highly functional."

"You think I'm a great actor?"

"I think you have the potential, but you can't be truly great as long as you keep playing the same part."

"That's bull. Every part has its own nuance, so don't tell me they're all the same. And actors have always loved playing villains. It gives them a chance to pull out the stops."

"We're not talking about actors in general. We're talking about you and the fact that you're not willing to play any other kind of part. Why is that?"

"I already told you, and it's too early in the morning for this discussion."

"Because you grew up with a distorted view of yourself. You were emotionally abused as a child, and now you need to be very clear about your motivation for choosing those parts." Another small rock to toss in his direction, and then she'd leave him alone. "Are you doing it because you love playing those sadists or because on some level you don't feel worthy to play the hero?"

He slammed his fist against the steering wheel. "As God is my witness, this is the last time I am *ever* dating a fucking shrink."

She smiled to herself. "We're not dating. And you're speeding."

"Shut up."

She made a mental note to give him a list of the Healthy Relationship Rules of Fair Combat, not one of which advocated yelling "shut up."

They'd reached town, and as they drove past the piazza, she noticed a few heads turning to watch. "I don't get it. Despite all your disguises, some of these people must know by now who you are, but they haven't been pestering you for autographs. Don't you think that's odd?"

"I told Anna I'd buy some new playground equipment for the local school if everybody left me alone."

"Considering the way you cultivate attention, hiding out must feel odd."

"Did you wake up this morning planning to irritate the hell out of me, or did it just happen?"

"Speeding again."

He sighed.

They left the town behind, and after another few kilometers they turned off the main road onto a much narrower one, where he finally condescended to speak to her again. "This leads to the abandoned castle on the hill above the house. We should have a decent view from there."

The road grew more rutted as they got closer. Finally it ended at the mouth of a trail, where Ren pulled off. As they began the climb through the trees, he grabbed the grocery sacks from her. "At least you didn't bring one of those sissy picnic baskets."

"I do know a few things about covert operations."

He snorted.

When they reached the clearing at the top, he stopped to read a battered historical marker at the edge of the site. She began to explore and discovered that the castle ruins weren't just those of a single building but a fortification that had once held many buildings. Vines curled over the crumbling walls and climbed up the remains of the old watchtower. Trees grew through fragments of arches, and wildflowers poked through what might once have been the foundation stones of a stable or a granary.

Ren abandoned the historical marker and joined her as she gazed over the vista of fields and woods. "This was an Etruscan burial site before the castle was built here," he said.

"A ruin on top of a ruin." Even with the naked eye she could make out the farmhouse below, but both the garden and olive grove were empty. "Nothing's happening."

He peered through the binoculars he'd brought. "We haven't been gone long enough. This is Italy. They need time to get organized."

A bird flew from its nest in the wall behind them. Standing so close disturbed the peace of this place, and she moved away. Her feet crushed some wild mint. The sweet scent enveloped her.

She noticed a section of wall with a domed niche. As she moved closer, she saw that it was the apse of what must have been a chapel. Faint traces of color were still visible in what was left of the dome— a russet that might once have been crimson, dusty shadows of blue, faded ocher. "Everything is so peaceful. I wonder why they left."

"The sign mentioned a plague in the fifteenth century combined with overtaxing by the neighborhood bishops. Or maybe they were driven away by the ghosts of the Etruscans buried here."

He sounded irritable again. She turned her back on him and gazed up into the dome. Churches generally calmed her, but Ren was too close. She smelled smoke and spun around to see him light a cigarette.

"What are you *doing*?"

"I only smoke one a day."

"Could you do it when I'm not around to watch?"

He ignored her and took a deep drag, then wandered toward one of the portals. As he leaned against the stone, he looked moody and withdrawn. Maybe she shouldn't have forced him to poke around in his childhood.

"You're wrong," he said abruptly. "I'm perfectly capable of separating real life from the screen."

"I never said you weren't." She sat down on a section of wall and studied his profile, so well proportioned and exquisitely carved. "I was only suggesting that the view of yourself you formed in childhood, when you were seeing and doing things no child should be exposed to, might not fit the man you've become."

"Don't you read the papers?"

She finally understood what was really bothering him. "You can't stop brooding about what happened with Karli, can you?"

He inhaled, not saying anything.

"Why don't you hold a press conference and tell the truth?" She plucked a stem of wild mint and crushed it between her fingers.

"People are jaded. They'll believe what they want to."

"You cared about her, didn't you?"

"Yeah. She was a sweet kid . . . and, God, so talented. It was hard watching all that go to waste."

She wrapped her arms around her knees. "How long were you together?"

"Only a couple of months before I figured out how bad her drug problem was. Then I got suckered into a rescue fantasy and spent another few months trying to help her." He flicked an ash, took another drag. "I arranged an intervention. Tried to talk her into rehab. Nothing worked, so I finally walked."

"I see."

He shot her a dark look. "What?"

"Nothing." She lifted the mint to her nose and wished she could let people be themselves without trying to fix them, especially when it was becoming increasingly obvious that the person who needed the most fixing was herself.

"What's that 'I see' crap? Say what you're thinking. God knows that shouldn't be hard for you."

"What do you think I'm thinking?"

Smoke curled from his nostrils. "Suppose you tell me."

"I'm not your psychiatrist, Ren."

"I'll write you a check. Tell me what's on your mind."

"What's on my mind isn't important. It's what's on yours that counts."

"It sounds like you're judging me." He bristled with hostility. "It sounds like you think I could have done something to save her, and I don't like it."

"Is that what you think I'm doing? Judging you?"

He tossed down the cigarette. "It wasn't my fault that she killed herself, damn it! I did everything I could."

"Did you?"

"You think I should have stuck around?" He ground out the butt. "Should I have handed her the needle when she wanted to shoot up? Scored some blow for her? I told you I had drug problems when I was a kid. I can't be around that shit."

She remembered the joking reference he'd made to snorting cocaine, but he wasn't joking now.

"I cleaned up when I was in my early twenties, but it still scares the hell out of me to think how close I came to screwing up my life. Since then I've made sure I stay as far away from it as I can." He shook his head. "What happened to her was such a goddamn waste."

Her heart ached for him. "And if you'd only stuck around, you might have been able to save her?"

He turned on her, his expression furious. "That's bullshit. Nobody could save her."

"Are you sure?"

"Do you think I was the only one who tried? Her family was there. A lot of her friends. But all she cared about was her next fix."

"Maybe there was something you could have said? Something you could have done?"

"She was a junkie, damn it! At some point she had to help herself."

"And she wouldn't do that, would she?"

He stubbed his toe into the dirt.

Isabel rose. "You couldn't do it for her, Ren, but you wanted to. And you've been going crazy ever since she died trying to figure out what you could have said or done that would have made a difference."

He stuffed his hands in his pockets and gazed off into the distance. "There wasn't anything."

"Are you absolutely certain?"

His long sigh came from someplace deep inside. "Yeah, I am."

She moved next to him and rubbed the small of his back. "Keep reminding yourself."

He gazed down at her, the furrows between his eyebrows smoothing. "I really am going to have to write you a check, aren't I?"

"Consider it barter for the cooking lesson."

His lips curved ever so slightly. "Just don't pray for me, okay? Freaks me out."

"You don't think you deserve a few prayers?"

"Not when I'm trying to remember what the person who's pray-ing for me looks like naked."

Something hot leaped between them. He lifted his hand and took his time tucking a lock of hair behind her ear. "It's just my luck. I stay on my good behavior for months, but then, when I'm finally ready to raise some hell, I get marooned on a desert island with a nun."

"Is that the way you think of me?"

He toyed with her earlobe. "I'm trying, but it's not working."

"Good."

"God, Isabel, you send out more mixed signals than a bad radio." He dropped his hand in frustration.

She licked her lips. "It's . . . because I'm conflicted."

"You're not conflicted at all. You want this just as much as I do, but you haven't figured out how to work it into whatever your cur-rent life plan is, so you're dragging your heels. The same heels, by the way, that I'd like to feel propped on my shoulders."

Her mouth went dry.

"You're driving me nuts!" he exclaimed.

"And you think you're not doing the same to me?"

"The first good news I've had all day. So why are we standing around?"

He reached out, but she jumped back. "I—I need to get my bear-ings. *We* need to get our bearings. To sit down and talk first."

"Exactly what I don't want." Now he was the one who stepped back. "Damn it, I'm not getting interrupted again, and the minute I put my hands on you, someone's guaranteed to show up at the farmhouse. How about you grab that picnic lunch, because I need a distraction in a big way."

"I thought my picnic was too girly for you."

"Hunger's put me in touch with my feminine side. Sexual frustration, on the other hand, has put me in touch with my killer instincts. Tell me you didn't forget the wine."

"It's a stakeout, you pansy, not a cocktail party. Go use those binoculars while I put out the food."

For once he didn't argue, and while he kept watch, she unpacked her purchases from the morning. She'd bought sandwiches with wafer-thin slices of prosciutto set between rounds of freshly baked focaccia. The salad was made of ripe tomatoes, fresh basil, and farro, a barleylike grain that frequently appeared in Tuscan cuisine. She set it all on a shady section of wall that provided a view of the farmhouse, then added a bottle of mineral water and the remaining pears.

They both seemed to realize that they couldn't endure any more verbal foreplay, so they talked about food and books while they ate—everything but sex. Ren was intelligent, amusing, and better informed than she on a variety of subjects.

She'd just reached for one of the pears when he grabbed his binoculars. "Looks like the party's finally started."

She found her opera glasses and watched as the garden and olive grove gradually filled with people. Massimo and Giancarlo appeared first, along with a man she recognized as Giancarlo's brother Bernardo, who was the local *poliziotto*, or policeman. Anna took her place at the top of the wall with Marta and several other middle-aged women. All of them began to direct the activity of the younger people as they arrived. Isabel recognized the pretty redhead she'd bought flowers from yesterday, the good-looking young man who worked in the Foto shop, and the butcher.

"Look who else is putting in an appearance."

She turned her opera glasses in the direction of Ren's binoculars and saw Vittorio enter the garden with Giulia. They joined a group that had begun taking apart the wall, stone by stone. "I shouldn't be disappointed in them," she said, "but I am."

"Yeah, me, too."

Marta shooed one of the younger men away from her roses.

"I wonder what they're looking for? And why did they have to wait until I moved in to try to find it?"

"Maybe they didn't know it was lost until then." He set aside the binoculars and began stuffing their trash into the bags. "I think it's time to play a little hardball."

"You're not allowed to use anything with a blade or trigger."

"Only as a last resort."

He kept his hand on her arm to steady her as they made their way down the trail to the car. It took only a moment to toss everything inside and set off. He pushed the Panda hard. "We're making a sneak attack," he said as he circled Casalleone instead of taking the most direct route through town. "Everybody in Italy has a cell phone, and I don't want anyone at the farmhouse tipped off that we're heading back."

They abandoned the car on a side road not far from the villa and approached through the woods. He picked a leaf from her hair as they stepped out into the olive grove and walked toward the house.

Anna was the first to spot them. She set down the water pitchers she'd been carrying. Someone turned off a radio that had been playing pop music. Gradually the buzz of conversation stopped, and the crowd shifted. Giulia stepped to Vittorio's side and slipped her hand into his. Bernardo, dressed in his *poliziotto* uniform, stood beside his brother Giancarlo.

Ren stopped at the edge of the grove, surveyed the mess, then surveyed the crowd. He'd never looked more like a natural-born killer, and everyone got the message.

Isabel stepped back so he had plenty of room to work.

He took his time, letting his actor's eyes move from one face to the next, playing the bad guy as only he knew how. When the silence grew unbearable, he finally spoke. In Italian.

She should have realized that this conversation wouldn't be in English, but she hadn't thought about it, and she was so frustrated she wanted to scream.

When he stopped, they all began to respond. It was like watching an army of hyperactive symphony conductors. Gestures toward the heavens, the earth, toward heads and breastbones. Loud outbursts, shrugs, eye-rolling. She hated not knowing what they were saying.

"English," she hissed, but he was too busy sandblasting Anna to pay attention. The housekeeper moved to the front of the crowd, where she responded to him with all the drama of a diva performing a tragic aria.

He finally cut her off and said something to the crowd. When he was done, they began to disperse, muttering to one another.

"What are they saying?" she demanded.

"More nonsense about the well."

"Find their weak point."

"I already have." He stepped farther into the garden. "Giulia, Vittorio, you're not going anywhere."

1 4

Vittorio and Giulia glanced uncomfortably at each other, then moved reluctantly back into the garden. Anna and Marta disappeared, leaving only the four of them. Ren bore in for the kill.

"I want to know what's happening on my property. And don't insult me with any more crap about water problems."

Vittorio looked so uneasy that Isabel almost felt sorry for him. "It's very complicated," he said.

"Simplify it so we can understand," Ren drawled.

Vittorio and Giulia gazed at each other. A trace of stubbornness appeared in her jaw. "We have to tell them, Vittorio."

"No," he said. "Go to the car."

"You go to the car!" Giulia's hands flew. "You and your friends haven't been able to do this. Now it is my turn."

"Giulia . . ." His voice sounded a warning note, but she ignored it.

"This—this goes back to . . . Paolo Baglio, Marta's brother," she said in a rush.

"No more!" Vittorio had the helpless expression of a man who knew he was looking at disaster but couldn't figure out how to stop it.

Giulia pushed past him and faced Ren. "He was—he was the local . . . representative. For . . . the Family."

"The Mafia." Ren sat on the wall, much too comfortable with the subject of organized crime. Vittorio turned away as if his wife's words were too painful for him to hear.

Giulia seemed to be trying to decide how much to tell them. "Paolo was . . . he was responsible for making sure our local businesspeople did not meet with misfortune. You know what I mean by this? That a shopkeeper's windows were not broken at night or that the florist's delivery truck did not disappear."

"Protection money," Ren said.

"Whatever name you wish to give it." She twisted her hands in front of her. They were small and delicate, with a wedding band on one finger and smaller rings on the others. "We are only a country village, but everyone understood how this worked, and the businesspeople paid Paolo the first day of each month. Because of this, windows were not broken, the florist made his deliveries, and there was never any trouble." She turned her wedding band. "Then Paolo had a heart attack and died."

She bit her lip. "At first everything was fine—except for Marta, who missed him very much. But right before you arrived, Isabel, some men came to town. Not nice men. Men from *Naples.*" Her lips pursed, as if she'd tasted something sour. "They—they found our mayor and . . . it is too horrible. But when they were done, we understood that Paolo had been very foolish. He had lied to them about how much money he had collected, and then he had hidden away millions of old-fashioned lire for himself." She pulled in a deep breath. "They have given us a month to find the money and turn it over. And if we don't . . ."

Her words trailed off, and Vittorio came forward. Now that

Giulia had begun, he seemed resigned to finishing the story. "Marta is certain Paolo hid the money somewhere near the house. We know he didn't spend it, and Marta remembers that he was always working on the wall before he died."

"We are running out of time," Giulia said. "We didn't want to lie to you, but what else could we do? It is dangerous for you to be involved, and we only wanted to protect you. Do you understand now, Isabel, why we wished for you to move into town? We are very worried that the men will grow impatient and show up here. And if you should be in their way . . ." She made a sharp, cutting gesture.

"It is very bad, this thing that has happened," Vittorio said. "We must find the money, which means we must finish taking apart the wall as quickly as possible."

"*Sì.* These man are very dangerous."

"Interesting." Ren rose. "I need some time to think about this."

"Please don't take too long." Giulia beseeched him with her eyes.

"We are very sorry we had to lie to you," Vittorio said. "And, Isabel, I am also sorry about that ghost last night. It was Giancarlo. If I had known, I would have put a stop to it. You will still come for dinner next week, yes?"

"And the porcinis?" Giulia said to Isabel. "The next time it rains."

"Of course," Isabel replied.

When the couple left, Isabel sighed and sat down on the wall. For a moment she let herself drink in the peace of the garden, and then she gazed at Ren. "Do you believe them?"

"Not a word."

"Neither do I." She'd started to nibble her thumbnail but caught herself in time. "One thing I do believe: There's something hidden here."

"The country's crawling with buried artifacts." He patted the back pocket of his jeans, then seemed to realize he'd already smoked his daily cigarette. "When an artifact is found, even if it's on private land, it becomes the property of the government. Maybe the good people of Casalleone have a bead on something so valuable they don't want to turn it over."

"You think the entire town's in on a conspiracy? Bernardo's a cop. It doesn't seem too likely."

"Cops have been known to be crooked. Do you have a better idea?" He gazed out at the hills.

"It would have to be one heck of an artifact." A leaf landed on the wall beside her, and she brushed it away. "We need to go along with this, I think."

"I agree. I also intend to be around when they're tearing that wall apart."

"So do I." One of the cats came up and rubbed against her legs. She reached down to pet it.

"I need to get the car, and then I have to go up to the villa for a while, God protect me."

"Good. I have work to do, and you distract me."

"The crisis book?"

"Yes. And don't you dare say a word."

"Not me. So I distract you, do I?"

She tucked her thumbnail into her fist. "I mean it, Ren. Don't bother turning all that smolder on me, because this isn't going any further until we talk."

He sighed and looked resigned. "We can have dinner tonight in San Gimignano. And we'll talk."

"Thank you."

His lips curved in a cocky smile. "But the minute you're done talking, I get to put my hands anywhere I want. And wear something sexy. Preferably low-cut and definitely without underwear."

"You high school boys crack me up. Any other requests?"

"No, I think that about uncovers it." He whistled as he walked away, looking more like a gorgeous goof-off than Hollywood's favorite psychopath.

She took a quick bath, then grabbed a pad of paper and jotted down a few ideas for her book, but her brain wasn't working, so she set the pad aside and made her way up to the villa to see how Tracy was doing.

"Just peachy." Ren's ex-wife lay on the chaise by the pool, her eyes closed. "Harry and the kids hate me, and the new baby is giving me gas."

Isabel had spotted the children climbing out of Harry's car in the drive, their faces smeared with gelato. "If Harry hated you, I don't think he'd still be here."

Tracy raised the back of the chaise and put on her sunglasses. "It's only because he feels guilty about the kids. He'll leave tomorrow."

"Have the two of you tried to talk?"

"I mainly talked, and he acted condescending."

"Why don't you try again? Tonight, after the children are asleep. Pour him a glass of wine and ask him to list three things you could do for him that would make him happy."

"That's easy. Raise my IQ twenty points, get organized instead of pregnant, and change my entire personality."

Isabel laughed. "Feeling a little sorry for ourself, are we?"

Tracy squinted at her over the top of her sunglasses. "You're one weird shrink."

"I know. Think about it, okay? Ask the question, and make it sincere. No sarcasm."

"No sarcasm? You just lost me. So tell me about you and Ren."

Isabel slouched back in the chair. "I'd rather not."

"The good doc can dish it out, but she can't take it. Nice to see I'm not the only screwed-up female sitting around this pool."

"Definitely not. And what can I say other than noting the obvious—I've lost my mind."

"He does that to women."

"I am way out of my league."

"On the other hand, you have a low tolerance for bullshit, so you know exactly what you're getting into. That gives you a distinct advantage over his other women."

"I suppose."

"Mommyyyy!" Connor shot around the corner, his fat blue shorts bobbing from side to side as he ran.

"Hey, big guy!" Tracy rose, scooped him up, and covered his gelato-stained cheeks with kisses. He peered at Isabel over her shoulder and grinned, showing sparkly little teeth.

Something constricted around Isabel's heart. Tracy's life might be in disarray, but it still had its rewards.

Ren grabbed the FedEx envelope he'd been waiting for from the console in the villa's entrance hall and beat a hasty retreat to the master bedroom. He locked the door against small intruders and settled into a chair by the window. As he gazed down at the midnight blue cover with NIGHT KILL typed across it in unassuming letters, he felt a sense of anticipation he hadn't experienced in years. Howard had finally finished the script.

He knew from their initial discussions that Howard's intention was to challenge audiences with the film's fundamental question: Was Kaspar Street simply a psychopath, or, more disturbing, was he the inevitable by-product of a society that took violence for granted? Even Saint Isabel would have to approve of that message. He smiled as he remembered the way she'd looked less than an hour ago, with the sun shining in her hair and those beautiful eyes drinking him in. He loved the way she smelled, like spice, sex, and human goodness. But he couldn't think about her now, not when his entire career was about to open up. He settled back and began to read.

Two hours later he was in a cold sweat. This was the best work

Jenks had ever done. The part of Street had dark twists and subtle nuances that would stretch Ren's acting chops to the limit. It was no wonder every actor in Hollywood had wanted a shot at this film.

But there'd been a major change since they'd last spoken, a change Howard hadn't discussed with Ren. With one brilliant stroke he'd intensified the film's theme and turned it into an existential nightmare. Instead of being a man who preyed on the women he loved, Kaspar Street was now a child molester.

Ren leaned back and shut his eyes. The change was pure genius, but . . .

No buts. This was the part that would put him on the A-list of every top director in Hollywood.

He grabbed some paper to begin making notes on the character. This was always the first step for him, and he liked to do it immediately after his initial reading, while his impressions were still fresh. He'd jot down sensory memories, ideas about costume and physical movement, anything that came to mind that would eventually help him build the character.

He toyed with the cap of the pen. Usually the ideas flowed, but the change Jenks had made had thrown him off balance, and nothing was happening. He needed more time to absorb it. He'd try again tomorrow.

Several hours later, as he headed back to the farmhouse, he decided not to mention the change to Isabel. No sense in getting her all riled up. Not now. Not when their long waiting game was about to come to an end.

Isabel ignored Ren's suggestion that she wear something sexy and chose her most conservative black sundress, then added a black fringed shawl scattered with tiny gold stars to cover her bare shoulders. She was feeding the cats when she heard movement behind her. A tiny pulse jumped in her throat. She turned to see an angsty-looking intellectual standing in the doorway. With his rumpled hair, wire-rimmed glasses, clean but wrinkled shirt, well-worn khakis, and the backpack slung over one shoulder, he looked like Ren Gage's poetically inclined younger brother.

She smiled. "I was wondering who my date would be tonight."

He took in her subdued outfit and sighed. "I knew a miniskirt was too much to hope for."

Outside she saw a silver Alfa-Romeo parked behind her Panda. "Where did this come from?"

"My car won't be ready for a while, so I had this delivered to hold me over."

"People buy candy bars to hold them over, not cars."

"Only poor people like you."

The city of San Gimignano sat like a crown on the hilltop, its fourteen watchtowers dramatically outlined against the setting sun. Isabel tried to imagine how the pilgrims on their way from Northern Europe to Rome must have felt as they caught their first sight of the city. After the hazards of the open road, this would have looked like a haven of strength and security.

Ren's thoughts had apparently taken the same path as hers. "To do this right, we should really approach by foot."

"I don't think these heels were designed for pilgrimages. It's beautiful, isn't it?"

"The best-preserved medieval town in Tuscany. In case you didn't have time to read your guidebook, that's a lucky accident."

"What do you mean?"

"This was an important city until the Black Death wiped out most of the population."

"Just like the castle."

"Definitely a tough time to go without antibiotics. San Gimignano was no longer a major stop on the pilgrimage route and lost its status. Fortunately for us, the few citizens who survived didn't have the money to modernize the place, which is why so many of the watchtowers are still standing. Parts of *Tea with Mussolini* were filmed here." A tour bus whizzed by in the opposite direction. "That's the new Black Death," he said. "Too many tourists. But the town's so small that most of them don't stay overnight. Anna told me it clears out by late afternoon."

"You talked to her again?"

"I gave her permission to have the wall taken apart starting tomorrow, but only if I'm around to supervise."

"I'll bet she didn't like that."

"Ask me if I care. I put Jeremy in charge of guard duty."

Ren parked in the lot just outside the ancient walls and slung the backpack over his shoulders. Although his angsty intellectual's disguise didn't hide as much of him as his other disguises had, most of the sightseers had left, and he didn't attract too much attention as they toured the town.

He shared what he knew about the frescoes in the twelfth-century Romanesque church and was remarkably patient as she poked into the shops. Afterward they walked through the narrow, hilly streets to the Rocca, the town's ancient fortress, and climbed its surviving tower to gaze out at the view of distant hills and fields, spectacular in the fading evening light.

He pointed toward the vineyards. "They're growing grapes for vernaccia, the local white wine. What do you say we sample some of it with our dinner while we have that talk you're so keen on?"

His slow smile made her skin prickle, and she nearly told him she wanted to forget both the wine and their talk so they could go straight to bed. But she was too bruised to handle any more blows, and she needed to do this right.

The small dining room at the Hotel Cisterna had stone walls, peach linen tablecloths, and another of the spectacular views that Tuscany gave away for free. From their table tucked in a corner between a set of windows, they could look down on the sloping, red tile rooftops of San Gimignano and watch the lights come on in the houses and farms that surrounded the town.

He lifted his wineglass. "To talking. May this conversation be mercifully short and wildly productive."

As she took a sip of the crisp vernaccia, she reminded herself that women who didn't claim their own power got stomped on. "We're going to have an affair."

"Thank you, God."

"But we're doing it on my terms."

"Now, there's a surprise."

"Do you have to be sarcastic about everything? Because if you do, I need to tell you right now that it's not attractive."

"You're just as sarcastic as I am."

"Which is why I know how unappealing it is."

"Just go on, will you? I can tell you're dying to lay out your terms. And I'm hoping 'lay' is the operative word here, or is that too sarcastic for you?"

He was already enjoying himself.

"Here's what we need to be clear about." She ignored the fact that his eyes were flashing a dozen different kinds of amusement. She didn't care. Too many women lost their spirit to their lovers, but she wouldn't be one of them. "First . . . you can't criticize."

"Why the hell would I want to do that?"

"Because I'm not the sexual triathlete you are, and because I threaten you, which you don't like."

"Okay. No criticism. And you *don't* threaten me."

"Number two . . . I won't participate in anything kinky. Just straightforward sex."

Behind the lenses of those scholarly glasses, his silver-blue wolf's eyes grew cagey. "What's your definition of straightforward?"

"The accepted definition."

"Got it. No groups. No toys. No Saint Bernard. Disappointing, but I can live with it."

"Forget it! Just forget it." She threw down her napkin. "You are *way* out of my league, and I don't know why I entertained the notion, even for a moment, that we could go ahead with this."

"Sorry. I was getting bored." He leaned across the table to flip her napkin back into her lap. "Do you want strict missionary position, or would you rather be on top?"

Leave it to him to try to turn this into a joke. Tough. Men had dozens of ways of protecting the illusion of their superiority, but she wasn't buying into any of them. "We can be spontaneous about that."

"Can we take our clothes off?"

"You can. As a matter of fact, it's a requirement."

He smiled. "If you don't want to undress, that's fine with me. A nice pair of black fishnets and a garter belt should help retain your sense of modesty."

"You're all heart." She traced the rim of her wineglass with her finger. "Stating the obvious, this is only going to be about our bodies. There won't be an emotional component."

"If you say so."

Now came the tough part, but she wasn't backing off. "One more item . . . I won't engage in oral sex."

"And why is that?"

"It's just not my thing. A little too . . . earthy."

"You know, you're kind of limiting my options here."

She set her jaw. "Take it or leave it."

Oh, he was going to take it all right, Ren thought as he watched that delectable mouth set in a mulish line. He'd made love both on-screen and off- to the most beautiful women in the world, but not one of those exquisite faces had as much life going on behind it as Isabel's. He saw intelligence, humor, determination, and an over-riding compassion for the human condition. Even so, all he could think about was scooping her up right this minute and carrying her to the nearest bed. Unfortunately, Dr. Fifi wasn't exactly a scoopable sort of woman, not when she had an agenda. He wouldn't be surprised if she whipped out some kind of contract and made him sign it first.

The pulse fluttering lightly in her throat encouraged him. She wasn't nearly as self-possessed as she pretended to be. "I'm feeling a little insecure," he said.

"Why should you feel insecure? You're getting what you want."

He knew he was working with a short rope, yet he refused to let her call all the shots. "But what I want seems to have some big warning stickers plastered across it."

"You're just not used to women openly communicating their needs. I understand that might feel threatening."

Who would have figured a great brain could be so sexy? "Regard-less, my ego's getting pretty deflated."

"Metaphysically speaking, that's a good thing."

"Physically speaking, it isn't. I want to believe I'm irresistible to you."

"You're irresistible."

"Could you manage to sound a little more enthusiastic?"

"It's a sore point."

"My irresistibility?"

"Yes."

He smiled. This was more like it.

The waiter arrived with an antipasto that included sausage, olives, and golden bites of deep-fried vegetables. Ren chose one and reached across the table to hold it to her lips. "Okay, just to summarize the agenda: no criticism and no oral sex. That's what you said, right? Nothing too kinky."

He'd hoped he could get another rise out of her, but she was made of stronger stuff. "That's what I said."

He slipped the morsel between her lips. "I guess I shouldn't ask about whips or paddles."

She didn't even bother responding to that silliness. Instead, she took a delicate dab at the corner of her mouth with her napkin.

"Or handcuffs," he said.

"Handcuffs?" The napkin stalled halfway to her lap.

Was this a spark of interest? She looked flustered, but he wasn't stupid enough to let her see that he'd noticed. "Forget it. I was being disrespectful, and I apologize."

"A-apology accepted."

He heard that little stammer and fought down a chuckle. So, Ms. Control Freak might not be averse to a little light bondage. Even though he had a pretty good idea which one of them was going to end up in handcuffs, he decided it was a good start. He just hoped to hell she wouldn't lose the key.

Ren took every excuse he could find to touch her during the meal. His legs brushed hers under the table. He stroked her knee. He played with her fingers and fed her tidbits from his plate. In a corny move he must have picked up from one of his films, he rubbed his thumb over her bottom lip. How calculated could a man get? And every bit of it was working.

He pushed aside his empty cup of cappuccino. The meal had been delicious, but she couldn't remember a thing she'd eaten. "Are you finished?" he asked.

Oh, she was finished all right.

When she nodded, he led her from the dining room toward a crooked flight of stairs, but instead of descending, he steered her up.

"Where are we going?"

"I thought you might like a bird's-eye view of the piazza."

She'd seen enough views for today. She wanted to get back to the farmhouse. Or maybe he'd like to do it in the car. She'd never done it in a car, but tonight seemed like a good time for new experiences. "I think I'll pass on the view. Maybe we should head for the car."

"Not so fast. I know you're going to want to see this." With his hand on her elbow, he turned down a corridor and pulled a heavy European room key from his pocket.

"When did you get that?"

"You didn't really think I was going to give you a chance to change your mind, did you?"

The room was tiny, with gilt moldings, a swirl of cherubs frescoed over the ceiling, and a double bed with a simple white counterpane. "The only one they had left, but I think it'll do, don't you?" He set down his backpack.

"Very nicely." She kicked off her sandals, determined not to let him take over. After she'd dropped her shawl on a straight-backed chair, she set down her purse, pulled out a condom, and marched over to place it on the bedside table. Naturally, that made him laugh.

"Not too optimistic, are you?" He took off his glasses and tossed them aside.

"I have more."

"Of course you do." He turned to lock the door. "And so, by the way, do I."

She reminded herself that tonight had nothing to do with love or permanency. It was about sex, the predictable outcome of being around Lorenzo Gage. And right now he was her personal plaything. Oh, he did look delicious.

She tried to make up her mind where to start. Should she undress him first? Unwrap him like a birthday present? Or did she want to kiss him?

He set the key on the dresser and frowned at her. "Are you making a list?"

"Why do you ask?"

"Because you have that list-making look on your face."

"Makes you nervous, doesn't it?" She slipped across the carpet, wound her arms around his shoulders, and drew his head down far enough so she could reach that great mouth. Then she took a small nip at his bottom lip—*"Hey!"*—just to let him know he had a tiger to contend with.

She grinned, hugged him tighter, and gave him a big, sloppy open-mouth kiss to heal that little wound, all the time making certain it was her tongue that stayed in the driver's seat.

He didn't seem to mind.

She snaked one leg around his calves. He gripped her bottom and lifted her off the ground, which was perfect, because it made her taller than he was, and, oh, she did love a position of superiority. She put a little more of herself into the kiss and slipped one foot between his legs.

He definitely enjoyed that move, and he started walking her backward toward the bed, already trying to take over. "Strip first," she said into his mouth.

"Strip?"

"Uh-huh . . . and make it slow."

He set her on the edge of the bed and gazed down at her, all dangerous sex and raunchy intention. Those chiseled lips barely moved when he spoke. "You sure you're woman enough to deal with it?"

"Fairly certain, yes."

"I don't want you to get ahead of yourself."

"Give me your best shot."

She could tell he was enjoying himself, even though he didn't betray it by so much as a flicker of those dark, spiky eyelashes. She also knew there wouldn't be any muscle flexing or cheesy calendar-boy posing. He was the real thing.

Slowly . . . languidly . . . he unbuttoned his shirt. Taking his time, freeing each button with the barest twist of his fingers. The shirt fell open. Her whisper was husky. "Excellent. I do love having my own private movie star."

The shirt slithered to the floor. He dropped his hand to his belt buckle, but instead of opening it, he cocked an eyebrow at her. "Inspire me first."

She reached under her dress, pulled off her panties, and tossed them aside.

"Excellent," he said. "I do love having my own sexy guru."

By the time he'd cast his belt aside, lost his shoes and socks, and dragged his zipper down the first few inches, she was dry-mouthed. This was definitely a two-thumbs-up performance.

She waited for him to tug his zipper the rest of the way, but he shook his head. "A little more inspiration."

She reached behind herself and dragged her zipper down a lot farther than he'd opened his. Her dress slid off one shoulder. She unclipped her earrings.

"Pathetic." He discarded his slacks and stood before her in a pair of silky, midnight blue boxers, 190 pounds of rough trade, all for her. "Before you see any more, I'm going to require another dose of inspiration."

He was trying to take charge again, but what would be the fun of that for either of them? She crooked her finger in a come-hither gesture she'd never used in her life, never thought to use, and yet she wasn't a bit surprised when he came hither.

She leaned back into the pillows and held out her arms, so ready for him she felt as if she were melting into the covers. He reached down and flicked up her skirt. Not all the way, just to the tops of her thighs, which was far enough to make her skin steam. The mattress dipped as he settled over her. He braced his weight on his forearms so their chests weren't touching and dropped his head.

It was so tempting to answer the invitation of his kiss. But the idea of exerting her own kind of power over this dark-haired beast was too exhilarating to give up, so she scooted out from under and gave him a good push. He obliged by rolling to his back. "This just keeps getting better and better," he said.

"We aim to please."

When she settled on top of him, he couldn't quite keep the devil from his eyes. "Happy?"

She grinned. "Pretty much."

A nicer, more sensitive man would simply have let her do this on her own terms, but he wasn't a nice man, and he nipped her shoulder, biting just hard enough so she felt it, then sucking on the spot. "You shouldn't play with fire unless you're ready to feel the burn."

"You're scaring me." She slid her leg over his hips. "And when I get scared, I get a little hyper." Drawing up her knees, she settled on top of both him and his silky midnight blue boxers.

He sucked in his breath.

She wiggled. "Do I need to slow down a little? I wouldn't want to frighten you."

"Uh . . . no. Stay right where you are." He pushed his hands under her skirt and curled them around her bottom.

She'd never imagined how exquisite it would be to have both her mind and body so aroused at the same time. But she wanted to laugh, too, and the contrast made her dizzy.

"Are you going to sit there all night," he said, "or are you going to . . . get moving?"

"I'm thinking."

"About what?"

"Whether I'm ready for you to excite me."

"You need more *excitement*?"

"Oh, yes . . ."

"That does it!" He pushed her off him and flipped her to her back. "Never expect a woman to do a man's job."

Her skirt flew to her waist. He shoved her thighs apart. "Sorry, sweetheart, but this has to be done." Before she could object, he plunged down on her and buried his mouth.

Rockets shot off inside her head. She let out a low, hoarse cry.

"Hang on," he muttered against her wet flesh. "It'll be over before you know it."

She tried to clamp her legs together, but his head was there, and her knees wouldn't have shut anyway, because it was all too exquisite.

His tongue delved, his lips stroked, and wild shards of sensation made her feel as if she were floating up off the bed. He could have teased her, but didn't—and she flew.

When she came back to herself, the midnight-blue boxers were gone. He rolled her on top, then pushed inside, not quite all the way. His expression grew tender, and he reached up to brush a lock of hair from her face. "It was necessary."

To her astonishment, her voice worked, although it croaked. "I told you I didn't want you to do that."

"Punish me."

Oh, she wanted to laugh, but he'd stretched her full, and she was languid and hot and ready for more.

"I'm only wearing one." He tilted his head toward the condom wrapper on the bed. "You'll have to hope for the best."

"Go ahead and make fun of me, lover boy. You won't be laughing for long." She crossed her arms over her body and pulled off her dress, conscious of the feel of him embedded inside her, almost— but not quite—all the way.

He drew her fingers to his mouth and kissed them. Now she wore only a black lacy bra and her gold bangle with BREATHE engraved inside. Slowly, she began to move, reveling in her power, feeling every inch a woman who could satisfy a man like this.

His hands didn't stay still for long. They flicked open her bra and tossed it aside so he could claim her breasts. Then he gripped her bottom and stroked her where their bodies met. Finally he drew her down so he could have her mouth. His hips thrust beneath her, and she wanted it to be as wonderful for him as it was for her, so even as their mouths mated, she forced herself to hold back, move slower and slower, ignore her own body's fierce demand.

His skin gleamed with sweat. His muscles quivered. She moved slower . . . Slower still . . . She was dying, and so was he, and he could have driven into her to finish off, but he didn't, and she knew that the effort was costing him. Costing her . . . But she went even slower.

Slower still. Barely moving.

Only the slightest friction . . . The smallest contraction . . .

Until even that . . .

. . . was too much.

15

The bells of San Gimignano rang softly through the morning rain. The hotel room had grown chilly during the night, and Isabel huddled deeper into the covers, warm and safe, sheltered by the ancient watchtowers and ghosts of the faithful.

Last night had been a pilgrimage for her. She smiled into her pillow and rolled to her back. She'd been in control, out of control, mindless and mindful, and every bit of it had been wonderful. Ren had been an indefatigable lover—no surprise there. The surprise had been that she'd kept up with him.

Now she was alone in the room. With a yawn, she threw her feet over the side and made her way to the bathroom. She found his backpack lying unzipped on the floor beneath her black fringed shawl. Inside she located a toothbrush and a tube of toothpaste missing its top. He'd planned ahead, something she always appreciated.

After a quick bath she wrapped herself in one of the hotel's big towels and looked inside the backpack to see if he'd thought to bring a comb. No comb, but a red lace thong.

He poked his head in the door. "A small token of my affection. As soon as you put it on, I'll share breakfast with you."

"It's not even nine o'clock. You're up awfully early."

"Day's a-wastin'. Things to do." He smiled at her in a way that indicated exactly what those things might be.

"Leave me alone while I get dressed."

"And exactly why would you want to do that?"

Ren had never seen anything as cute as Dr. Fifi all rumpled and damp from her bath, curls everywhere, cheeks glowing, nose shiny with freckles. But there wasn't anything innocent about her curvy body or that bright red thong dangling from her competent little fingers.

Last night had been crazy. She was either ordering him around like a dominatrix or lying limp and pliable in his arms. It had been more fun than he'd ever had with a woman, and he couldn't wait for the fun to start all over again. "Come here."

"Oh no you don't. I'm hungry. What did you bring me?"

"Nothing. Drop that towel."

She twirled the thong on her finger. "I smell coffee."

"Your imagination."

"I don't think so. Pour. I'll be out in a minute."

He shut the door, smiled again, and retrieved the white paper sack containing the coffee and rolls he'd bought. The guy behind the counter had recognized him, which had forced Ren into signing autographs for the man's relatives, but he'd been feeling too good to mind.

The bathroom door swung open, and he nearly spilled his coffee. She stood framed in the doorway wearing only her black fringed shawl and the lacy red thong he'd bought on impulse yesterday.

"Is this what you had in mind?"

"Even better."

She smiled, flicked her shoulders, and let the shawl drop.

By the time they got to the coffee, it was stone cold

"I love San Gimignano," she said as they drove home through the rain. "I could have stayed there forever."

He hid his smile and turned the windshield wipers up a notch. "You're going to give me money again, aren't you?"

"Dude, if anybody's handing out money for sexual favors, it should be you, because I was pretty darned good. Admit it."

She looked so happy with herself he didn't even think of disputing her. "You were world-class."

"I thought so, too."

He laughed and wanted to kiss her again, but she lectured when he took his hands off the wheel.

She let one sandal swing from her toes as she crossed her legs. "If you were to give me a number, what would it be?"

"A number?"

"A ranking."

"You want me to *rank* you?" Just when he thought she'd lost the ability to surprise him, she hit him in the head with her personal clapper board.

"Yes."

"Don't you think that's a little demeaning?"

"Not if I'm the one asking."

He was no fool, and he recognized a snake pit when he saw it. "Why do you want this ranking?"

"Not because I'm being competitive—don't flatter yourself. I just want an idea of my current level of competence from the viewpoint of a recognized authority. How far I've come. And—in the interest of self-improvement—how far I have to go."

"That 'coming' part . . ."

"Answer the question."

"Okay." He relaxed back into the seat. "I have to be honest. You weren't number one. Are you all right with that?"

"Go on."

He took a hairpin turn. "Number one was a highly accomplished French courtesan."

"Ah, well, a Frenchwoman."

"Number two spent her formative years in a Middle Eastern harem, and you can hardly expect to compete with that, right?"

"I suppose not. Although I do think—"

"As for number three, that's iffy. Either a bisexual contortionist for the Cirque du Soleil or a pair of red-haired twins with an interesting fetish. Number four—"

"Just cut to the chase."

"Fifty-eight."

"Go ahead. Have your fun."

"Oh, I am."

She gave him a cute smirk and wiggled deeper in her seat. "I wasn't serious anyway. I have way too much confidence in myself to care how you rank me. I just wanted to make you squirm."

"I don't seem to be the only one squirming. Maybe you're feeling a little more insecure than you're letting on."

"It's the thong." She tugged at it through her skirt. "Truly a garment for desperate women."

"I enjoyed it."

"I noticed. You understand, don't you, that you have to move back to the villa now?"

Just like that, she'd slammed him with the clapper board again. "What are you talking about?"

"I'm prepared to have an affair with you, but I'm not prepared for us to live together."

"We were living together yesterday."

"That was before last night."

"I'm not stumbling back to the villa at five o'clock in the morning." He punched the accelerator harder than necessary. "And if you think we won't be sleeping together again, then you must have a short memory."

"I didn't say you couldn't stay overnight occasionally. I just said you couldn't keep living at the farmhouse."

"A fine distinction."

"An important one." Isabel understood the difference, and she suspected he did, too. She touched her bangle. She couldn't stay centered unless she had plenty of time alone to catch her breath. "Our affair is only about having sex." He took his eyes off the road long enough to shoot her his killer's scowl, but she ignored it. "Living together complicates that."

"I don't see what's so complicated about it."

"When two people live together, they're making an emotional commitment."

"Wait a min—"

"Oh, stop looking so horrified. You're only proving my point. We're having a short-term physical relationship, with no emotional component. All you're getting from me is my body. That should be good news."

His expression grew blacker, something she didn't understand, since she'd just outlined a perfect relationship from his point of view. He must be balking because she was the one who was laying out the terms. Predictable gender-driven behavior. But she couldn't take anything for granted when it came to this man, and she plunged on. "Just to make certain we're clear about this . . . as long as we're having sex, we'll both be faithful."

"Will you stop talking about 'having sex'? You make it sound like a flu strain. And I don't need any lectures about fidelity."

"I'm not lecturing."

That made him laugh.

"All right," she conceded. "Maybe I was lecturing. Go ahead. It's your turn."

"I get a turn?"

"Of course. I'm certain you have some conditions."

"Damn right."

She watched him try to think of a few and resisted the urge to make suggestions.

"Okay," he said. "I'll move my stuff out as soon as we get back. But if we're 'having sex,' I'm not going home afterward."

"All right."

"And if we're *not* 'having sex,' and I'm forced to spend the night at the villa with those hooligans you foisted on me, then don't expect me to be in a good mood the next day. If I want to pick a fight, I get to."

"Fine." She uncrossed her legs. "But you can't say 'shut up.'"

"Shut up."

"One other thing . . ."

"No other thing."

"Last night you crossed a boundary. And just because I was mistaken about establishing that particular boundary, that doesn't mean I want you to keep doing it."

His eyes grew sly. "Tell me which boundary I crossed."

"You know which boundary."

"Talk dirty to me. Was it the one where you had your knees locked around—"

"That would be it."

"Baby, when you're wrong, you're wrong." He gave a diabolic chuckle. "*Really* wrong. And it has me wondering—"

"I don't know. I'm thinking about it."

"How do you even know what I'm going to ask?"

"I'm extremely perceptive. You're a man, and you'd like a little reciprocity."

"It's not a deal breaker. I'm more than happy with the way things are."

"That's nice to know."

"And I don't want you to feel pressured."

"Thank you. I won't."

"The only reason I'm even bringing this up is to reassure you. I just wanted you to know that if you ever decided to . . . get adventurous, I promise I'll be a perfect gentleman."

"How could you be anything else?"

"You understand me so well."

The rain kept all of them trapped inside the villa through the morning and into the early afternoon. Harry roamed from one room to another with his cell phone pressed to his ear, avoiding only those rooms Tracy happened to be in. Tracy played Barbies until she wanted to rip the little anorexic bitch's head off. She tried to keep Jeremy entertained with card games he didn't want to play. The kids fought, Connor was pulling on his ear, and her ankles had started to swell, which meant that she needed to lay off salt, and what was the point of life without salt? Just thinking about it made her want to lick her way through a bag of potato chips.

She finally got Connor down for a nap, the rain stopped, and the other kids ran outside to play. She was ready to weep with gratitude, except that watching Harry place yet another call on his cell made her upset all over again. She thought about what Isabel had said—the question she was supposed to ask—what three things could she do that would make him happy? What about the things he could do to make her happy? At that moment she hated Isabel Favor nearly as much as she hated Harry.

He made the mistake of walking past her just as she tripped over the case to his laptop that Connor had been dragging around. She picked it up and threw it at him. He didn't yell, but then Harry never yelled. She was the yeller in the family. He simply ended his call and gave her his disapproving look, the same one he turned on the children when they misbehaved. "I'm sure you had a reason for that."

"I'm only sorry it wasn't a chair. It's been raining like hell all morning, and you haven't once helped with the kids."

"I had an emergency conference call. I told you that. I've canceled all my meetings and rescheduled two presentations, but I needed to take care of this."

She knew he was at a critical point in the project, and he'd already stayed around longer than she'd ever dreamed he would. He'd also spent more hours with the kids since he'd arrived than she had, but she hurt too much to care about being fair. She only cared about being right. "I wish I had the luxury of deciding I could pick up the phone anytime I wanted." When had she turned into such a shrew?

When her husband had stopped loving her.

"Just calm down, will you? For once in your life could you at least pretend to be reasonable?"

Distancing her . . . always distancing her. Pretending her feelings didn't count just so he wouldn't have to deal with them. "What's the point, Harry? Why pretend anything? I'm pregnant again, you can't stand being around me, you don't even like me. God, I'm sick of you."

"Stop being so melodramatic. I'll get used to having another kid. You blow things out of proportion just because you get bored and want to entertain yourself."

All he did was belittle her. She couldn't tolerate another minute of his cool detachment, another second of knowing how little their love meant to him.

"This overreacting is because of your pregnancy," he said. "Your hormones have made you completely irrational."

"I wasn't pregnant a year ago. Was I irrational when we took that trip to Newport and you spent all your time on the phone?"

"That was an emergency."

"There's always an emergency!"

"What do you want me to do? Tell me, Tracy. What can I do to make you happy?"

"Just show up!"

His expression was cold and flat. "Try to get control of yourself, will you?"

"So I can turn into a robot like you? No thanks."

He shook his head. "This is all a waste of time. My staying here. I'm just wasting my time."

"So leave! It's what you want to do anyway. Drive away so you don't have to deal with your fat, hysterical wife."

"Maybe I will."

"Go!"

"You've got it! As soon as I say good-bye to the kids, I'm out of here." He kicked aside the laptop case and stalked away.

Tracy dropped into the chair and began to cry. She'd finally done it. She'd finally driven him off for good.

"Tell me, Tracy. What can I do to make you happy?"

For a moment she wondered if Isabel had gotten to him, too. But no, his question had been a whiplash. Still, she wished she'd told him the truth.

Love me, Harry. Just love me like you used to.

Harry found his oldest son and youngest daughter in front of the villa. As he pulled Brittany down from one of the statues Jeremy had dared her to climb, he realized he was sweating underneath his shirt. He couldn't let his children see his despair, and he forced a smile. "Where's Steffie?"

"Dunno," Jeremy said.

"Sit down, guys. I have something to tell you."

"You're leaving again, aren't you?" Jeremy's bright blue eyes, exactly the same color as his mother's, regarded him accusingly. "You're going back to Zurich, and you and Mom are getting a divorce."

"We're not getting a divorce." But that was the next logical step, and Harry's chest hurt so much he could barely breathe. "I need to get back to work, that's all."

Jeremy looked at him as if Harry had shot out the sun.

"It's no big deal. Really." Harry hugged them both and drew them down onto one of the benches, where he said all the right things, except he couldn't tell them when he'd see them next or whether it would be here or in Zurich. He couldn't plan, couldn't think. He hadn't slept well in months. The past two nights, with the kids curled against him, he'd been able to sleep a little, but it hadn't been that deep, peaceful state he could fall into when Tracy threw her arms over his chest and his dreams held the sweet, exotic scent of her wild black hair.

"I'll be seeing you again before you know it."

"When?" Jeremy had always been more like Tracy than Harry. His oldest son had a tough exterior, but beneath that he was emotional and very sensitive. What would this do to him?

"I'll call you every day," Harry said, giving him the best answer he could.

Brittany stuck her thumb in her mouth and kicked off her shoes. "I don't want you to go."

Thank God Connor was still asleep. Harry couldn't have borne the feeling of those trusting little arms wrapped around his neck, those sticky kisses plastering his jaw. All that unconditional love from the son he hadn't wanted. How could he expect Tracy to forgive him for that when he hadn't forgiven himself? And the new pregnancy had stirred it all up again.

He knew he'd love this baby once it was born. Damn it, Tracy understood him well enough to know that, too. But he hated the fact that only more children could make her complete. Never just him.

He needed to find Steffie, but he dreaded breaking the news to her. She was a natural worrier like him. While the other children clamored for his attention, she held back, a little pucker of concern on her forehead, as if she weren't sure she deserved her place with the rest of them. Sometimes she broke his heart. He wished he knew how to toughen her up.

Jeremy started kicking the bench. Brittany pulled on her sundress. He couldn't think about what he was doing to either of them right now. "Go look for Steffie, will you? I'll be back in a few minutes."

He gave them a reassuring smile and set off for the farmhouse and Tracy's ex-husband. He should have done this two days ago, but the son of a bitch had been elusive.

Ren stood by the farmhouse door and watched Harry Briggs coming toward him. The rain had cooled the air, and Ren had been about to go for a run, but it seemed that would have to wait.

He'd always had a secret admiration for guys like Briggs, mathematical whizzes with high-powered brains and low-key emotions. Men who didn't have to spend their workday digging into their internal cesspools looking for memories and emotions they could draw on to help them convince an audience they were capable of murder. Or of molesting a child.

Ren pushed the thought aside. He'd simply have to find another way to look at it. This evening he'd sit down with his notebook and get to work.

He met Harry next to Isabel's Panda. Harry wore a pin-striped shirt, slacks with a knife-edge pleat, and polished loafers, but there was a smudge on his glasses that looked like a tiny thumbprint. Ren slouched like a badass against the side of the Panda just to irritate him. Since Briggs had made Tracy miserable, he didn't deserve anything better, the cheating bastard.

"I'm going back to Zurich," Briggs said stonily. "But before I leave, I'm warning you to watch yourself. Tracy's vulnerable right now, and I don't want you doing anything to upset her."

"Why don't I just leave that up to you?"

The cords in Briggs's neck tightened. "I mean it, Gage. If you try to manipulate her in any way, you'll regret it."

"You're boring me, Briggs. If you cared so much, you wouldn't have screwed around on her, now, would you?"

Not even a flicker of guilt crossed his face, which seemed odd for an uptight guy like Briggs. Ren remembered that Isabel had reservations about Tracy's story, and decided to poke around a little. "Funny, isn't it, that she came running to me when she started to hurt? And you know what else is funny? I might have been a shitty husband, but I stayed away from other women when we were married." Pretty much anyway.

Harry began to respond, but whatever he'd been about to say got lost as Jeremy shouted from the top of the hill. "Dad, we've looked everywhere, and nobody can find Steffie."

Harry's head shot up. "Did anybody check the pool?"

"Mom's there now. She said to come right away!"

Briggs started to run.

Ren took off after him.

16

S teffie wasn't in the pool or hiding in the gardens. They fanned out to search every room of the house, including the attic and the wine cellar, but she wasn't anywhere. Harry's complexion took on an ashen hue as Ren made the call to the local police.

"I'll take the car and look along the road," Harry said after Ren had hung up. "Jeremy, I need another set of eyes. You come with me."

"I'll search the grove and the vineyard," Ren said. "Isabel, maybe Steffie's hiding in the farmhouse. Why don't you check that out? Tracy, you have to stay here in case she comes back."

Tracy reached for Harry's hand. "Find her. Please."

For a moment they simply gazed at each other. "We'll find her," he said.

Isabel had her eyes closed, so Ren knew she was praying, and for once he was glad. Steffie seemed too timid to wander off. But if she hadn't wandered off, and there hadn't been some kind of accident, that left only one alternative. He pushed away the ugly thoughts that had started working overtime in his brain. The *Night Kill* script was doing a number on him.

"She'll be fine," Isabel whispered to Tracy. "I know it." With a reassuring smile, she set off for the farmhouse.

Ren headed through the wet garden toward the vineyard, the muscles in his neck growing more tense with every step. That damned script . . . He reminded himself that this wasn't the city, where predators skulked in alleyways and hung out in abandoned buildings. They were in the country.

But Kaspar Street had found one of his victims in the country, a seven-year-old girl, riding her bicycle down a dirt road.

It's a movie, for chrissake!

He forced himself to concentrate on the real instead of the imaginary and mentally divided the vineyard into sections. It was barely three o'clock, but so cloudy it was hard to see. The mud from the earlier rainstorm tugged at his running shoes as he began making his way along the rows. Tracy said Steffie had been wearing red shorts. He kept his eyes peeled for a flash of color. Wherever she was, he hoped there weren't any spiders.

Street would have used spiders.

The back of his neck tightened. He absolutely could not think about Street now. *Come on, Steffie. Where are you?*

Tracy gave Bernardo a photo of Steffie she kept in her wallet when he showed up in response to Ren's call. She asked Anna to stay by her side as an interpreter so there wouldn't be any miscommunication. Occasionally she stopped to reassure Brittany and cuddle Connor, but nothing could keep her terror at bay. Her precious little girl . . .

Isabel searched the farmhouse, but no child had hidden herself away there. She checked the garden, peered beneath the wisteria that grew over the pergola. Finally she grabbed a flashlight and headed for the pie-shaped section of woods that ran close to the road, between the villa and the farmhouse. As she walked, every step she took was a prayer.

Harry inched along the road, with Jeremy keeping watch on the right while he watched the left. The clouds had begun to boil in the sky, and visibility was growing more limited by the minute.

"Do you think she's dead, Dad?"

"No!" He swallowed the lump of fear in his throat. "No, Jeremy. She just went for a walk and got lost."

"Steffie doesn't like walks. She's too afraid of spiders."

Something Harry had been trying to forget.

A splatter of raindrops hit the windshield. "She's fine," Harry said. "She's just lost, that's all."

The rain was coming down so hard that Ren wouldn't have noticed the storehouse door if a bolt of lightning hadn't flashed just as he slogged past it. Two days ago it had been locked. Now it wasn't shut all the way.

He swiped the rain from his eyes. It was unlikely that a child with a fear of spiders would go inside, at least not voluntarily. He remembered how the door had dragged in the dirt. She wouldn't have been strong enough to open it herself. But someone else could have opened it and carried her inside. . . .

Kaspar Street had him spooked. He headed for the door. As he pulled on it, he noticed it didn't drag nearly as much as it had. The rain must have washed away some of the dirt. He pushed it back on its hinges.

Inside, it was dry and dark as hell, even with the door open. As he skirted a pile of boxes, he wished he had a flashlight.

"Steffie?"

There was no sound except the thud of rain. He banged his shin against one of the wooden crates. It shifted on the dirt floor, making just enough noise that he nearly missed it.

The sound of a sniffle.

Or maybe he'd imagined it. "Steffie?"

There was no response.

Resisting the urge to push through the clutter, he stayed where he was and let several seconds tick by, until he finally heard it again, a muffled sob coming from the back, just off to his left.

Relief shot through him. He started to move, then hesitated. He didn't know what he'd find, and if he weren't careful, he'd frighten her more. God, he didn't want to do that.

"You don't want to frighten the little ones. Not until it's too late for them to get away."

His stomach lurched. He'd read the script only once, but he had a good memory, and too many lines had stuck.

"Steffie?" He spoke softly. "Everything's going to be okay."

He heard a rustle, but no response. "It's all right," he said. "You can talk to me."

A tiny, frightened whisper traveled through the gloom. "Are you a monster?"

He squeezed his eyes shut. *Not now, sweetheart, but give me another month.* "No, honey," he said quietly. "It's Ren."

He waited.

"P-please, go away."

Even in the face of her terror, she'd remembered her manners. *"Polite little girls are the easiest victims,"* Street said in the script. *"Their need to please outweighs their survival instincts."*

He was cold and clammy from the rain, but he started to sweat. Why did *he* have to be the one to find her? Why couldn't it have been her father or Isabel? He moved as quietly as he could. "Everybody's looking for you, honey. Your parents are worried."

He heard something shift in the dirt. She was moving also, too frightened, he suspected, to let him come closer. But what had frightened her?

He hated the feeling that he was stalking her. Even more, he hated the way he automatically added that emotion to the teeming garbage heap inside him that made up his actor's stockpile—the place he visited when he needed to access the ugliness of the human condition. Every actor had one of those stockpiles, but he suspected that his was more squalid than most.

Only an act of desperation could have forced her in here. Unless she'd been given no choice. . . . "Are you hurt?" He kept his voice calm. "Did anybody hurt you?"

Her breath caught on a soft, frightened hiccup. "There are . . . lots of spiders in here."

Instead of going after her and upsetting her more, he moved back toward the door so there was no chance she could slip past him. "Did you . . . did you come in here by yourself?"

"The d-door was open, and I squeezed in."

"By yourself?"

" 'Cause I was afraid of the thunder. But I didn't know it would be so . . . dark."

He couldn't shake off the shadow of Street. "Are you sure you didn't come here with somebody?"

"No. By myself."

He let himself relax. "That door's pretty heavy. How did you close it?"

"I pulled real hard with both hands."

He drew a full breath. "You must be really strong to do that. Let me feel your muscles."

A sucker was born every minute, but she wasn't one of them. "No thank you."

"Why not?"

"Because . . . you don't like kids."

You've got me there. He was definitely going to have to work on his relationship with children before the cameras started to roll. One of the things that made Street such a monster was the way he could enter their world. They didn't sense his evil until it was too late.

He forced himself back to reality. "Hey, I love kids. I used to be a kid myself. I wasn't a good kid like you, though. I got into a lot of trouble."

"I think I'm going to be in trouble."

You can bet on that. "Naw, they're going to be so happy to have you back that you're not going to be in any trouble at all."

She wasn't moving, but his eyes had adjusted enough for him to see a dim shape huddled near what looked like an overturned chair. One more time, just to be absolutely certain. "Tell me again, honey. Are you hurt? Did anybody hurt you?"

"No." He saw a slight movement. "Spiders in Italy are very big."

"Yeah, but I can kill them for you. I'm good at that."

She didn't say anything.

While Steffie made up her mind about him, Tracy and Harry were going through the torments of the damned. It was time to get serious. "Steffie, your mom and dad are really scared. I need to take you back to them."

"No thank you. C-could you please go away?"

"I can't do that." Once again he started toward her, taking it slow. "I don't want you to be scared, but I have to come and get you now."

A sniffle.

"I'll bet you're hungry, too."

"You're gonna r-ruin everything." She started to cry. Nothing dramatic. Just a few miserable gulps that tore at him.

He stopped to give her a little time. "What am I going to ruin?"

"E-everything."

"Give me a hint." He slipped sideways between some crates.

"You wouldn't understand."

He was nearly close enough to touch her now, but he didn't. Instead, he crouched in the dirt about five feet away, doing his best to compress his height. "Why is that?"

"J-just because."

He was overcome by his own inadequacy. He didn't know a damn thing about kids, and he had no idea how to handle this. "I've got an idea. You know Dr. Isabel? You like her, don't you? I mean, a lot better than you like me."

Too late, he realized that probably wasn't the best way to phrase a question for an overly polite little girl. "It's okay. My feelings won't be hurt. I like Dr. Isabel a lot, too."

"She's very nice."

"I was thinking . . . She's the kind of person who understands things. Why don't I take you to her so you can tell her what's wrong?"

"Would you go get her for me?"

Tracy hadn't raised a fool. This was going to take a while.

He propped himself against one of the wine crates. "I can't do that, honey. I have to stay with you. But I promise I'll take you to her."

"Would my d-daddy have to know?"

"Yes."

"No thank you."

What was this about? He kept his manner casual. "Are you afraid of your dad?"

"My daddy?"

He heard the surprise in her voice and relaxed. "He seems like a pretty nice guy to me."

"Yes." The word held a universe of misery. "But he's going away."

"I think he just needs to get back to his job. Grown-ups have to work."

"No." The word trailed off on a wispy sob. "He's going away forever and ever and ever."

"Who told you that?"

"I heard him. They had a big fight, and they don't love each other anymore, and he's going away."

So that's what this was about. Steffie had overheard Tracy and Briggs fighting. Now what was he supposed to do? Hadn't he read somewhere that you should help kids verbalize their feelings? "Bummer."

"I don't want him to go," she said.

"I've just met your dad, so I don't know him real well, but I can tell you this: He'd never leave you forever and ever."

"He won't leave at all if I get really lost. He'll have to stay and look for me."

Bingo.

She was a gutsy kid, he'd give her that. She was willing to face her worst fear to keep from losing her father. In the meantime, though, her parents were going crazy with worry. He wasn't proud of himself, but it had to be done. "Don't move! I see a giant poisonous spider!"

She hurled herself at him, and the next thing he knew, she was plastered against his chest, trembling all over, her clothes damp, bare legs icy. He pulled her into his lap and held her close. "It's gone. I don't think it was a spider. I think it was a dust ball."

Little girls didn't smell like big girls, he noticed. She smelled sweaty, but it wasn't unpleasant, and her hair smelled like bubblegum shampoo. He rubbed her arms, trying to get some warmth into her. "I tricked you," he felt bound to confess. "There wasn't really a spider, but your mom and dad are upset, and they need to see that you're all right."

She started to struggle a little then, but he kept rubbing her arms to calm her. At the same time he tried to figure out how Isabel would handle this. Whatever she said would be just right—sensitive, insightful, perfect for the occasion.

Screw it.

"Your plan sucked, Steffie. You couldn't stay hidden forever, right? Sooner or later you'd have to get something to eat, and then you'd be right back where you started from."

"I was worried about that."

She relaxed a little, and he smiled over her head. "What you need is a new plan. One without so many loopholes. And the place to start is by telling your mom and dad what got you so bent out of shape."

"I might hurt their feelings."

"So what? They hurt your feelings, didn't they? A word to the wise, kid: If you go through life trying not to hurt anybody's feelings, you'll turn into a big wimp, and nobody likes a wimp." He could almost see Isabel frowning at him, but what the hell? She wasn't here, and he was doing his best. Still, he offered an amendment. "I'm not saying you should hurt people on purpose. I'm just saying you have to fight for what's important to you, and if somebody's feelings get hurt in the process, that's their problem, not yours." Not much better, but it was the truth.

"They might get mad."

"I didn't want to mention this earlier, but frankly, I think your mom and dad are going to be mad anyway. Not at first. At first they'll be so happy to see you they're going to slobber all over you. But after that wears off—now, I'm just taking a guess here—after that I think you're going to have to do some fancy footwork."

"What's that mean?"

"It means being smart about how you handle yourself so you don't get in too much trouble."

"Like what?"

"Like . . . when they finally stop the slobbering, they're going to start getting upset with you for running away, and that's when you're in the danger zone. You're going to need to lay on the guilt about how you heard them fighting, and—this is the important part—while you're doing that, you should probably cry a little and look pitiful. Can you do that?"

"I'm not sure."

He smiled to himself. "Let's go over to the door, where the light's a little better, and I'll show you. Is that okay?"

"Okay."

He picked her up and carried her to the door. The toes of her sandals banged into his shins. She clung to his neck, too big to be carried but feeling the need. When they reached the door, he crouched down again, ignoring the mud to sit with her on his lap. It had stopped raining, and there was enough light to make out a very dirty, tear-streaked face and solemn, expressive eyes gazing at him as if he were Santa Claus. If she only knew.

"Okay, the idea here is to keep from getting grounded for the rest of your life, right?"

She nodded solemnly.

"So once they calm down, they're going to decide they have to punish you to make sure you never do anything like this again." He whipped her a lethal-weapon look. "And just so we're clear, if you ever *do* decide to pull this crap again, I won't be half as easy to manipulate as your parents, so you'd better promise me right now that you'll figure out a smarter way to solve your problems."

Another solemn nod. "I promise."

"Good." He pushed a little spike of hair away from her face. "When your parents start talking to you about taking the consequences for your actions, that means they're thinking about punishment, so you have to start telling them about why you ran away. And make sure you don't forget to say how bad it made you feel when you heard them fighting because, face it, that's your ace in the hole. Naturally, talking about it is going to make you sad again, which is good, because you're going to use that emotion to look as pitiful as you can. Got it?"

"Do I have to cry?"

"It wouldn't hurt. Let me see how you're going to do it. Give me a real pitiful look."

She gazed up at him, all big sad eyes, just about the most pitiful thing he'd ever seen, except he realized she hadn't started yet, and he nearly laughed as she screwed up her face, pinched her lips, and took a huge, dramatic snuffle.

"You're overplaying your hand, kiddo."

"What d'you mean?"

"Make it more real. Just think about something sad, like being locked in your room for the rest of your life with all your toys taken away, and let it come out on your face."

"Or about having my daddy go away forever?"

"That should do it."

She mulled it over for a minute, and before long she'd worked up some pretty good misery, complete with a lip quiver.

"Excellent." He needed to put a quick end to the acting lesson before she got carried away. "Now give me a quick summary of the script so far."

She dabbed at her nose with the back of a skinny arm. "If they start to get mad, I have to tell them about hearing them fighting and how I feel about Daddy leaving, even if it hurts their feelings. And I can cry when I tell them. I just think about something really sad, like my daddy going away, and look pitiful."

"You got it. Gimme five."

They smacked hands, she grinned, and it was like watching the sun come out.

As he led her by the hand through the wet grass up the hill, he remembered his earlier promise and grimaced. "You don't still need to talk to Dr. Isabel, do you?" The last thing he wanted was for Reverend Feelgood to undermine all his hard work with what would surely be talk of honest repentance. Soon the lip quiver would be yesterday's news.

"I think I'm okay now. But"—she gripped his hand a little tighter—"would you . . . Could you stay with me when I talk to them?"

"I don't think that's a good idea."

"I think it is. If you stayed with me, you could, you know, look pitiful, too."

"Everybody wants to direct."

"What?"

"Trust me when I tell you that I'd only screw up your big scene. But I promise to check in on you. And if they decide to lock you up in a dungeon or anything, I'll smuggle you some candy bars."

"They wouldn't do that."

Her look of mild reproof reminded him of Isabel, and he smiled. "Exactly. So what are you scared of?"

Briggs had just arrived back at the house to check in, so they were all gathered in front when Ren came up the path from the farmhouse with her. The minute they saw her, both parents started to run. Then they were on their knees in the gravel, half smothering the poor kid.

"Steffie! Oh, my God, Steffie!"

They kissed her, checked her over to make sure she wasn't hurt, and then Tracy jumped up and tried to slobber Ren with kisses. Briggs actually reached out to hug him, something Ren managed to avoid by bending over to tie his shoelace. Isabel, in the meantime, stood there looking proud, which annoyed the hell out of him. What had she expected him to do? Kill the kid?

That's when it occurred to him that at some point during his time with Steffie, he'd mercifully stopped thinking about Kaspar Street.

Isabel's attitude didn't keep him from aching to sink into her again, even though it had only been a few hours since he'd done just that. And even though he wasn't crazy about those terms she'd laid out in the car this morning. Not that he wanted too many emotional entanglements—God knew he didn't—but did she have to be so cold-blooded about it? Then there was the matter of Kaspar Street. She hadn't liked the fact that he was in the business of killing young women. What would she do when she found out about the kids?

He finally managed to get her away by reminding her that he was soaked to the skin, cold as hell, and hungry. That kicked in her female instincts, just as he'd hoped, and within an hour he had her in bed.

"Are you mad?" Steffie whispered.

Harry had a lump in his throat the size of Rhode Island. Since he couldn't talk, he brushed the hair back from her forehead and shook his head. She lay curled in bed with her oldest teddy cuddled to her cheek. She was clean from her bath and wearing her favorite blue cotton nighty. He remembered her as a toddler, waddling toward him, arms out. She looked so small under the covers and so very precious.

"We're not mad," Tracy said quietly from the other side of the bed. "But we're still upset."

"Ren told me if you locked me in a dungeon, he'd sneak me some candy bars."

"What a wild and crazy guy." Tracy smoothed the sheet. Her makeup had vanished hours ago, and she had dark circles under her eyes, but she was still the most beautiful woman Harry had ever seen.

"I'm sorry I scared you so much."

Tracy looked stern. "So you've said. But you're still spending tomorrow morning by yourself in this bedroom."

Tracy was made of stronger stuff than Harry was, because he wanted to forget all about discipline. But then Steffie hadn't run away on account of her. It was him. He felt defeated and disoriented. But he also felt resentful. How had he managed to become the bad guy?

"All morning?" Steffie looked so little and miserable he could barely keep himself from overriding Tracy and promising to take her for ice cream instead.

"All morning," Tracy said firmly.

Steffie thought it over, and then her lip started to quiver. "I know I shouldn't have run away just because I got so sad when I heard you and Daddy fighting."

Harry's stomach twisted, and Tracy's forehead crumpled. "Until ten-thirty," she said quickly.

Steffie's lip stopped quivering, and she sighed one of those grown-up sighs that usually made him laugh. "I guess it could be a lot worse."

Tracy tugged on a lock of her daughter's hair. "You bet it could. The only reason we're not locking you in that dungeon Ren mentioned is because of your allergies."

"Plus the spiders."

"Yeah, that, too." Tracy's voice got thready, and Harry knew they were thinking the same thing. Having her parents together was so important to Steffie that she'd been willing to face her worst fear. His daughter had more courage than he did.

Tracy leaned down to kiss her, clutching the headboard to support her weight. She stayed there for a long time, eyes closed, her cheek pressed to Steffie's. "I love you so much, punkin. Promise you won't ever do anything like this again."

"I promise."

Harry finally managed to find his voice. "And promise that the next time you get upset about something, you'll tell us what's bothering you."

"Even if it hurts your feelings, right?"

"Even then."

She tucked her bear under her chin. "Are you . . . still going away tomorrow?"

He didn't know what to say, so he simply shook his head.

Tracy went to check on Connor and Brittany, who were sharing a room, at least until they woke up and crawled in with their father. Jeremy was still downstairs playing a computer game. Harry and

Tracy hadn't been alone since their disastrous argument that afternoon, and he didn't want to be alone with her now, not while he felt so raw, but parents couldn't always do what they wanted.

She shut the door and stepped back into the hallway. Then she pressed the small of her back against the wall, something she did late in her pregnancies to ease the strain. With her other pregnancies he'd massaged her there, but not with this one.

The weight of his guilt grew heavier.

She cupped her hand over her belly. The brazen, overly confident rich girl who'd led him on such a merry chase a dozen years ago had disappeared, and an achingly beautiful woman with haunted eyes had taken her place. "What are we going to do?" she whispered.

What are you going to do? he wanted to say. She was the one who'd left. She was the one who was never satisfied. He took off his glasses and rubbed his eyes. "I don't know."

"We can't talk anymore."

"We can talk."

"No, we just start hurling insults."

Not the way he remembered it. She was the one with the sharp tongue and atomic temper. All he tried to do was dodge. "No insults from me." He slipped his glasses back on.

"Of course not."

She said it without any bite, but the knot inside him tightened. "I think what happened this afternoon pushed us past the insult stage, don't you?"

Despite his good intentions, he sounded accusatory, and he braced himself for her retaliation, but she simply shut her eyes and rested her head against the wall. "Yes, I think so, too."

He wanted to wrap her in his arms and beg her to let this go, but she'd made up her mind about him, and nothing he'd said so far had been able to change it. If he couldn't make her understand, they had no chance at all. "Today proved what I've been saying all along. We have to buckle down. I think we both know that now. It's time for us to buckle down and do what we have to."

"And what's that?"

She seemed genuinely perplexed. How could she be so obtuse? He tried to hide his agitation. "We can start behaving like adults."

"You always behave like an adult. I'm the one who seems to have trouble."

It was true—exactly what he'd been trying to tell her—but the expression of defeat on her face tore him apart. Why couldn't she just adapt to things so they could move forward? He searched for the right words, but too many feelings lay in his way. Tracy believed in digging through those feelings whenever the whim struck, but not Harry. He'd never seen the benefit, only the downside.

She closed her eyes for a moment. Spoke softly. "Tell me something I can do to make you happy."

"Be realistic! Marriages change. We've changed. We get older, and life catches up with us. It can't always be like it was in the beginning, so don't expect that. Be satisfied with what we have."

"Is that what it comes down to? Just settling?"

All the emotional jumble inside him had come together in his stomach. "We have to be realistic. Marriage can't be moonlight and roses forever. I wouldn't call that settling."

"I would." Her hair flew. She thrust herself away from the wall. "I'd call it settling, and I'm not doing it. I'm not phoning in this marriage. I'm going to fight for it, even if I'm the only one with the guts to do that."

She'd raised her voice, but they couldn't have another argument, not with Steffie so close. "We can't talk here." He took her arm, pulled her away, steered her down the hall. "You don't make sense. You've never once—never once in our entire marriage—made sense to me."

"That's because you have a computer for a brain," she railed at him as they rounded the corner into the next wing. "I'm not afraid to fight. And I'll do it until we're both bleeding if I have to."

"You're just trying to create another one of your dramas." He was appalled at how angry he sounded, but he couldn't seem to calm down. He shoved open the nearest door, hauled her inside, and hit the switch. Big room, big furniture. The master bedroom.

"Our children aren't going to be raised by parents who have a ghost marriage!" she cried.

"Stop it!" It was anger he felt—that's what he told himself. Anger, not desperation, because anger was something he could control. "If you don't stop it . . ." A monster sucked at his bones. "You can't do this." He drew in air. "You have to stop it. You have to stop it before you ruin everything."

"How can I ruin—"

An explosion went off in his head. "By saying things we can't ever take back!"

"Like what? That you've stopped loving me?" Angry tears filled her eyes. "Like the fact that I'm fat, and the novelty of screwing a pregnant woman wore off three kids ago. Like the fact that I can't ever balance the checkbook, and I misplace your car keys, and you wake up every morning wishing you'd married somebody neat and tidy like Isabel. Is that what I'm not supposed to say?"

Leave it to Tracy to go off on some ludicrous tangent. He wanted to shake her. "We can never work this out if you won't be logical."

"I can't be any more logical than this."

He heard the same desperation in her voice that he felt inside, but why should she feel desperate when she was saying such stupid things?

She never remembered to carry tissues, and she wiped her nose with the back of her hand. "Today you asked me what you could do to make me happy, and I lashed out instead of saying what I wanted to. Do you know what I wanted to say?"

He knew, and he didn't want to hear. He didn't want her to tell him how boring he was, and that he was losing his hair, and that he wasn't even close to being the man she deserved. He didn't want her to tell him that he'd served his purpose by giving her children and now she wished she'd chosen differently, someone more like her.

Tears made silver streaks on her cheeks. "Just love me, Harry. That's what I wanted to say. Love me like you used to. Like I was special instead of a cross you have to bear. Like the differences between us are good things instead of something awful. I want it to be the way it used to be when you looked at me as though you couldn't believe I was yours. Like I was the most wonderful creature in the world. I know I don't look the way I did then. I know I have stretch marks everywhere, and I know how much you used to love my breasts, and now they're halfway to my knees, and I hate this, and I hate that you don't love me like you used to, and I hate the fact that you're making me beg!"

This was absurd. Completely illogical. This was so wrong he couldn't figure out what to say to set it straight. Of all the . . . He opened his mouth, but he didn't know where to start, so he closed it, tried again. It was too late. She'd already fled.

He stood there, numb, trying to figure out what had hit him. She was everything to him. How could she think, even for a moment, that he didn't love her? She was the center of his world, the breath of his life. It wasn't him . . . She was the one who couldn't love enough.

He sagged down on the side of the bed and dropped his forehead into his hands. She didn't think he loved her? He wanted to howl.

A door creaked, and the hairs stood on the back of his neck, because the noise hadn't come from the hallway. It had come from across the room.

He lifted his head. There was a bathroom. . . . Dread pooled in his stomach as the door opened and a man stepped out. Tall, good-looking, with a full head of hair.

Ren Gage shook his head and looked at Harry with pity. "Man, you are so screwed."

And didn't he just know it.

1 7

P *orcini!"*

A wet branch slapped Isabel in the face as Giulia shot ahead of her through the underbrush. Her sneakers would never be the same after the morning's excursion through the woods, which were still soggy from yesterday's rainfall. She hurried toward a fallen tree and crouched next to Giulia in front of a circle of velvety brown porcini, their toadstool tops large enough to shelter a fairy.

"Mmm . . . Tuscan gold." Giulia pulled out the pocketknife she'd brought with her, cut a mushroom neatly at the base, and laid it in her basket. Plastic sacks were never used by the *fungaroli*, Isabel had learned, only baskets that allowed spores and bits of root to fall to the ground so next year's crop would be ensured. "I wish Vittorio could have come with us. He complains when I wake him so early, but he loves the hunt."

Isabel wished Ren were with them, too. If she hadn't asked him to go back to the villa yesterday evening after they'd made love, she could have nagged him out of bed this morning and made him come along. Even though they'd been lovers only a little over twenty-four hours, she'd found herself reaching for him last night, then waking up when he wasn't there. He was like a drug. A dangerous drug. Crack cocaine topped off with heroin. And she was going to need a twelve-step program when their affair ended.

She slipped her fingers beneath the cuff of her sweater and tugged at her gold bangle. *Breathe. Stay centered and breathe.* How often would she be able to hunt porcini in the woods of Tuscany? Despite the damp, Ren's absence, and what felt like a permanent crick in her back from crouching down to look for mushrooms, she was enjoying herself. The morning had dawned bright and clear, Steffie was safe, and Isabel had a lover.

"Smell. Is it not indescribable?"

Isabel inhaled the pungent, earthy scent of the *funghi* and thought about sex. But then everything made her think about sex. She was already looking forward to returning to the farmhouse and seeing Ren again. The people from the town would be gathering at ten o'clock to finish dismantling the wall, and he would be there to help.

She remembered how moody he'd gotten last night just before he'd left. At first she'd thought it was because she was kicking him out, but he'd been fairly good-humored about that. She'd asked him what was wrong, but he'd said only that he was tired. It had seemed like more than that. Maybe he'd been having a leftover reaction from finding Steffie. One thing was certain: Ren was a master dissembler, and if he didn't want her to know what was going on inside him, she had very little chance of figuring it out.

They set off again, eyes peeled, using the walking sticks Giulia had brought along to push away undergrowth near the tree roots and beside rotting logs. The rain had revitalized the parched landscape, and the air was heady with the scent of rosemary, lavender, and wild sage. Isabel found a velvety cache of porcini under a pile of leaves and added them to the basket.

"You are very good at this." Giulia spoke in the whisper she'd been using all morning. Porcini were precious, and mushroom hunting was a secretive operation. Their basket even had a lid to conceal their treasure should they happen to pass someone in the woods, not that anyone was going to be fooled. Giulia yawned for the fourth time in as many minutes.

"A little early for you?" Isabel said.

"I had to meet Vittorio in Montepulciano last night and in Pienza the night before that. I didn't get back until very late."

"Do you always meet him when he's out?"

Giulia poked at some weeds she'd just finished looking beneath. "Sometimes. Certain nights."

Whatever that meant.

As it neared ten o'clock, they returned to the farmhouse, taking turns carrying the full basket. The villagers had begun to appear, and Ren stood in the garden studying the wall. The way he wore his dusty boots, jeans, and faded T-shirt turned them into a fashion statement. When he saw her, his smile took away the last of the morning's chill, and it grew even wider when he spotted the basket. "Why don't I put these someplace safe?"

"Oh, no you don't."

But she was too late. He'd already snagged the basket from Giulia and headed inside with it.

"Hurry." She grabbed Giulia's arm and pulled her into the kitchen, arriving there on his heels. "Give that back right now. You're not trustworthy."

"You hurt my feelings." His con man's eyes were as innocent as an altar boy's. "And just when I was getting ready to suggest cooking up a little dinner for the four of us tonight. Nothing elaborate. We could start with some sautéed porcini on top of toasted crostini. Then maybe spaghetti al porcino—a light sauce, very simple. I'll sauté the mushrooms in olive oil and garlic, add some fresh parsley. We could grill the larger ones and use them on an arugula salad. Of course, if I'm being presumptuous . . ."

"Yes!" Giulia hopped like a child. "Vittorio will be home tonight. I know it is our turn to invite you, but you are a better cook, and I accept for both of us."

"We'll see you at eight." The porcini disappeared into the cupboard.

Satisfied, Giulia slipped back out to the garden to greet some of her friends. Ren glanced at his watch, lifted an imperious eyebrow, and jerked a very arrogant thumb toward the ceiling. "You. Upstairs. Now. And make it fast."

He wasn't the only one who knew how to have fun. She yawned. "I don't think so."

"Apparently I'm going to have to get rough."

"I knew this was going to be a good day."

With a laugh, he dragged her into the living room, pressed her to the wall, and gave her a kiss that made her dizzy. Much too soon, Giulia called out to them from the kitchen, and they were forced to break away.

While they worked, the townspeople spoke with heart-wringing emotion and dramatic gestures about how relieved they would be when old Paolo's secret money stash was found and they no longer had to live in mortal fear. Isabel wondered if an entire town could win an Academy Award.

Tracy waddled down with Marta and Connor. Harry appeared

half an hour later with the older children. He looked frazzled and depressed, and Isabel was surprised to see Ren walk over and speak with him.

Steffie stayed at her father's side except when she scampered away to talk to Ren. He seemed to enjoy her company, a surprise after all the complaining he'd done about having the children around. Maybe the incident yesterday had changed his outlook. He even crouched down to talk with Brittany, despite the fact that she'd taken off her T-shirt.

When Jeremy saw his sisters getting so much attention, he began to misbehave, something his parents seemed too dispirited to notice. Ren complimented him on his muscles, then set him to work carrying stone.

Isabel decided she preferred food service to manual labor, so she helped make sandwiches and keep the water pitchers filled. Marta chided her in Italian, although not unkindly, for slicing the panforte too thinly. One by one, the people who'd caused her trouble managed to find their way to her side to make amends. Giancarlo apologized for the ghost incident, and Bernardo, off duty for the morning, took her to meet his wife, a sad-eyed woman named Fabiola.

Around one o'clock a handsome Italian with thick, curly hair appeared. Giulia brought him to meet Isabel. "This is Vittorio's brother, Andrea. He is our very excellent local doctor. He closed his office for the afternoon to help in the search."

"*Piacere, signora.* I'm happy to meet you." He tossed away his cigarette. "A bad habit, I know, for a doctor."

Andrea had a small scar on his cheek and a rogue's practiced eye. As they chatted, she grew aware of Ren watching from the wall, and she tried to convince herself he was being possessive. Unlikely, but a nice fantasy.

Tracy wandered over. Isabel introduced her to Andrea, and she asked him to recommend a local obstetrician.

"I deliver the babies of Casalleone."

"How fortunate for their mothers." Tracy's reply was flirtatious, but only, Isabel suspected, because Harry was near enough to overhear.

By midafternoon the wall had been taken apart stone by stone, and the festive mood had disappeared. They'd found nothing more exciting than a few dead mice and some shards of broken pottery. Giulia stood alone at the top of the scarred hillside, head down. Bernardo looked as though he were comforting his sad-eyed wife. A woman named Tereza, who seemed to be another of Anna's relatives, linked arms with her mother. Andrea Chiara went off to speak with one of the younger men, who was smoking and kicking the dirt with his boot.

Just then Vittorio arrived. He took in the mood of the group and immediately headed to Giulia's side. Isabel watched as he steered her into the shadows of the pergola, where he pulled her close.

Ren joined Isabel by one of the gravel paths. "I feel like I'm at a funeral."

"There's something more at stake here than a missing artifact."

"I sure would like to know what."

Giulia drew away from Vittorio and approached them, looking teary. "You will excuse us from dinner tonight, yes? I am not feeling so good. This will leave more porcini for you to eat."

Isabel remembered Giulia's earlier excitement about the meal. "I'm so sorry. Is there anything I can do?"

"Can you make a miracle?"

"No, but I can pray for one."

Giulia gave a wan smile. "Then you must pray very hard."

"It might be easier if she knew what she was praying for," Ren said.

Vittorio had remained by the pergola, and Giulia turned her head just enough to give him an imploring look. He shook his head. Isabel saw resentment cloud Giulia's features and decided it was time to step up the pressure. "We can't help if you won't be truthful with us."

Giulia rubbed one hand with the other. "I do not think you could help anyway."

"Are you in some kind of trouble?"

Her arms flew. "Do you see a child in my arms? Yes, I am in trouble."

Vittorio heard her, and he shot forward. "That's enough, Giulia."

Ren seemed to read Isabel's mind, which at that moment was telling her they needed to divide and conquer. As Isabel slipped an arm around Giulia's shoulders, he stepped into the path to cut Vittorio off. "Why don't we talk?"

Isabel quickly steered Giulia around the side of the house to her car. "Let's go for a ride."

Giulia got into the Panda without protest. Isabel backed out and headed for the road. She waited a few minutes before she said anything.

"I suspect you have a good reason for not telling us the truth."

Giulia rubbed her eyes wearily. "How do you know I'm not telling the truth?"

"Because your story sounded too much like one of Ren's movie scripts. Besides, I don't think stolen money would make you so sad."

"You are a very smart woman." She combed her fingers through her hair, hooking it behind her ear. "No one wants to look foolish."

"And that's what you're afraid of? That the truth will make you look foolish? Or is it just that Vittorio has forbidden you to talk?"

"You think I keep silent because Vittorio has told me to?" She gave a tired laugh. "No. It is not because of him."

"Then why? It's obvious you need help. Maybe Ren and I could provide a different perspective."

"Or maybe not." She crossed her legs. "You've been so kind to me."

"What are friends for?"

"You have been a better friend to me than I have to you."

As they passed a small farmhouse where a woman worked in the garden, Isabel felt the weight of Giulia's internal battle.

"It is not my story to tell," Giulia finally said. "It is the whole town's, and they will be angry with me." She grabbed a tissue from a pack Isabel had left on the seat and blew her nose with an angry bleat. "I don't care. I am going to tell you. And if you think it is foolish . . . well, then, I cannot blame you."

Isabel waited. Giulia's breasts rose and fell before she gave a sigh of resignation. "We are looking for the *Ombra della Mattina*."

It took a few moments for Isabel to remember the votive statue of the Etruscan boy from the Guarnacci Museum, *Ombra della Sera*. She eased up on the accelerator to allow a truck to pass. "What does it mean? *Ombra della Mattina?*"

"*Shadow of the Morning.*"

"The statue in Volterra is called *Shadow of the Evening*. That isn't a coincidence, is it?"

"*Ombra della Mattina* is its mate. A female statue. Thirty years ago our village priest found it when he was planting rosebushes at the gate of the cemetery."

Just as Ren had suspected. "And the people of the village don't want to turn it over to the government."

"Do not think this is an ordinary case of greedy people trying to hide an artifact. If only it were that simple."

"But this is a very valuable artifact."

"Yes, but not only in the way you are thinking."

"I don't understand."

Giulia tugged on her small pearl earring. She looked drawn and exhausted. "*Ombra della Mattina* has special powers. This is why we do not speak of it to outsiders."

"What kind of powers?"

"Unless you were born in Casalleone, you cannot understand. Even those of us born here did not believe." She made one of her small, graceful gestures. "We laughed when our parents told us stories about the statue, but now we are no longer laughing." She finally turned to look at Isabel. "Three years ago *Ombra della Mattina* disappeared, and since then not one woman within thirty kilometers of this town has been able to conceive."

"No one has gotten pregnant in three years?"

"Only those who have been able to conceive away from the town."

"And you really believe that the disappearance of the statue is responsible?"

"Vittorio and I were educated at the university. Do we believe it rationally? No. But the fact remains . . . The only way any couples have been able to get pregnant is to do so beyond the borders of Casalleone, and this is not always so easy."

Finally Isabel understood. "That's why you're always traveling to meet Vittorio. You're trying to have a child."

Giulia's hands twisted in her lap. "And why our friends Cristina and Enrico, who want a second child, must leave their daughter with her *nonna* night after night so they can get away. And why Sauro and Tea Grifasi drive far out into the country to make love in their car, then drive back home afterward. Sauro was fired from his job last month because he kept sleeping through his alarm clock. And this is why Anna is sad all the time. Bernardo and Fabiola can not get pregnant to make her a grandmother."

"The pharmacist in town is pregnant. I've seen her."

"For six months she lived in Livorno with a sister who always criticizes. Her husband drove back and forth every night. Now they are getting divorced."

"But what does all this have to do with the farmhouse and old Paolo?"

Giulia rubbed her eyes. "Paolo is the one who stole the statue."

"Apparently Paolo had a reputation for disliking children," Isabel told Ren that evening as they stood in the kitchen together, gently wiping the dirt from the porcini with damp cloths. "He didn't like the noise they made, and he complained that having so many children meant they had to spend too much money on schools."

"My kind of guy. So he decides to cut the town's birthrate by stealing the statue. And what part of your mind did you lose when you started to believe this story?"

"Giulia was telling the truth."

"I don't doubt that. What I'm having trouble comprehending is the fact that you're taking the supposed powers of this statue seriously."

"God works in mysterious ways." Ren was making a mess of the kitchen as usual, and she began clearing space on the counter.

"Spare me."

"No one has conceived a child in Casalleone since the statue was stolen," she said.

"And yet I'm not feeling any compulsion to throw away your condoms. Doesn't this offend your academic sensibilities just a little?"

"Not at all." She carried a stack of dirty bowls to the sink. "It supports what I know. The mind is very powerful."

"You're saying there's some kind of mass hysteria going on? That women aren't conceiving because they believe they can't conceive?"

"It's been known to happen."

"I liked the Mafia story better."

"Only because it had guns."

He smiled and leaned down to kiss her on the nose, which led to her mouth, which led to her breast, and several minutes passed before they came back up for air. "Cook," she said weakly. "I've been waiting all day for those mushrooms."

He groaned and grabbed his knife. "You got a lot more out of Giulia than I got out of Vittorio, I'll give you that. But the statue disappeared three years ago. Why did everyone have to wait until now to dig up this place?"

"The town's priests kept the statue in the church office. . . ."

"And isn't it charming the way paganism and Christianity can still coexist?"

"Everyone knew it was there," she said, rinsing out a bowl, "but the local officials didn't want a rebellion on their hands by reporting it, so they looked the other way. Paolo had done odd jobs at the church for years, but no one made the connection between him and the statue's disappearance until he died a few months later. Then people started remembering that he didn't like children."

Ren rolled his eyes. "Definitely suspicious."

"Marta always defended him. She said he didn't hate children. That he was just *imbronciato* because of his arthritis. What does '*imbronciato*' mean?"

"Grouchy."

"She pointed out that he'd been a good father to his daughter. He'd even flown to the States years ago to see his granddaughter when she was born. So people backed off, and other rumors started to fly. I guess it got fairly ugly."

"Any guns?"

"Sorry, no." She wiped up a small section of the counter. "The day before I arrived, Anna sent Giancarlo down here to clean up a rubbish pile that had gotten out of hand. And guess what he found tucked in a hole in the wall when he accidentally knocked out one of the stones?"

"I'm holding my breath."

"The marble base the statue had always stood on. The same base that disappeared the day the statue was stolen."

"Well, that does explain the sudden interest in the wall."

She dried her hands. "Everyone in town went crazy. They made plans to take the wall apart, only to have the fly in the ointment show up."

"You."

"Exactly."

"Things would have been a lot easier if they'd just told us the truth from the beginning," he said.

"We're outsiders, and they had no reason to trust either one of us. Especially you."

"Thanks."

"What good would it do for them to find the statue if we spread the word that it was here?" she said. "It's one thing for local politicians to turn a blind eye to a priceless Etruscan artifact sitting around in a church office, but officials in the rest of the country weren't going to be quite that cavalier. Everyone was afraid the statue would end up locked away in a glass case in Volterra right next to *Ombra della Sera*."

"Which is where it should be." He whacked a clove of garlic with the flat of his knife.

"I did some snooping while you were working out, and look what I found." She retrieved the yellowed envelope she'd discovered in the living room bookcase and spread the contents on the kitchen table. There were several dozen photographs of Paolo's granddaughter, all carefully identified on the back.

Ren wiped his hands and came over to look. She pointed toward a color photograph showing an older man holding a baby on the front porch of a small white house. "This is the oldest photo. That's Paolo. It must have been taken when he went to Boston not long after his granddaughter was born. Her name is Josie, short for Josephina."

Some of the photographs showed Josie at camp, others on vacation with her parents at the Grand Canyon. In some she was alone. Isabel picked up the final two. "This is Josie on her wedding day six years ago." She had curly dark hair and a wide smile. "And this one with her husband was taken not long before Paolo died." She flipped it over to show him the date on the back.

"It doesn't seem like the collection of a child hater," Ren admitted. "So maybe Paolo didn't take the statue."

"He was the one who built the wall, and he was also the one responsible for the rubbish pile."

"Not exactly hard evidence. But if the statue's not in the wall, I wonder where it is?"

"Not in the house," she said. "Anna and Marta have searched it from top to bottom. There's talk of plowing up the garden, but Marta says she'd have noticed if Paolo hid it there, and she won't allow it. There are lots of places near the wall or the olive grove, maybe even the vineyard, where he could have dug a hole and hidden it. I suggested to Giulia they bring in some metal detectors."

"Gadgets. I'm starting to like this."

"Good." She whipped off the tea towel she'd wrapped at her waist. "Now, that's enough talk. Turn off the stove and get naked."

He yelped and dropped his knife. "You nearly made me slice off my finger."

"As long as it's just your finger." She grinned and began unbuttoning her blouse. "Who says I can't be spontaneous?"

"Not me. Okay, I've got my breath back." He watched the buttons open. "What time is it?"

"Almost eight."

"Damn. Company's coming any minute." He reached for her, but she frowned and dodged.

"I thought Giulia and Vittorio canceled on us."

"I invited Harry."

"You don't like Harry." She took another step back and began fastening up her buttons.

He sighed. "What gave you that idea? He's a great guy. Would you mind leaving a few of those open? And Tracy's coming, too."

"I'm surprised she accepted. She wouldn't even look at him today."

"I didn't exactly tell her I'd invited him."

"And isn't this going to be a pleasant evening?"

"It couldn't be helped," he said. "Things bottomed out between them this morning, and Tracy's been dodging him ever since. He's pretty upset."

"He told you all this?"

"Hey, guys share. We have feelings, too."

She lifted an eyebrow.

"Okay, maybe he's a little desperate and I'm the only one around he can talk to. The guy's a total screw-up when it comes to women, and if I don't help him out, they're going to be here forever."

"Yet this total screw-up managed to stay married for eleven years and father five children, while you—"

"While I have an idea I think you'll like. An idea, by the way, that has nothing to do with the Battling Briggses, other than the fact that we have to get rid of them to pull it off."

"What kind of idea?" She leaned down to pick up some mushroom stems he'd dropped on the floor.

"A little sexual costume drama. But we need the villa to do it justice, which means that the whole family and their baby-sitters have to go."

"A costume drama?" She let the stems fall back to the floor.

"A *sexual* costume drama. I'm thinking nighttime. Candlelight. A thunderstorm if we're lucky." He picked up her glass and rolled the stem in his fingers. "It seems the unscrupulous Prince Lorenzo has caught sight of a feisty peasant woman in the village, a woman no longer in the first blush of youth—"

"Hey!"

"Which makes her all the more appealing to him."

"Darn right."

"The peasant woman is known throughout the land for her virtue and good works, so she fights off his advances, despite the fact that he's the best-looking dude in the region. Hell, in all of Italy."

"Only Italy? Still, you should always put your money on a virtuous woman. He doesn't have a chance."

"Did I mention that Prince Lorenzo is also the smartest dude in the region?"

"Oh, well, that definitely complicates things."

"So what does he do but threaten to burn the entire village if she won't submit to him."

"The cad. Naturally she says she'll kill herself first."

"Which he doesn't believe for a minute, since good Catholic women don't kill themselves."

"You do have a point."

He drew a descriptive arc with his knife. "The scene opens on the night she delivers herself to the prince's deserted, candlelit villa. The same villa, coincidentally, that sits at the top of this hill."

"Amazing."

"She arrives in the dress he sent her that afternoon."

"I can see it. Simple and white."

"Bright red and slutty."

"Which only makes her virtue more apparent."

"He wastes no time in preliminaries. He drags her upstairs—"

"Scoops her up in his arm and carries her upstairs."

"Despite the fact that she's not exactly a featherweight—but luckily he works out. And once he gets her into his bedroom, he makes her take off her clothes slowly . . . while he watches."

"Naturally he's naked as he watches, because it's very hot in the villa."

"And even hotter in that bedroom. Did I tell you how good-looking he is?"

"I believe you mentioned it."

"So the time comes when she's forced to submit to him."

"I don't think I'm going to like this part."

"That's because you're a control freak."

"And, coincidentally, *so is she.*"

He bowed to the inevitable. "Just as he's ready to force himself on her, what should she catch sight of out of the corner of her eye but a pair of handcuffs?"

"They had handcuffs in the eighteenth century?"

"Manacles. A pair of manacles lying just within her reach."

"Convenient."

"While his lust-glazed eyes are focused elsewhere"—Ren's own lust-glazed eyes focused on her breasts—"she reaches behind him, grabs the manacles, and snaps them around—"

"I knocked, but nobody answered."

They pulled apart and saw Harry standing in the doorway looking miserable. "We used to do that thing with the handcuffs," he said glumly. "It was great."

"Ah." Isabel cleared her throat.

"You could have knocked," Ren grumbled.

"I did."

Isabel grabbed a fresh bottle of wine. "Why don't you open this? I'll get you a glass."

He'd barely finished pouring when Tracy came in. She bristled with hostility at the sight of her husband. "What's he doing here?"

Ren pecked her cheek. "Isabel asked him. I told her not to, but she thinks she knows everything."

In another lifetime Isabel would have defended herself, but she was dealing with insane people, so what was the point?

"This seemed the best way," Harry said. "I've been trying to talk to you all day, but you keep running away."

"Only because you make me sick."

He flinched but persevered. "Come outside, Tracy. Just for a few minutes. There are some things I need to say to you, and I have to do it privately."

Tracy turned her back to him, wrapped an arm around Ren's waist, and rested her cheek on his arm. "I should never have divorced you. God, you were a great lover. The best."

Ren glanced over at Harry. "Are you sure you want to stay married to her? Because right now I've got to say I think you could do a lot better."

"I'm sure," Harry said. "I'm very much in love with her."

Tracy lifted her head like a small animal sniffing the air, only to decide that what she smelled was unpleasant. "Yeah, right."

Harry hunched his shoulders and turned to Isabel, the shadows in his eyes making him look like a man with nothing left to lose. "I'd hoped to do this privately, but apparently that's not going to happen, and since Tracy won't listen, I'll tell you, if you don't mind."

Tracy seemed to be listening, and Isabel nodded. "By all means."

"I fell in love with her the moment she dumped her drink in my lap. I thought it was an accident. I'm still not sure whether to believe her that it wasn't. There were all kinds of good-looking guys at that party tripping over each other to get her attention, but it hadn't occurred to me even to try, not just because of her physical beauty—and God knows she was the most beautiful woman I'd ever seen—but because of her . . . because of this *glow* she had. This energy. I couldn't take my eyes off her, but at the same time I didn't want her to know I was watching. Then she dumped her drink, and I couldn't think of one thing to say."

"He said, 'My fault.'" Tracy's voice caught on a little hitch. "I dump the drink, and the idiot says, 'My fault.' I should have known right then."

He still paid no attention to her, focusing on Isabel instead. "I couldn't think. It felt like my brain had gotten a shot of novocaine. She was wearing this silver dress that dipped low in the front, and she had her hair up, except it wouldn't stay up and these curls had fallen down her neck. I'd never seen anything like it. Anything like her." He gazed into his glass. "But as beautiful as she was that night . . ." His voice grew thick. "As beautiful as she was then . . ." He swallowed. "I'm sorry. I can't do this." He set his glass on the counter and disappeared through the garden door.

Tracy's eyes were bleak, but she shrugged as if it didn't matter. "See what I have to put up with? The minute I think he's finally ready to talk, he shuts down. I might as well be married to a computer."

"Stop acting like an ass," Ren said. "No guy wants to spill his guts in front of an ex-husband. He's been trying to talk to you all day."

"Big deal. I've been trying to talk to him for years."

Isabel glanced toward the garden. "He doesn't seem like a man who's too comfortable with his feelings."

"I've got a news flash for both of you," Ren said. "No man is comfortable with his feelings. Get over it."

"You are," Tracy said. "You talk about how you feel, but Harry has terminal emotional constipation."

"I'm an actor, so most of what comes out of my mouth is bullshit. Harry loves you. Even a fool can see that."

"Then I'm a fool, because I'm not buying it."

"You're not fighting fair," Isabel said. "I know it's because you're hurt, but that doesn't make it right. Give him a chance to say what's on his mind without an audience." Isabel pointed at the door. "And listen with your brain when you talk to him, because your heart's too bruised right now to be reliable."

"There's no point! Don't you understand? Don't you think I've tried?"

"Try again." Isabel gave her a firm push toward the door.

Tracy looked mulish, but she went outside.

"I already want to kill them both," Ren said, "and we haven't even had the appetizers."

Harry stood by the pergola, hands shoved in his pockets, the frames of his glasses picking up the last rays of sun. Tracy felt that familiar dizziness that had first plagued her twelve years ago, right before she'd dumped her drink in his clueless lap.

"Isabel made me come out here." Tracy heard the hostility in her voice, but she'd begged him once today, and she wasn't going to do it again.

He pulled his hand from his pocket and braced it on the side of the pergola, not looking at her. "What you said this morning . . . Were you just throwing up another one of your smoke screens? About being fat and having stretch marks, when you know damned well you get more beautiful every day? And saying I don't love you when I've told you a thousand times how I feel?"

Words uttered by rote. *"I love you, Tracy."* No emotion behind them. Never, *"I love you because . . ."* Just, *"I love you, Tracy. Don't forget to buy more toothpaste when you go to the store."*

"There's telling and there's believing. Two different animals."

He slowly turned to her. "It's never been *my* love in question, not from the beginning. It's always been *yours*."

"Mine? I *picked* you! If it had been up to you, the two of us would never have happened. I found you, I stalked you, and I reeled you in."

"I wasn't that big a prize!"

Harry never yelled, and just the surprise of it silenced her.

He pushed himself away from the pergola. "You wanted kids. And I had 'Daddy' written all over me. Don't you get it? For you, it wasn't about us. It was all about your need to have kids. About me being the father you wanted for them. Someplace in my subconscious I always knew that's what you were after, but I kept fooling myself. And it was easy to do when there were only Jeremy and Steffie. Even when Brittany came along, I could pretend it was still about us, that you wanted me for me. I might have been able to keep on pretending, but then you got pregnant with Connor, and you walked around with this cat-that-ate-the-canary smile on your face. Everything was about being pregnant and the kids. I tried to swallow it, to keep on pretending I was the great love of your life and not just your best source of sperm, but it got harder. Every morning I'd look at you and want you to love me the way I loved you, but I'd done my job, and you didn't even see me. And you're right. I did start shutting down. So I could keep going. But when you got pregnant this time and you were so happy, I couldn't even go through the motions. I wanted to, but I couldn't." His voice broke. "I just . . . couldn't."

Tracy tried to take it in, but so many conflicting emotions were barreling through her that she couldn't begin to sort them out. Relief. Anger at him for being so obtuse. And joy. Oh, yes, joy, because it wasn't completely hopeless after all. She didn't know where to begin, so she decided to start small. "What about the toothpaste?"

He stared at her as if she'd grown a second pregnancy from her forehead. "Toothpaste?"

"The way I don't always remember to buy toothpaste. And the way it drives you crazy when I lose my keys. You told me if I screwed up the checking account one more time, you were going to take away my checkbook. And do you remember that dent in the fender of your car that you thought happened when you took Jeremy to Little League? I put it there. Connor threw up in my car, and I didn't have time to clean it up, so I took yours instead, and I was yelling at Brittany in the parking lot at Target and drove my shopping cart into it. What about that, Harry?"

He blinked. "If you'd keep an organized shopping list, you wouldn't forget to buy toothpaste."

In typical Harry fashion, he didn't get it. "I'll never keep an organized shopping list or stop losing keys or get much better at any of those other things that drive you wild."

"I know that. I also know there are a thousand men who'd line up for the chance to buy you toothpaste and let you run a shopping cart into their car."

Maybe he did get it.

Isabel had told her to think with her brain instead of her heart, but that was hard to do when it came to Harry Briggs. "I did know you'd be a great father, and that might have been part of the reason I fell in love with you. But I'd have kept on loving you even if you hadn't been able to make a single baby. I found all my missing parts with you. I don't keep wanting to have more babies because you're not enough for me. I keep wanting them because my love for you gets so big it needs more places to go."

Hope flickered in his eyes, but he still looked sad. She realized that his insecurities ran even deeper than her own. She'd always regarded him as the most intelligent person she knew, so it was difficult to adjust to the idea that she might be the smarter partner. "It's true, Harry. Every word."

"A little hard to believe." He seemed to be drinking in her face, even though he knew every pore. "Just look at us. I'm the kind of guy you could pass on the street a dozen times and never notice. But you . . . Men walk into mailboxes when they see you."

"I never knew a man so hung up on appearance." She forgot all about thinking with her head and smacked his jaw to get his attention. "I love the way you look. I could stare at you for hours. I used to be married to the most gorgeous man in the galaxy, and we made each other miserable. And you're right—I could have had any man in the room at that party, but I wasn't attracted to a single one of them. And when I dumped that drink in your lap, I definitely wasn't thinking of you as anybody's father."

She sensed his spirits begin to lighten, but she wasn't nearly done. "Someday I'm going to be old, and if you'd seen my grandmother, you'd know there's a good chance I'll be ugly as sin by the time I'm eighty. Are you going to stop loving me then? Is appearance all it comes down to with you? Because if it is, we're in just as much trouble as I thought."

"Of course it isn't. I didn't . . . I never . . ."

"Talk about throwing up smoke screens. I've always believed that you were so clear-thinking, but even on a bad day I'm thinking more clearly than you. God, Harry, next to me you're an emotional basket case."

That made him smile, and he looked so goofy that she realized she was finally getting through. She wanted to kiss away his fears, but she still had too many fears of her own to deal with, and their troubles were too big to be kissed away. She didn't want to have to spend the rest of their marriage reassuring him. She also didn't like how important her looks were to him. The face he loved so much was already showing signs of wear and tear. How was he going to feel when it went south with the rest of her body?

"After all these years of marriage, you'd think we'd understand each other better," he said.

"I can't keep living like this. We need to get whatever is broken between us permanently fixed."

"I don't know how we're going to do that."

"With a good marriage counselor, that's how. And the sooner we get one, the better." She stood on tiptoe, kissed him hard, and turned to the farmhouse. "Isabel! Could you come out here?"

18

I sabel and Ren lay naked together outside on the thick comforter, where they kept each other warm in the chilly night air. She gazed up at the sputtering candles in the chandelier that hung from the magnolia tree. He brushed her hair with his lips. "Too heavy for you?"

"Mmm . . . In a minute." Funny, but lying beneath him didn't bother her at all. Odd to feel so safe with such a dangerous man.

"Just for the record—that one sexual hang-up you used to have? I think we can safely say it's a thing of the past."

She smiled into his hair. "I was just trying to be polite."

"Do unto others?"

"A philosophy I try to live by."

He chuckled.

She trailed her fingers along his spine. He turned his lips into the pulse at her wrist, then nudged her bangle. "You always wear this."

"It's a reminder." She yawned and traced the outline of his ear with her index finger. " 'Breathe' is engraved inside."

"A reminder to stay centered, I remember. I still think it sounds boring."

"Our lives are so hectic that it's easy to lose our serenity. Touching the bangle keeps me calm."

"It would have taken a lot more than a bracelet to keep me calm tonight. And I'm not just talking about the last hour on this blanket."

She smiled. "The porcini weren't completely ruined."

"Just about."

He eased off her. She propped herself on an elbow and trailed her fingers across the hard landscape of his chest. "Your spaghetti al porcino was the best thing I ever tasted."

"It would have been even better an hour earlier. They've been fighting for months. I don't know why they decided they had to go into marriage counseling tonight."

"They needed some emergency triage. I'm not really a marriage counselor."

"You're sure not. You made them swear on their children's lives not to have sex."

"You weren't supposed to hear that."

"Pretty hard to go deaf when you're in the next room and everybody keeps telling you not to leave."

"We were hungry, and we were afraid you'd take our dinner with you. Physical communication is easy for them. It's the verbal that's causing them trouble, and they need to concentrate on that right now. They looked happy during dinner, didn't they?"

"As happy as two people can look who know they aren't going to get any for a while. And aren't you afraid those lists you told them to make will only stir things up again?"

"We'll see. One thing I didn't have a chance to mention to you— and I think you'll be happy about this . . ." She nibbled on his shoulder, not just to be manipulative, although that was part of it, but because it was right there in front of her and looked particularly tasty. "We're going to live together for a while."

He lifted his head far enough to regard her suspiciously. "Before I start dancing the tango, let me hear the rest of it."

The chandelier above their heads swayed in the night breeze. She used the tip of her finger to trace a ripple of shadow that meandered across his chest. "I'm moving into the villa tomorrow morning. Just for a few days."

"I've got a better idea. I'll move down here."

"Actually . . ."

"You didn't!" He sat up so fast he nearly knocked her over. "Tell me you didn't invite those two neurotics to stay in this farmhouse."

"Only for a few days. They need privacy."

"*I* need privacy. *We* need privacy." He fell back onto the comforter. "I'm going to kill you. Really. This time I'm going to do it. Do you have any idea how many ways I know to *take a human life?*"

"Quite a few, I'm sure." She slid her hand down over his stomach. "But I'm hoping you'll find something more productive to do."

"I'm cheap, but I'm not that easy." His breath caught.

"You sound easy." She let her fingers move lower, until they located a particularly sensitive region.

He groaned. "Okay, I'm cheap *and* easy. But let's try it on a bed this time?" He caught her head as she pressed her lips to his stomach. "We definitely need a bed." He moaned.

She nuzzled his navel. "I couldn't agree more."

"You're killing me, Doc. You know that, don't you?"

"And I haven't even shown you my vicious streak."

Ren spent the next day trying to talk Harry and Tracy out of staying at the farmhouse, but he had no luck. His only satisfaction lay in the last-minute lecture he inadvertently witnessed Isabel giving them.

"Remember," she said, just as he walked into the room at the villa that was supposed to be *his* office, "no sex. The two of you have a lot of work to do first. That's why I'm offering you the farmhouse. So you have time alone every evening to talk without any interruptions."

Ren backed into the hallway, but not before he saw Tracy give Harry a longing glance. "I guess," he heard her say. "But you have no idea how hard this is. Don't you think—"

"No, I don't." Isabel's voice trailed after him. "Sex has allowed the two of you to mask your problems. It's easier to get it on than talk it out."

He winced. *"Get it on."* Why did she have to put it that way? Less than two weeks ago she'd talked about sex being sacred, but she'd loosened up a lot since then. Not that he was complaining. He loved her responsiveness. He loved the way she enjoyed him, enjoyed them. At the same time, though, something about her attitude was beginning to stick in his craw.

He was being unreasonable, and he knew it. Maybe he had a guilty conscience. Not telling her about the change in the *Night Kill* script bothered him, and the fact that he felt guilty about it bothered him even more. Isabel had nothing to do with his career, nothing to do with *him* beyond the next few weeks. She was the one who'd spelled out the terms, and she'd been right, as usual. This was only about sex.

When it came right down to it, they were using each other. He was using her for companionship, for entertainment. He was using her to help him deal with Tracy and to work through his guilt over Karli. And, God knew, he was using her for sex, but that didn't qualify as a sin in the Book of Isabel.

Damn it, he didn't want to hurt her, not when he already had more sins on his soul than she could imagine—the drugs, the women he'd treated so callously, all the debris of his early years that still left a slimy trail behind him wherever he went. Sometimes when she gazed at him with those innocent eyes, he wanted to remind her that he didn't know how to play the good guy, but he never said a word, because he was a selfish son of a bitch and he didn't want her to walk away. Not yet. Not until he'd gotten what he needed and was ready to let her go.

One thing was certain: As soon as she found out about the new script and Kaspar Street's twisted desire for little girls, she'd be on her way out the door, and right before she got there, Ren had a feeling all four of those Cornerstones were going to be dropped on his head.

After dinner Tracy told the kids that she and Harry would be back in time for breakfast and that Marta would take care of them if they needed anything during the night. Ren spent the rest of the evening feeling resentful. He wanted Isabel in a bedroom that didn't have half a dozen people lurking outside the door. Instead, she'd excused herself and gone off to make notes on her book.

He headed for his office and tried to work on a character study of Street, but he couldn't concentrate. He lifted some weights and played with Jeremy's GameBoy for a while. Then he took a walk that didn't do a damn thing to work off his sexual frustration. Finally he gave up and went to bed, only to end up punching his pillow and cursing the senior Briggses, who were curled up in the farmhouse bedroom where he and Isabel should be.

Eventually he drifted off, but he hadn't been asleep for long before something warm cuddled next to him. It was about time. He loved to touch Isabel's bare skin while she slept. He smiled and drew her close— But something was very wrong. His eyes flew open, and he sat upright with a yelp.

Brittany's face puckered. "You yelled. Why'd you yell?" She lay curled on top of the covers, naked as a jaybird.

"You cannot sleep here!" he croaked.

"I heard a noise. I'm scared."

Not half as terrified as he was. He started to jump out of bed, then remembered she wasn't the only one naked. He grabbed the blanket and wrapped it around his waist.

"You're too wiggly," she protested. "I'm sleepy."

"Where's your nightgown? Never mind." He tucked the sheet around her so tightly she looked like a mummy, then picked her up.

"You're squishing me! Where we goin'?"

"To see the good fairy." He tripped over his blanket and almost dropped her. "Shit."

"You said—"

"I know what I said. And if you repeat it, your tongue'll fall out." Somehow he managed to maneuver her through the door, down the hall, and into Tracy's former bedroom without losing his blanket, but he made so much noise Isabel woke up.

"What . . . ?"

"She's scared, she's naked, and she's all yours." He dropped Brittany next to her.

"Who's that?" Steffie popped up from Isabel's other side. "Brit'ny?"

"I want Daddy!" Brittany wailed.

"It's all right, sweetheart." Isabel looked warm and tousle-haired. He'd never known a woman like her, one who was so unconscious of her sexual allure, although most men didn't seem to be as aware of it as he was. Vittorio's brother, the oily Dr. Andrea, saw it, though. He hadn't fooled Ren one bit today when he'd shown up with that phony excuse about telling Isabel that they'd rounded up the metal detectors. *Punk*.

Her nightgown dropped low on one shoulder, revealing the rounded top of a breast that should, at that exact moment, have been in his hand. She nodded toward his blanket. "Nice skirt."

He mustered his dignity. "We'll discuss this in the morning."

As he headed back to his room, he reminded himself that he'd come to Italy to get away from everything. Instead, he was throwing a frigging house party and adding another black mark to his soul.

Right before dawn it got worse. He pried open his eyelids and saw a foot stuck in his mouth. Not his.

A tiny toenail dug into his bottom lip. He winced and tried to move, only to have the other foot punch him in the chin. Then he felt the damp spot by his hip. And how could life get any better than this?

Diaper Boy cuddled closer. So much for Marta's taking over during the night. Ren weighed his options. Waking the kid meant a hassle, something Ren had no intention of dealing with at—he checked the clock—four in the morning. Resigned, he moved to dryer territory and willed himself back to sleep.

A few hours later he got a poke in the chest. "Want my *daddy!*"

The light filtering through his eyelids told him it was morning, but just barely. Where the hell was Marta? "Go back to sleep," he mumbled.

"Want my mommy *now!*"

Ren gave in to the inevitable, opened his eyes, and finally understood the reason parents went through this. Diaper Boy looked cute as hell. His dark curls stuck up all over the place, and his cheeks were rosy from sleep. A quick check of the mattress showed no new wet spots. Which meant . . .

Ren jumped out of bed, whipped on a pair of shorts, and grabbed him. Connor gave a startled yowl. Ren hauled him like a potato sack to the bathroom.

"Want Jer'my!"

"No more BS, kid." He gingerly pulled off the diaper, stared at it for a moment, then threw open the shutters and tossed it out the window. "Belly-up-to-the-bar time." He pointed down at the toilet. "That's the bar."

Connor thrust his lower lip and scowled, looking exactly like his mother during most of her marriage to Ren. "Potty bad."

"Tell somebody who cares."

Connor screwed up his face. "I want my mommy!"

He flipped up the toilet seat. "Do your business, and then we'll talk."

Connor stared at him.

Ren offered his most heartless sneer.

Connor walked backward to the tub and climbed in.

Ren crossed his arms and leaned against the door.

Connor poked the faucet.

Ren scratched his chest.

Connor picked up the soap.

Ren inspected his fingernails. "You might as well cut out the BS, tough guy, because I've got all day."

Connor gazed at the soap for a moment, then set it down and started to pee in the tub.

"No way." Ren grabbed him under the arms and stood him in front of the toilet. "Right here. Right now."

Connor craned his neck to look up at him.

"You heard me. Are you a man or a girl?"

Connor took his time thinking it over. He stuffed his finger up his nose, inspected his belly button. Then he peed in the toilet.

Ren grinned. "Way to go, dude."

Connor grinned back, then started to run for the door, only to stop in his tracks. "Poopy!"

"Aww, man . . . you sure?"

"Poopy!"

"I could do without this, you know." Ren picked him up, flipped the seat back down, and plunked him on top.

"Poopy!"

Sure enough . . .

When the kid was done, Ren held him under the tub faucet for a while, then headed for the bedroom, where he located a big safety pin and his smallest pair of stretch bikini briefs—a pair he seemed to remember Isabel admiring. He fastened them on the kid as best he could, then gave him the hairy eyeball. "These are mine, and if you get 'em wet, you're going to regret it. Understand?"

Connor stuck his thumb in his mouth, bent his head to inspect, then gave a deep, satisfied chortle.

The briefs stayed dry.

The next few days fell into a routine. Harry and Tracy appeared around breakfast time to attend to the children. Ren and Isabel spent part of the morning at the farmhouse, where they helped the others begin the laborious task of sweeping the area with metal detectors. Afterward Isabel headed off with her notebook, and Ren went to meet Massimo in the vineyard.

Massimo had been growing grapes all his life, and he didn't need any supervision, but Ren found something satisfying about strolling through the shady rows and feeling the hard clay soil of his ancestors beneath the soles of his shoes. Besides, he needed to get away from Isabel. He liked being with her too much for his own good.

Massimo gave him a grape to crush. "Are your fingers sticking together?"

"Not yet."

"Still not enough sugar. Maybe two more weeks, and then we will be ready for the *vendemmia*."

In the late afternoon, when Ren got back to the villa, he'd invariably find Jeremy hanging around waiting for him. The kid never said anything, but it hadn't taken Ren long to figure out that he wanted to practice his martial-arts moves. The boy was smart and well coordinated, and Ren didn't mind. Harry and Tracy were usually sealed away with Isabel for their daily counseling, but if the session ended in time, Harry liked to join them. Ren got a kick out of watching Jeremy teach his father what he'd learned.

Sometimes Ren found himself wondering how he'd have turned out if he'd had a father like Harry Briggs. Even Ren's success hadn't won his father's approval. Being an actor, especially a successful one, was too public, too vulgar—this from the man who'd been married to Ren's playgirl, pothead mother.

Fortunately, Ren had stopped caring about his father's opinion a long time ago. There was nothing useful about having the approval of a man he'd never respect.

Anna began pestering him about holding a *festa* after the harvest was in. "This was done for many years when I was a girl. Everyone who helped with the *vendemmia* would come to the villa on the first Sunday after the grapes were picked. There would be much food and laughter. But your Aunt Philomena decided it was too much trouble, and the tradition ended. Now that you are living here, we can begin again, yes?"

"I'm only living here temporarily." He'd been in Italy nearly three weeks. He had to go to Rome next week to meet with Jenks for a few days, and filming would start a couple of weeks after that. He hadn't discussed any of this with Isabel—not the meeting in Rome nor how much longer he'd be staying at the villa—and she hadn't asked. But then, why should she? They both knew that this was short-term.

Maybe he'd invite her to come with him. Seeing familiar sights through her eyes gave him a whole new view. Except he couldn't invite her. All the disguises in the world wouldn't keep some sharp-eyed paparazzo from spotting them, and being seen with him would finish off what little was left of her good-girl reputation.

There was also the inescapable fact that she'd refuse to go along once she discovered what *Night Kill* was really about.

His resentment resurfaced. She'd never understand what this role meant to him, just as she refused to understand that it wasn't some distorted image of himself he carried around that made him want to play bad guys. He simply couldn't identify with heroes, and that didn't have a freakin' thing to do with his demented childhood. Well, not much anyway. And since when did someone who hired crooked accountants and got engaged to an asshole have the right to sit in judgment?

It was a wonder their affair hadn't already fizzled out, although it was hard to picture anything simply fizzling where Isabel was concerned. No, when this affair ended, it would go out with a bang. The idea was so depressing that it took him a moment to realize Anna was still talking to him.

". . . but this is your home now—your family's home—and you will keep coming back. So we will hold the *festa* this year to begin a new tradition, yes?"

He couldn't imagine coming back, not when Isabel wasn't here, but he told Anna to go ahead with her plans.

"You're not one of those people who thinks pregnant women don't need sex, are you?" Tracy regarded Isabel accusingly. "Because if you are, take a good look at this man and tell me how any woman, pregnant or not, could resist him?"

Harry managed to appear both embarrassed and happy. "I don't know about that. . . . But really, Isabel, it's not necessary any longer. *Definitely* not necessary. We've had more than enough time to talk, and the lists you've asked us to make have been very helpful. I hadn't quite realized . . . I just didn't know . . ." A smile melted his face. "I never imagined all the ways she loves me."

"And I had no idea he admired so many things about me. *Me!*"
Tracy gave a shiver of delight. "I thought I knew everything about
him, but I'd only scratched the surface."

"Let's give it a little longer," Isabel said.

"What kind of marriage counselor are you?" Tracy retorted.

"No kind. I'm winging it. I told you that from the beginning.
You're the ones who insisted on this, remember?"

Tracy sighed. "We just don't want to screw things up again."

"Then let's discuss today's lists. Did each of you come up with
twenty attributes the other one has that you wish you had yourself?"

"Twenty-one," Tracy said. "I included his penis."

Harry laughed, and they kissed, and the pang of envy Isabel felt
made her ache. Marriage had its rewards for those who could survive the chaos.

"Hurry up! They're gone."

Isabel dropped her pen as Ren entered the villa's rear salon,
where she'd been sitting at a beautiful eighteenth-century desk
writing a note to a friend in New York. Since the Briggs family had
just left for dinner in Casalleone, she didn't have to ask Ren whom
he was talking about.

She reached down to pick up her pen, but he pulled her out of
the chair before she could grab it. He'd been so moody lately, one
minute acting as though he wanted to snap her head off, the next
minute looking as he did now, full of devilry. The more she was with
him, the more she sensed the battle he had going on inside him
between the person he believed himself to be and the man who was
no longer comfortable living inside his bad-guy skin.

He jerked his head toward the door. "Let's go. I figure we've got
two hours before they come back."

"Anyplace in particular?"

"The farmhouse. Too many people around here."

They raced down the hill, through the door, and up the farmhouse stairs. As they got to the top, she pushed him toward the smaller bedroom. "Clean sheets."

"Like that's going to last for long."

She pulled off her clothes while he locked the door, closed the shutters, and flipped on a lamp. Its low-wattage bulb cast the small room into shadow.

He tossed the contents of his pockets onto the nightstand and undressed. She lay on the narrow bed, then rolled to her side as he settled next to her. He nuzzled her neck and slipped off her bangle. "I want you completely naked for me." Her nipples pebbled at the husky, possessive note in his voice. She shut her eyes as he buried his lips in the palm of her hand. He spoke against her skin. "Naked except for this . . ."

He reached toward the nightstand. Seconds later cold metal snapped around her wrist.

Her lids shot open, and she let out a squeal of alarm. "What are you doing?"

"Taking charge." He snagged both wrists, the one that was free and the cuffed one, and drew them over her head.

"Well, stop it right now!"

"I'd rather not." He fed the chain through one of the bars in the headboard, then clamped the free cuff to her other wrist.

"You handcuffed me to the bed!"

"I'm so rotten I even surprise myself sometimes."

She tried to decide how upset she was, but couldn't quite get a bead on it. "These are real handcuffs."

"I had them FedExed." He slid his lips along the underside of her arm, just above the armpit. As she strained against the cuffs, her skin prickled with delicious waves of response.

"Don't you know there are rules for bondage?" She gasped as he found a nipple, drew it deep into his mouth, and sucked. "There's a . . . protocol!"

"I've never paid much attention to protocol."

He continued to abuse her poor, defenseless nipple, but she wouldn't let herself succumb to the delicious tremors until she'd made her point. "You're not ever supposed to use real handcuffs, only something that can be easily unfastened." She suppressed a moan. "At the very least they should be padded. And your partner has to *agree* to being tied up—did I mention that?"

"I don't believe you did." He settled back on his heels, pushed her knees apart, and gazed down at her.

She licked her lips. "Well, I'm mentioning it now."

His fingers played in the curls. "Duly noted."

She caught her lip between her teeth as he opened her. "I did . . . *ah* . . . a research paper when I was working on my master's."

"I see." The erotic timbre of his voice vibrated through her nerve endings. The motion of his thumb felt like a warm, wet feather stroking and probing. "You also need . . . a code word to use . . . *ahhhh* . . . if things go too far."

"We can do that. I even have a few ideas." He abandoned his caress too soon, moved up on her body, and whispered in her ear.

"They're not supposed to be sexual words." She slid her knee along his inner thigh.

"Now, what's the fun of that?" He cradled her breasts, lifted and molded them in his hands, feasted.

She gripped the bars of the headboard. "They're supposed to be words like 'asparagus' or 'carburetor.' I mean it, Ren. . . ." A moan slipped out before she could repress it. "If I say . . . 'asparagus,' it means you've . . . *ahh* . . . gone too far and you have to stop."

"If you say 'asparagus,' I'm going to want to stop, because I can't think of a bigger turn-off." He pulled away from her breast.

"Couldn't you say something like 'stud'? Or 'stallion'? Or . . ." Once again he whispered in her ear.

"That's sexual." She shifted her thigh ever so slightly to rub against him. He was so hard she shivered. He brushed her armpit and made another suggestion. She strained against the cuffs. *"Very* sexual."

"How about this?" His whisper changed to a dark purr.

"That's obscene."

"Great. Let's use it."

Her hips arched off the bed. "I'm using 'asparagus.' "

Just like that, he abandoned her. He settled back on his heels between her splayed feet so their bodies were no longer touching, and waited.

Despite the diabolic glint in his eye, it took her a moment to get the point. When was she going to learn to keep her mouth shut? She searched for a bit of dignity, not easy to do in her current, vulnerable position. "You can disregard that."

"Are you sure?"

And wasn't he just Mr. Smug? "I'm sure."

"Positive? In case you haven't quite taken it in, you're naked, handcuffed to the bed with no chance of rescue, and about to be violated."

"Uh-huh." She slid her knee higher on the bed.

He traced the soft curls with his thumb, enjoying the view. She felt his desire, burning as hot as her own, and heard the dark, husky note beneath his teasing. "I don't just make my living abusing women, you know. I threaten everybody who represents truth, justice, and the American way. And—not to put too fine a point on it—your only protection from me is a vegetable."

She moved her legs farther apart to show him she wasn't entirely defenseless. At the same time she promised herself that when this was over, she wouldn't rest until she'd used those handcuffs on him. Unless she missed her guess, he wouldn't put up much of a struggle.

"I see what you mean." His finger slipped inside her. "Now, be quiet so I can violate you."

Which he did. Masterfully. First with his fingers and then with his body. Moving on top of her, pushing inside. Torturing her until she heard herself beg. At the same time she'd never felt safer or more cherished than now, a prisoner to his exquisite care.

"Not yet, sweetheart." He gave her another fierce, possessive kiss and thrust deeper. "Not till I'm ready."

He was more than ready. His muscles strained as though he were the one in bondage. This fierce pleasure was costing him even more than it was costing her. He sank deeper into the cradle of her thighs. She wrapped her legs around him. They moved together, cried out together . . .

The shackles that held them to the earth broke free. In the end he became as much a prisoner as she.

While he dozed, she slipped out of bed and picked up the handcuffs that lay on the floor along with the discarded key. She gazed down at him. His thick lashes formed spiky crescents against his cheekbones, and strands of dark hair fell over his forehead. The contrast between his exotic olive skin and the white of the sheets gave him the look of a gorgeous infidel.

She made her way to the bathroom, where she stuffed the handcuffs and key under a towel. She should have hated what he did to her, but she hadn't, not for a moment. What had happened to the woman who needed to stay in control? Instead of feeling helpless and angry, she'd given him everything she had.

Including her love.

Her fingers constricted around the edge of the sink. She'd fallen in love with him. She stared at herself in the mirror, then dropped her eyes. Who wanted to look at someone that stupid? They'd barely known each other three weeks, yet she, the most cautious of women when it came to romantic relationships, had tumbled head over heels.

She splashed her face and tried to detach so she could consider the business of male-female attraction from a biological level. Early humans were attracted to their opposites as a method of ensuring that the strongest of the species survived. Some of that instinct still remained in most people, and obviously it still remained in her.

But what about her survival as a modern woman? What about her survival as a woman who'd been determined to engage in healthy relationships, a woman who'd vowed she'd never repeat her parents' tempestuous patterns? Her affair with Ren was supposed to have been about claiming her sexuality and liberating it. Instead, she'd liberated her heart.

She stared glumly down at the soap dish. She needed a plan.

Right. As if any of her other plans had worked.

For now she simply wouldn't let herself think about it. She'd go into total denial. Denial wasn't always bad. Maybe if she didn't dwell on her feelings, they'd disappear.

And maybe not.

19

W ould you like chocolate cake or cherry pie?"
Isabel stopped at the edge of the villa's garden and
watched Brittany extend a clay saucer toward Ren.

He gave the assortment of leaves and twigs all his concentration.
"I believe I'll have the cherry pie. And maybe a glass of scotch if it
wouldn't be too much trouble."

"You can't say that," Steffie admonished him. "You have to say
tea."

"Or a Slurpee," Brittany said. "We can have Slurpees."

"No, we can't, Brit'ny. Only tea. Or coffee."

"Tea will be fine." Ren took an imaginary cup and saucer from
her, his pantomime so skillful that Isabel could almost see it in
his hand.

She lingered for a few moments to observe. His concentration
when he played with the girls was oddly intense. He wasn't like that
with the boys. When he tossed Connor around or poked under the
hood of the recently repaired Maserati with Jeremy, he did it

casually. Equally odd was the fact that he seemed willing to play whatever game the girls decided to force on him, including imaginary ones like this tea party. She'd have to ask him about it.

She headed for the farmhouse to see if they'd made any progress since yesterday with the metal detectors. Giulia spotted her and gave a weary wave. She had a smudge on her cheek and shadows under her eyes. In the background three men and one of the women were methodically scanning the olive grove. Others stood around with shovels, ready to dig whenever the detectors beeped, which was much too frequently.

Giulia handed off her shovel to Giancarlo and came over to greet Isabel, who immediately asked for an update.

"More coins, nails, and part of a wheel," she said. "We found something bigger about an hour ago, but it was only part of an old stove."

"You look tired."

Giulia rubbed her cheek with the back of her hand, spreading the dirt. "I am. And my business is suffering because I am here all the time. Vittorio, he does not let this affect his work. He takes his groups out right on schedule, but me . . ."

"I know you're frustrated, Giulia, but try not to take it out on Vittorio."

She gave Isabel a wan smile. "I have been telling myself the same thing. Vittorio, he has to put up with so much from me."

They moved into the shade of one of the olive trees. "I've been thinking about Josie, Paolo's granddaughter," Isabel said. "Marta's talked to her about the statue, but apparently Josie's Italian isn't very good, so who knows how much she understood? I was thinking about calling her myself to see how much she knows, but maybe you should call. You know more about the family than I do."

"Yes, this is a good idea." She glanced at her watch, calculating the time difference. "I need to get back to the office. I will call her from there."

After Giulia left, Isabel took her turn with one of the metal detectors before she handed it over to Fabiola, Bernardo's wife, and returned to the villa. She fetched her notebook, then tucked herself away on one of the chairs in the rose garden.

The seclusion of the garden made it one of her favorite places. It lay on a narrow terrace of land below the formal gardens but was sheltered from view by a small grove of fruit trees. A horse grazed in a field by the woods, and the late-afternoon sun made a golden halo around the ruins of the old castle on the hilltop. It was warm today, more like early August than late September, and the scent of roses hung in the air.

She looked at the notebook in her lap but didn't open it. All the ideas she jotted down seemed to repeat her earlier books. She was getting the uneasy feeling that she'd already written everything she knew about overcoming personal crisis.

"There you are." Ren ambled toward her, wearing a blue-and-white-striped rugby over a pair of shorts. He propped his hands on the metal chair she was sitting in, and leaned down to give her a long kiss. Then he cupped her breasts. "Right here. Right now."

"Tempting. But I don't have the handcuffs with me."

He abandoned her breasts and sprawled in the chair next to her, looking sulky. "We're doing it in the car tonight just like everybody else in this town."

"You're on." She turned her face to the sun. "Assuming, that is, your female fan club doesn't find you."

"I swear those little girls have radar."

"You've been amazingly tolerant. I'm surprised you're spending so much time with them."

His eyes grew chilly. "What do you mean by that?"

"Just what I said."

"I don't want to talk about them."

She raised her eyebrows. He knew how to distance people just as effectively as he knew how to charm them, although she couldn't imagine why he felt the need to do it now. "Somebody's in a cheery mood."

"Sorry." He stretched out his legs and crossed them at the ankles, but the posture seemed more calculated than carefree, almost as if he were forcing himself to relax. "Did Tracy tell you she and Harry were going to rent a house in town?"

She nodded. "That apartment in Zurich was contributing to their troubles. It's too small for all of them. They decided it would be better if she and the kids stayed here, where they feel more at home, and let Harry commute on weekends."

"Am I the only one who finds it unnerving that my current lover is doing marriage counseling for my ex-wife?"

"It's not as if there's much confidentiality involved. One or the other seems to tell you everything we talk about."

"Something I've been trying my best to discourage." He picked up her hand and absentmindedly played with her fingers for a while. "Why are you putting yourself out like this? What's in it for you?"

"It's my job."

"You're on vacation."

"I don't have the kind of job that allows vacations."

"Every job allows vacations."

"You can't punch a time clock on what I do."

He frowned. "How can you be sure you're helping? Isn't there something arrogant in assuming you always know what's best for other people?"

"Do you think I'm arrogant?"

He gazed off at a row of ornamental grasses drifting in the breeze. "No. You're pushy and opinionated. But no, you're not arrogant."

"You're right, though. There is a kind of arrogance in thinking you know what's best for other people."

"Yet you persevere."

"Sometimes we focus on others' flaws so we don't have to focus on our own." She realized that her thumbnail had crept toward her teeth, and she dropped it back into her lap.

"Is that what you think you've done?"

She didn't use to, but now she had to wonder, didn't she? "I guess that's what I came to Italy to find out."

"How're you doin' so far?"

"Not too well."

He patted her leg. "If you need any help finding your flaws, you'll be sure to let me know. Like your neat fetish and the way you try to manipulate everything so you're in charge."

"I'm touched, but this is something I have to sort out for myself."

"If it's any consolation, I think you're a damn fine person."

"Thanks, but your standards are lower than mine."

He laughed, then squeezed her hand and gave her a sympathetic look. "Poor Dr. Fifi. Being a spiritual leader's a real bitch, isn't it?"

"Not as much as being a clueless spiritual leader."

"You're not clueless. You're just evolving." He brushed her cheek with his thumb.

She didn't want him turning sensitive on her. For days now she'd been trying to convince herself she wasn't really in love with him, that her subconscious had invented the emotion so she didn't have to feel guilty about the sex. But it wasn't true. She loved him, all right, and this moment explained why. How could someone who was her polar opposite understand her so well? She felt a sense of completion when they were together. He needed someone to remind him of his decency, and she needed someone to keep her from becoming self-righteous. But she knew he didn't see it the same way.

"Ren!" Two little girls came bursting through the shrubbery.

He dropped his head back and groaned. "They do have radar."

"We've been looking everywhere for you," Steffie said. "We built a house, and we want you to play with us."

"Time to get to work." He squeezed Isabel's hand and rose. "Hey, go easy on yourself, okay?"

As if that would ever happen . . . She watched him disappear. One part of her wanted to will away her love for him, but the other part wanted to hold on to it forever. A little well-deserved self-pity bubbled inside her.

Way to go, God. You couldn't have thrown somebody like Harry Briggs at me for a soul mate. Oh, no. You had to give me a man who murders women for a living. Nice going, Pal.

She threw aside her notebook. She was too distracted to write anything, so she might as well go down to the farmhouse and take a turn with a shovel. Maybe she could work off some of her negative energy.

Andrea Chiara was there when she arrived. He and Vittorio were cut from the same rogue's cloth, but Dr. Andrea wasn't quite as harmless, which made the immature part of her wish Ren were around to witness the way he kissed her hand in greeting.

"With another beautiful woman to inspire us," he said, "the work will go faster."

She glanced surreptitiously toward the villa, but alas, Ren was nowhere to be seen.

Tracy showed up as Isabel was finishing her shift. Her eyes danced with excitement. "I just heard from Giulia, and the house we're renting in town is going to be ready for us in three days."

"I'm so glad."

"It'll be hard being away from Harry so much, but we'll talk on the phone every night, and he can work eighteen hours a day if he wants without feeling like he has to hurry home at night or I'll bitch at him. Best of all, when he flies down on weekends, we'll have him all to ourselves, no cell phone."

"I think it's a good plan."

"As we get closer to my due date, he's going to work from here. The kids are over the moon, knowing they don't have to go back to Zurich. They're picking up Italian a lot faster than I am, and they've gotten attached to Anna and Marta. You'll be here for another month, and Ren's going to be around for almost three weeks. We'll be so much happier here."

Three weeks. He hadn't told her. She could have asked, but she'd hoped he'd say something instead of acting as though the future didn't exist for them, even though it didn't. Ren was hardly the serial womanizer the media depicted him to be, but different times in his life seemed to be marked with different relationships. Years from now he'd remember her only as his Tuscan affair. She didn't like how vulnerable she'd made herself, but she hadn't figured out any other way to live.

Tracy had stopped talking long enough to regard her with amusement. "You're the only person I've ever met who can do manual labor and not get dirty."

"Years of practice."

Tracy gestured toward the olive grove, where Andrea was smoking a cigarette as he finished his turn with a metal detector. "I made an appointment with Dr. Wet Dream for next week. Anna said he's a wonderful doctor, despite his playboy reputation. I might as well enjoy myself while my feet are in the stirrups."

"Let me add some more good news, then. I think it's time to lift the sex ban."

Tracy rubbed her stomach and looked thoughtful. "Okay."

This was hardly the reaction Isabel had expected. "Is there a problem?"

"Not exactly." She reached under her knit top to scratch. "But . . . would you mind not telling Harry you lifted the ban?"

"Your marriage is about open communication, remember?"

"I know, but—oh, Isabel, I love the talking. Last night we talked about whales—and not the shape of my body either. We were trying to think of how many species we could name. And the scariest movie we could remember from when we were kids. He let me tell him about this argument I had with my roommate in college that still makes me mad, and all this time I thought chocolate ripple was his favorite ice cream, but it's butter pecan. We listed every present we could remember that we'd ever given each other and whether we really liked it or not. Even though I've been walking around with my legs crossed all week because I'm so horny I can't stand it, I don't want to give up the talking. It's not just my looks after all. He loves the whole package."

Isabel felt another pang in the vicinity of her heart. For all their emotional disorder, Tracy and Harry shared something precious. "I'm lifting the ban," she said. "As far as telling Harry, let your conscience be your guide."

"Great," Tracy said glumly.

Tracy exchanged a few words with Andrea, then set off for the villa. She worked with the girls on their reading for a while and tried to give Jeremy a history lesson, but she had trouble concentrating. What was she going to do about Isabel's decision to lift the sex ban?

She was still wrestling with the problem that night as she and Harry walked hand in hand back to the farmhouse. She was a spoiled rich girl, and she hated moral dilemmas, but her marriage wasn't going to work if she didn't have the courage to face the challenges straight on. As they entered through the kitchen door, she decided this would be a good time to use a few of the new skills Isabel had been teaching them, so she took both his hands and looked him straight in the eye.

"Harry, there's something I'm supposed to tell you, but I don't want to. I have a very good reason, and I'd like your permission to withhold the information."

She knew he'd want some time to think this over, and she was more than happy to study his dear, familiar face while she waited.

"Does it involve life and death?" he finally asked.

Now she was the one who needed to think. "Almost, but not quite."

"Is it something I want to know?"

"Oh, yes."

"But you don't want to tell me."

"I really don't. Not right now. Soon. Very soon."

He lifted one eyebrow ever so slightly. "Because . . . ?"

"Because I love you so much. I love talking to you. Talking is important to me, and once you know this thing that I don't want you to know yet, I'm afraid we won't talk so much, and I'll start thinking you only love me for my face."

His eyes lit up. "Isabel lifted the sex ban!"

She dropped his hands and stomped away. "I hate honest communication."

He was chuckling as he caught up with her. He scooped her into his arms and kissed her forehead. The baby kicked between them. "Hey, you're not the only one who loves talking. And you know by now that I'd love you if you were as ugly as my Uncle Walt. Let's make a deal: For every minute we spend naked, we'll triple that time in conversation. Which, with the way I'm feeling now, means a lot of conversation."

She smiled into his neck. Just the smell of his skin made her blood rush. But what if they slipped back into old patterns? They'd had a brutal lesson in what it took to make their relationship work.

Maybe it was time to trust in the tough new fabric of their marriage.

"First you've got to make out with me," she said. "Clothes on. No hands below the waist."

"Deal. And the first one who breaks down has to give the other a full-body massage."

"You're on." What the heck. She loved giving him full-body massages.

He grabbed her and pulled her onto the couch in front of the fireplace, but she'd barely leaned into the cradle of his shoulder before she groaned. "I have to pee. I always have to pee. If I ever even mention getting pregnant again, leave me on a mountaintop to die."

He laughed and hoisted her up. "I'll come along."

As Harry followed his wife upstairs, he couldn't think of one thing he'd done in his life that made him deserve this woman. She was tempest to his calm, quicksilver to his base metal. He followed her into the bathroom. She didn't protest when he took a seat on the side of the tub. Until Isabel and her lists, Tracy hadn't known that he made excuses to join her when she was on the toilet simply because he loved the intimacy of it, the everyday coziness. Tracy'd laughed like hell when he'd tried to explain it, but he knew she understood.

"Favorite vegetable?" she said. She hadn't forgotten how much he wanted her, and she was making sure he remembered her concern. "Never mind. I know. It's peas."

"Green beans," he replied. "Not cooked too much. A little crisp." He reached over and cupped her calf. He knew now that he had to say what he was feeling instead of assuming that Tracy already understood what was so obvious to him.

"I love the talking, too, you know." Honesty compelled him to add, "But right now I'm a lot more interested in sex. God, Trace, it's been so long. Do you know what you do to me? Just being with you?"

"Yes, because you've told me." They smiled at each other, and a few moments later headed for the bedroom. Once inside the door she gave him her coquette's sly gaze. "What if you get me pregnant?"

"Then I'll marry you. As many times as you like."

He kissed her awhile before she drew back. "This baby's the last one, I swear. I'm getting my tubes tied."

"If you want to keep having babies, it's okay with me. We can afford a few more."

"Five's gonna do me. I always wanted five." She nibbled at the corner of his mouth. "Oh, Harry, I'm so glad you're not mad about this baby."

"It was never the baby. You know that now." He touched her face. "I hate being so insecure."

"I thought I'd driven you away."

He followed the line of her jaw with his thumb. Her lips were puffy from their kisses, and he suspected his were, too. "We're not taking any more chances, okay? Marriage counseling every six months, whether we need it or not. And I still think we should let Isabel know that we refuse to work with any shrink but her."

"She'll figure it out when we show up on her doorstep twice a year."

They'd reached the bedroom, and they were ready to get down to the serious business of making out. At first they kept their mouths closed, but that didn't last for long. When her lips went slack, he pressed his advantage, slipping his tongue into the honey-sweet recess of her mouth. They played that way for a while, but it wasn't enough. His hand grew greedy, and he curled his palm around her breast. "From the waist up," he whispered.

"Waist up is fair."

He slipped her top over her head. She was studying his face as he unclasped her bra. She'd told him she never got tired of looking at him.

Her breasts fell free, and his mouth went dry as he gazed down at her swollen nipples. He knew they were tender, just as he knew she liked having them touched anyway. He remembered her shock when she saw how high her pregnancy breasts ranked on his turn-on list. It had never occurred to him to tell her. He'd assumed she would have figured it out from the way he couldn't keep his hands off them.

She made a throaty exclamation as he dropped his head to suckle. Then she slipped her hand between his legs. "Oops. I lose."

His control broke, and their clothing flew. She gave him a hard shove, and he fell back on the bed. Her hair tumbled in an inky cloud over one shoulder as she mounted him, and then she lifted a bit so he could have the access she knew he craved. He stroked her with his fingers, moving up and down the wet, musky valley before he delved inside.

The memory of what they'd almost lost made them fierce. He touched her everywhere, and she did the same to him. They gazed into each other's eyes, treasuring what they saw.

"I love you forever," he whispered.

"And ever," she whispered back.

Then their bodies found a perfect rhythm, and speech became impossible. Together they tumbled into the beautiful darkness.

20

T he villa's two-hundred-year-old dining room table groaned
with food. Ornate oval platters offered up a roast leg of lamb
as well as guinea hens stuffed with garlic and sage. Escarole
leaves fried a golden brown held a pungent cargo of pine nuts, olives,
anchovies, and raisins, while slivers of pancetta flavored a simple
bowl of green beans. Fresh loaves of pane toscano spilled from a
basket lined with antique linen towels bearing the family crest.

Despite the room's grand arches and religious frescoes, the
atmosphere was informal. The Briggs children chased tiny meat
ravioli around their plates and stuffed themselves with wedges of
homemade pizza. Ren demanded a second helping of the chestnut
pasta, and Isabel indulged in an extra slice of polenta, grilled crisp
on the outside but soft and steaming inside. There were creamy
wedges of pecorino, chocolate-dipped figs, and wine—a lively red
from their own vineyard and a fruity white Cinque Terre.

Ren was inherently Italian, therefore a man who enjoyed a good
party, and he'd used the Briggs family's impending departure the

next morning as an excuse to invite company for dinner. Vittorio and Giulia sat at the table, along with the various members of Massimo and Anna's family. Dr. Andrea Chiara was noticeably absent, even though Isabel had suggested he be invited.

Massimo talked about the *vendemmia*, the grape harvest that would begin in two days, while Anna and Marta jumped up and down to bring more food to the table. No one spoke of the statue. They'd finished searching the olive grove with the metal detectors and turned up nothing.

"You are always so nice to her," Giulia said quietly to Isabel, so that Tracy, who was at the other end of the table, wouldn't overhear. "If she had been Vittorio's wife before me, I would hate her."

"Not if Vittorio had tried to get rid of her as hard as Ren did," Isabel replied.

"Even so . . ." Giulia flicked her hand. "Ah, I am not fooling you, I know. It is my jealousy that makes me not like her. Some women, they get pregnant just by looking at a man. Even Paolo's granddaughter Josie is pregnant again."

"I was with the children when you told Ren you'd spoken with her. What did she say?"

Giulia picked at a bread crust. "That she's pregnant. Her second." She gave Isabel a watery smile. "Sometimes I think everybody else in the world is pregnant. It makes me feel sorry for myself, which is not a good thing."

"She didn't know anything about the statue?"

"Very little. It wasn't so easy for Josie to talk with Paolo after her mother died, because her Italian is not very good. But they still kept in touch, and he always sent her gifts."

"Gifts? Do you think—"

"No statue. I asked, especially after she said she had a hard time getting pregnant with her first baby."

"It might be good to have a list of everything he sent. There could be a clue somewhere. A map tucked in a book, a key—something."

"I did not think of that. I will call her back tonight."

"Potty!" Connor shrieked from his booster seat at the bottom of the table just as an apple cake appeared.

Harry and Tracy jumped up at once.

"I want man!" He jabbed his finger at Ren, who grimaced.

"Gimme a break, dude. Go with your dad."

"Want you!"

Tracy flapped her arms like a frantic chicken. "Don't argue with him. He'll have an A-C-I-D-E-N-T."

"He wouldn't dare." Ren gave the toddler his death glare.

Connor plopped his finger in his mouth and chuckled.

Ren sighed and gave in to the inevitable.

"It took him a while to get the idea, but he potty-trained in a day," Tracy bragged to Fabiola as Ren carried Connor from the table. "I guess after four kids you finally figure out how to get the job done."

Ren snorted from the next room.

One hour slipped into the next. A throat-searing grappa appeared along with a sweeter vinsanto for dipping the hazelnut-studded cantucci. The breeze coming in through the open doors had turned chilly, but Isabel had left her sweater at the farmhouse when she'd moved her things back that morning. She rose and touched Ren's shoulder, briefly interrupting his discussion with Vittorio about Italian politics. "I'm going upstairs to borrow one of your sweaters."

He nodded absentmindedly and returned to the conversation.

The villa's master bedroom held dark, heavy furnishings, including a hand-carved wardrobe, gilded mirrors, and a bed with four fat posts. Yesterday afternoon she and Ren had stolen an hour between those posts while the Briggs family had gone sight-seeing.

As a little shiver passed through her, she considered the possibility that she might be turning into a sex addict. But she knew that it was more likely an addiction to Lorenzo Gage.

She headed for the dresser, only to stop short as she spotted something on the bed. She moved closer to see what it was.

Ren had drunk more than enough wine, so he passed on the grappa. He intended to be sober tonight when he got down and dirty with Dr. Isabel. He felt as if a giant clock had begun ticking over their heads, counting off the time they had left. In less than a week he had to leave for his meetings in Rome, and not long after, he'd be going for good. He looked around for her, then remembered that she'd gone to his bedroom to borrow one of his sweaters.

An alarm sounded in his brain. He shoved back from the table and made a dash for the stairs.

Isabel recognized his footsteps in the hallway. He had a distinctive walk, measured steps, light and graceful for such a tall man. He ambled through the doorway and stuffed his hands in his pockets. "Find a sweater?"

"Not yet."

"There's a gray one in the bureau." He wandered across the carpet. "It's the smallest one I've got."

She sat on the side of the bed holding the script she'd found. "When did you get this?"

"Maybe you'd rather have my blue sweater. That? A couple of days ago. The blue one's clean, but I wore the gray a few times."

"You didn't say anything about it."

"Sure I did." He rummaged through the drawer.

"You didn't tell me you'd received the script."

"It's been a little crazy around here, in case you haven't noticed."

"Not that crazy."

He shrugged, pulled out a sweater, then dug for another.

She ran her thumb over the label. "Why didn't you mention it?"

"There's been a lot going on."

"We talk all the time. You didn't say a word."

"I guess I didn't think about it."

"I find that a little hard to believe, since I know how important this is to you."

Although the motion was subtle, his body seemed to uncoil, almost like a snake before it struck. "This is starting to sound like an interrogation."

"You told me how anxious you were to read the final script. It seems strange that you never mentioned it was here."

"It doesn't seem strange to me. My work is private."

"I see." Moments before, she'd been remembering their love-making with pleasure, but now she felt sad and a little cheap. She was the woman he slept with—not his friend, not even a real lover, because true lovers shared more than their bodies.

He didn't quite meet her eyes. "You don't like my films anyway. Why should you care?"

"Because you care. Because we talked about it. Because I tell you about my work. Pick one." She tossed down the script and rose from the bed.

"You're making too big a deal out of this. I just—Jenks changed directions a little, that's all. I'm still processing. You're right. I should have said something. But I guess I didn't want to have to get into it with you again. Frankly, Isabel, I'm a little tired of having to defend what I do for a living."

First his anger, then his guilt, and now he'd gone on the attack. Classic. She wanted to retaliate, but that's not how healthy relationships were built, and she needed this relationship to be healthy so much she couldn't breathe.

"All right. That's fair." She fingered her bangle and took a deep breath. "I have been judgmental, and I need to stop. But I don't like being shut out."

He pushed in the bureau drawer with his knee. "Jesus, you make it sound like we're—like we have— Shit."

"A relationship?" Her palms were clammy. "Is that what you're trying to say? I'm making it sound like we have a relationship?"

"No. We do have a relationship. A great relationship. I'm glad about it. But . . ."

"It's just sex, right?"

"Hey! You're the one who set the rules, so don't turn this back on me."

"Is that what you think I'm doing?"

"What I think you're doing is treating me like one of your goddamn patients."

She couldn't do this anymore. She couldn't stay calm and listen. She couldn't feed back what he was telling her, then process it using the principles she believed in so deeply. He was right. She'd made the rules, and now she was violating them. But those rules had been set an emotional lifetime ago.

She crossed her arms over her chest and hugged herself. "Excuse me. Apparently I've overstepped."

"You expect too much, that's all. I'm not a saint like you, and I've never pretended to be, so lay off, will you?"

"Of course." She made her way to the door, but before she got there, he called out from behind her.

"Isabel—"

A saint would have turned back so they could settle this, but she was no saint, and she kept walking.

Ren stood in the darkened doorway gazing out at the marble statues faintly lit by the moonlight washing the garden. The villa was quiet except for Dexter Gordon's heartbreaking saxophone playing behind him. Harry and Tracy had moved back in for the night so Isabel could have the farmhouse to herself again, but they'd gone to bed hours ago. Ren rubbed his eyes. Dr. Isabel Favor, the great believer in talking things out, had turned her back on him and walked away. Not that he blamed her. He'd been a prick.

His amazon had too many tender spots, and he was starting to bruise every one of them. But it was either bruise or get bruised, right? And he couldn't let her poke around in his psyche again, delving into all those pockets of self-disgust he'd been carrying around for as long as he could remember. She'd set the conditions of their relationship. *"This is only about sex,"* she'd said. *"A short-term physical commitment."*

He lit a cigarette. Why did she have to be so damned pushy? She'd go ballistic when she realized he'd be playing a child molester. Not only that, but she knew how much time he'd spent with the girls. She'd put two and two together in a heartbeat and figure out he'd been playing with them as part of his research. Then all hell really would break loose, and just like that he'd lose what little of her respect he'd been able to gain. The story of his life . . .

He took a deep drag. This was his punishment for getting involved with a righteous woman. All that nutty goodness had sucked him in, and now he was suffering for it. Food didn't taste as good when they weren't together; music didn't sound as sweet. He should be getting bored with her. Instead, he was bored without her.

He could get back into her good graces with a simple apology. *Sorry I held out on you.* It wouldn't occur to her to hang on to a grudge, and unlike him, she didn't know how to sulk. She deserved an apology, but then what? God help her, she was falling in love with him. He hadn't wanted to acknowledge it, even to himself, but she telegraphed her emotions. He could see it in her eyes, hear it in her voice. The smartest woman he knew, and she was falling in love with a man who was leaving invisible smudge marks on her skin whenever he touched her. And the worst thing—the thing he couldn't forgive himself for—was how good it felt to receive the love of a righteous woman.

His anger, as misplaced as it was, resurfaced. In so many ways she knew him better than anyone, so why hadn't she protected herself? She deserved someone with a clean past. A Boy Scout, a student-council president, someone who'd spent spring break building houses for the poor instead of getting wasted.

He took a final drag and flicked the butt onto the loggia. Acid burned in the pit of his stomach. Any villain worth his stripes would take advantage of the situation. Enjoy what he could get and walk away without a qualm. Villains were easy to figure out. But what would the hero do?

The hero would walk away before the heroine could get hurt anymore. The hero would make the break as clean as he could and do it in a way that would leave the heroine with a sense of relief that she'd escaped disaster so easily.

"I heard music."

He whipped around and saw Steffie padding across the marble floor toward him. This was her last night here. With the kids gone, he'd finally have some peace and quiet, except he'd already told them they could come back every day to swim.

She wore a faded yellow nightgown printed with some kind of cartoon character he supposed he should be able to identify but couldn't. Her dark, pixie cut was sticking up at the cowlick, and she had a crease on her cheek. As she came to his side, he knew he'd have to rely on all the acting technique he'd ever learned to play Street, because no matter how much research he did, he'd never be able to understand how anyone could hurt a kid. "What are you doing up?"

She pulled her nightdress to her thighs, and he saw a thin scratch on her calf. "Brit'ny kicked me while she was sleeping and cut my leg with her toenail."

He needed a drink. He didn't want pixie-haired little girls coming to him for comfort in the middle of the night. During the day it was different. He could detach and observe. But not at night, when he already felt a thousand years old. "You'll live. Go back to bed."

"You're crabby."

"Go see your mom and dad."

Her dark brows slammed together. "They *locked* their door!"

He had to smile. "Yeah, well, life's tough."

"What if I saw a spider?" she said indignantly. "Who'd kill it?"

"You would, pal."

"Nuh-uh."

"You know what I used to do when I was a kid and saw a spider?"

"Stomp on it hard."

"No. I'd scoop it up and take it outside."

Her eyes grew round and horrified. "Why'd you do *that*?"

"I like spiders. I had a pet tarantula once." It had died, of course, because he'd stopped taking care of it, but he wasn't going to tell her that. "Most spiders are pretty nice bugs."

"You're weird." She squatted down to pick at some chipped blue glitter nail polish on her big toe. Her vulnerability worried him. Just like Isabel, she needed to toughen up.

"Time to cut the crap, Stef. That spider stuff is old news. You're smart, and you're strong enough to handle it without running to Mommy and Daddy in the middle of the night like a big baby."

She gave him the haughty look she'd learned from her mother. "Dr. Isabel says we need to talk about our feelings."

"Yeah, well, we all know how you feel about spiders, and we're tired of hearing it. You're doing some kind of emotional transfer thing anyway."

"That's what she said. Because I was worried about my mom and dad."

"You sure don't need to worry about them now."

"You don't think I should be scared of spiders anymore?" She looked both accusatory and skeptical, but he also thought he detected a hint of hope.

"You don't have to like them, but stop making them so important. It's better to face what's scaring you than to keep running from it."

Hypocrite. When had he ever made himself face that decades-old emptiness inside him?

She scratched her hip. "Did you know we get to go to school here?"

"I heard." Jeremy had apparently led his sisters in a rebellion against Tracy's homeschooling attempts, which had ended up with Harry writing a check to the local officials so the kids could attend the school in Casalleone until they left at the end of November. When Harry had asked his opinion, Ren had pointed out that they already spoke enough Italian for minimal exchanges, and he thought it would be a good experience for them.

"Are you going to marry Dr. Isabel?"

"No!"

"Why not? You like her."

"Because Dr. Isabel is too nice for me, that's why."

"I think you're nice."

"That's because you're a pushover."

She yawned and slipped her hand in his. "Tuck me back in bed now, okay?"

He gazed down at the top of her head, then pulled her to his side for a quick squeeze. "Okay, but only because I'm bored."

They all gathered in front of the villa the next morning to see the Briggses off, even though they weren't going far. Ren slipped Jeremy a couple of CDs he knew the kid liked, accepted a sticky kiss from Connor, admired Brittany's final cartwheel, and gave Steffie a last-minute pep talk about not being a wimp. Isabel stayed busy, talking to everyone but him. He wasn't surprised she was still pissed. In her world the fact that he hadn't mentioned the arrival of the script counted as a major betrayal.

As the car disappeared down the lane, she waved at Anna, then turned to head back to the farmhouse. Marta was moving in with Tracy to help take care of the kids, and Isabel would be alone there. As he watched her walk toward the path, the roll he'd eaten for breakfast settled into a hard lump in his stomach. He might as well get this over with. "Hold on," he said. "I've got something for you."

She turned. He took in the black sweater she'd knotted around her waist, the sleeves neatly crossed. Everything about her was tidy, except her feelings for him. Hadn't she figured out yet that she'd gotten caught up in the lure of the forbidden? And she wasn't the only one.

He picked up the script he'd left between the rails of the balustrade, carried it over to her, and held it out. "Take it."

She didn't say anything. She just looked at it.

"Go on. Read it."

She didn't get sarcastic as he would have. Instead, she nodded and tucked it under her arm.

As he watched her walk away, he reminded himself he was doing the right thing. But, God, he'd miss having her in his life. He'd miss everything about their time together . . . except the nagging certainty that he'd somehow corrupt her.

He spent the rest of the morning in the vineyard so he could avoid smoking his way through the nearest pack of cigarettes. As he listened to Massimo, he tried not to think about which scene Isabel might be reading at that moment or how she'd be reacting to it. Instead, he watched the old man glance at the sky and ruminate on all the disasters that could still transpire before the next day's *vendemmia*—a sudden squall, an early frost that would turn the ripe fruit into dripping slime.

When he could no longer handle Massimo's gloom, he headed back to the villa, but it felt depressingly empty without the kids running around. He'd just decided to go for a swim when Giulia showed up looking for Isabel.

"She's at the farmhouse," he told her.

"Would you give this to her? She wanted me to call Paolo's granddaughter again and ask about the gifts he sent. I talked to Josie last night, and this is everything she remembered."

Ren took the piece of paper she held out and studied the list. It was made up of practical items, things for the house and garden: clay pots, a set of fireplace tools, a bedroom lamp, a key rack, bags of dried porcini, wine, olive oil. He tapped the paper with his finger. "This lamp . . . maybe the base . . ."

"Alabaster—and too small. I asked."

"It was worth a try." He folded the paper and put it in his pocket. Even though he had no belief in the statue's powers, he didn't like the fact that he hadn't been able to help them find it. As the current lord of the manor, he somehow felt as if he should have come up with a way to get it done.

After Giulia left, he headed for the pool to swim some laps. The water was chilly, but not cold enough to numb him, something he would have welcomed. When he got tired, he flipped to his back, and that was when he saw Isabel sitting by the umbrella.

She'd crossed her ankles and tucked them off to the side. Her straw hat shaded her face, and the script lay in her lap. He dove under, then resurfaced as far away from her as he could get in a cowardly desire to postpone the inevitable. Finally he pushed himself up onto the deck and grabbed his towel.

She watched him come toward her. Normally her battle to keep her eyes from drifting to his crotch would have amused him, but today he didn't feel like laughing.

"It's a great script," she said.

Apparently she'd decided to lull him before she went in for the kill. He played the world-weary movie star, sprawling down next to her, tilting his head back, and shutting his eyes against the sun. "Yeah."

"It's not too difficult to figure out why you didn't want me to see it."

A surly attitude was the quickest way to bring this to its ugly conclusion. "I'm not looking for any lectures."

"I won't give you any. This isn't a film I'd stand in line to watch, but I know I'll be the exception. The critics are going to love it, and so will audiences."

He popped open one eye. Instead of coming at him directly, she was setting him up for a sneak attack.

"I can see why you're excited about it," she went on. "This part is going to push you to your limits. You're at the place in your career right now where you need that."

He couldn't take any more, and he shot out of his chair. "He's a child molester!"

She blinked her eyes. "I know that's not what you signed on for, but it'll be an amazing performance challenge." She had the balls to smile at him. "You're sublimely talented, Ren, and you've been waiting your whole career for something like this."

He shoved a chair out of his way and headed across the pool deck. At that moment he almost hated her. She was so relentlessly reasonable, so unmercifully fair, and now he was going to have to spell out the details. "It seems to have escaped your attention that I was spending all that time with Tracy's girls because I've been using them for research."

"Yes, I figured that out."

He whirled on her. "Steffie and Brittany! Those great little girls. Don't you understand? I've been trying to get inside Street's skin and see them through his eyes."

The brim of her hat shaded her face, so he thought he mistook her expression. Then she shifted her head, and he saw he hadn't been mistaken at all. Her eyes were filled with sympathy. "I can only imagine how difficult that must have been for you."

Right then he lost it. It wasn't enough for her to rip his skin off. She had to gnaw at his bones, too. "Goddamn it!" He hated her goodness, her compassion. He hated everything that set her apart from him. He had to get away, except his feet wouldn't move, and the next thing he knew, she had her arms wrapped around his waist.

"Poor Ren." She lay her cheek to his chest. "For all your sarcasm, you adore those little girls. Getting ready for this part must be awful."

He wanted to push her away, but she was balm to his wounds, and he drew her close instead. "They're so damn trusting."

"And you're completely trustworthy."

"I've been using them."

"You're scrupulous about your work. Of course you need to understand children to play the part. You haven't been a threat to those girls, not for a second."

"God, I know that, but . . ." She wasn't going to walk away. In the back of his mind he knew that meant he'd have to start all over again. But not today, not right now.

It defied logic, but he wanted to talk to her about it. He took a few steps back, putting just enough distance between them so he didn't have to worry about corrupting her. "The script . . . It's much better than Jenks's original concept. There are times the audience will actually be rooting for Street, even though he's a monster."

"That's what makes it brilliant and horrifying."

"It shows how seductive evil can be. Everybody who sees the film is going to have to look inside themselves. Jenks is brilliant. I know that. I just . . ." His mouth seemed to dry up.

"I understand."

"I'm turning into a goddamn wimp."

"Don't swear. And you've always been a wimp. But you're such a wonderful actor nobody's figured that out."

Isabel had hoped to make him smile, but he was too caught up in his inner turmoil for smiles. This explained why he'd been so prickly lately. As much as he wanted to play the part, he was also repulsed by it.

"It's Street's film," he said. "Nathan, the hero, is basically white wallpaper."

"You've never had any problem detaching from your characters in the past, and you won't have a problem detaching from this one."

She'd intended her words to comfort him, but he looked even more troubled.

"I don't understand you," he said. "You should hate this. Aren't you the big proponent of only sending good fairy dust out into the world?"

"That's the way I want to live my own life. But nothing's simple when it comes to art, is it? Artists have to interpret the world as they see it, and their vision can't always be beautiful."

"Do you think this film is art?"

"Yes. And so do you, or you wouldn't be putting yourself through this."

"It's just . . . I wish . . . Hell, I wish my agent had forced them to put my name over the title."

His bluster didn't fool her, and her heart ached for him. The fact that he was so obviously conflicted might mean he'd finally gotten tired of skulking down dark alleys. Maybe he'd be ready to play someone heroic when this was over. It was time he moved past his narrow view of himself, both as an actor and as a human being.

Now, however, his gaze held nothing but cynicism. "So you're giving me absolution for the sin I'm about to commit."

"Making this film isn't a sin. And I'm hardly in a position to offer absolution."

"You're the best I've got."

"Oh, Ren." She walked over to him and reached up to brush a lock of hair from his forehead. "When are you going to start seeing yourself for who you are instead of who you think you are?"

"Man, are you ever a pushover."

She reminded herself she was his lover, not his therapist, and it wasn't her job to fix him, especially when she hadn't made a dent in healing herself. She began to take a step backward, but he snagged her arm, his grip so tight it almost hurt. "Let's go."

She saw something that looked almost like desperation on his face. He pulled her to the farmhouse, to the bedroom. She knew that something was wrong, but she caught his fever anyway and tore at her clothes as urgently as he tore at his.

As they fell onto the mattress, she drew him upon her. She wanted him to drive away the premonition that it was all coming to an end faster than either of them could stop it. He gripped her behind the knees and spread her legs. Her orgasm was shattering but not joyous—a shadow racing across the sun.

Ren wrapped a towel around his waist and headed down to the kitchen. He'd expected a lot of reactions out of her after she'd read the script, but acceptance—not to mention actual encouragement—hadn't been on the list. Just once he'd like her to behave the way he expected, but the fact that she never did was one more reason he couldn't seem to get enough of her.

He'd begun to feel something like . . . the word "panic" crept into his head, but he pushed it away. He didn't *do* panic, not even at the end of the film when he was enduring a predictably violent death. He just felt . . . unsettled, that was it.

Upstairs he heard water running as she began to fill the tub. He hoped she scrubbed hard at the smudge marks he'd left on her skin—the ones she couldn't see but he knew were there.

He tapped his hip, looking for cigarettes, only to remember he was wearing a towel. As he made his way to the sink to get a glass of water, a stack of letters lying on the counter caught his attention. Next to them a padded mailing envelope bore the return address of her New York City publisher. He glanced at the one on top.

Dear Dr. Favor,

I've never written to a famous person before, but I heard your lecture when you came to Knoxville, and it changed my whole attitude toward life. I started going blind when I was seven . . .

He finished the letter and reached for the next one.

Dear Isabel,

I hope you don't mind if I call you by your first name, but I feel like you're my friend, and I've been writing this letter to you in my head for a long time. When I read in the paper about all the trouble you've been having, I decided I needed to write it for real. Four years ago when my husband left me and our two kids, I got so depressed I couldn't get out of bed. Then my best friend brought me this audiotape of one of your lectures she got at the library. It was all about believing in yourself and it changed my life. I have my GED now, and I'm taking classes . . .

He rubbed his stomach, but the queasiness he felt there had nothing to do with the fact that he'd forgotten to eat.

Dear Mrs. Favor,

I'm sixteen and a couple months ago I tryed to kill myself because I think I might be gay. Somebody left this book you wrote at Starbucks, and I picked it up. I think you might of saved my life.

As he settled down at the table, he realized he'd started to sweat.

Dear Isabel Favor,

Could you send me an autographed picture of yourself? It would mean alot. When I got laid off at work . . .

Dr. Favor,

My wife and I owe our marriage to you. We were having money problems, and . . .

Dear Miss Favor,

I never wrote a famous person before, but if it hadn't of been for you . . .

All the letters had been written after Isabel's fall from grace, but the writers didn't care about that. They only cared about what she'd done for them.

"Pretty pathetic, right?" Isabel stood in the doorway, knotting her robe at the waist.

The constriction in his stomach had risen to his throat. "Why would you say that?"

"Two months. Twelve letters." She sank her hands into the robe's pockets and looked unhappy. "In my golden days, sonny boy, they came in by the boxload."

The letters hit the floor as he shot up from the table. "Saving souls is based on quantity rather than quality, is that it?"

She regarded him oddly. "I only meant that I had so much, and I blew it."

"You didn't blow anything! Read these letters. Just read the fucking things, and stop feeling so goddamn sorry for yourself."

He was acting like a bastard, and any other woman would have torn into him. But not Isabel. Not the fucking Holy Woman. She didn't even wince. She just looked sad, and it cut right through him.

"Maybe you're right," she said.

She turned away slightly. He was starting to apologize when he saw her eyes drift shut. He couldn't handle this. He knew how to deal with women who cried, women who yelled, but how was he supposed to deal with a woman who prayed? It was time to think like a hero again, no matter how much it went against his nature. "I have to get back. I'll see you in the morning at the *vendemmia.*"

She didn't look at him, didn't answer, and who could blame her? Why talk to the devil when God was your companion of choice?

21

Only Massimo beat Ren to the vineyard the next morning, and not because Ren had gotten up so much earlier than everybody else, but because he'd never gone to bed. Instead, he'd spent the night listening to music and thinking about Isabel.

She appeared as if he'd conjured her, stepping out of the early-morning mist like an earthbound angel. She wore new jeans that still had fold marks across the knees. The flannel shirt she'd buttoned over her T-shirt belonged to him, and so did her Lakers cap. Still, she somehow managed to look tidy. He remembered the fan letters she'd received, and something burned in his chest, right behind his breastbone.

A car door slammed and Giancarlo arrived, sparing Ren the need to do more than give her a brief hello. As the others appeared, Massimo started issuing orders. The *vendemmia* had begun.

Isabel discovered that harvesting grapes was a messy business. As she tossed the heavy clusters into the basket, or *paniere* as it was called, juice threatened to trickle under her sleeves, and her pruning shears became so sticky they might as well have been glued to her palms. They were also treacherous, mistaking flesh for the tough grape stems. It wasn't long before she had a Band-Aid on the end of one finger.

Ren and Giancarlo traveled the rows picking up the overflowing baskets and dumping them into the plastic crates that had been stacked on the small flatbed hitched to the tractor. They unloaded these at the old stone building beside the vineyard, where another group began crushing the grapes and pouring the must into vats to ferment.

The day was overcast and cool, but Ren had stripped down to a T-shirt printed with the logo from one of his films. He appeared beside her to collect the basket she'd just filled. "You don't have to do this, you know."

In the next row one of the women held two bunches of grapes in front of her breasts and jiggled them, making everybody laugh. Isabel waved away the bee that kept buzzing her. "How many chances do I get to harvest grapes in a Tuscan vineyard?"

"The romance is going to wear off pretty quickly."

It seemed that it already had, she thought, as he wiped his forehead and walked away.

She stared at the bee that had landed on the back of her hand. He hadn't come to her last night. Instead, he'd phoned from the villa and told her he had work to do. She needed to work, too, but she'd brooded instead. The dark side of Ren's past clung to him like cobwebs, getting in the way of any hope they had of a future together. Or maybe he'd just decided she was too much for him.

She was grateful when one of the younger women appeared to work next to her. Since the woman's English was as limited as Isabel's Italian, their conversation took all her attention.

By evening, with half the vineyard picked, she headed back to the house. She didn't speak to Ren, who'd gone to share a bottle of wine with some of the men. When Tracy called to invite her to dinner, she declined. She was too tired to do more than eat a cheese sandwich and fall into bed.

Morning arrived before she was ready, and her muscles protested as she rolled over. She considered staying in bed, but she'd enjoyed the camaraderie yesterday. She'd also liked the sense of accomplishment she'd felt. It was something she hadn't experienced for a long time.

The job went faster the second day. Vittorio showed up to help. Tracy appeared with Connor and filled Isabel in on the children's first day of school, as well as Harry's phone call from Zurich the previous night. Fabiola used her limited English to tell Isabel about her struggles to get pregnant. But Ren barely spoke to her. She wondered if he was working harder than everyone else because he owned the vineyard or because he wanted to avoid her.

The sun sank closer to the horizon. When there were only a few rows left, she made her way to the water table. As she filled her cup, a burst of laughter made her look up. She saw a group of three men and two women approaching from the villa.

Ren set down the crate he'd been unloading and waved as he walked toward them. "It's about time you got here."

Two of the three men were of the Adonis species, and they both spoke with American accents.

"When the big guy calls, the cavalry comes to the rescue."

"Where's the beer?"

An expensive-looking redhead with a pair of pricey sunglasses pushed on top of her hair threw Ren a kiss. "Hey, babe. We've missed you."

"Glad you made it." He brushed her cheek, then did the same to the other woman, a Pamela Anderson look-alike.

"I'm dying for a diet Coke," she said. "Your heartless agent wouldn't stop."

The fourth man was small and thin, maybe in his mid-forties. His sunglasses dangled from a sport strap around his neck, and he held a cell phone pressed to his ear. At the same time he managed to pantomime to Ren that the caller was an idiot and he'd be off in a minute.

The redhead gave a throaty laugh and ran her index finger down Ren's bare chest. "Oh, my God, sweetie, look at you. Is this real dirt?"

Indignation swept through Isabel. That was Ren's chest the woman was making free with. Isabel took in the redhead's low-riding pants, killer shoes, endless legs, and perfectly exposed belly button. Why hadn't Ren mentioned that he'd invited these people?

She was standing just far enough away that he could easily have ignored her, but he called her over instead. "Isabel, I want you to meet some friends of mine."

Tracy had teased Isabel about always looking tidy, but she didn't feel tidy at the moment. As she moved toward them, she wished she could freeze time just long enough to take a bath, do her hair, put on makeup, slip into something elegant, and saunter over with a martini in her hand. "You'll forgive me if I don't shake. I'm a little the worse for wear."

"These are friends of mine from L.A.," Ren said. "Tad Keating and Ben Gearhart. The bozo on the cell is my agent, Larry Green." He indicated the redhead first. "This is Savannah Sims." Then the Pamela Anderson look-alike. "And that's Pamela."

Isabel blinked.

"I just look like her," Pamela said. "We're not related."

"This is Isabel Favor," Ren said. "She's been staying in that farmhouse over there."

"Oh, my God!" Pamela shrieked. "Our book club did two of your books last year!"

The fact that someone who looked like Pamela was also smart enough to belong to a book club could have given Isabel another reason to detest her, but she rose above it. "I'm glad to hear it."

"You're a writer?" Savannah drawled. "That's so cute."

Okay, this one she was allowed to detest.

"I don't know about all of you," Ren said, "but I'm ready to party tonight. Isabel, why don't you come to the villa after you get cleaned up? Unless you're too tired."

She hated it when anyone over the age of twenty-one used "party" as a verb. Even more, she hated the way he was making her feel like an outsider. "I'm not tired at all. As a matter of fact, I can't wait. *Woo, woo.* Party hearty."

Ren looked away.

When she got back to the house, she took a bath, then lay down for a quick nap, only to fall into a deep sleep. By the time she awakened, it was after nine. She shook off the cobwebs and began to dress. Since she couldn't compete with the women in the hottie department; she didn't try. Instead, she wore her simplest black dress, brushed her hair smooth, fastened on her bangle, grabbed her shawl, and set off for the villa with a sense of dread.

Because she felt like a guest, she rang the bell instead of simply walking in as she'd been doing. A blast of music hit her as Anna opened the door. "It is good you are here, Isabel," she said, her posture stiff with disapproval. "These people . . ." She made a sound like air escaping from a tire.

Isabel gave her a sympathetic smile, then followed the music to the back of the house. When she got to the archway leading to the rear salon, she paused.

Ren's agent lay facedown on the carpet with Pamela straddling him, her skirt riding to the top of her thighs as she gave him a back rub. The lights were low, the music loud. Abandoned food lay all around, and a black bra draped the marble bust of Venus. Next to it, Tad the Adonis was making out with the sultry young woman who worked in the cosmetic shop in town. Ben, the other Adonis, held a gnawed drumstick like a microphone and sang drunkenly along with the music.

Ren was dancing with Savannah and didn't seem to notice Isabel's arrival, maybe because the redhead's breasts were plastered to his chest and she had both arms wrapped around his neck. A crystal tumbler filled with something lethal-looking dangled from his fingers as he rested his hand at her waist. Isabel watched his other hand slip down along her bony hip.

So . . .

"Hey, girlfriend!" Pamela waved from her perch on Larry Green's back. "Larry loves twozies. Want to do his feet?"

"No, I don't believe I do."

Ren turned languidly as she spoke, and Savannah moved with him. He was elegantly dissolute in a pair of tailored black slacks and a white silk shirt open one button more than necessary. He took his time letting Savannah go. "There's food on the table if you're hungry."

"Thanks."

A lock of hair fell over his forehead as he made his way to the chest and refilled his glass from one of the liquor bottles that sat on a silver tray. He took a sip, then lit a cigarette. Smoke curled around his head like a tarnished halo. "I didn't think you were coming."

She slipped off her shawl and laid it over the back of the chair. "Miss a chance to party? No way. Just tell me I'm not too late for spin the bottle."

His eyes swept over her, smoke trickling from his devil's nostrils. Savannah of the haughty expression and endless legs regarded Isabel's simple black dress with cool amusement. Pamela laughed and hopped off Larry Green's back. "Isabel, you're too funny. Hey, did you ever play that drinking game when you were in college where every time Sting sings 'Roxanne,' you chug?"

"I think I missed that one."

"You were probably studying while I was hanging out in bars. I wanted to be a vet because I love animals, but the classes were really hard, and I finally dropped out."

"Basic math is such a drag," the Queen of the Bitches drawled.

"No, it was organic chemistry I couldn't handle," Pamela replied good-naturedly.

Adonis Ben abandoned his drumstick microphone for some air guitar. "Come on over here an' love me, Pammy, 'cause I'm an animal."

Pamela giggled. "Take over with Larry, will you, Isabel?"

Savannah curled herself around Ren like a python. "Let's dance."

He slipped his cigarette into the corner of his mouth and gave Isabel a shrug. This time he locked his hands at the back of Savannah's waist and began a slow grind.

Larry gazed up at Isabel from the floor. "I'll pay you a hundred bucks to take over where Pam left off."

"I think we should talk first to see if we're compatible."

Ren snorted.

Larry groaned and eased up. "Jet-lagged. The rest of them slept on the plane." He shook her hand. "I'm Larry Green, Ren's agent. I was on the phone when we were introduced. I haven't read any of your books, but Pam was filling me in on your career. Who handles you?"

"Until recently, Ren."

Larry laughed, and she noticed that his eyes were shrewd but not unkind. The rhythm of the music changed, and Ren slid his palm a few inches lower on Savannah's hip.

Larry tilted his head toward the liquor chest. "Can I get you a drink?"

"Wine would be nice." She took a seat on the couch. Her last meal had been eight hours ago, and she needed to eat, not drink, but she'd lost her appetite.

The music changed to a rhythmic ballad, and Savannah rubbed herself against every part of Ren she could reach. Larry handed Isabel a drink and took a seat next to her on the couch. "So I hear your career's in the crapper."

"On its final flush."

"What are you going to do about it?"

"That seems to be the million-dollar question."

"If you were my client, I'd tell you to reinvent yourself. It's the fastest way to get the energy back. Create a new persona."

"Good advice, but unfortunately I seem to be a one-persona person."

He smiled, and they began to talk about careers while she tried not to watch Ren and Savannah. She asked Larry about his work as an agent, and he asked her about life on the lecture circuit. Ren stopped dancing to show Savannah some of the antiques in the room, including the pistol he'd terrified Isabel with during her first visit. To her relief, he put it away, but as he moved closer, she realized that his speech had gotten slurred. He gestured toward Larry with his liquor glass. "Why th' hell didn't you bring some grass with you?"

"An irrational fear of foreign prisons. And since when do you . . . ?"

"Next time bring some goddamn grass." He refilled his glass, not caring that he splashed half of it onto the tray as he poured. He took a swig, then curled his hands around Savannah's hips. They began another slow, sexual dance. Isabel decided it was a good thing she hadn't eaten, because anything she'd swallowed would have come right back up.

"You want to dance?" Larry asked, more because he felt sorry for her, she was certain, than from any desire to move beyond the couch. She shook her head.

One of Ren's hands curved around Savannah's bottom. Savannah tilted her face and parted her lips. That was all the encouragement Ren needed, and he dove right in.

Isabel had seen enough. She rose purposefully from the couch and gathered up her shawl. Then she spoke just loudly enough so she could be heard over the music. "Ren, would you step outside with me for a moment?"

An uneasy silence fell over the room. Ren slowly disengaged himself from Savannah's lips. "Don't be a drag," he drawled.

"Yes, well, Drag is my middle name, and this won't take long."

He picked up his drink, looking bored and very drunk, took a deep swig, then set it down. "All right, let's get this over with." As he made his way unsteadily toward the doors that led to the loggia, he lit another cigarette.

Which she promptly snatched from his mouth as soon as they were outside.

"Hey!"

She stomped it out. "Kill yourself on your own time."

He bristled with drunken belligerence. "I'll kill myself any goddamn time I want."

"I'm so annoyed with you."

"You're *annoyed*?"

"Did you expect me to be happy?" She drew her shawl tighter. "You've actually given me a headache. As for eating . . . I couldn't swallow a bite."

"I'm way too drunk to care."

"You're not drunk. Those drinks were mainly ice, and you spilled every time you poured. If you want to walk away from me, just come out and say so."

His lips tightened. The drunken swagger faded, and his speech rang clear as a bell. "All right. I want to walk away."

She gritted her teeth. "You have no idea what you want."

"Who says?"

"I do. And right now I seem to be the only one of us even remotely in touch with our feelings."

"Did you open your eyes in there?" He jabbed his hand toward the doorway, and his words shot out like bullets. "That's my real life. This time in Italy has been a *vacation*. Don't you get it?"

"That's not your real life. It might have been at one time, but not now. Not for a while. That's what you want me to believe is your real life."

"I live in freakin' L.A.! Women tuck their panties in my pockets when I go to clubs. I have too much money. I'm shallow and egotistical. I'd sell my fucking *grandmother* for a *Vanity Fair* cover."

"You also have a potty mouth. But nobody's perfect. I can be starchy."

"*Starchy?*" He looked like he was going to erupt. He took a step toward her, gritting his teeth. "You listen to me, Isabel. You think you know everything. Well, try this on for size. Suppose what you're saying is true? Suppose I invited them here—went through all this—just to show you it's over. Don't you get it? The bottom line stays exactly the same. I'm trying to get rid of you."

"Obviously." She couldn't quite keep the quiver out of her voice. "The question is, why put yourself through all this to do it? Why not just give me a '*hasta la vista*, baby'? You know what I think? I think you're scared. Well, so am I. Do you think I'm comfortable with this relationship?"

"How the hell should I know what you think? I don't understand anything about you. But I do know this: When you put a saint and a sinner together, you're asking for trouble."

"A saint?" She couldn't take it anymore. "Is that really what you think I am? A saint?"

"Compared to me, you sure as hell are. You're a woman who needs to have all her ducks in a row. You don't even like having your hair messed up. Look at me. I'm chaos! Everything about my life is insane. And I like it that way."

"You're not that bad."

"Well, I'm no walk in the park, sister."

She hugged herself. "We care about each other, Ren. You can try all you want to deny it, but we really care." Her feelings weren't shameful, and she wouldn't treat them as if they were. Still, she had to take a deep breath before she could go on. "I more than care. I've fallen in love with you. And I'm definitely not happy about it."

He didn't bat so much as an eyelash. "Come on, Isabel, you're smart enough to know what's going on. It's not really love. You're a woman who has 'savior' plastered all over you. You see me as a big rescue project."

"Is that so? Well, what exactly am I supposed to rescue? You're talented and competent. You're one of the most intelligent men I've ever known. Despite that little soap opera you wanted me to believe, you're not a womanizer, you don't do drugs, and I've never seen you drunk. You're great with children in your own bizarre way. You have steady employment and the respect of your peers. Even your ex-wife likes you. Other than a weakness for nicotine and a foul mouth, I don't get what's so terrible about you."

"You wouldn't. You're so blind to people's faults it's a wonder you're still allowed outside without a leash."

"The fact is, you're afraid of what's happening between us, but instead of trying to work through it, you decided to behave like an idiot. And as soon as you get inside, you'd better scrub your mouth and brush your teeth to get rid of that woman's germs. You also need to apologize to her. She's a very unhappy woman, and it wasn't right to use her the way you were."

He shut his eyes and spoke in a whisper: "God, Isabel . . ."

The moon slithered from under a cloud, casting angular shadows over his face. He looked tortured and somehow defeated. "The scene in there. It isn't all that much of an exaggeration."

She resisted the urge to touch him. She couldn't solve this for him. He had to work it through, either his own way or not at all. "I'm sorry. I know how sick you are of living like that."

He made a soft, almost inaudible sound and pulled her hard against him, but she barely felt the heat of his body before he released her.

"I have to go to Rome tomorrow," he said.

"Rome?"

"Howard Jenks is there now finalizing locations." He patted his hip, searching for a missing cigarette pack. "Oliver Craig is flying in—the Brit who's playing Nathan—and Jenks wants us to read together. We've got costume fittings, some makeup tests. I promised to do a couple of interviews. I'll be back in time for the feast."

The feast was a week away. "I'm sure Anna will appreciate that."

"In there"—he tilted his head toward the house—"you didn't deserve that. I just . . . You needed to understand, that's all. I'm sorry."

And so was she. More than he could imagine.

22

Tracy's eyes filled with hormone-driven tears. "Have I said thank you for giving Harry back to me?"

"Several times."

"If it hadn't been for you . . ."

"The two of you would have worked it out. All I did was speed up the process."

She wiped her eyes. "I don't know. Until you came along, we weren't having a lot of luck. Connor, keep the ball away from the flowers."

Connor looked up from the soccer ball he was rolling around in the tiny garden behind the Briggs house in Casalleone and grinned at them. One side of the yard sloped toward a row of houses on the street beneath, the other toward a section of the old Roman wall that used to surround the town.

"Ren left for Rome today," Isabel said, the hollow place inside her aching. "He wants to get rid of me."

Tracy set aside the ratty pink child's denim jacket she'd been mending. "Tell me what's happening."

Isabel filled her in on last night's party. When she was finished, she said, "I haven't seen him since. Anna told me that he and Larry drove off around noon."

"What about the L.A. parasites?"

"They left for Venice. Pamela's nice."

"If you say so." Tracy rubbed her abdomen. "He has a pattern of taking the easy way out, which is why he married me. The only place he tolerates emotional messiness is on the screen."

"It doesn't get much more emotionally messy than being involved with me." Isabel attempted a smile, but it wouldn't quite take shape.

"Not true."

"You're just saying that to be nice. He thinks I'm judging him, which I am, but only about his work. I tried not to show it, because I know it's not fair, especially since I have so many of my own flaws to deal with. The only reason I challenge him is that I care so much about him. Most of the time he comes out so high on my private rating scale that it shocks me."

"Are you sure lust hasn't clouded your judgment?"

"You've known him for so long that you don't see the amazing man he's grown into."

"Shit." Tracy sagged back in her chair. "You really are in love with him."

"I didn't think it was a secret." Certainly not from Ren after she'd thrown her heart at him last night.

"I knew you were attracted to him. What red-blooded woman wouldn't be? And every look he throws at you is X-rated. But you're so wise about people. I thought you understood that any relationship with Ren has to stay at an animal level. The only thing he's ever really serious about is his work."

Isabel felt a pathetic need to defend him. "He's serious about a lot of things."

"Name one."

"Food."

"There you go," Tracy drawled.

"I mean everything about food. He likes cooking it, creating with it, serving it. Food means community to him, and you know better than anyone how little of that he grew up with. He loves Italy. He adores your children, whether he'll admit it or not. He's interested in history, and he knows art and music. And he's serious about me." She took a deep breath, and her voice lost its assurance. "Just not as serious as I am about him. He's got this maddening thing about how wicked he is and how saintly I am."

"Ren lives in an alternate universe, and maybe it has made him wicked. Women throw themselves at him. Studio executives practically beg him to take their money. People can't say yes fast enough. It gives him a distorted view of his place in the world."

Isabel started to say that she found Ren's view of his place in the world fairly clearheaded, if a little cynical, but Tracy wasn't finished.

"He doesn't like hurting women, but somehow he always ends up doing exactly that. Please, Isabel . . . don't let yourself get sucked in."

Good advice, but it had come too late.

Isabel tried to stay busy, only to find herself staring off into space or washing the same dish over and over. When she realized she was hanging around the farmhouse in case the phone rang, she was so angry with herself that she grabbed her datebook and began planning every minute. She visited Tracy, played with the children, and spent hours at the villa helping get ready for the *festa*. Her affection for Anna grew as the older woman told her stories about the history of the villa and the people of Casalleone.

Three days passed, and she didn't hear a word from Ren. She felt rudderless, heartsick, and increasingly despondent about the course her life was taking. Not only had she failed to find a new direction, but she'd made the old one even more difficult.

Vittorio and Giulia took her to Siena, but despite the beauty of the old city, the trip wasn't a success. Whenever they passed a child, Giulia's sadness became almost palpable. Although she put up a good front, their failure to find the statue had devastated her. Vittorio did his best to cheer them up, but the tension had begun to take its toll on him, too.

The next day Isabel volunteered to baby-sit Connor at the farmhouse while Tracy kept her doctor's appointment and Marta went up to the villa to help Anna with the cooking. As they walked through the olive grove, she concentrated on his happy chatter instead of the sharp wedge of pain that had poked a hole through her heart. Afterward they played with the cats, and when it began to grow chilly, she took him inside and let him draw at the kitchen table with some crayons she'd bought for him.

"I drawed a dog!" Connor held up his picture for her to admire.

"A perfect dog."

"More paper!"

She smiled and pulled one of her empty notebooks from the stack of papers she'd left on the table. Connor, she'd quickly discovered, didn't believe in conserving natural resources. How dear he was. She'd never thought much about having children, relegating them to the unspecified future. How casually she'd treated so much of what was important in life. She blinked away the sting of tears.

Tracy appeared just as Connor began to grow restless. She picked him up and blew into his neck, then settled at the table with him on her lap while Isabel fixed them a cup of tea. "Dr. Andrea is definitely a hunk. I still can't decide whether it's creepy or not to get a pelvic from a great-looking doctor. He asked about you."

"He's a serial flirt."

"True. Has Ren called?"

She stared at the cold fireplace and shook her head.

"I'm sorry."

A coil of anger singed the edges of her pain. "I'm too much for him. Too much of everything. Well, that's just tough. I wish he weren't coming back at all."

Tracy's forehead knit with concern. "I don't think you're too much. He's being an ass."

"Horse!" Connor shouted from the doorway, holding up another drawing.

While Tracy turned to admire it, Isabel tried to make herself breathe, but the coil of anger had lit a flame inside her that was using up all the oxygen.

Tracy gathered up Connor's things, then gave her a hug as she got ready to leave. "It's his loss. He couldn't find a better woman than you, present company included. Don't you dare let him see you cry."

Fat chance of that, Isabel thought.

After they left, she grabbed her jacket and went outside to try to calm herself down, only to realize that anger felt better than pain. She'd been dumped twice in four months, and she was sick of it. Granted, getting rid of Michael had turned out to be a blessing, but Ren was a coward of a different sort. God had dangled a precious gift in front of the two of them, but only one of them had the guts to grab for it. So what if she was too much of everything? So was he. And when she saw him, she intended to tell him exactly that.

She stopped herself. She wasn't going to tell him a thing. She'd challenged him once, but she wouldn't do it again. And not because of her pride. If he couldn't come to her on his own, she didn't want him at all.

The wind shifted to the north. She was chilled and miserable by the time she got back to the house, so she lit a fire. After it caught, she went into the kitchen to make tea she didn't want. While she waited for the water to boil, she busied herself cleaning up the papers Connor had left scattered on the table. He didn't like drawing more than one figure on a page, she noticed. When he'd run out of the paper she'd given him, he'd commandeered the backs of the fan mail she still hadn't attended to.

She made her tea, then carried the cup, along with the letters, back into the living room. She'd always been diligent about answering her correspondence, but she wanted to throw this batch in the fire. What was the point?

She remembered Ren's disgust when she'd pointed out how few there were. *"Saving souls is based on quantity rather than quality, is that it?"* She'd seen the tiny pile as another symbol of how far she'd fallen, but he'd seen something else.

She leaned back on the couch and shut her eyes. The letters felt warm in her fingers, as if they were alive. She picked up the first one and began to read. When she was done, she moved on to the second, then the third, until she'd read them all. Her tea cooled. The fire crackled. She curled deeper into the couch, and slowly, she began to pray. One by one, she held each letter in her hand and prayed for the person who'd written it.

Then she began to pray for herself.

Darkness slipped over the cottage. The fire burned lower. She prayed the prayer of the lost.

Let me see the way.

But when she finally opened her eyes, all she could see were her colossal missteps.

She'd created the Four Cornerstones as a way of fighting her own insecurities. Someplace inside her, the frightened little girl who'd grown up at the mercy of unstable parents still craved stability so badly that she'd constructed a system of rules to make herself feel safe.

Do this and this and this, and everything will be all right. Your address won't change from one month to the next. Your parents won't get so drunk they forget to feed you. No one will scream hateful words or run off in the middle of the night, leaving you alone. You won't get sick. You won't grow old. You'll never die.

The Four Cornerstones had given her the illusion of security. Whenever something happened that didn't fit neatly inside them, she'd simply shoved in another building block to try to shore them up. Finally the whole structure had grown so unwieldy it had crashed in on her. She'd been living a life of desperation, all in an attempt to control the uncontrollable.

She rose from the couch and gazed out at the darkness on the other side of the window. The Four Cornerstones combined sound psychology, common sense, and the spiritual wisdom of the masters. She'd heard too many testimonials not to understand how useful they were. But she'd wanted to believe they were more than that. She'd wanted to believe they were some kind of rabbit's foot that offered protection from the dangers of being alive. If you follow these rules, you'll always be safe.

But life refused to follow any rules, and all the organizing, reorganizing, goal-setting, calculating, and meditating in the world wouldn't whip the universe into shape. Nor would a thousand Cornerstones, no matter how well conceived.

That was when she heard it. A tiny voice that came from deep inside her. She closed her eyes and strained to hear, but she couldn't quite make out the words. Frustrated, she stayed where she was, eyes shut, cheek resting against the window frame, but it was no use. The voice had slipped away.

Although the room was warm, her teeth began to chatter. She felt lost, alone, and very angry. She'd done everything right. Well, almost everything, if she didn't count falling in love with a gutless coward. She'd done everything too right. She'd been so busy imposing order on her life that she hadn't taken the time to live it. Not until she'd come to Italy. And look what a mess that had turned out to be.

Once again the voice whispered inside her, but she still couldn't hear the words, only the pounding of her heart.

"Ren?"

He snapped to attention. "Yes. That'll be fine. Whatever you think."

"Are you sure?" Howard Jenks sank his burly frame deeper into his chair, looking increasingly like someone who was having second thoughts about his choice of leading man. And Ren couldn't blame him. He kept having these attention lapses. One minute he'd be right there on top of the conversation, and the next minute he'd drift off.

He also knew he looked like shit. His eyes were bloodshot, and only a master makeup artist could have gotten rid of the circles underneath them. But how good could you look when you hadn't had a decent night's sleep in days? *Damn it, Isabel, leave me the hell alone.*

Larry frowned at him from the opposite chair of Jenks's suite at Rome's St. Regis Grand. "Are you sure about that, Ren? I thought you'd decided you didn't want to use a double for the scenes on the Golden Gate."

"I don't," Ren replied, as if that's what he'd meant to say all along. "It'll just complicate things, and I'm comfortable with heights." He meant to stop there, but the words kept on coming. "Besides, how tough can it be to catch a six-year-old girl?"

An uncomfortable silence fell over the room. Oliver Craig, the actor who was playing Nathan, lifted an eyebrow.

Craig looked like a choirboy, but he had the acting chops of a pro. He'd studied at the Royal Academy and done rep at the Old Vic. A low-budget romantic comedy had brought him to the attention of Jenks.

"Those stunts on the bridge involve more than chasing little girls," Jenks said stiffly. "As I'm sure you're aware."

Craig came to his rescue. "Ren and I were talking last night about the balance between the action scenes and the quieter moments. It's quite extraordinary."

Larry picked up the conversation—how glad Ren was to finally have a part that would display his amazing talent, how brilliantly Ren and Oliver were going to work together—blah, blah, blah. Ren excused himself and headed for the bathroom. When he got there, he leaned over the sink to splash his face with cold water. He needed to pull himself together. Last night Jenks had taken Larry aside and asked him if Ren was using.

He grabbed a towel. This was the biggest break of his career, and he was blowing it, all because he couldn't concentrate. He wanted to hear Isabel's voice so badly he'd nearly called her a dozen times. But what would he say? That he missed her so much he couldn't sleep? That his need for her had grown into an ache that never went away? If he hadn't agreed to attend the harvest feast, he could have slunk off into the night like the reptile he was. Instead, he was going to have his guts wrenched out all over again.

Yesterday he'd run into an American reporter who wanted to know if the rumor he'd heard was true. "Word is, you and Isabel Favor are an item."

Savannah and her big mouth had already gotten busy. Ren had denied everything, pretended he barely knew who Isabel was. Her fragile reputation could never survive a public liaison with him.

He told himself the same thing he'd been saying for days. At some point an affair either had to end or take the next logical step forward, and there was no next step for two people who were so different. He should have left her alone from the beginning, but the attraction had been more than he could resist. And now, when it was time to walk away, some needy part of him still wanted her to think well of him afterward. Maybe that was why he was trying so hard to come up with at least one good memory he could hand her before they said their last good-bye.

He flushed the toilet he hadn't used and went back out. The conversation stopped when he appeared, which took away the mystery of what they'd been talking about. Oliver, he noticed, had left. Not a good sign.

Jenks pushed his half glasses on top of his head. "Sit down, Ren."

Instead of dropping into a chair as he should have to show that he understood the gravity of the situation, Ren wandered over to the bar and popped a bottle of Pellegrino. Only after he'd taken a slug did he sit. His agent shot him a warning look.

"Larry and I have been talking," Jenks said. "He keeps reassuring me that you're totally committed to this project, but I'm having some serious doubts. If there's a problem, I want you to put it on the table so we can deal with it."

"No problem." A bead of sweat had formed near his hairline. He knew he had to say something that would reassure Jenks, and he tried to find the right words, only to hear himself come out with the opposite. "I want a child psychologist on the set whenever the kids are there. The best you can find, got it? I'll be damned if I'm going to be responsible for any little girls' nightmares."

Except that was his job, being responsible for people's nightmares. He wondered how Isabel was sleeping.

The furrows in Jenks's jaw grew deep enough to plant wheat, but before he could respond, the phone rang. Larry picked it up. "Yeah?" He gazed at Ren. "He's not available at the moment."

Ren whipped the receiver from his hand and brought it to his ear. "Gage."

Jenks exchanged a long look with Larry. Ren listened, then shoved the phone back into the cradle and headed for the door. "I have to go."

Isabel's anger stayed with her. It simmered beneath the surface as she chopped vegetables in the villa's kitchen and pulled serving dishes from the cupboard. By late afternoon, when she met Giulia in town for a glass of wine, it still hadn't gone away. She stopped to see the Briggs children, but even as she listened to them talk, the anger bubbled inside her.

She'd just started to drive home when a splash of color in the window of the local boutique caught her attention. The dress shimmered there, a flaming red-orange confection that burned as hot as her anger. It was like nothing she would ever wear, but her Panda didn't seem to know that. It swung into the No Parking space directly in front of the store, and ten minutes later she emerged with a dress she couldn't afford and couldn't imagine wearing.

That evening she began to cook in a frenzy of hostility. She turned up the flame on the stove until the skillet sizzled and fried the spicy sausage she'd bought earlier. Her knife pounded the cutting board as she rough-chopped onion and garlic, then threw in hot peppers from the garden. When she realized she hadn't boiled water to cook the pasta, she poured her fiery sauce over a thick wedge of day-old bread, then carried everything out to the garden, where she sat on the wall and devoured the food with two glasses of Chianti. That night she washed dishes to the blare of Italian rock and roll on the radio. She broke a plate and threw it into the trash. It hit so hard the pieces shattered.

The phone rang.

"Signora Isabel, it is Anna. I know you said you would come up tomorrow morning to help arrange the tables in the tent, but it is not necessary. Signore Ren is taking care of it."

"He's back?" The pencil that had found its way into her hand snapped in her grip. "When did he arrive?"

"This afternoon. You have not spoken with him?"

"Not yet." She put her thumbnail to her teeth and clipped it off.

Anna began going on about last-minute details for the *festa*, the girls she'd hired to help, the fact that she didn't want Isabel to do anything but have a good time. Isabel's anger burned so hot she could barely manage a response.

Later that night she gathered up the pages of notes she'd written for her book on overcoming personal crisis and tossed them into the fire. When everything had turned to ash, she swallowed two sleeping pills and went to bed.

In the morning she threw on her clothes and drove to town. Generally she felt groggy after taking sleeping pills, but her anger was still with her, and it burned away the cobwebs. She downed a lethal cup of espresso in the bar on the piazza, then walked the streets, but she was afraid to look into the shop windows for fear she'd crack the glass. Several of the villagers stopped her, anxious to talk about the missing statue or the feast that afternoon. She dug her fingernails into the heels of her hands and kept her responses as brief as possible.

She didn't return to the farmhouse until a short time before the *festa*. She headed for the bathroom, turned the shower water to cold, and stood under it trying to make her skin stop sizzling. When she began applying makeup, her fingers pressed more firmly than usual on her eyeliner pencil, and the bronzing brush took an extra swipe at her cheekbones. Foundation, eye shadow, mascara—each seemed to have a will of its own. Tracy had left behind a lip wand filled with bloodred gloss, and Isabel slid it over her mouth. When she was done, her lips glimmered like a vampire's.

She'd hung the dress she'd bought on the door of the wardrobe, and it beckoned from its hanger. The fabric fell straight from bodice to hem in a slim, fiery column. She never wore bright colors, but now she yanked it from the hanger and pulled it on. Only after she'd jerked up the zipper did she remember to put on a pair of panties beneath.

She turned to look at herself in the mirror. The scattering of tiny amber beads hidden in the fabric glowed like banked embers. The slashed bodice left one shoulder bare, and the jagged, scarf-point hem flickered like flame tips from midthigh to calf. The dress wasn't right either for the occasion or for her, but she intended to wear it anyway.

She needed dangerously high stiletto heels with gilded beads across the toes, but she didn't have any, so she pushed her feet into her bronze sandals. *All the better to stomp your heart into a thousand pieces.*

She gazed into the mirror. Her scarlet lips clashed with the dress, and her sandals didn't match, but she didn't care. She'd forgotten to dry her hair after her shower, and her wild blond curls looked like her mother's at her most reckless. She remembered the men, the screaming, all the excess that had marked her mother's life, but instead of reaching for a headband, her fingers closed over her manicure scissors. She stared at them for a moment, then lifted them to her hair and began to snip away.

Little chopped ends curled around her fingers. The scissors made angry clicks, moving faster and faster until her sleek bob became a riot of disheveled wisps. Finally she pulled off her bangle, tossed it on the bed, and left the room.

As she made her way up the path from the farmhouse, the heels of her sandals sent the stones scattering. The Villa of the Angels came into sight, and she spotted a dark-haired man climbing into a dusty black Maserati. Her heart gave a lurch, then settled back into its normal rhythm. It was only Giancarlo moving the sports car off to the side of the drive to make more room for the cars of the guests who were still arriving.

The day was too cool for such a bare dress, but even as the sun disappeared behind a high bank of clouds, her skin burned. She made her way through the formal gardens to the back of the villa, where the villagers had already begun to gather. Some of them stood chatting beneath the canopy that had been erected, others gathered on the loggia. Jeremy and a few of the older boys were kicking a soccer ball through the statuary while the younger boys got in their way.

She'd forgotten her purse. She had no money with her, no tissues or lipstick, pens or breath mints. She didn't have Tampax, car keys, or her pocket screwdriver set—none of the objects she carried to protect herself from the messy reality of being alive. Worst of all, she didn't have a gun.

The crowd parted.

Ren sensed that something unusual had happened even before he saw her. Tracy's eyes widened, and Giulia made a soft exclamation. Vittorio lifted his head and muttered a familiar Italian phrase, but when Ren saw what had captured everyone's attention, his brain lost its ability to translate.

Isabel had set herself on fire.

He took in the glowing conflagration of her dress, the heat in her eyes, the angry energy that radiated from her, and his mouth went dry. Gone were her tidy neutrals—all those comforting blacks, whites, and beiges that defined her world. And her hair . . . Disorderly curls blazed around her head in a style that Beverly Hills hairdressers charged hundreds of dollars to produce.

Her lipstick was wrong and her shoes didn't match, but she burned with a sense of purpose that put him on high alert. He'd spent a year on *The Young and the Restless*. He'd studied the scripts, and he knew exactly what was happening.

Isabel's evil twin had come to town.

23

I sabel watched Ren watching her. He was dressed entirely in black. Under the canopy behind him, bright blue linens covered the rows of tables, each of which held a terra-cotta pot spilling with pink geraniums. But the splashes of color did nothing to soothe her. Music played from the speakers Giancarlo had set up on the loggia, and the serving tables already held platters of antipasti, trays of cheeses, and bowls of fruit.

As Isabel held Ren's gaze, the flames of her anger crackled. This man had been her lover, but she had no idea what was going on behind his silvery eyes, and she no longer cared. For all his physical strength, he'd proved to be an emotional coward. He'd lied to her in a thousand ways—with his seductive cooking and winning laughter, with his furious kisses and soul-wrenching lovemaking. Whether he'd intended it or not, each had been an unspoken promise. Maybe not of love, but of something important, and he'd betrayed that.

Andrea Chiara was coming toward her through the garden. She turned away from Ren with his black clothing and equally dark heart and went to meet the town's doctor.

Ren wanted to punch something as he watched Isabel greet Vittorio's smarmy brother. He heard her say his name, her voice sounding as breathy as a 1950s starlet's. Chiara gave her an oily look, lifted her hand, and kissed it. *Punk.*

"Isabel, *cara.*"

"Cara," *my ass.* Ren watched Dr. Lovebutt take her arm and steer her from one group to the next. Did she really think she could beat Ren at his own game? She wasn't any more interested in Andrea Chiara than he'd been interested in Savannah. So why didn't she at least glance his way to see if her poison was working?

He willed her to look over, just so he could yawn, which was all the proof he needed that he'd finally turned into a certified prick. He wanted to end it with her, didn't he? He should be relieved that she was flirting with someone else, even if she was only doing it for effect. Instead, he felt like killing the son of a bitch.

Tracy appeared and dragged him just far enough away from the others so she could give him hell. "How does it feel getting some of your own medicine back? That woman's the best thing that ever happened to you, and you're throwing her away."

"Well, I'm not the best thing that ever happened to her, and you damn well know it. Now, leave me alone."

He'd no sooner gotten rid of her than Harry ambled over. "Are you sure you know what you're doing?"

"Better than anyone."

He missed her passion, her kindness, her infinite sense of certainty. He missed the way she almost made him believe he was a better man than he knew himself to be. He gazed over at her gorgeous, messy doppelgänger and wanted his tidy, patient Isabel back, the same one he was trying so hard to get rid of.

As Chiara set his hand on her shoulder, Ren forced himself to swallow his jealousy. He had a mission this afternoon, a mission that he'd been hoping would give him a bittersweet redemption. He wanted her to know that the emotional investment she'd made in him had been at least a little worthwhile. Maybe he'd even hoped to earn one of her smiles, although that no longer seemed likely.

He'd originally planned to wait until the meal was over for his big announcement, but he no longer had the patience. This was something he needed to do now. He motioned for Giancarlo to turn down the music.

"Friends, could I have your attention?"

One by one, people stopped talking and turned to him: Giulia and Vittorio, Tracy and Harry, Anna and Massimo, everyone who'd helped with the harvest. The adults shushed the children. Ren moved into a shaft of sunlight next to the canopy, while Isabel stayed at Andrea's side.

He spoke first in Italian, then in English, because he wanted to make sure she didn't miss a word. "As you know, I'll be leaving Casalleone soon. But I couldn't go without finding a way to show my appreciation for your friendship." As everyone beamed at him, he switched to English. Isabel listened, but he could feel her anger coming at him in waves. The undertow sucked at his legs and threatened to swamp him.

He pulled out the box he'd hidden beneath the serving table and set it on top. "I hope I've found the right gift." He'd planned to build the suspense by making a long speech, teasing them a little, but he no longer had the heart for it. Instead, he opened the lid.

Everyone moved closer as he pushed away the packing material. He slipped his hands inside and pulled out *Shadow of the Morning* for all of them to see.

A few seconds of stunned silence ticked by, and then Anna gave a muffled shriek. "Is it real? Have you found our statue?"

"It's real," he said.

Giulia gasped, then flung herself into Vittorio's arms. Bernardo lifted Fabiola off the ground. Massimo threw his hand to the heavens, and Marta started to weep. Everyone surged closer, blocking his view of the one person whose reaction he'd most wanted to witness.

He held *Ombra della Mattina* high so everyone could see. The fact that he had no faith in the statue's magical powers didn't matter. They believed, and that was all that counted.

Like *Ombra della Sera*, this statue was about two feet high and only a few inches wide. It had the same sweet face as its male counterpart, but the hair was a bit longer and a tiny pair of breasts marked it as female. The questions about how he'd found it began to fly.

"Dove l'ha trovata?"

"Com'è successo?"

"Dove era?"

Vittorio put his fingers to his teeth and whistled for silence. Ren set the statue on the table. Tracy moved a few inches to the side so that he could finally catch a glimpse of Isabel. Her eyes were wide, her fingers pressed to her lips. She gazed at the statue, not at him.

"Tell us," Vittorio said. "Tell us how you found it."

Ren began by recounting Giulia's phone call to Josie for a list of the gifts Paolo had sent. "At first I didn't see anything unusual. Then I noticed that he'd given her a set of fireplace tools."

Vittorio drew a sharp breath. As a professional tour guide, he understood before the rest. *"Ombra della Sera,"* he said. "I never thought . . ." He turned to the others. "The farmer who found the male statue in the nineteenth century was using it as a fireplace poker until someone recognized its value. Paolo knew this story. I heard him tell it."

Ren had studied the list several times before he'd remembered how the other statue had been found. "I called Josie and asked her to describe the fireplace tools. She said it was an old set and very unusual. A shovel, some tongs, and a poker shaped like a woman's body."

"Our statue," Giulia whispered. *"Ombra della Mattina."*

"Josie had been trying to have a child. Paolo knew this. When she couldn't get pregnant, he took the statue from the church and packaged it with the other things so she wouldn't suspect what she had. He told her it was a valuable antique set, and that if she kept it by her fire, it would bring her good luck."

"And it did," Anna said.

Ren nodded. "Three months after she received the statue, she was pregnant with her first child." A coincidence, but no one here was going to believe that.

"Why did Paolo go to all the bother of making the statue look like it was part of a set?" Tracy asked. "Why didn't he just send it to her as it was?"

"Because he was afraid she'd mention it to Marta, and he didn't want his sister to know what he'd done."

Marta twisted her apron and began telling everyone how much her niece had wanted to have a baby and how it broke Paolo's heart to hear of her sadness. Even though her brother was dead, she still felt a need to defend him, and she insisted that Paolo would have returned the statue to the town after he'd learned of his grand-daughter's pregnancy, but he'd died too soon. The crowd was in a magnanimous mood, and they all nodded their agreement.

Giulia picked up the statue and held it in her arms. "It's only been a little more than a week since I got the list from her. How were you able to get this so quickly?"

"I asked a friend of mine to go to her house and pick it up. He shipped it to me at my hotel in Rome two days ago." His friend also had efficient methods of bypassing customs.

"She did not mind giving it back to us?"

"She has two children now, and she knew how important it was."

Vittorio grabbed Ren and kissed his cheeks. "I know I speak for everyone in Casalleone when I say that we can never thank you enough for what you've done."

From then on it was a free-for-all. From men and women, old and young—he was smothered with kisses. From everyone but Isabel.

The statue made its way from one set of hands to another. Giulia and Vittorio glowed. Tracy shrieked good-naturedly as Harry tried to draw her closer to it. Anna and Massimo gazed with pride at their sons and with love at each other.

Ren was too miserable to enjoy any of it. He kept glancing at Isabel, trying to see if she understood that, at least in this one thing, he hadn't failed her. But she didn't seem to be getting the message. Even as she smiled and laughed with the others, he felt her anger scorching him.

Steffie leaned against his side. "You look sad."

"Who me? Never been happier. Look around. I'm a hero." He wiped a dab of chocolate from the corner of her mouth with his thumb.

"I think Dr. Isabel's mad at you. Mom says . . ." Little pucker marks formed in her forehead. "Never mind. Mom's cranky. Daddy told her she has to be patient with you."

"Here, have a breadstick." He pushed it into her mouth to shut her up.

Anna and the older women started herding the crowd to the tables. As the statue was passed from one family to the next, the toasts began, all of them directed at him. An unaccustomed tightness gripped his throat. He was going to miss this place, these people. He hadn't planned it, but he'd somehow managed to grow roots here. Ironic, since he couldn't come back, not for a very long time. Even if he waited until he was an old man to return, he knew he'd still see Isabel walking in the garden, her eyes shining just for him.

She'd seated herself at the opposite end of the table, as far from him as she could get. Andrea sat on one side of her, Giancarlo on the other. Neither could take his eyes off her. She was like a film running on fast forward. Her curls skipped about her head as she gestured. Her eyes flashed. Everything about her was charged with energy, but only he seemed able to feel the anger behind it.

The excitement had stirred appetites, and the soup quickly disappeared. The wind developed a chilly edge, and some of the women reached for their sweaters, but not Isabel. Her bare arms glowed with angry heat.

Oversize bowls of linguini with a red mussel sauce appeared on the table, along with a creamy risotto, and everyone dug in. This was the kind of occasion he most enjoyed, surrounded by friends, good food, great wine, and yet he'd never been more miserable. Giulia and Vittorio stole a kiss. Judging from the expression on Tracy's face, Harry was groping her under the table. Ren wanted to grope Isabel.

Clouds rolled in, and gusts of wind rattled the trees. Isabel's angry energy kept her from sitting still, but every time she jumped up to grab a serving platter, he expected it to shatter in her hands. One person after another demanded her attention, drawn to her as if her skin had been magnetized. She splashed wine on the table-cloth when she refilled glasses. She knocked the butter dish to the ground. But she wasn't drunk. Her own glass had barely been touched.

The sun settled lower in the sky, the clouds darkened, but the town had its statue back, and the mood grew more festive. Giancarlo turned up the music, and some of the couples began to dance. Isabel leaned against Andrea's side, listening to him as if each word coming from his mouth were a drop of honey she wanted to lick up. Ren cracked his knuckles.

As the bottles of grappa and vinsanto appeared, Andrea rose. Ren heard him address Isabel over the music. "Come dance with me."

The canopy snapped in the wind. She stood and took his hand. As they began walking toward the loggia, the points of her fiery skirt sparked at her knees. She tossed her head, and her curls flew. Andrea's eyes nudged her breasts as he lit his cigarette.

Just like that, she plucked it from his mouth and stuck it between her own lips.

Ren jumped up so quickly he knocked over his chair. Before she could cough out her first inhalation, he'd covered the ground between them. "What in the *hell* do you think you're doing?"

She took a mouthful of smoke and blew it in his face. "Partying."

He shot Andrea the look he'd been saving up all afternoon. "I'll have her back to you in a few minutes, pal."

She didn't fight him, but as he dragged her away, the heat of her skin made his fingers burn. He ignored the amused expressions of the people they passed, and towed her behind the farthest statue. "Have you lost your mind?"

"Fuck you, loser." She hit him with another cloud of smoke.

He wanted to wash her mouth out with soap, except he was the one who'd done this to her. Instead of kissing all the anger out of her, he drew himself up like a pompous asshole. "I'd hoped we could talk, but you're obviously not in a mood to be rational."

"You've got that right. Now, get out of my way."

He never defended himself, but this time he had to. "Isabel, it wasn't going to work. We're too different."

"The saint and the sinner, right?"

"You expect too much, that's all. You keep forgetting I'm the guy who has 'No Redeeming Social Value' tattooed across his forehead." He clenched his hands at his sides. "A reporter found me when I was in Rome. He'd heard a rumor about us. I denied everything."

"You want a Boy Scout badge?"

"If the press finds out that we've had an affair, you're going to lose what little credibility you have left. Don't you understand? It's all gotten too complicated."

"I understand that you make me sick. I understand I gave you something important, and you didn't want it. And I understand I don't ever want to see you again." She flicked the cigarette at his feet, then stalked away, her dress flaming around her in a bonfire of rage.

For a few minutes he stood there trying to get his equilibrium back. He needed to talk to someone with a clear head—get some advice—but a glance toward the loggia told him that the wisest counselor he knew was dirty dancing with an Italian doctor.

The wind cut through his silk shirt, and his sense of loss nearly brought him to his knees. Right then he understood. He loved that woman with all his heart, and walking away from her was the biggest mistake of his life.

So what if she was too good for him? She was the strongest woman he knew, tough enough to tame the devil himself. If she put her mind to it, she'd eventually whip him into shape. Hell no, he didn't deserve her, but that only meant he'd have to do everything in his power to keep her from figuring that out.

Except Isabel was smart about people. She wasn't some emotionally needy female who was taken in by a pretty face. What if the things she said about him were true? What if she was right, and he'd grown so used to seeing himself through an old, worn-out lens that he couldn't see the man he'd become?

The idea made him dizzy. The freedom that a new view of himself could bring opened up too many possibilities to think about right now. First, he had to try to talk to her again, tell her how he felt, and he had a sinking feeling she wouldn't make it easy.

Until today he would have sworn that she had an unlimited

capacity to forgive, but he was no longer so certain. He studied her as she danced. There was something different about her tonight that went well beyond the chopped hair, the dress, even her anger. Something . . .

His eyes settled on her bare wrist, and the panic he'd been trying to hold off hit him like a sucker punch. Her bangle was missing. His mouth went dry as all the changes she'd made in herself suddenly fell into place.

Isabel had forgotten to breathe.

Isabel's hands curled into fists, and she couldn't draw enough air into her lungs. She pulled away from Andrea and stumbled through the dancers to the edge of the loggia. All around her, faces shone with happiness, but instead of calming her, their joy became gasoline to her anger.

The children raced past in a rowdy, noisy group. Andrea was heading toward her to see what was wrong. She turned away from him and stumbled into the garden. A shutter had come loose in the wind, and it banged against the side of the house.

Her anger consumed her, no longer directed just at Ren but at herself. Her orange dress burned like acid against her skin. She wanted to tear it off, to grow her hair smooth again, to scrub the makeup from her face. She wanted her calmness back, her control, her certainty about the order of life—everything that had been snatched away from her three nights ago when she'd read those letters and prayed by the fire.

The canopy snapped like a sail in a storm. The children shrieked, boys against girls, racing too close to the posts. They darted past the table where the statue stood. She stared at it, a solitary female figure holding the power of life.

EMBRACE . . .

The word hit her like an assault, no longer the quiet whisper from her prayers by the fire that night, the whisper she hadn't quite been able to hear. This was a shout.

EMBRACE . . .

She gazed at the statue. She didn't want to embrace. She wanted to destroy. Her old life. Her old self. But she was too afraid of what lay on the other side.

Ren started to come toward her from across the garden, concern etched on his face. The racing boys catcalled; the girls squealed. Isabel made her way across the path toward the statue.

EMBRACE . . .

There was more. She knew it. The voice had more to tell her.

EMBRACE THE . . .

Anna cried out, ordering the swarming children to stay away from the canopy. But her warning came too late. The boy in the lead stumbled and crashed into the corner post.

EMBRACE THE . . .

"Isabel, watch out!" Ren shouted.

The canopy wobbled.

"Isabel!"

The voice roared in her head, and joy surged through her.

EMBRACE THE CHAOS!

She grabbed the statue from beneath the falling canopy and ran.

24

I sabel's orderly world had split open, and she rushed into the
heart of it. The voice snapped at her heels, rang in her head.
Embrace the chaos!

She raced around the side of the house, the glorious statue
clutched to her chest. She wanted to fly, but she had no wings, no
plane, not even her Panda. All she had was . . .

Ren's Maserati.

She ran toward it. The top was down, and on this day of chaos she
saw keys dangling from the ignition where Giancarlo had left them.
She skidded to a stop next to it, kissed the statue, tossed it into the
passenger's seat. Then she lifted her skirt and climbed over the door.

The powerful engine roared to life as she twisted the key in the
ignition.

"Isabel!"

Cars blocked her on three sides. She wrenched the wheel,
stepped on the accelerator, and shot across the lawn.

"Isabel!"

If this had been one of his films, Ren could have swung up onto a balcony, then dropped into the car as she drove beneath. But this was real life, and she had all the power.

She kept the car on the grass, racing between the rows of shrubbery toward the road. Branches lashed the sides, and turf flew. A limb took off the outside mirror as she shot between the cypresses to reach the drive. The tires spit gravel. She shifted gears, and the Maserati fishtailed as she turned out onto the road, leaving them all behind on her way to the mountaintop.

EMBRACE THE CHAOS. The wind tore at her hair. She glanced over at the statue next to her and laughed.

A wooden sign splintered against her fender as she took the first turn. On her next she destroyed an abandoned henhouse. The dark clouds swirled lower in the sky. She remembered the way to the castle ruins from the day she and Ren had driven there to spy, but she overshot the road she was looking for and had to make a U-turn through someone's vineyard. When she found the right road, the deep ruts jarred the car. She pushed hard as she climbed. For a while the Maserati lurched along, then bottomed out just before she reached the top. She turned off the engine, grabbed the statue, and jumped out.

As she hit the trail, her sandals slipped on the stones. The wind blew stronger at the higher elevation, but the trees protected her from the worst of it. She gripped the statue tighter and kept climbing.

When she reached the end of the trail, she stepped out into the clearing. A gust caught her, and she stumbled but didn't fall. Ahead of her the ruins loomed against the stormy sky, and the dark clouds swirled so close overhead she wanted to sink her fingers into them.

She bent into the wind and made her way through the crumbling archways and fallen watchtowers to the wall at the very edge. She clutched the stones with one hand, the statue with the other, and climbed on top. Fighting the gusts, she rose to her feet.

A sense of ecstasy gripped her. Wind ripped at her skirt, clouds

boiled above her, the world lay at her feet below. Finally she understood what had escaped her before. She had never thought too
small. No, she had thought too big and lost sight of everything she
wanted her life to be about. Now she knew what she had to do.

With her face turned to the sky, she surrendered to the mystery
of life. The mess, the uproar, the glorious turmoil. Bracing her feet,
she lifted the statue high above her head and offered herself to the
gods of chaos.

The confusion after the canopy's collapse had slowed Ren down,
and Isabel was already climbing into his Maserati by the time he
reached the front of the villa. Bernardo had been on his heels, but
since he wasn't on duty, he was driving his own Renault instead of
the town's police car. They threw themselves inside and set off
after her.

It hadn't taken Ren long to figure out where she was heading, but
the Renault was no match for his Maserati. When they finally
reached the base of the trail, he was in a cold sweat.

He managed to convince Bernardo to stay with the cars and went
after her himself, racing from the mouth of the trail out into the
castle's ruins. The hair rose on the back of his neck as he saw her in
the distance. She stood on top of the crumbling wall, silhouetted
against a sea of furious clouds. The wind battered her body, and the
jagged hem of her dress flew around her like orange flames. Her
face was turned to the heavens, and she had both arms raised, the
statue held aloft in one hand.

In the distance a bolt of lightning split the sky, but from where
he was standing it seemed to come from her fingertips. She was a
female Moses receiving God's second set of Commandments.

He could no longer remember a single one of his well-reasoned
arguments for walking away from her. She was a gift—a gift he

nearly hadn't found the guts to claim. Now, as he watched her standing fearless against the elements, her power stole his breath. Cutting her out of his life would be like surrendering his soul. She was everything to him—his friend, his lover, his conscience, his passion. She was the answer to all the prayers he'd never had enough sense to pray. And if he wasn't as perfect for her as he wanted to be, she'd just have to work harder to improve him.

He watched as another bolt of lightning shot from her finger-tips. Drops of rain began to pelt him, and the wind cut through his shirt. He began to run. Over the aged stones. Across the graves of the ancients. Across time itself to become part of her tempest.

He pulled himself up next to her on the wall. The wind was making too much noise for her to hear his approach, but only mortals were caught unprepared, and she didn't jump when she realized she was no longer alone. She simply lowered her arms and turned to him.

He yearned to touch her, to calm those furious wisps of hair that flew about her head, to draw her into his arms and kiss her and love her, but something had changed forever, and his blood ran cold at the thought that it might be her love for him.

Another bolt of lightning shattered the skies. She had no concern for her safety, but he did, and he pulled the statue from her stiff fingers. He began to toss it to the ground where it could no longer serve as a lightning rod. Instead, he found himself staring at it in his hand, feeling its power vibrating through him. She wasn't the only one who could make a covenant, he understood. It was time for him to make one of his own, a covenant that went against every male instinct he possessed.

He turned as she had, faced outward, and lifted the statue back to the sky. First she belonged to God—he understood that. Next she belonged to herself, no doubt about that. Only afterward did she belong to him. This was the nature of the woman he'd fallen in love with. So be it.

He lowered the statue and turned back to her. She watched him, but her expression was unreadable. He didn't know what to do. He had vast experience with mortal women, but goddesses were another matter, and he'd angered this particular deity beyond reason.

Her dress whipped the legs of his trousers, and the raindrops had turned into angry warheads. A terrible frenzy gripped him. Touching her would be the biggest risk of his life, but no power on earth could hold him back. If he didn't act, he would lose her forever.

Before his courage deserted him, he pulled her hard against him. She didn't turn to ash as he'd feared. Instead, she met his kiss with a punishing fire. Peace and love, he somehow understood, were currently the province of her tamer sisters. This goddess was driven by conquest, and her sharp teeth sank into his bottom lip. He'd never felt so close to death or life. With the wind and rain raging around them, he used his strength to pull her down from the wall and set her against the stones.

She could have resisted, she could have fought him—he expected her to—but she didn't. Her fingers pulled at his clothes. He was the mortal she'd chosen to service her.

He pushed her skirt to her waist and ripped away her panties. The part of him that could still think wondered at the fate of one who tried to claim a goddess, but he no longer had a choice. Not even the threat of death could hold him back.

The stones bit into his arms and the backs of her legs, but she opened her thighs for him anyway. She was wet. Wet and fierce beneath his fingers. He spread her legs wider, and then he drove deep.

She tilted her face to the rain as he worked inside her. He kissed her neck, the column of her throat. She set her legs around his hips and drew his power deeper, using him as he was using her.

They struggled together, climbed together. The storm lashed

their bodies, urged on by the ghosts of the ancients who themselves had once made love within these walls. *I love you*, he shouted, but he kept the words inside his head, because they were too small to express the immensity of what he felt.

She gripped him tighter and whispered against his hair: "Chaos."

He waited until the very end, the last moment before they lost themselves, that sliver of time that separated them from eternity. Then he closed his hand around the statue and pulled it hard against her side.

A bolt of lightning split the sky, and they flung themselves into the fury of the storm.

She didn't speak afterward. They moved away from the wall into the shelter of the trees. He straightened his clothes. They began walking through the ruins toward the trail. Not touching.

"The rain stopped." His voice was hoarse with emotion. He had the statue in his hands.

"I thought too big," she finally said.

"Did you, now?" He had no idea what she was talking about. He swallowed the lump in his throat. If he didn't get this right the first time, there was no guarantee of a retake. "I love you. You know that, don't you?"

She didn't respond—didn't even look at him. It was too little too late, exactly what he'd feared.

They made their way down the trail accompanied by the steady drip of rainwater from the trees. At the end Ren saw Bernardo standing by the Maserati. He'd gotten it out of the ruts, and he came forward, looking unhappy but determined. "Signora Favor, I regret to tell to you that you are under arrest."

"Surely that's not necessary," Ren said.

"She has damaged property."

"Hardly anything," he pointed out. "I'll take care of it."

"But how do you take care of the lives she has endangered with her reckless driving?"

"This is Italy," he said. "Everybody drives recklessly."

But Bernardo knew his duty. "I do not make the laws. *Signora*, if you would come with me."

If this had been a film, she would have clung to Ren's arm, quivering in fear, but this was Isabel, and she merely nodded. "Of course."

"Isabel—"

She slid into the backseat of Bernardo's Renault without acknowledging Ren. He stood alone and watched them disappear.

He gazed at his Maserati. The side mirror was gone, the fender dented, a scrape marred the black paint on one side, but he couldn't bring himself to care about anything except the knowledge that he was the one who had pushed her to such dangerous recklessness.

He stuffed his hands in his pockets. He probably shouldn't have bribed Bernardo with the promise of a top-of-the-line computer for the police station if he arrested her, but what else could he do to make sure she didn't get away before he'd had a chance to set things right? With his heart in his throat, he made his way to the car.

The only light in the cell came from a flickering fluorescent fixture set inside a wire cage. It was past nine o'clock, and Isabel hadn't seen anyone since shortly after her arrival, when Harry had appeared with some dry clothes that Tracy had gathered up. She heard footsteps approaching, and she looked up to see the door swing open.

Ren came in. His presence filled the small cell. Even here he managed to take center stage. She didn't try to read his expression. He was an actor, and he could show whatever emotion he wanted.

The door closed behind him, and the lock clicked. "I've been frantic," he said.

He didn't look frantic. He looked purposeful but tense. She set aside the pad of paper she'd propped on her knees, the one she'd made Bernardo give her. "That must be why it took you three hours to get here."

"I had to make some phone calls."

"Well, that explains it."

He came closer and studied her, looking uneasy. "That insanity on top of the mountain . . . It got a little rough up there. Are you all right?"

"I'm pretty tough. Why, did I hurt you?"

His lips thinned. Smile or grimace, she wasn't sure which. He slipped a hand in his pocket, then immediately withdrew it. "What did you mean when you said you thought too big?"

She knew her place in the world now, and there was no reason not to explain. "My life. I've always told people to think big, but I finally realized that sometimes we can think too big." She moved to sit on the edge of the cot.

"I don't know what you mean."

"I thought so big that I lost sight of what I want my life to be about."

"Your life is about helping people," he said fiercely. "You've never for a single moment lost sight of that."

"It was the scope." She curled her hands in her lap. "I don't need to fill auditoriums. I don't need a brownstone near Central Park or a closetful of designer clothes. In the end, all that suffocated me. My career, my possessions—all of them stole the gift of time from me, and I lost my vision."

"Now you have it back." It was a statement, not a question. He understood that something important had changed inside her.

"I have it back." She'd gotten more satisfaction helping Tracy and Harry than she'd gotten from her last lecture at Carnegie Hall. She didn't want to be a guru to the masses anymore. "I'm opening a small counseling practice. No place fancy—a working-class neighborhood. If people can't pay, that's all right. If they can, so much the better. I'll be living simply."

His eyes narrowed with his hit man's gaze. "I'm afraid I have some news that's going to put a crimp in those simple plans."

She'd embraced the concept of chaos, and she waited to hear what he had to say.

He moved close enough to loom over her, something she now found more interesting than threatening. "You managed to piss everybody off when you stole the statue."

"I didn't steal it. I borrowed it."

"Nobody knew that, and now the locals want to lock you up for the next ten years."

"Ten years?"

"More or less. I thought about talking to the American embassy, but that seemed risky."

"You could mention how much money I gave the IRS this year."

"I don't think it's a good idea to bring up your criminal past." He rested a shoulder against the graffiti-covered wall, looking more confident than when he'd arrived. "If you were an Italian citizen, you probably wouldn't have been arrested, but the fact that you're a foreigner makes it more complicated."

"It sounds like I might need a lawyer."

"Lawyers tend to confuse things in Italy."

"I'm supposed to stay in jail?"

"Not if we follow my plan. It's a little drastic, but I have every reason to believe it should get you out fairly quickly."

"Yet I find myself curiously reluctant to hear what it is."

"I have dual citizenship. You know that my mother was Italian, but I don't know if I told you I was born in Italy."

"No, you didn't."

"She was at a house party in Rome when I was born. I'm an Italian citizen, and I'm afraid that means we'll have to get married."

That brought her up off the bed. "What are you talking about?"

"I've spoken to the local officials, and in their own way they let it be known that they wouldn't keep you in jail if you were the wife of a citizen. And since you're pregnant anyway . . ."

"I'm not pregnant."

He regarded her steadily from beneath those angled eyebrows. "Apparently you've forgotten what we were doing a few hours ago and exactly where that statue was when we were doing it."

"You don't believe in the statue."

"Since when?" He threw up one hand. "I can't imagine what kind of hell-raiser we conceived up there. When I think about that storm . . ." He shuddered, then bore down on her. "Do you have any idea what it's going to take to raise a child like that? Patience, for one thing. Luckily, you've got a lot of that. Toughness—God knows, you're tough. And wisdom. Well, enough said about that. All in all, you're up to the challenge."

She stared at him.

"I intend to do my part, don't think I don't. I'm damn good at potty training."

This was what happened when you welcomed chaos into your life. She refused to blink. "I'm supposed to forget that you ran off like a coward when I got to be too much for you?"

"I'd appreciate it if you would." He regarded her with something like entreaty. "We both know I'm still a work in progress. And I've got a great present to help you forget."

"You bought me a present?"

"Not exactly bought. One of those phone calls I made after you were thrown in jail was to Howard Jenks."

Her stomach sank. "Don't tell me you're not going to make that film."

"Oh, I'm going to make the film. But Oliver Craig and I are switching parts."

"I don't understand."

"I'm playing Nathan."

"Nathan's the hero."

"Exactly."

"He's a dweeb."

"Let's just say he's testosterone-challenged."

She sank down onto the bed and tried to envision Ren as the bookish, bumbling, mild-mannered Nathan. Slowly, she shook her head. "You'll be perfect."

"I think so, too," he said with satisfaction. "Fortunately, Jenks is a man of vision, and he got it right away. Craig's doing cartwheels. Wait till you see him. I told you he looks like a choirboy. Just thinking about him playing Street gives me the chills."

She looked up at him. "You did this for me?"

He wrestled with his answer, then looked vaguely embarrassed. "It was mostly for me. I'm not giving up playing bad guys, don't think that for a minute, but I couldn't handle Street. Besides, I need to stretch. I'm not all bad. It's time I accepted that. And you, my love, are not all good. Witness which one of us is currently incarcerated."

"It's giving me a chance to think about an idea for a new book."

"What happened to the old one? The one on crisis management?"

"I finally figured out that not every crisis can be managed." She gazed at the cell around her. "As much as we want to keep ourselves safe, we can't protect ourselves from everything. If we want to embrace life, we also have to embrace chaos."

"Getting married to me sounds like a good start."

"Except that chaos has its own way of finding us. We don't have to set ourselves up for it."

"Still . . ."

"I can't imagine how difficult a marriage between us would be," she said. "The logistics alone are impossible. We both have our careers. And where would we live?"

"You'll figure it out in no time. You can start making lists. You still remember how, don't you? And while you're doing that, I'll take care of the really important stuff."

"Such as?"

"I'm designing our kitchen. Everything's going to be state-of-the-art. I want a low counter at one end so our kids can cook, too, although we're keeping that little bugger you're carrying away from knives. A big eating area with—"

"I'm not pregnant."

"I'm fairly sure you are. Chalk it up to male intuition."

"Why the change of heart, Ren? What happened to you?"

"You happened to me." He came over and sat next to her on the cot, not touching her, just looking deep into her eyes. "You scare me to death, you know. When you stormed into my life, you turned everything inside out. You upset all the things I believed about myself and made me think in new ways. I know who I used to be, but I'm finally ready to figure out who I am. Cynicism gets tiring, Isabel, and you've . . . rested me." The cot springs squawked as he shot up, turning fierce without warning. "And don't you dare tell me you've stopped loving me back, because you're still a better person than I am, and I'm counting on you to take more care with my heart than I took with yours."

"I see."

He began to pace. "I know that marriage to me is going to be a mess. Two careers. Kids. Conflicting travel schedules. You'll have to deal with the fallout from the press I've been trying so hard to avoid. There'll be paparazzi hiding in the bushes, tabloid stories every six months saying I'm beating you or you're doing drugs. I'll have location shoots and women coming on to me. Every time I do a love scene with some beautiful actress, you'll give me all the reasons it doesn't bother you, and then I'll find the sleeves cut off my favorite shirts." He rounded on her and jabbed a finger in her direction. "But the woman who stood on that wall this afternoon is strong enough to face an army. I want to hear you tell me right now that I didn't leave that woman behind on the mountaintop."

She threw up her hands. "All right. Why not?"

"Why not?"

"Sure."

His arms fell to his sides. "That's it? I pour my heart out. I love you so much I've got freakin' tears in my eyes. And all I get in return is 'Why not'?"

"What did you expect? Am I supposed to fall all over you just because you've finally come to your senses?"

"Would it be too much to ask?"

Pride went along with chaos, and she gave him a quelling look.

He'd begun to glare at her again, his eyes growing stormier by the minute. "When do you think you might be ready? To fall all over me, that is."

She took her time thinking about it. Her arrest had been his doing. She'd known that immediately. As for that ridiculous story about having to marry him to get out of jail, even an idiot wouldn't buy that. Still, dirty tricks were part of what made him Ren Gage, and how much did she want him to change?

Not a bit, because his basic decency went bone deep. He understood her in ways no one else ever had, in ways she hadn't understood herself. And what better guide could she find into the world of chaos? Then there was the inescapable fact that her heart overflowed with love for him, although it didn't speak well of her that she was taking so much pleasure watching those furrows of worry etch themselves in his brow. What a mess of contradictions she was. And how lovely not to fight them anymore.

She still had to pay him back for the arrest, and she decided to make things messier. "Maybe I should tell you all the reasons I don't love you."

He went pale, and little rainbows of happiness danced through her. What a horrible person she was.

"I don't love you because you're gorgeous, although God knows I'm grateful for it." The wave of relief that crossed his face nearly melted her, but what was the fun in tidying up too soon? "I don't love you because you're rich, because I've been rich, too, and it's harder than it seems. No, your money's a definite drawback. I definitely don't love you because you're an amazing sex partner. You're amazing because you've had too much practice, and I'm not happy about that. Then there's the fact that you're an actor. You're deluding yourself if you think I'll be able to rationalize those love scenes. Every one of them will drive me wild, and I *will* punish you."

Oh, he was smiling now, was he? She tried to think of something terrible enough to take that smile off his face, but the same tears filling his eyes had begun to fill her own, so she gave up. "Mostly I love you because you're decent, and you make me feel like I can conquer the world."

"I know you can." His voice was thick with emotion. "And I promise to cheer you on the whole time you're doing it."

They gazed at each other, but they both wanted to prolong this moment of anticipation, and neither moved closer. "Do you think you could get me out of jail now?" she asked, then hid a smile as he shifted his weight and looked uncomfortable again.

"See, the thing is, it took me a little longer to make all those phone calls than I'd planned, and everything's closed down for the night. I'm afraid you're in the slammer until morning."

"Correction. *We're* in the slammer until morning."

"That's one possibility. The other is a little more exciting." They still weren't touching, but they'd each taken a step closer. He lowered his voice and patted his side. "I have a little firepower tucked away. I admit it's a long shot, but we could always shoot our way out."

She smiled and opened her arms. "My hero."

The game had gone on long enough, and they could no longer resist each other. They had pledges to make.

"You know you're the breath of my life, don't you?" he whispered against her lips. "You know how much I love you?"

She pressed her palm against his chest and felt a skipped heartbeat.

"Actors are needy creatures," he said. "Tell me how long you'll love me back."

"That's easy. Eternally."

As he smiled into her eyes, all his goodness shone through. "I guess that'll be long enough."

They kissed, deep and sweet. He tunneled his fingers into her hair. She reached between the buttons of his shirt to touch his skin. They drew back just far enough to gaze into each other's eyes. All the barriers between them were gone.

She tilted her face to his. "This is the place where the music comes up and the credits start to roll."

He cupped her cheek and smiled into her eyes. "You're so wrong, sweetheart. The film's just beginning."

Epilogue

The wicked *principessa* had been lusting after her poor but honest groom for months, but she waited until a stormy February night before she summoned him to the master bedchamber at the Villa of the Angels. She was dressed in scarlet, her favorite color. The scandalous gown fell off her shoulders, revealing a small tattoo on the curve of her breast. Her untidy blond hair curled about her head, big gold hoops swung at her ears, and iridescent plum toenails peeked out from beneath the hem of her gown.

He entered more simply dressed, as befitted his station, in fawn-colored workman's breeches and a white shirt with long, loose sleeves. "My lady?"

His deep voice sent her senses reeling, but as a *principessa* she knew better than to display weakness before underlings, so she addressed him imperiously. "Did you bathe first? I do not like the smell of horse in my bedchamber."

"I did, my lady."

"Very good. Let me look at you."

While he stood quietly, she circled him, tapping her chin with her index finger as she took in the hard symmetry of his body. Despite his humble status, he stood proudly under her scrutiny, which further aroused her. When she could no longer resist, she touched his chest, then curled her fingers around his buttocks and squeezed. "Undress for me."

"I'm a virtuous man, my lady."

"You're merely a peasant, and I'm a *principessa*. If you don't submit to me, I will have the village burned to the ground."

"You would burn down the village merely to satisfy your evil lust?"

"In a New York minute."

"Well, then, I suppose I must sacrifice myself."

"Darned right."

"On the other hand . . ." Without warning, the wicked *principessa* found herself upended on the bed with her scarlet skirts tossed over her head.

"*Hey!*"

His breeches hit the floor. "Unbeknownst to you, my lady, I'm not really your poor but honest groom. Instead, I'm your long-lost husband in disguise, come back to claim his rights."

"Shucks."

"Some days it doesn't pay to be evil." He settled between her legs, stroking, but not entering. As she lifted her arm, a wide gold bangle engraved with the word CHAOS fell from its mate at her wrist, the one that reminded her to breathe—two parts of her life come together at last. "Please be gentle," she said.

"And have you complain? No way."

They finally stopped talking and got down to what they did best. Loving each other with passionate touches and soft, sweet words that carried them away to a secret place only they inhabited. When they were finally drained, they curled together in the big bed, secure against the winter winds that buffeted the old house.

She laid her foot over his calf. "One of these days we're going to have to start behaving like grown-ups."

"We're too immature. Especially you."

She smiled.

They were quiet for a while. Content. His whisper drifted over her cheek. "Do you have any idea how much I love you?"

"Oh, yes." With a sense of absolute certainty, she pressed her lips to his, then fell back against the pillow.

He stroked her skin as if he still couldn't quite believe she was his. "You're doing it, aren't you?"

She heard the smile in his voice, but she continued her prayers. They'd become as essential as her breathing. So many prayers of thanksgiving.

When she was done, she gazed across the firelit room to the mantel top, where his gold Oscar for *Night Kill* perched. Ren hadn't even begun to test his limits, and unless she missed her guess, another would someday sit next to it.

She hadn't tested her limits either. *Living an Imperfect Life* had been a runaway bestseller—so much for thinking small—and *The Imperfect Marriage* would be coming out in a few months. Her publisher wanted *Raising the Imperfect Child* as soon as possible, but that book was still very much a work in progress, and she didn't intend to complete it for some time.

Thanks to an excellent referral network, she was keeping her counseling practice small. Just as she'd promised herself, she made certain she had time each day to think, to pray, to have fun. Marriage to Lorenzo Gage was messy but fulfilling. Definitely fulfilling.

He slipped out of bed, cursing softly as he stepped on a plastic action figure. Tomorrow they were attending the christening of Giulia and Vittorio's second child, a boy born just fourteen months after his sister. They'd welcomed the excuse to come back to Tuscany. As much as they loved their home in California, this always felt like a journey back to their roots. In the summer they'd spend a month here, along with Harry, Tracy, and the children, including Annabelle, their fifth and last, who'd been born the day after Ren and Isabel's wedding, which had taken place in the garden below their bedroom window.

Ren picked up the clothes they'd discarded, and tossed them into the trunk where they kept an assortment of interesting costumes along with a few devilish props.

Thank you, God, for gifting me with an actor.

He reached into the wardrobe, pulled out her nightgown, and handed it to her. "As much as I hate to give you this . . ."

She slipped it over her head while he shoved his legs into gray silk pajama bottoms. Then he walked over to the door, gave a long-suffering sigh, and unlocked it.

"Did you read the script?" he asked as he slid back under the covers.

"I did."

"You know, don't you, that I'm not going to do it."

"I know that you are."

"Jesus, Isabel . . ."

"You can't turn it down."

"But *Jesus*?"

"I admit it'll be a stretch. He was celibate and preached nonviolence. But you both love kids."

"Especially ours."

She smiled. "The twins are demons. You were so right."

"They're potty-trained demons. I held up my end of the bargain."

"You're very good at it."

He silenced her with a kiss, his favorite form of conflict resolution. They held each other. While the wind howled in the chimney and the shutters rattled, they whispered their love all over again.

They'd just begun to drift off when the door creaked open and two pairs of small feet scampered across the carpet, fleeing all the monsters who lived in the dark. Ren reached out and drew the invaders into the warmth of the bed. Their mother cuddled them close. For the next few hours peace reigned in the Villa of the Angels.